RED ENEMIF[...]

Big Oak could hear the Brit[...] [...]d crackle of rifle shots, call[...] [...]. And good soldiers that they [...] [...]e lightly burdened riflemen merely [...] on the run, then turned and fired at the c[...] [...]s red target they could see. By now the screams [...] [...]s of fallen redcoats had added a chorus to the dea[...] symphony of gunfire, shouted orders, and battle cries.

The British were confused. Too many men were down. Already some of the reinforcements had been bloodied. If they kept trying to go forward, by the time they had conquered this little section of woods, none of them would be left.

The riflemen saw the British waver, saw some of them retreat, saw stranded pockets of worried redcoats. And then one of Morgan's men, not an officer, shouted, "Let's go get 'em, boys!" Suddenly the retreating riflemen were the shock troops, dashing forward, firing one well-aimed shot, then continuing the dash, waving hatchets and screaming the bloodcurdling cries they had first heard from their red enemies . . .

SHADOWS ON THE LONGHOUSE

MIKE ROARKE

ST. MARTIN'S PAPERBACKS

SHADOWS ON THE LONGHOUSE

ISBN: 0-312-95322-4

Printed in the United States of America

St. Martin's Paperbacks edition / October 1994

10 9 8 7 6 5 4 3 2 1

❧ I ❧

HE SIGHED AND LEANED HIS BACK UP against the sycamore tree, pulled on his cane pole and flicked the hooked cricket out across the surface of the pond. It hit the water with the softest of sounds. Almost immediately a fish struck.

Big Oak pulled quickly up on the cane pole. Not quickly enough. The hook flew into the air, with half a cricket left on it, and came to rest on the earth next to Big Oak. He laughed quietly, as if the woods around him might still be filled with demonic French *couriers de bois*. But no, he knew that such a thing could not be. The last war with the French had removed their threat forever.

He looked around him, at the glorious green hills filled with majestic oaks, maples, beeches, and elms, and then at his pond, green from the reflections of trees that marched right to the shore. This was *his* pond. He was not certain that aside from his wife, his three half-Tuscarora children, his half-Seneca son Thad, and a handful of friends, anybody on God's green earth knew that his pond existed. Oh, he was certain that at one time a small group of Mohicans had called this place home. There were signs all around. But the Mohicans were gone, scattered to the winds like chaff.

He stretched his lean six-foot-two-inch frame. This was a good day. Sunny, with just the hint of a chill in the air. The twinges in his joints were not bad today, he observed. When a man was late into his fifties, days like this were to be treasured.

He turned his body to the right and peered up the hill toward his log house. Again he laughed quietly and shook his head. It had been such a simple house when he built it. But as the children came, they needed more space, and the trading company he had built with his son and his son's father-in-law was thriving, so he had the money to hire a couple of skilled helpers and redo it right. It had three fireplaces that drew beautifully. The logs of the home were all perfectly chinked, and the windows had *glass* in them! His wife could only stand in wonder as the additions were built and the house was reinforced. Now, no matter how the winds howled, most of the house stayed warm as toast as long as he and his sons continued to drag in the seasoned logs from the huge pile they kept by the front porch.

He pulled out his pipe and sucked on it, cold, but filled with the aroma of many smokes. He had been without tobacco now for over a month. Sometime next week Paul Derontyan would come up from Albany with provisions for the family. Big Oak chuckled. Imagine the family of Samuel Watley—his own Christian name—lying around in their forest cabin, waiting for someone else to bring them their necessities. Not so long ago he could have run fifty miles in a day to the nearest town for some tobacco and salt pork. Well, he admitted to himself, he still could, he just didn't feel like it. After his last war, more than ten years ago, and his marriage to Cilla, domestic life had become a habit. Only the need to stretch his legs along the forest trails in search of fresh deer meat kept his frame spare and well-muscled. Occasionally did he take to the rivers on a trade mission for Wendel and Watley. Otherwise he stayed pretty close to home, raising his children and loving his wife.

So he sucked his cold pipe and imagined the bite of fragrant tobacco on his tongue. One more time he let his eyes roam the hills and smell the summer smells of all the trees and grasses around him. These were real, and he knew too well that another war might be coming that would make peaceful home life as unreal as the taste of tobacco sucked from a cold, empty pipe.

There was a crunching sound in the woods, the footfalls of a carefree child plunging headlong through the low-hanging branches of the trees that bordered the lake. The boy was Ken, named for an old Indian brave, Big Oak's first son's grandfather, who was murdered in a long ago massacre on the Genesee River. Ken was eleven summers old and already an accomplished hunter. He wore woodsman's skins from head to foot, as Big Oak had in the days when he was a legendary hunter and warrior himself, before he had bought himself a set of civilized work clothes and settled down on Big Oak Pond.

The boy tripped over a sycamore root and almost toppled into the pond, but saved himself neatly by grabbing a hanging branch. He stopped next to his father's reclining figure.

"Pa," he said. "Uncle Paul's here. Ma's feedin' him. He says you better hurry on up to the house. There's things he needs to talk to you about."

Big Oak nodded to his son and set out on a long-legged walk up the hill to the house whose view commanded the approaches of four paths.

"What's he so all-fired anxious about?" he asked the boy. He expected a coherent answer. Even though Ken was only the second of three tightly spaced boys, he was observant, alert, and intelligent.

"Says there's gonna be fightin' around here soon," replied the boy.

"I know that."

"He means real soon, and real close, maybe, Pa."

Big Oak thought silently for several moments, sucking on his pipe.

"Tell you what I want you to do, son," he said to the boy.

"You tell that Oneida beggar that when he gets through eatin' up all the food we got, he should get himself down to the pond here, okay?" Big Oak stopped his climb up the hill.

The boy nodded without expression, turned and began to run back to the house.

"Oh, and Ken, one thing more. Tell Paul that on his way to the pond, he should cut himself a pole. No sense him comin' down here without something to fish with. I've got some line and hooks here. Go along, then."

The boy turned and started to run, then turned back to Big Oak. "Pa, can I stay 'n' fish with you and Uncle Paul?"

Big Oak thought again, for a moment. The talk would not be pretty, but the boy had an old head on his shoulders, and he had a gift that was rare for an eleven-year-old. He knew to keep his mouth shut when the men were speaking in council. Without smiling, he looked at the boy and nodded.

The boy vanished into the woods. Big Oak turned to look toward the house, and soon he saw the boy emerge from the woods at the top of the hill on the run and head for the front porch.

The old trader returned his concentration to the pond, rebaited his hook and flicked his line out to a tiny cove ten feet away. He sat back and watched the little stick that served as a bobber, sucked on his empty pipe, and thought about his friend Paul, and the Oneidas.

He had met Paul on a trading mission to the Tuscarora village where his wife's people lived. Many years ago the Tuscaroras had come up from North Carolina to live with their Iroquois cousins, after the English had stripped the Tuscaroras' land from them in a series of wars. In council the Tuscaroras were always warning the Senecas and the Mohawks not to trust their greedy English allies.

And now that there were two kinds of English, who were the English that the Iroquois most had to fear? Big Oak knew that when Paul sat down beside him and tossed his hook into the water, that question would be the topic of conversation. Big Oak didn't like that conversation. After Pontiac's rebellion in 1763, he had retired from the warpath, and although deep in the fastness of his hillside hideaway he had heard news of this new rebellion, and then of war, his blood did not boil with martial ardor. It was time to let the others do the fighting, while he warmed his bones in the pondside sun and watched with pride as his children grew up strong and honest.

Not only was he through with war, he was through with politics. Let someone else decide which were the worse, the Tories or the rebels. Over the years, he had fought beside stupid English officers who refused to learn a thing about the new land into which they so blindly led their troops. But at least the king and his advisors had had some idea of justice for their red subjects. The rebels, on the other hand, had no need of justice, they had need only of land, especially Indian land.

He loved it when the wind blew ripples across the pond in the afternoon. Then a million little suns would sparkle on the waters and it no longer mattered to him if the fish were nibbling at his hooked insects. Like the flickering flames of an Indian campfire, sunlight on the water was a drug that drew from him all the painful memories that were the legacy of anyone who had spent his life on the New York frontier, watching reds and whites in their unending struggle with each other and among themselves. Mindless, unblinking, he could stare for long minutes at the glimmering sparks of white light as they marched across the pond.

And on this drowsy late summer afternoon, he did.

"Sam, my brother," came the voice, soft, almost reverent, behind him.

The voice did not startle him. A distant corner of his brain, the silent sentinel that stood guard every minute of every day, had caught Paul Derontyan's approach in the woods and recognized the footfalls as friendly. The words came at almost the exact moment the sentinel knew it would, and it knew what the words would be. Most whites and nearly all the Iroquois—or Ganonsyoni, as they called themselves—knew him as Big Oak, but Paul Derontyan, educated with the Reverend Kirkland in New England, had taken on many English ways.

Paul's imitation was imperfect. In his mouth "Sam" became "Semm." He still wore a single earring, and though he had let his hair grow in, he wore it free-flowing, Indian fashion. Nor could he change the shade of his skin or the features of his face. These attributes touched Sam's heart with the realization that even for a man like Paul, who was ready to give up his entire Iroquois birthright in exchange for peace with his white neighbors, his destiny was bound to be long on grief, short on satisfaction. To his white neighbors, after all, Paul would forever be a heathen, no matter how devout his Christian faith.

"Hello, Paul, my brother," said Sam. "Where's your pole?"

Paul smiled but did not laugh. "I cannot sit still to fish," he said. "I need your wisdom.

"Please," he added.

Sam handed Paul his cold pipe. "I am wiser when I see smoke before my face," he said.

Paul dug into his pouch and produced a clump of kinnikinick, which he packed into Sam's pipe.

There was no fire at hand to light it, but Sam was pleased just to draw some air through the fragrant Indian tobacco mixture and imagine himself strolling back to the house, pulling a coal from the fireplace, and feeling the comfort of the smoke.

Paul saw that his friend was willing to listen, but not willing to urge himself into his own state of worry. Not yet. Not until there was good reason. Paul sighed and sat down next to the old trader. "There is war," he said.

Sam nodded. "Bunch of New England hotheads bound to get us all fighting amongst ourselves," he muttered. "If the rest of us just hunker down a bit, maybe they'll get some sense into them and this thing will go away."

Paul shook his head. "I'm just a poor Indian," he said, but got no further. Sam, normally the politest of men, would not abide such talk, and interrupted.

"You think you're talking to an English general? Am I your brother or just another white man that you have to flatter so you can get through his village without him taking a whip to you?"

His words hurt Paul, because they struck so close to home. "I am sorry, my brother. I forget who you are. When I see your big house, and your children who will be white men, then I see you like I see the rest. We are the trees and you are the fire of the forest, and when you are done with us there will be nothing but ashes. But we are not like the forest. After the fire, the forest grows back, greener than ever, but we will not grow back. Your diseases will see to that."

"Honest words from an honest man, Paul. But if this is so, then why are you Paul instead of Derontyan, and why do you stay close to the white man? Beyond the mountains the king says the white man cannot go. Many of your brothers are finding homes in the valley of the Spay-Lay-Wi-Theepi, where the English are not burning down the forests and building their cabins and filling them with whelps. Take your wife and your children and go where my people cannot."

For a moment Paul dropped his mask of dignity. Sam saw sadness, and maybe guilt, in the lines of the Oneida's face, so much younger and yet older than his own.

"The white disease is not just the pimple sickness," Paul said. "Nor is it just the strong water he makes that we love so. The white sickness is his guns and his strouds, his kettles and his houses. Even his Jesus." He went silent for a moment, stunned by his own words. Sam knew Paul Derontyan was a devout Christian. Now, for a few short breaths, both men watched the sun dance on the wind ripples of the pond.

"I remember my grandfather," Paul said. "He was an

Oneida brave. He knew who he was. He had no doubt. He wore the skins of deer. He lived in his mother's longhouse by a fire many years old, and when he married, he lived in his wife's mother's longhouse. He could shoot a rifle, but he could still shape the flint for arrowheads. He never begged a crumb from the forts. He never went near the forts. 'Stay away from the white people,' he told us, 'except when you need one to make your rifle shoot again.'

"Look at me," Paul went on. "I do not even wear a blanket. I wear a shirt made of cloth that I do not understand. I wear breeches like yours. I wear no metal in my nose or feathers in my hair. Nor do I dare the enemy with a scalp lock. I have forgotten the Indian gods. I preach the gospel to children. I am a white man to everyone but the white men. I am nothing."

"When the war comes to us, Paul, everything will change. And when the war is over, then you and I and everybody else will have to think what to do with our lives. No matter who we are—you, me, Thad, my son James— our lives will be different. Till then it is not time to worry. Till then it is only time to survive."

Big Oak's rod suddenly bent, but before he could jerk the line to set the hook, he could tell that the pull was not that of a fish. Gently he pulled on his pole, then on the string. Resting before him, his head, legs, and tail pulled way into his shell, was a painted turtle, perhaps five inches from the front to the back of the shell.

"Say, there, little brother," murmured the old trader softly as he picked up the shell and almost tenderly used the hook to draw the turtle's head out from within his shell house. Carefully as he could, he slipped the hook from the mouth of the turtle. "I am sorry, little brother, if I have caused you pain," he said, staring into the eyes of the creature. The turtle did not withdraw into his shell, but seemed to stare back.

Big Oak laid the turtle down at the edge of the pond, facing toward the water. The turtle stood on its bowed legs for a few long moments, then crawled into the water and swam off. Big Oak hooked another cricket and tossed his line into the shining water.

Paul stood before Big Oak, who remained seated, his back up against his tree. "I remember that your son is of the Turtle clan," he said. "You may think that, like the turtle, you can sit up here in your shell." He pointed up the hill to the cozy log house. "While around you the Longhouse falls down. But you cannot. Sooner or later the war will come to you, and when it does, you must know where you stand."

"And where do you stand, my brother Paul, or is it my brother Cansadeyo?"

"I stand with my people the Oneida," Paul replied. "We stand with the rebels, may God help us. Against the mighty Seneca. Against our man-eating brothers, the Mohawks. I see the twilight of my people in the flash of English guns. Were it only me, I would put on my loincloth and die on the warpath. But my brother, when this war is over, my people will be scattered by the Mohawks, and then, will my family be slaves in a mocking Ganiengehaka village? I cannot stand the thought."

Big Oak pulled his line from the pond, dropped his pole and stood up, placing his hands on the shoulders of his friend. He smiled. "Then take heart, my brother. I believe the rebels may yet win."

If anything, the expression on Paul's face became sadder still. "And if the rebels win, what will happen then?" he asked. "Their hunger for our land is even greater than that of the king's people. Our land will look as fair to them as the land of the Mohawks that is now nearly all theirs. If they win, then my people are surely lost. You, my brother, know the heart of the white man, and you know the heart of the Ganonsyoni." He flexed the thick biceps of his right arm.

"This is the last great war of the Longhouse. Will my own brothers feel the bite of my tomahawk? Or I theirs?"

* * *

Degata was loping up a steep slope when he smelled the white man's smoke. Reacting from long and careful habit, he dropped into a squat beside a large elm tree and looked around. His eyes told him nothing that he did not already know. His nose told him that the smoke had water in it. After a week of dry weather, any fool could find dry wood for a campfire during wartime. This had to be white man's smoke.

He crawled forward along the forest floor, then decided the fire was too far to crawl to. The woods would soon be darkening, and he wanted to know where his enemy was, if indeed it was an enemy making this obscene smoke. Life was more complicated now than it used to be. Years ago if you found a red man and he was not of the Longhouse, then he was an enemy and you killed or captured him. If he was an Englishman, maybe you scared him a little and got him to give you something, then you pounded him on the back and called him brother.

Now if you saw a white man, you had to try to figure out whether he was an Englishman or something else.

The smoke was strong now. A veteran warrior, Degata had caught the scent of a prey. He stopped walking, unshouldered his pack, and pulled his bullet pouch and powder horn around so they rested on his back. He crept along on his stomach until he could see the smoke and the fire, and a lone white man with a bright shock of red hair piled atop his head, leaning back against a tree, watching something cook in a little pot that was just sitting on the fire.

The man wore a shirt and breeches made of butternut-colored homespun. His clothes were trail-worn but not tattered. His legs were stretched straight out. His eyes were half closed. His left arm cradled an earthenware jug. His rifle, Degata noted, was leaning against a tree on the other side of the campfire, and his pack was sitting on the ground beside him.

Somewhere in the back of his mind Degata knew he should either pass this one by or try to figure out what kind

of a white man he was. But here was a temptation no true
Seneca warrior could resist. What was he anyway? A trader?
Where were his goods? A trapper? No, there were not
enough beaver left on this land to lure a trapper. A deer
hunter? A farmer? Maybe he was just lost. Degata didn't
care who he was. It was wartime, and he was a warrior. And
besides, there was that jug. It was a big jug. Degata hoped
there was plenty of rum left in it. He crept closer.

Slowly the man's head turned and his dark eyes fastened
squarely on the Seneca. He had not been too drunk to pick
up the sound of Degata's nearly noiseless approach. As
Degata raised his rifle, the man shifted his body and put the
tree between him and Degata's line of fire.

A grim smile split Degata's round face. Standing tall, he
walked toward the white man, rifle at the ready, now moving toward the side to get an angle on his enemy. The
white man reached into his pack and pulled out something,
then stepped around the tree to keep it between himself
and the Seneca. The man was a big, broad-shouldered giant. For a moment Degata played with the thought of
breaking off their little duel and heading north for Irondequoit. But then he realized that the moment he stopped
being the hunter, he might well become the hunted. Besides, he had the rifle, loaded and primed, and he was only
twenty yards away from his foe. He was confident that he
could take this man and make him his.

Confident he may have been, but his senses were not
asleep. He saw the man's right hand move and he dropped
quickly to one knee, his rifle at his shoulder. The man had a
pistol. The range was close enough and he was exposed.
Quickly Degata cocked his rifle and pulled the trigger, just
as the muzzle of the pistol exploded fire. He felt the bullet
pass him by, but he did not wait for the smoke to clear
before he charged through it, his tomahawk suddenly in his
grasp.

Ten running steps and he was nose to nose with the
redheaded giant. With his pistol, the man deflected

Degata's arm as the tomahawk descended. Degata aimed a knee at the man's groin, but the man stepped back adroitly and drew his knife. Degata's nostrils flared with the thrill of battle. Forward he came, tomahawk against knife, and the relentless momentum of his charge caught the giant off stride. He stepped back one, two steps, pulled his head out of the way of Degata's tomahawk, then stumbled and went down. His left hand reached out and grabbed at Degata's ankle. The Indian pulled away from the huge hand, and the white man was on his feet in an instant.

His dark eyes held a look of fury Degata had never before seen in a white man. There was no fear here, only wild hostility.

"Come on, Injun," he murmured softly. "Come to me where I can cut your guts out!"

Degata did not answer, though he understood most of what the man said. The white man towered over him by at least four inches and must have outweighed him by forty pounds. Degata had never before seen a neck or forearms such as this man had, but his size and strength did not cow him. The first thing his father had ever taught him was that a tomahawk can chop anything down to size.

They stood ten feet apart glaring at each other. "Come on you sonofa—" the white man said. Degata had heard that word before at the forts, never did know what it meant, but knew that white men used it when they were mad at an animal. He stepped forward suddenly, as if he were going to attack hand-to-hand. He raised his tomahawk, but instead of taking the last step or two and then chopping down, he flung the tomahawk at the man's chest. The redhead raised his right arm to fend off the blow. The tomahawk bit into his forearm. He screamed and dropped his knife. Degata now drew his knife and plunged it deep into the giant's chest, between his ribs, into his heart.

With its last few beats it pumped a great gush of blood out over his chest. Degata watched the man's eyes widen, then cloud over just before he toppled face first to the floor of the forest. The Seneca leaned over, then with his knife cut to the bone around the man's scalp. He put his knee on the back of the man's head, reached his fingers under the scalp and pulled it back with a grunt. He held it high in his bloodsoaked hand.

He sat on the back of his fallen foe and waited for his heart to slow down. Beneath him the dry, porous soil of the forest floor soaked up all the white man's blood without even a brief puddle. Finally Degata stood up and sang his victory song, slid the scalp into his belt, and walked over to the tree beneath which he had first spotted the man. There lay the earthenware jug, in pieces. The forest floor around them was still damp. As it had absorbed the blood, the earth had absorbed every drop of the man's rum.

It was almost dark, but Degata had no desire to linger long where an enemy had released his spirit. Stolidly he slung his pack on his shoulders, then did the same with the dead man's pack. He reached for his tomahawk and slid it back in his belt, picked up his rifle and reloaded it, and headed north, to the big conference at Irondequoit.

Degata was not surprised to see so many Senecas in one place. The English knew how to promote large convocations of Indians. All it took was the promise of presents and rum, and the Indians would be there. That was one promise the English always kept. They knew they had better. The only thing was, what would the English want in return? They'd say one thing before the council, but it would often turn out to be another. They were clever, thought Degata, who had also met many clever Indians in the course of his thirty summers.

There were more than just the sachems and warriors present on this day. The women and children were there too, and the old men would not be left behind either. There was a great feeling of anticipation among them, but Degata knew that underneath the excitement lay tremendous anxiety.

The women weren't there just for the festivities. They were also there to keep an eye on their men, because they knew that every time their men went into council with the English, they came away with less than they went in with. And yet, Degata thought, the white men knew how to turn the women's heads too.

On this day Major Butler would be asking the people for more than he had a right to ask. But then, that was what the English did. They were always very persuasive. And they almost always got their way. They had the goods to buy their way. Degata dreaded this day.

How great was the price? Probably more than the Senecas could afford to pay. Degata knew this was true only because the price was usually more than they could afford.

Then he thought about the enemy. He had always been confused about the English. On one hand they were their allies, on the other hand they were always pushing them farther west. That was why he had joined the Seneca renegades who went to war against the English during the great rebellion fourteen summers back.

The Senecas were milling around the provisions stacked up for them, and settling themselves on the grounds. The smell of beef roasting over large open pits made mouths water. English soldiers were distributing ample portions of flour to the women. And now here came the rum. Oh yes, the rum. Always the rum, Degata thought. And Degata ignored the meat, and the flour, and his family, as he queued up for the rum, his mouth already beginning to water in anticipation of a good day.

Major Butler had prepared this conference with great care. The Senecas were important to him. They were by far the most numerous of the Iroquois. If he won them over, he believed he could win over the other five nations of the great confederacy. And he had to win their hearts, not just their promises. So this would not be a simple get-them-drunk-pull-out-the-document-have-the-chiefs-stagger-forward-and-sign-here agreement.

All day he let them drink and feast, until their bellies were content. Then they slept. And the next day, what did he do but feed them again, this wonderful beef that they had come to love well, and pour out the rum, until he thought that by now every red man and woman in the camp would be convinced that the King of England was indeed the finest, richest, most generous man on the face of the earth.

The third day, speaking through an interpreter who had a very strong voice, Major Butler addressed the Senecas.

"Everybody here knows of the ancient covenant chain that you took hold of so many years ago, when we took you by the hand and helped you defeat your enemies to the north that the French had given guns when you had none," he began. And they all knew that what he said was true.

"And we all remember how faithful the king has been to you, and you to the king, over these many years." And they all knew that this was sort of true, give or take a few betrayals on both sides over those many years. And they gave their cries of assent.

"We know," he said, "how bad it is when some of your people grow rebellious and no longer listen to their proper leaders." Actually, the Senecas knew nothing of the sort. When some people no longer wanted to heed the village chiefs, they simply went their own way, either a few miles away or on to the next village or out to the Spay-Lay-Wi-Theepi, the valley of the Ohio River, with the Mingoes. They didn't think that was bad at all. But they listened politely to Major Butler because they knew it was good manners.

"It is your duty to take a firm hold of the covenant chain and fight on the side of the king against those who would break the chain," he continued. "Think of these rebels. They are the ones who cross the line set by the king. They are the ones settling your lands when the king would have them in the east where they belong. They are bad, and you must help us teach them a lesson. Look around you at the gifts the king has prepared for you. He is a very rich man. If you fight for him, he will reward you so that you will never again have to worry about a hungry winter for your children. The king will be there for you. That is how he is with those who fight for him. A generous man. A great chief.

"This war is already nearly over. Think how every time we attack them they run from us. We chase them all over the woods, and all they know how to do is lose and die. They do not know how to fight back. Think about these rebels. How poor they are. How weak they are. Scattered little groups of disobedient children that we must teach to behave."

He had raised the hatchet above his head and was exhorting the Senecas to take it, but the chiefs would not be bullied or bribed, at least not then and there. With great dignity they stood up, told Butler that his words had entered them, and that their men would this night meet in council to discuss Major Butler's request.

This was the night that the sachems and the chiefs and the principal warriors arranged themselves around the council fire sober, not sated. They knew that what they decided on that night would be important. Now it was not the gray-hairs and the big-bellies counseling caution and the young warriors questing for glory. This was not glory, this was white man's war. "What were these fools fighting over anyway?" asked one of the warriors, and even the wisest men in the Seneca nation could not answer.

"Besides," reminded another, "do you all not remember that a few moons ago we met with the rebels and promised to keep out of the war? I like them. They do not ask us to risk our lives for their war, like the English do. All they wish is for us to stand aside and not help the English."

Everybody else liked that too. "If the English king is so strong and the rebels are so weak, why is it that the king needs our warriors to fight for them and the rebels do not?" asked Sayengaraghta, a warrior well respected by his Seneca comrades. "And if this is to be such a short war, if the

rebels are already on their knees, then why do they need us
to win the final victory? I am not so sure this white chief is
telling us the things he should tell us. Let us wait a while
and see where the truth lies." And it soon became clear that
almost every Seneca in Irondequoit on that day, from the
most powerful chief down to the youngest women, did not
want to follow Major Butler or the King of England into
war.

The next evening the formal council between Butler and
the leading Seneca chiefs was scheduled. They puffed the
pipe, talked the talk, and threw down strings of wampum
each time they made an important point. But Butler was a
tough, stubborn man. He looked up at the moonlit clouds
that scudded across the night sky.

"These rebels," he said, "are nobody. They disappear, like
that cloud running across the moon. Would you make a
treaty with that cloud just because it had words to throw
down at you? No. The Keepers of the Western Door make
their treaties with important people, like the King of England, who is very rich, who can do so much for his children.

"Is rum precious to you? It is like water to us. Are your
warriors precious to you? Our men are like the grains of
sand on the shores of Lake Ontario. When your men are
away claiming glory on the warpath against those who
would take your land, we will be there to protect your
women and children in the villages. The king will watch
over his faithful red children. They shall never want for
anything." He went on in that vein for many minutes.

The council continued for hours, until finally, judging
that he had made his impression, Butler bade them return to
their councils to consider his words.

They must have been powerful words, because this time
the warriors were split on which side they wished to be
faithful to. The women were now stirred up too. All
through the next morning there were arguments and
harangues throughout the camp. The whites had all with-

drawn from sight, to let the Indians have it out by themselves.

And while the Senecas debated, their ship came in. It was a two-masted schooner, not one of his majesty's more majestic vessels, but big enough to the Indians of the lakes. It wasn't the ship that impressed them most, however, it was what came down the gangplanks of that ship.

Without fanfare the sailors began carrying bundles from the ship and dropping them in a cleared area by the dock. That was enough to draw half the Senecas in the camp. They knew the bundles had something to do with them. And then, when all the bundles had been beached, Major Butler commanded the sailors to open them up. And what glorious wonders to behold! First, there were ostrich feathers. Who of them had ever seen an ostrich feather? Who of them had ever seen a bird one-fourth the size of the birds that must have worn such feathers? It was as if somebody had docked in Albany and started passing around emeralds and rubies as big as hens' eggs.

And then there were thousands of tiny little bells that tinkled softly and beautifully. Butler knew how these Indians loved bells, how Mohawks would kill a cow just to get a big clunking cowbell. But these pretty-sounding things that could be sewn into the hems of dresses—the women were enchanted! What fine people these English were to share such things with them. Nor were the warriors unmoved by such generosity.

Then came the beads, thousands upon thousands of smooth, shining glass and porcelain beads. The Senecas had beads, of course, wampum beads carefully ground from seashells by Long Island Indians who paid them as tribute to their Iroquois lords. But those beads were so precious that in the upper counties of gold-starved New York, even the whites used strings of these beads as a form of money. To the Senecas it was as if a ship had docked in New York and its captain had begun to shower purest gold over all the inhabitants. Many on that beach were now certain that a

new day had dawned. Starting from that day, surely the
king who loved them enough to be so generous would care
for all their needs, so that never again in the depths of a
frigid winter would a child cry for want of a warm blanket
or a morsel.

Major Butler watched the Senecas while they played
with the strange and beautiful goods like children. Some of
them had their hands over their mouths, so astonished were
they. Others touched the bells and the ostrich feathers gingerly, as if they were afraid of being bitten. As they gathered up these things for themselves, Butler could not help
but notice that none of them attempted to take huge quantities. There was an innate sense of decency when it came
to sharing.

He knew he had them now, and he was glad, not only
because they were a fierce enemy to have at his back and
good fighters to have at his side, when they felt like fighting. He wanted them on the English side because he had
few doubts about who the final victors would be, and he did
not want to see these Senecas suffer for having sided with
the wrong people.

As for the suffering they might have to endure in the
course of this war, that was not his concern. Everybody was
suffering in this war. That's what war did to people. Meanwhile, he could see that he had softened them up quite a
bit. They were only too glad to resume their council with
him that evening. Having seen how incredibly generous the
king had been with them in the matter of trinkets, they
imagined an incredible bounty of necessities that would be
theirs once the treaty was concluded.

By the time they had assembled, they were feeling so
good about themselves and their benefactors that their
minds were wide open to the golden possibilities of their
future. To remind them that their self-interest was also their
duty, Major Butler brought with him the big old wampum
belt that all Iroquois knew as the covenant chain. This belt
was designed with the symbolism that helped the learned

elders to recall the ancient alliance between them and the
English, an alliance so much older than their treaty with the
rebels. This was a real treaty, with a great people. Butler
reminded them that there was much glory and booty to be
gained on the warpath while they helped the English to
secure the final easy victories over these miserable rebels
who seemed to long for their own destruction, else how
would you explain their perverse desire to separate themselves from such a caring, generous king?

It was a seductive moment. Even Degata and others who
had fought the English during Pontiac's rebellion forgot the
days after the last war with France, when the king seemed
to have gone to sleep. Now for the feast, with more beeves
roasting over slow fires, and enough rum for them all to
drink themselves into oblivion, a night worth remembering,
but few of the warriors and sachems would.

The next afternoon, having obtained such relief as sleep,
bathing in the lake, and their favorite remedies would provide, the warriors were treated to another off-loading of
goods. Every man received a white man's suit. Fine new
tomahawks and scalping knives were passed out, along with
shiny brass kettles and money for the chiefs. Most important was the ammunition and guns that suddenly appeared
in abundance. And the word went around that the warriors
would be rewarded for every prisoner or scalp they brought
in.

Now they knew they were loved and trusted, for most of
them remembered another time when ammunition was
scarce and new firearms were unavailable. Those were the
hungry times, when the king truly must have been sleeping.
The women and children and old men went home, but
many of the warriors, including Degata, stayed at Irondequoit. He was hungry for action, and he did not have long
to wait.

❧2❧

IT WAS JUST A SINGLE CANOE, BUT IT WAS THE biggest one in the Wendel and Watley fleet. Once a year Thad and his son Jinja paddled sixty miles or so up the river from Albany to the falls, where they traded with a small group of Abnaki trappers. Although the furs were high quality, the trip was never extremely profitable for them. Thad had a soft spot in his heart for the men of this poor little village on the northeast shore of Lake Champlain. He always gave them a better deal than he gave anybody else, and then dared his father-in-law to complain about it.

Thad generally avoided spending time on the trails and rivers. Although he was half Seneca, and had been raised in a Seneca village in western New York, he did not maintain the same adoration of the wilderness as did his father Big Oak or his son Jinja. But this was a sort of outing for Thad, a short jaunt up the Hudson to be with old friends who had long ago agreed to meet them more than halfway. Thad felt that since the Abnakis traveled so far, they deserved to get a better deal, and besides, they had a lot of people to support and worked hard to support them.

It was early in the spring, but the woods on the upper reaches of the Hudson River had not heard about it yet. The poplars on the hillsides still stood stark and bare-limbed in contrast to the lush green growth of the pines and spruces around them. But Thad and Jinja had already felt the lessening of the chill. It was a still day, with no annoying wet wind in their faces as they bent their backs and worked the canoe up against the current, which was stronger in the upper, narrower regions of the river. Theirs was not a logy Iroquois elm-bark canoe. Just before the war had started, Thad had arranged for a shipment of birch bark from Lake Ontario. They had constructed a large and a small canoe sheathed in that fine material.

The canoe cut through the waters like a sharp trade hatchet, surging with each powerful stroke, slowing as the paddlers recovered, then surging again as the muscles of the two strong men rippled and the paddle blades swept along the sides of the canoe.

They were getting close to their rendezvous point below the falls. Now was the time to be extra careful. Any skulking Tory or Mohawk might find them vulnerable as they paddled their canoe into the creek that was always their meeting place. The canoe climbed the creek with only seven or eight feet to spare on each side, and then only about five hundred feet inland before the creek became too shallow to navigate.

As soon as the canoe scraped bottom, the two men leaped onto the bank, seized their rifles, tied the boat to a nearby sapling, and ran quickly into a thick clump of assorted young trees. There they waited silently, on one knee, watching and listening, their rifles at the ready.

The wind stirred the bare branches around them. Thad, who was watching the creek, felt the wind dry his eyes, and he blinked several times to moisten them again. Generally these meetings came off like clockwork, as if it were scheduled for two o'clock in the Musket and Arrow Tavern three blocks from Thad's house.

They had been waiting for less than two minutes when they heard the call of the mourning dove. To make certain of what they had heard, they continued to wait, still as death, and shortly it came again. Thad responded in kind, then paused for several seconds and repeated the call.

"Little Oak!" came a voice from across the creek, using Thad's Seneca name.

"Here, Petit Roi," Thad hissed. Dubbed the little king by the French traders, the English-speaking colonials rendered his name as "Pettyroy."

The little Abnaki turned quickly, his rifle raised, until he saw his friend Thad. The corners of his mouth turned up, just a little.

"Ah, Little Oak. I see you have Jinja with you." Behind Petit Roi an empty forest came alive as seven more Abnakis suddenly materialized. Although Thad had been raised in a village of Seneca warriors and taught the mysteries of woodland invisibility, it never failed to amaze him when he saw Indians appear abruptly, as if they had been dropped from the heavens.

The traders and the Abnakis examined each other's wares. The Abnakis were satisfied with the trade goods, as Thad knew they would be. Thad was pleased with the quality of the Abnakis' furs, but as always he wished that there had been more. He knew that the Indians had been fair, that they had brought all their pelts and withheld none.

They sat together and smoked around a very small campfire, with guards posted, warmed by small amounts of rum supplied by Thad.

"My friend," said Petit Roi, "I have heard that it will be a bad summer along the River Flowing Through Mountains." He was referring to the Mohawk River, which flowed eastward almost from Lake Oneida to the Hudson River. "I have heard that there will be a big battle there, and here, and that when the battle is over, the king's men will march into Albany and choke all the rebels with a rope."

"I have also heard that the English will attack," Thad agreed.

"I am worried about you," Petit Roi continued. "What will you do?"

Thad had been trading with this band of Abnakis for years and enjoyed their company, but he did not intend to take them into his confidence. Poverty makes for desperate people. The English had bribed better men than these with their free trade goods.

"We will certainly not be going west to fight. We have our business to take care of," he said, neglecting to tell the little chief that Wendel and Watley was one of the principal smugglers and suppliers for the Continental Army. "What will you do?" he asked.

"My friend." Petit Roi smiled. "Maybe it is better that neither one of us knows what the other is doing in this war."

Barry St. Leger should have been a general. Unfortunately, he had to depend on military skill rather than friends in court to get him where he wanted to be in the British army, and of course, skill was not enough. And so he was Lieutenant Colonel Barry St. Leger.

This little war was not exactly the opportunity he was seeking. What glory could there be in some woods, skirmishing against a gaggle of rude bumpkins who couldn't even march in formation, much less engage with courage the hard steel of British bayonets? But at least it gave him the opportunity to be a brigadier general, even if the promotion was only temporary.

His force was an interesting blend that included a couple of hundred veteran English foot troops, a small Tory regiment, some German riflemen, a handful of Canadians, and best of all, close to a thousand genuine wild Iroquois led by Joseph Brant, or Thayendanegea, a Mohawk who had been to England and benefited from the experience, at least from the English point of view.

Among the Iroquois horde, which included Mohawks, Senecas, Cayugas, and Onondagas, was Degata, who was not certain he wanted to be there. For one thing, he had no desire to fight under a Mohawk. According to Iroquois tradition, they should have been commanded by Seneca war chiefs. For another, he didn't care very much for Mohawks.

And then, like most other Senecas, he was not convinced that he wanted to fight on either side in this war. Once the gifts were in the lodges, and the rum was all drunk, and the party was over, there was reality. Once more they were caught in the middle of a white man's war, and every time they got caught in a white man's war, they lost, even when their white men won. It didn't make any sense.

And this white general was not making any sense. He had his Englishmen wasting their time chopping a path through the woods so that he could bring his big boom guns with him. What were they going to do with cannon in the woods? Degata didn't like cannon no matter whose side they were on, and before he even thought about getting into the fight, he'd make sure he was nowhere near one of those roaring monsters.

Thanks to his scouts, and to the noisiness of the rebels, St. Leger knew the enemy was on the way to Fort Stanwix, which was just a few miles away. So he told Brant to rig an ambush for him, which Brant was only too glad to do. Brant found a pair of wooded hillsides that looked down on Oriskany Ravine along the route the rebels must take, and there he stationed his warriors. Degata lay hidden behind a big old elm and snickered. Just like a stupid Mohawk to think that a whole army would just stumble into his trap. Instead of watching the ravine, Degata kept his eyes roaming to his left and behind him, searching for rebel scouts and flankers. This didn't feel right at all, he thought. He'd be much happier in his lodge with his woman, that was certain.

And yet here they came, in a jumbled mass of militia following some fool on a white horse. Ah, of course, Brant had been around these people much more than he. One last time Degata checked the priming in his pan, then he tightened his hold on the trigger and waited. Above, dark clouds were moving in. Good thing this was going to be a quick fight.

Brant fired first, then the valley exploded with the impact of good British muskets and rifles. Below, dozens of rebels fell, but the rest reacted well, taking cover behind trees and looking for targets.

To veteran Iroquois warriors, battles had a rhythm. It never took them long to figure out the rhythm, and if it seemed to favor them, they were quick to dance to it. In this case they discovered the rhythm almost immediately. Degata loaded his weapon and waited for a rifle to fire from down below. He then rushed down the hill, a dash that took only a few seconds, and while his target was struggling desperately to ram his charge home, Degata seized his tomahawk, raised it above his head and brought it down with manic force on the skull of the rebel. The blood poured out and the rebel crumpled without a sound. Around him other Ganonsyoni were doing the same, and once they had been blooded, there was no stopping them.

But the militiamen were game for a fight. They too had tomahawks and rifle butts, and they swung them with all the desperation of cornered men. When they lost their tomahawks and rifles, they turned to their knives, and then their bare hands, until it seemed the two armies were locked in a death grip strangling the life out of each other. Somehow the survivors disengaged, picked up their rifles and started blasting each other again from behind trees.

The forest echoed with the smoky explosions of black powder and the wild screeches of Iroquois and militiamen alike. The air beneath the forest canopy misted over with gray smoke. The smell of powder and rancid bear grease choked the nostrils of the rebel defenders. The shock of the initial attack had been absorbed. But as the minutes went by and men on both sides continued to topple, the rebel situation got more and more desperate, until suddenly, as if in response to the pandemonium on the forest floor, thunder split the heavens and the rains came. Rebels, Indians, English, Germans, Canadians, and Tories alike hunkered down beneath the cloudburst and concentrated on keeping their powder dry.

Through a curtain of water Degata could see militia officers going from man to man, positioning them in a sort of a circle, facing out in pairs, behind the trees. Degata's comrades either failed to notice or did not care. As soon as the rain stopped, the firing began, and once again came the charges down the hill. To Degata's horror, brave warriors, many of them Senecas, were stopped mid-flight by the sharpshooters they hadn't counted on. Veteran though he was, Degata had never been in such a bloody fight. One rebel would fire and then, when a warrior would rush the position to dispatch the frantically loading militiaman, his partner behind the tree would shoot the warrior down. And they were good shots, those rebels. The Indians were paying a heavy price.

"Oonah!" came a cry through the woods. He could not believe it. The greatest warriors of the Iroquois confederacy were retreating, beaten back not by the great British army with their iron discipline and gleaming bayonets, but by this gaggle of farmers; the like of whom Degata had so often before seen give their lives up easily to painted braves. Degata looked around quickly, swallowing his panic, making sure he wasn't being left alone. Then, with a single swift movement, he dove from his spot behind a tree into some underbrush, running doubled over, zigzagging around trees and rocks until he had gained the top of the hill.

Then he and others near him stopped and turned to fire at the advancing militiamen. They had an uphill climb. If the Senecas let them fire, then came boiling down the hill, they could literally chop the militiamen to pieces. But once again came the cry—"Oonah! Oonah!" Degata was not bound to obey the call, but neither was he willing to be the last fighting Ganonsyoni on the hillside while his cohorts had run off. There had to be a reason. So the Senecas left the militiamen in possession of the battlefield, for whatever that was worth.

The militia did not pursue. Their losses had been staggering, hundreds of men killed, nearly all of them neighbors who lived in or near the Mohawk Valley. Degata had seen many of his own people fall too. As he loped through the forest, following those Iroquois who had earlier left the fight, he sensed that they were not so much fleeing from the battlefield as heading somewhere. Around him were men he did not know. Cayugas, Onondagas, Mohawks. He peered through the woods and saw far ahead a Seneca scalp lock, and he sprinted forward to overtake him.

The warrior proved to be an old campaigner known as Ganaysa, and he was wounded in his upper chest. One quick look convinced Degata that the wound was serious. His bare chest was covered with blood. Even as Degata watched, he could see the old warrior weakening. Gradually his smooth gait became ragged. His body bobbed from side to side as he tried to will himself to continue forward. He reeled for a moment, caught himself, and continued on, but his staggering movements were now in slow motion. Slowly, unwillingly, he sank to one knee, then to both knees, as Degata finally caught up to him.

"If you can help me, I think I can make it home," said the old warrior, and then his eyes closed and he sank to the forest floor. As badly as Degata wanted to be gone, he could not leave the old warrior, not then. He looked around and spotted some moss, which he scraped off the ground and plastered over the wound. He held his water skin to Ganaysa's mouth and was glad to see the warrior swallowing some of the liquid, even though most of it dripped down his chin.

Ganaysa was pure warrior. If he had ever had a family of his own, Degata had never heard of it. The old brave lived for the hunt and the warpath, a loyal, staunch son of the Longhouse. On the backs of men like him had the powerful Iroquois Confederation been built.

The old warrior swallowed a few more times, then took a deep breath and regained consciousness.

"Help me, Degata," he said, and Degata blinked with surprise. It had never occurred to him that the old warrior knew his name. Degata hoisted Ganaysa to his feet. To his amazement, Ganaysa still had some strength in his legs, although Degata had to hold onto him because the man's sense of balance was gone. Slowly they made their way ahead, while around them men streamed past, not in panic, but in retreat nevertheless.

They had not gone much farther before Degata began to feel Ganaysa weakening again. Step after step they struggled on, until finally they had reached the area where they had camped the night before, and where the British had kept their supplies. What they found was a smoking ruin with a few bodies and a lot of bare earth where tents and supplies had stood only a few hours before. Soldiers and Indians were milling about, looking confused, waiting to be told what to do next and unnerved that nobody there appeared to care about giving orders. British officers were standing around, hands on hips, looking stupid, as if wondering whether the supplies had burned the camp and walked away.

Ganaysa's knees buckled then. Slowly Degata lowered him to the ground and propped him up against a tree. Ganaysa coughed and blood flowed from his mouth. He gasped and coughed up more blood. Degata found that he cared whether or not Ganaysa lived, even as he knew that the old warrior was dying.

The old warrior raised his hand feebly to his mouth. "Uhh," he breathed, trying to ask for water. Degata pulled Ganaysa's head back and tried to pour a trickle of water down his throat, but Ganaysa could not swallow. He didn't know it, though, and he smiled, just before his eyes closed.

More men came streaming in, mostly either wounded or helping the wounded. Degata was appalled by what he saw. Some of the finest warriors of the Seneca nation were lying in the clearing, and like Ganaysa, their lives drained from them drop by drop. Others lay in the forest, waiting for their tribesmen to come back and reclaim their bodies. Degata sat by Ganaysa and listened to the survivors talk.

Among the Iroquois, the sachems, their most renowned statesmen, had no authority in battle, but in times of trouble they had the right to fight in the ranks, so to speak, as warriors. Degata had rejoiced that many of these men of great heart had chosen to join the war chiefs against the rebels. He had faith in the wisdom of the sachems, and if they felt the cause was worth their lives, then it must be a worthy cause. But now, while the afternoon faded to twilight and warriors were coming in with the dead, he could feel an ache behind his eyes as he saw two sachems brought in, their lives spent, and laid side by side.

A French scout Degata knew only as Leon sat down on the other side of Ganaysa and studied his wound. He put his ear to the old warrior's chest and listened to his shallow, labored breathing, then shook his head.

"About ready for the spirit world, eh, Degata?" he said sadly. "Well, anyway, we showed those damned rebels a real fight, damned if we didn't." Degata understood Leon's French from his long years of dealing with French traders, better men with worse trade goods. If only there had been more of them, then maybe this fight would have been to get the king's Englishmen out of their forest, instead of rebels who looked and acted so much like Englishmen.

Degata did not dislike the Frenchman, but he was not about to let a white man know of the sadness in his heart. He watched as several more Seneca warriors were brought in and placed on the ground beside the others. Many years had passed since the Senecas had fought in the great wars of conquest against the surrounding tribes. They had fought little in the last war against the French. Those who had fought in the rebellion on the big lakes against the English had suffered few casualties. He had never witnessed the demise of so many fine warriors. His heart felt like a stone, and here was this Frenchman smiling and boasting of the way they had whipped the rebels.

Degata wanted to ask the Frenchman if he had any brandy, but at that moment Ganaysa gave a deep sigh, his last. Without Degata having to ask, Leon took a flask from beneath his buckskin shirt, threw his head back and drank deeply, then handed the flask to Degata. He understood that Leon meant for him to have the rest, but the flask seemed so light that he expected only a scant taste remained for him. He was pleasantly surprised to find four full-throated swallows warming his belly.

"Thank you," he said to Leon, not in French, but in sign. "Thank you, my friend." Slowly he stood up and began to walk around the camp, looking for a man from his own village, a man to help him care for Ganaysa's body, a man with whom to share the long walk home. There would be more battles, he knew. And he was certain that the British would defeat the rebels. But this war would not be like others, when the Senecas did a little scouting, found the enemy, then sat around and smoked their pipes while the white armies slaughtered each other. The English had been very generous up at Irondequoit. But Degata knew from past experience that when the British paid, they always received more than their due in return.

In this case, more than their due was the precious blood of the Seneca people.

❖3❖

THAD WATLEY'S AGING FATHER-IN-LAW stomped around the balcony above the trading floor of Wendel and Watley, the finest of all the mercantile establishments in Albany. Now approaching the age of seventy, his heavy frame still stood on a pair of sturdy legs that pounded the hardwood floor as he walked across his office above the shop. The people on the floor below could not hear his footsteps. There were so many shoppers, and their voices were so loud that they would not have heard if a cannon had been fired off the balcony.

"You cannot go, Thad! Not now," he half hollered, half begged. "Please!" he added with an insistence that demonstrated not courtesy but command. "Especially, you cannot go alone. Only a fool runs through the woods alone these days."

Thad was dressed in the fashion of the times, from his three-cornered hat to his buckled shoes. His waistcoat was fawn-colored, while his coat and breeches were a woodsy brown. His body was lean and muscular and his face had a youthful look to it, although he was nearly forty years old. He stood loose-limbed and relaxed as he listened to his father-in-law rail at him. In fact, he appeared so detached that a witness would have thought the old man's anger was directed at a fool many miles distant.

"It is time I brought Big Oak and his family back to Albany," Thad insisted. "I don't think he knows just how bad the situation is."

"He knows, he knows!" the old man hollered back at him. "The trees and the animals tell him everything." In times of stress the old Dutchman still occasionally let a hint of old world accent come through. "Tad, I need you here now. You are not to go!"

"I'll leave just before dawn in the morning," Thad answered, as if he hadn't heard a word the old man said. "We'll be back in a few days."

"Hah! What is that 'we'? Why are you so sure your fadder will come running with you back to Albany? Him and that wild squaw of his? And his three dirty wild kids—your 'brudders'!" The sarcasm was thick, but it only made Thad's smile grow wider.

"I know you want to see him as much as I do," Thad said. "And you're right. A man should not travel alone. I'll take Jinja with me. He's a good boy to have on a trail."

"You'll do no such thing," the old man shouted, so loudly that finally the people buying goods on the crowded floor below did hear. Abruptly, the noise of trade below subsided. A few snickers indicated that Dieter Wendel's tirades were nothing new to the customers at Wendel and Watley.

"I won't haf my grandson running around the woods in the middle of a war," said the old man in a hissing whisper.

"He's my son and he's going with me, Dieter," Thad retorted. And before the old Dutchman could answer, Thad was descending the stairs two at a time with his long legs, on his way home to pack for the morning.

Thad's oldest son, like Thad and his father, had two names, a white one and an Indian one. But whereas Thad and his father had been named Little Oak and Big Oak by the Senecas of Tonowaugh, where Thad had spent his childhood, Jinja—David to his white friends and family—received his Longhouse name from his grandfather, after an honored old friend, the Mohawk chief Gingego.

Dieter spent the next five minutes pacing back and forth across his balcony office. "Jinja!" he muttered bitterly. "Jinja! Demmit! Demmit! Demmit!"

The hour before dawn was Thad's favorite hour of the whole day. At that time he considered that he was getting a jump on the rest of the human world. His heart soared like that of a child as he and his oldest son walked softly in the rutted dust of the Albany streets, through the town and out across the long clearing that led to the woods north of town.

Thad's six-foot-three frame towered above most of those he knew in that town or any other, and Jinja missed matching him by an inch. Although Jinja was already eighteen years old, his lanky body had yet to gain the bulky muscle that characterized his father. In that way he was more like his all-white grandfather, Big Oak, and like Big Oak, he leaned toward the lifestyle of the Ganonsyoni. His half-Seneca father, on the other hand, preferred to live like a white man, as a prosperous businessman in Albany.

Already Jinja was an active employee in the firm of Wendel and Watley, learning the business from the bottom up, from the trading trails to the warehouses to the counting houses to the big store. In his five years of employment, he had learned to sit still when his work called for sitting still. But he didn't like it. As restless as a Seneca warrior, he longed for the trail. Every night his dreams would be filled with it. So when his father had told him that soon they would be leaving the stinking streets of Albany for the sweet-smelling hardwoods and hemlocks of the north trail, his heart nearly leaped from his chest.

They spent the evening before their departure on the back porch, cleaning their weapons, filling their pouches with food and ammunition, checking out their trail skins and moccasins, and arguing with his mother, who pleaded with them not to go.

"This will be a short, fast trip," Thad had told Katherine.

"We hope that when we return, we will have my father and his family with us, so I would like you to see that their rooms are ready for them."

Katherine nodded and smiled with anticipation. She loved the old woodsman and his Tuscarora wife, who was close to her age. She loved their "wild Indian children," and so did her father, no matter what he said. In times of war, she thought, it was good to have your family around you, especially when they included strong men like Big Oak, Thad, and her own David. Still, of late she had been thinking more and more that her life had little in common with these people. As Wendel and Watley had continued to profit, and her husband and her friends' husbands had become men of means, Indians had become less and less relevant to her world. Sometimes she even forgot that when she had met her husband, clad head to toe in deerskins, nut-brown from his months on the trail, she had thought him the handsomest Indian she had ever seen.

"You will be careful with the boy?" she asked Thad as they lay together that night in the flickering light of a candle.

"He is also *my* greatest treasure," Thad replied. "But he knows the woods too. We are safe there. It is the others who must take care." Katherine caught the fierce glint in her husband's eye as he spoke. His years of business as a white man had not dulled his warrior instincts. It still amazed her to think that the hands that had stroked her with such loving tenderness over all these years had sped many enemies, red and white, to an early appointment with their creator.

"I will have everything in readiness for Sam and his family," she said. "Just make sure to get them down here quickly. They say that it will be a bloody summer. My heart would break if we should lose any of them."

Once outside the town, Thad and Jinja broke into a long-legged lope that quickly took them past the old wagon road and onto the north trail. They ran silently, with little effort, while their eyes became used to seeing what they had to see in the forest. The beams of light that filtered through the green canopy above fell on the irregular shapes of nature—rocks, bushes, felled tree trunks, ragged stumps, occasional skittering creatures and startled birds. Those beams of light would be the beacons that would save their lives if they fell upon an object that did not belong and revealed it to Thad or Jinja. See before being seen.

The day was windless, and Thad was pleased. Wind in the forest covered up the sounds made by other people. Thad and Jinja made little noise themselves, only the regular sigh of their breath and the occasional movement of a rock or a twig beneath their feet.

Within an hour of leaving Albany they were so into the rhythm of their journey that what little effort they had felt at the beginning had disappeared. They might have been floating from hill to hill, for all the energy it cost them. The mosquitoes and gnats of the forest hovered but did not bite, repelled by the rancid bear grease they had smeared on their faces, necks, and hands.

Five hours out of Albany they topped a hill and found a rock shelf off the trail that commanded a view of the next twenty miles of their journey. From their pouches they extracted some pieces of cold goose that Katherine had prepared for them the day before. The two men gnawed away, relishing the rich meat. While either one could live on spare trail food for weeks at a time, neither preferred to if they could help it.

The hilltop caught a breeze that dried the perspiration on their faces as they sat silently eating and looking across the green forest canopy that spread below them. The breeze carried the scent of summer wildflowers, various conifers—and smoke. They studied the canopy to the horizon but could see nothing. Invisible smoke meant Indian smoke, Thad thought, but said nothing. When the whites are at war, each side wants the Indians on their side. Thad knew it wasn't because the Indians were dependable allies, but because they were fierce, undependable enemies.

"Come on," Thad said to Jinja. The two men stood up and resumed their journey north. Those two words were the only ones that had passed between them since they had entered the woods north of Albany.

They skittered down the trail toward a creek, and walked along the bank until they found a good fording place, just before a noisy little rapid. Thad crossed over first, dry over a trio of handy rocks, then waited, crouched, while Jinja followed. Before Jinja had taken his final step across the creek, Thad seized him and pulled him into some nearby underbrush.

He pointed back across the creek. Through the trees, maybe fifty yards from where they lay, he could see flashes of red. British troops, cloaked like cardinals for visibility on the open European battlefield. Thad and Jinja pointed their rifles toward the soldiers and waited for the attack. Thad looked around to see if they were being surrounded. All he saw were the motionless leaves of the forest. He turned back and watched the redcoats approach. There were three of them, plus two men in civilian clothing. The two civilians were leading horses.

Thad took a quick glance sideways at Jinja, who lay motionless, staring down his barrel without a blink. Good boy. His first look at the enemy in the field. No more than Thad had expected. Jinja was quiet, steady, unemotional. Jinja was his son.

The soldiers were now about fifty yards upstream, above the rapids, still on the other side. They walked down the bank until they were opposite where Thad and Jinja lay concealed. They continued downstream, followed by the civilians. It was obvious they had not seen the trader and his son. They were not looking for men, Thad now understood. This place was where a north-south trail crossed an east-west trail, and the soldiers were hoping to strike the trail east. They were close to it now, Thad knew, and sure enough, the one in front gave a shout and the others followed. Soon all Thad could see was their backs, and then only the rear ends of horses as they followed the trail.

They waited another two minutes before they rose from their hiding place and took the west trail, which would bring them closer to the ancient Mohican trace that would lead them to the home of Big Oak.

Just a few pink fingers of sunlight remained on the horizon when Thad and Jinja topped the final rise. Then, as they descended into the valley, the pink horizon vanished. The woods were all dark save for the faint yellow glow through the trees on the side of the next hill. Both had made the journey many times before, always arriving near nightfall, hungry, tired, and knowing they would be receiving warm hospitality and hot food within moments of their arrival.

Dark as it was, they knew the path up the side of the hill and followed it with sure feet. Still they maintained silence, a habit gleaned from Thad's long experience of woods travel in time of war.

For a while the woods hid the house lights from the two travelers. Soon, however, they were coming up the sloping path that passed by the side of the house and led to the three front steps.

There was a crude chair on the front porch, but no one was occupying it. That surprised Thad because he knew that this late at night Big Oak normally sat on it, its back leaned up against the cabin, and whittled pine sticks. He put a hand on Jinja's shoulder and made him stop at the side of the house while he climbed up on the porch and took a peek through one of the front windows.

There was an enormous fire in the fireplace, lighting up most of the front room, but there was nobody inside. Thad felt a chill. This was strange. He had expected that Big Oak would somehow observe their arrival, and half expected the family to be out on the front porch beating their rifle butts on the floor in celebration. Instead there was a ghastly silence, and an untended fire throwing sparks up the chimney. Instinctively, his right hand sought out the trigger and hammer of his rifle.

"Ease that hand on down," came a voice from behind him. Thad froze. "It's a sad situation when a man gets caught sneaking up on his father's house in the middle of the night."

Thad let a silent chuckle escape his mouth. Sheepishly he looked over toward where Jinja was standing. There was a hand over Jinja's mouth but his eyes were smiling. The hand was small, belonging to his stepmother, Cilla. The voice, of course, was Big Oak's.

He turned around and hugged his father while three young boys scampered up on the porch laughing or giggling, according to their ages. "And now I suppose I have to hug the child uncles of my son," muttered Thad in sham grumpiness. "It's not right, you old vulture. A man should not have to go through part of his life calling children 'Uncle.' Anyway, you've had enough children."

"Sure enough, you bet," came the voice of Cilla as she climbed the stairs to the porch. She had put on some weight since Thad had last seen her, but her round face still bore the strong look of determination he had seen the night the three of them made their desperate escape by canoe from a Huron village so long ago. "Get in the house, you two," she continued. "Come on."

She pulled the latchstring, opened the door, watched while everybody walked in, closed the door and pulled the latchstring in, then bolted the door. Thad and Jinja took turns hugging the three boys. Two of them hugged back. The third one was too young to have remembered them from their last visit a year ago, but when he saw what his brothers were about, he caught the spirit.

"What you got for us Thad, huh?" said Caleb, the oldest.

Ken, the second one, focused on Jinja, begging plaintively. These were unspoiled children, used to basic toys they made themselves or their father made for them. City toys were things they only saw and touched when Thad and Jinja came up to visit.

"Children, you go to bed. You two sit down at the table. I will feed you and talk to you. Semm, I don't care what you do," Cilla said good-naturedly.

The children groaned, but all it took was one word from Thad to send them scurrying up the ladder to the loft. The word was "tomorrow."

Big Oak laughed and pulled an extra chair up to the table while Cilla began filling large wooden bowls with the stew she had been cooking all day in the fireplace. She placed the bowls with spoons in front of Thad and Jinja, then produced two huge hunks of bread and put them on a clay dish in the middle of the table. Finally she brought them mugs of branch water, stood back, and watched them dig in.

Big Oak sat tall in his chair and observed as the next two generations begin to fill themselves. He waited until they were well into their meal before he spoke. In the meantime, a series of giggles revealed that the children were witnessing the scene from the loft.

Everybody ignored them.

"Then you did see us coming," Thad said.

"I saw someone on the next hill just over the night shadow," Big Oak replied. "I didn't know who it was, but I knew they were coming our way, so I got everybody out of the house, just in case."

"Just in case what?"

"Well, I don't know for sure. These days it's hard to tell who your friends are. So I decided to be careful. Ten years ago I would have known it was you when I saw you across the valley. My eyes ain't what they were, which you know. Anyway, you know more than me what's happening, so you can tell me—after you tell me what you're doing here. These days, no one goes for social visits in the woods."

His day in the woods had given Thad a ravenous appetite. The stew and the bread were ambrosia to him. With difficulty he tore his mind away from the food and focused it on his message.

"We think it's time you came into town with us. It's gettin' dangerous out here, and we're spending so much time thinking about your family that it's hard for us to do our work."

Big Oak nodded seriously, but Thad could see the corners of his mouth twitch just a bit.

"What's so funny?" he asked.

"What makes you think Albany is so safe?" This time Big Oak did laugh, an abrupt chuckle that stopped in his throat as if he'd been throttled.

"At least we've got the militia down there and—"

"Mi-li-sha." Big Oak pronounced each syllable distinctly, ironically, scornfully. "After all you and I have been through with militia . . . Let me tell you something, my boy. The word I get is that General Burgoyne is about to march right down the Hudson into Albany with his reg'lars, and his Tories, and his Hessians . . . and his Mohawks. Now let me ask you, should we be moving in down there or would it be safer if you and yours moved in with us up here?"

"How could we be safe up here?"

"The Mohawks won't attack me because I am a Ganonsyoni. The English won't attack because everybody knows I haven't gone over to the rebellion, and the rebels—hell, the rebels won't attack because I'd pin their ears back if they did."

"Well now, Pa, I've been meanin' to talk to you about your attitude concernin'—"

"My attitude? My *attitude*? You sound like one of them damn Sons of Liberty that's makin' life miserable for everybody. Are you gettin' the tar ready for me, is that it? You oughta know me, boy." He fixed a furious eye on his son and leaned forward in his chair until his chin stood poised directly over Thad's bowl of stew. I don't jump into anything until I know what it is I'm jumpin' into. Now I know you and your business friends don't like taxes, but I have to tell you, I live a pretty good life up here. Nobody bothers me for taxes or anything else. I've seen the rabble that calls itself the Continental Army, and to tell the truth, son, they ain't much. I don't just mean they can't fight. The ones I've seen, I wouldn't trust my back to them."

Thad and Jinja sat quietly and let the old man's temper run its course. "By the way," Big Oak said, his voice suddenly descending from the strident to the soft, sly, insinuating. "Just what would there be for me to do if I took the family into Albany?" He reached into a pouch, pulled out a pipe, and began to puff on it, cold and empty.

Thad sopped his bread in the stew and took a large bite, then followed it with a heaping spoonful.

"I thought you might—"

The old man leaned forward still farther. "Either I don't hear so good anymore or you're mumblin' through your food."

Thad swallowed, raised his spoon again, then put it down. "We're doin' pretty good smugglin' furs and weapons," he said. "Thought you might want to join us."

"Now why would I want to do that? For money I don't need that ain't worth nothin' anyway?"

"We need the guns if we're gonna lick the British."

"I told you, I am no patriot. Rebels are no damn good. The English are no damn good. Neither are the damn Mohawks anymore. Gettin' hard to find company these days. I guess that's why I stick around here with my family. So why should I go floatin' down the river with a boatload of beaver skins?"

"How about for the fun of it? You just about fished out that pond of yours down there."

"You got any tobacco? Cilla can grow just about anything, but I tell you, tobacco will not grow around here and I cannot figure why."

Thad fished into his pouch, pulled out a large clump and placed it on the table in front of Big Oak. Big Oak gave a grateful grunt and packed some in his pipe. He rose, walked over to the fireplace, grabbed a splint, and carried a bit of fire from the hearth to the bowl of his pipe.

"Tell you what," he said between satisfied puffs. "I'll go with you, but first we have some business to take care of on the trail."

"What's that?" Thad asked suspiciously.

"I get plenty of news here. Mostly from Paul Derontyan. Your friend John Burgoyne is on the march south. Takes those boys forever to march, especially when they've got them damn Hessians with them. They're worse than Yankee militia. We're gonna make them even slower."

Thad looked at his father. Same old Sam, full of tricks, and you never knew where he was gonna jump next. "I thought you didn't give a hoot about either side, and now you're gonna go out in the woods and risk your old scrawny neck for the sake of some mangy Continental Army?"

His father shook his head. "I know you think I've forgotten, but I haven't. Them boys up there," he pointed straight up to where the oldest one was hanging half off the loft, taking in the whole conversation, "ain't my only family. You're still my oldest son. This long tall thing," he gestured toward Jinja, who had finished his stew and was staring at Thad's with the eye of a famished wolf, "is my only grandson. If the English win, they'll prob'ly hang both you boys. Cilla wouldn't stand for that, and I'd never have a bit a peace around here again."

The Tuscarora woman carried Jinja's bowl to the fireplace, filled it, and topped it with an even bigger hunk of bread than the first one. Jinja accepted his second helping as if she had just granted him eternal salvation.

Thad looked at his father, then at his son. His father was a bit of a magician, he realized, when it came to staving off the effects of age. But no man ran the woods forever. Sooner or later would come his last warpath.

"Paul will be coming in tomorrow morning. By tomorrow night we'll be out on a lobster hunt. Are you interested?"

Thad gave his father a grim smile. "We'll be there." He turned to look at Jinja, but Jinja's eyes were cast down at the bowl of stew, which he was putting away in an unending series of spoon movements from bowl to mouth. As before, his long dark eyelashes did not blink. If he was thinking of action or excitement, he certainly did not show it.

He tilted the bowl backward and took a last spoonful. "Cilla," he said. "If you would point out a corner where I could pull up a blanket . . ." Cilla pointed to a spot in front of the fireplace. Jinja smiled. Although it was summer, the nights were mostly cool. "Thank you, Cilla."

She smiled back. She had always loved this young man, so quiet and courteous, like her own brother who lived in a Tuscarora village south of Ontario lake. "I'd love to listen all night to the two of you butting heads, but I'd sooner get some sleep," Jinja said, unrolling his blanket and putting his pack down for a pillow.

Immediately he fell asleep.

Big Oak looked at Thad with raised eyebrows.

"Never seen anything yet that twisted his tail," Thad said.

❧4❧

PAUL DERONTYAN WAS IN A BIGGER HURRY than usual. While the red eastern sun balanced itself on a bloody horizon, he took the creek below the house in one leap and did not slacken his pace as he climbed the side of the hill to the house.

He found the entire household awake and stirring around on the porch in the brisk morning air. He was pleased that Thad and Jinja had arrived, but had no desire to wait silently while they played with the toys they were handing to the children.

He need not have worried. As soon as Thad saw his head appear over the rise at the side of the house, he gave the youngest boy, Joshua, a light pat on the head and stepped off the porch to meet Derontyan. They hugged and shook hands quickly. Paul hurried only when he had to, Thad recalled, and yet his blue woolen shirt bore signs of sweat in spite of the morning coolness. Big Oak stopped his play with the children with an expression so severe that everybody on the porch turned to Paul and waited for him to present the news.

"We must go now," he said, and that was enough for Thad and Big Oak. They and Jinja immediately dashed into the house, and a minute later were out on the porch adjusting their packs, blankets, and pouches, and checking the priming in the pans of their rifles. The oldest boy, Caleb, made a brief squall about wanting to go with them, but a single look from his father silenced him. Big Oak and Thad each gave Cilla a quick hug and kiss, and then the three generations of woodsmen fell in line behind Paul as he headed down the hill and struck an easterly path.

"Burgoyne's army is on the other side of the river," he explained as they eased into their usual ground-eating lope. "He's heading south, and Gates has men in front of them slowing them down."

"I'm not so handy with an ax as I used to be," Big Oak commented, but he knew that he wasn't needed to chop down trees. No further words were spoken until they reached the bank of the Hudson four hours later and pushed off in Paul's canoe. It was a sturdy Iroquois canoe sheathed in elm bark, equipped with four paddles, so they made good time along the western shore of the river, stroking in unison, in cadence, as if they'd been doing it together for years, which they had. By mid-afternoon they had crossed the river, hidden the canoe, and located the route the British army was expected to follow.

Now they stopped and listened. Sure enough, in the distance they could hear chopping and then the hissing, crackling sound of a falling tree. They made for the noise and soon found themselves at the bank of a large creek. Three brawny men stripped bare above the waist were at work chopping the main beams of a bridge over the creek, while a fourth was using a bar to pry boards off the bridge and toss them downstream. Just north of them a dozen more men were felling trees and arranging them into huge, tangled obstacles. One of the men, on seeing Paul and the woodsmen, dropped his ax and slipped into a buckskin shirt.

"Lieutenant Simpson," said Paul, "these are—"

"Later, Paul," came the answer. "I've got five men protecting our rear who need to be choppin' trees. Send 'em on back to me if you will. Bound to be an advance party coming through here soon, and unless they're too big to handle, I'd like you to handle them yourself, if you would."

Paul nodded and the four men trotted north for about fifteen minutes, until they spotted two men who looked more or less like woodsmen, staring northward motionlessly, like hounds on the point.

On closer look it became obvious that one of them was at least part Indian. It was he that Paul approached, to say that the lieutenant wanted them back at the bridge to help them finish the wrecking job as quickly as possible.

The Indian nodded, signaled the leader of the party, and then gathered the others. When the five men had come together, they took a long look at the men who were replacing them. What they saw must have satisfied them. "Good hunting," they said as they started down the trail toward the wood-chopping party.

"What do you think?" Paul asked Big Oak as they looked up the trail.

"Let's spread out in pairs," Big Oak suggested, taking command as naturally as if he had a commission in his pocket. You and me on the left and Thad and Jinja on the right, far enough apart that when the advance party comes they won't flank us by accident."

Three of them knew exactly what to do, and the fourth was willing to learn. While Paul and Big Oak found a well-concealed vantage point to the left of a huge tangle of elms and maples that had been chopped down an hour before, Thad found a position behind a giant old oak. And there they waited. "Just do what I do," Thad whispered to his son. "We won't fire unless they see us or Big Oak fires first. Wait till you see a target before you fire, and then don't get excited, put him in your sights and squeeze the trigger."

Jinja said nothing. He just nodded and took a position. Thad noticed that the boy pointed not his eyes up the trail, but his right ear. Makes sense, he thought. For a minute he watched his son. Again he noticed that the boy seemed to sense no great danger to his health and well-being. Thad remembered how frightened he had been before his first fight, and he could not understand how his son could be so calm.

Thad focused his eyes on a clearing about a hundred yards down the trail. And they waited. The mosquitoes buzzed and the gnats swarmed around them in the late afternoon, and in spite of the bear grease, some of the insects landed and feasted.

Not having eaten all day, they each swallowed a handful of corn and some water as they waited. An hour went by and all they did was sweat. Jinja looked across the trail for any sign of his grandfather or Paul, but they were well-concealed. The sun dipped farther, until Thad could catch an orange glow through a clear spot in the forest to the west of them. He shifted his position to put a tree trunk between him and the direct glare. And they waited.

It was Jinja who spotted the pair of birds that suddenly beat their way out of a bush somewhere up the trail. He didn't react, not just then. Birds have their own reasons for what they do. But he kept his eyes on the spot and soon caught a motion he hadn't seen before. He kicked his father in the leg and pointed. Thad nodded.

They waited and watched as one by one, single file, seven men appeared on the trail. The lead one was stripped, and might have been a Caughnawaga. Thad was not sure. Then came a short, slight man in a green uniform. Tory. Good. Thad had no desire to shoot at friends, but neither did he want to step out of cover and ask who they were. The loyalist green uniform was the giveaway. Then came five men dressed in varied combinations of skins and linsey-woolsey. One of them wore his dark hair long and unbound with earrings. He may have been a Canadian. The Tory carried a Brown Bess musket. The rest carried rifles. Thad knew that his father would take the man behind the Tory and that Paul would take the one behind him. The Caughnawaga, who probably felt little allegiance to the men he was guiding, would likely run away and not stop

running until he had made it back to Canada. The Tory
with his musket would be unlikely to hit anything. They'd
net him last.

So Thad picked out the last one in line and pointed out
the one before him as Jinja's target. The young man nodded. There was one man in the middle they could not account for on the first shot. You can't have everything.

They waited while the men came closer, even though
their fields of fire were excellent. Thad knew that Big Oak
was waiting to see if seven were all they had to contend
with. It was important that he make sure, and anyway, the
closer the better.

There were no more, but still Big Oak waited for them to
come closer. Thad took a last look around, checking for a
flanker or two, but if there were any, they were better
woodsmen than he. He turned back and laid his man in his
sights, waiting.

Big Oak fired, and the other three fired almost in unison
a split second after. Three bodies crumpled while a fourth
spun around then crawled behind a tree. A moment later
two weapons flashed from the direction of the ambushed
party, and right after that, a third. From across the trail
came a shrill war cry as Paul sprang to his feet and rushed
toward a place where he had seen smoke. And it was here
that Thad received the biggest surprise of his life. A chilling
whoop pierced his ears from right beside him. His quiet-
spoken son leaped from his place of concealment and
sprinted down the trail toward where the Tory had disappeared in the underbrush. Thad rose, quickly reloaded, and
moved forward, watching Jinja leaping over rocks and
roots. He was vaguely aware of a struggle off to his right as
Paul pounced on his man. Jinja had dropped his rifle and
drawn his tomahawk. He knew he had just so much time
before the Tory reloaded. Paul and his quarry were struggling in the dust, and Big Oak was still combing the area
for any sign of the Caughnawaga when he saw the Tory
arise in panic and sprint down the trail. Twenty yards be-

hind was a screaming Jinja, his hatchet cocked above his head. The distance closed to ten yards, then five, and then, just before they reached a bend in the trail that would have taken them out of sight, Jinja screeched again, the hatchet fell, and so did the Tory.

Now, suddenly, all was silence. Not a blade of grass moved. Not an animal stirred. The sun itself appeared to teeter on the horizon. All because a single violent action that seemed to have taken forever to unwind actually was over less than two minutes after the first shot had been fired.

Now came a groan from beneath a big old pine tree, followed by another a few yards away. Thad and Jinja walked from body to body while Big Oak and Paul searched the underbrush for the Caughnawaga. Four of the ambushed scouts were dead, none deader than the poor Tory that Jinja had decided to make his own. Thad had never seen so much damage from one swing of a tomahawk. He looked up at his son, who was solicitously bending over one of the wounded men. After he had killed the Tory, he had not bothered to stay and admire his work, but simply cleaned his hatchet on his leather breeches and walked away, his eyes once again sleepy and unconcerned.

"What have I raised up?" Thad muttered to himself.

"Pa," came his son's calm voice. "Would you help me with this fella? I don't think he looks too good."

And indeed he didn't. A bullet had entered and exited his left side, without piercing his lungs or stomach, but he was bleeding badly, and his face was dead white. It was his good fortune that he had lapsed into unconsciousness. Thad shook his head, tore two pieces of cloth out of the man's shirt and attempted to stanch both the wounds. He might have spared himself the effort. Even as he worked, the scout's lifeblood drained away and the breathing became shallower and shallower, until, like a candle going out, it ceased.

Thad moved on to the next one, the Canadian, who was

sitting up against a tree. Jinja had torn the man's shirt off around his wounded arm and poured some canteen water on the wound, which was more painful than it was severe. The man apparently had witnessed Jinja's attack on the Tory. His eyes were big and round as he watched the youngster work on his arm. At one point Jinja wrapped his wound and pulled the cloth tight. The Canadian grimaced with pain, but he dared not utter a sound. When Thad approached and Jinja took a step backward, the wounded man's expression abruptly went from panic to relief.

Big Oak and Paul gave up their search. Somehow the Caughnawaga had made his escape, and it didn't matter much that he had. Big Oak walked up to the little group with a funny little smile on his face.

"What you been teaching this boy, Thad? All the time I thought he was over at the counting house with the old Dutchman, you was out in the woods teachin' him to chop up Tories." Turning around to look at the bloody heap in the green jacket, Big Oak said, "Now don't you go carryin' that man home to your mother, Jinja." He shook his head. "Thad, did you have any idea what a terror your boy would be on the warpath?"

Thad took a deep breath. "He ain't any worse than you, you old frog killer. That's what you called Gingego once, a long time ago, I remember. But I seen you collect a couple of French scalps once about as easy as pullin' a couple of ears of corn."

Big Oak suddenly looked stern. "I don't do that anymore, son. I'm a Christian man with a good Christian family." He looked at Jinja and smiled. "But yes, you remind me of me," he said. "A lot more than this one does." He returned his gaze to Thad, who could only wonder why his half-wild father, whom he seldom got to see, would have more of an influence on the boy than a father who lives with him.

"Anyway," said Big Oak, "Let's find out what this man knows."

Meaning to give the man a little water to drink, Jinja

stepped toward him. The man's look of relief turned back into one of panic. "Would you get him away from me?" he asked.

"Where is Burgoyne?" Big Oak asked.

In truth, the man was so frightened that for a moment he couldn't even remember who Burgoyne was, much less where he was, and Big Oak took his silence for resistance. Big Oak looked at Jinja, and that look was all that was necessary to loosen the man's tongue.

"He's about twenty mile north of here."

"Where's he going?"

"Albany."

"Your grandfather would be excited to hear that," Big Oak said to Jinja. "Let's take him up to the tree choppers. They ought to be about through with their day's work, and we'd better move on. Oh, say, how many men you reckon Burgoyne has with him?"

THEIR JOB NOW WAS TO FIND BURGOYNE'S army. Gentleman Johnny, as Burgoyne was known in some places, was a playwright and poet who had come to America expecting easy glory. He was on his way south, heading toward Albany with a large, mixed broth of English, loyalist, and German soldiers, but nobody seemed to know exactly where he was. So the four woodsmen turned north and spent the following day prowling through the woods, making good time but finding nothing. That night Big Oak sat in the dark with his cohorts, scratching his head and wondering. Was he slipping so badly that he couldn't find an army as big as Burgoyne's wandering around in the woods? As slow as they were bound to march with the ponderous German soldiers stopping every mile to dress their ranks, they would have had to stop altogether not to have come this far.

The little group had eaten their cold trail food and laid down just about an hour after dark so as to be fresh at dawn, when Big Oak suddenly sat upright and muttered a nasty oath, which surprised everybody and made them think that perhaps he had been bitten by a copperhead.

"Everybody up," he hissed. They obeyed, and in five minutes' time he had them tearing through the underbrush for the bank of the river. Directly across the river it was dark, but when they looked farther up the river and studied the opposite bank closely, they could see winking firelight through the marsh vegetation on the other side.

"We didn't figure that they might have crossed the river already. But there they are," Big Oak said.

They stole up the river until they were directly opposite the enemy. The little campfires stretched for miles along the river, and the buzz of conversation was constant.

"I'd say they're pretty confident, don't you think?" Big Oak asked Thad and Paul.

"I think we're a little closer to them than I'd like to be," suggested Thad.

His father nodded, pulled them back from the river to the trail, and they began their careful lope south, by the light of the moon. As they ran down the dimly lit path, their feet ever alert for roots and rocks that their eyes could not see, Thad turned around and grabbed a quick look at Jinja, who was directly behind him. The moonlight revealed a young man obviously thrilled with the whole thing, eyes wide and alert, lips parted and relaxed, the slightest trace of a smile on his face.

Suddenly Thad felt terribly sorry for the young man. Each day in the counting house and the store must have been pure agony for Jinja. He was too much like his grandfather to be able to stand being cooped up all day in a place with four walls and a roof. And yet, during the five years he had been working for Wendel and Watley, they had never heard him voice a complaint. That poor, split-skulled Tory must have been the recipient of all the anger and frustration Jinja had accumulated behind desks and counters over the years. Thad counted himself lucky that the boy hadn't decided to take his frustrations out on him, for he had, after all, been the one to suggest Jinja's long apprenticeship in the business of the trading company.

About five miles down the river they found the landmarks that brought them to the ditch where they had hidden their canoe.

"Quiet," Big Oak whispered, as they carried it to the bank, to lay it gently on the waters of the upper Hudson. "They may have scouts this far ahead."

Big Oak and Paul paddled so softly that the only sound Thad could hear was the drip of water off the paddles when they were lifted from the water. Thad and Jinja fastened their keen eyesight on the shadows of the opposite bank. They saw nothing. They looked north, toward where Burgoyne's army would be coming from the following day. They saw nothing, and heard nothing but the nighttime forest noises and the occasional splash of a water creature of the Hudson.

Thad took a look at the stars, both in the original and reflected off the choppy water of the river. Again he leaned forward and listened. Again he heard nothing. How interesting, he thought, that death could be so close and yet, on this night, seem worlds away.

They paddled just far enough out into the river to avoid snagging the canoe bottom on a submerged rock or tree. Then they turned the canoe south and began to paddle downriver, silently, deliberately, yet swiftly, considering the limited vision they had. They couldn't travel too far south, for then they might miss the rebel army, which was also camped on the other side of the river, but would be far more cautious about revealing their whereabouts.

They decided instead to catch about five hours of sleep on the east side of the river and then cross over to the other side just before dawn.

They saw him before he saw them. That was always good. Before a battle, Big Oak thought, a scout was just as likely to get shot at by a friend as a foe. They had crossed the river, traversed a good deal of marshy ground, and climbed a long, wooded slope that seemed to command a pretty fair view of the area. At the edge of the woods he found himself staring at a clearing filled with tents and with shaggy men just beginning to stir after a night's repose. Some army, that you could sneak up on it so easily, Big Oak thought. The dawn was still tentative when he motioned for the other three to get down while he crept toward where a lone rebel dressed in woodsman's garb stood chewing on a pipe stem, and otherwise more or less dozing on his feet. Near dawn after a night watch, it was hard not to.

"Micah," he whispered into the ear of the dreamer.

The woodsman jumped as if he had been struck by light-ning. An expletive leaped from his throat and he whirled around with his rifle. Big Oak seized the weapon, stuck his face in front of the woodsman's and smiled.

"Mornin', Micah," he said.

"Damn it, Sam! You scared me out of three years' growth."

"Only way you're gonna grow is old, you miserable ex-cuse for a bird dog," Big Oak said affectionately.

The woodsman, who was almost as tall as Big Oak, but narrower, stuck his bearded chin out and collected his dig-nity. "You here to help us beat that dandy general the Brit-ish sent over here?"

"I'm here to tell you he's comin'. Ain't more than fifteen mile up the river."

Micah scowled. "We know where he is, you fool. We always know where he is. Now, if you want to be useful, hie yourself and that ol' Dutch rifle of yours over to Colonel Dan Morgan and let him plant you where you'll do some good."

"Not just me," Big Oak responded. "This is my son, and my grandson, and Paul Derontyan, who's an Oneida preacher."

"Mmh," the woodsman grunted. "Well, get ye over to Colonel Morgan there." He pointed toward a big, weath-ered, rawboned man in his early forties, then turned away and headed for a soft spot under an elm, where he could catch some real sleep.

"Not one of your best friends?" Thad asked.

"Good enough friend," his father answered. "He was just

a bit miffed that I was able to sneak up on him like that. Got a lot of pride, that Micah. But maybe he's too old to still be fightin' battles."

"Which reminds me, Pa. What are we doin' here? I came up to your place to get you and bring you and your family back to Albany so we can do some honest smuggling, and here you've got me in the middle of the war."

"Listen, son, first you're peeved at me because I won't take sides, and then you're peeved because I'm ready to pull a trigger for the cause." He gave a silent chuckle. "For a while I thought I'd finally fought my last battle. Settin' up there on a hill with a wife and kids, fishin' a little, doin' a little business for you—very little business, I might add. As long as there was a war nearby, I guess I just had to feel the sting of one more battle. I know you understand. You're my son."

"I understand all right. Now, how do I keep this one"— he grabbed Jinja by his buckskin shirt—"from doing something foolish and gettin' killed doing it?"

Big Oak bit his lip for a moment and drilled his gray eyes into the dark ones of his grandson. "Now you listen carefully," he said. "We're probably gonna have a fight today, and when we do, I want you to fight like a real Ganonsyoni would fight. The life of a Ganonsyoni is precious. There's so few of them, you see, and they have got the whole Iroquois confederacy to protect. After they fight, they want to go home and tell their war stories to their family and their fellow warriors around the campfire. They're not in it hoping that their friends'll spend their time talkin' about what a brave guy Little Britches was the day he got his head blown off by a French cannon, if you get my drift. So I want you to stick by me.

"By the way," he said to his son and grandson. "I don't know if you've thought about this, but if we get licked today, they'll be marching into Albany the day after tomorrow. And we don't want that, now, do we?"

It was full morning now, and the rebel army of General

Horatio Gates was ready for action, though Thad could see only a small portion of it. The four of them were part of the left wing, that part of the army farthest from the river and holding the highest ground. They spent most of the morning waiting for word, sharpening tomahawks and knives, and checking out their rifles. Dan Morgan's outfit were men at home in the woods, all sharpshooters, the kind of men that played the very devil with British troops. They couldn't wait to get some redcoats and Germans in the sights of their rifles. There would be good hunting today, they were certain, if only Burgoyne would come down.

The English, Micah explained, had gotten roughed up pretty good at Bennington, but you can't teach an Englishman nothin', he said, all you could do was kill him and kill him until there weren't any left, and then *maybe* they'd give up and go home. Big Oak laughed, remembering that the Indians used to say pretty much the same thing about the English soldiers. Micah told them about General Gates, nearsighted and fussy, frumpy and dumpy, organized as hell, but it took him forever to march from one place to another. Thad and Big Oak listened carefully. Their vast knowledge of war-making did not include the details of the great men who would lead them into battle.

Big Oak was sitting on a big rock fiddling with his powder horn when word came that Burgoyne was coming on fast, at least for Burgoyne. Quickly, Morgan got his men formed up in formation, more to get everybody moving at the same time than to define the order of march. Not long after noon he had them marching along the heights northward. Big Oak and his group did not volunteer to scout. Rather, they tagged along with Morgan's woods fighters, feeling secure with men like themselves.

It was a summer day, but the heat was not at all unbearable. A good day for fighting, thought Big Oak. For one of the rare times in his life the thought crossed his mind that even a smart fighter can sometimes catch an unlucky bullet, and he sent up a rare prayer toward the heavens as they moved forward into the woods and swept on toward the sounds of gunfire.

"That's our boys out front," exclaimed Micah. "They've found 'em for sure. Now let's get at 'em and kill us a few."

Over the years, Big Oak had pulled trigger on many red men and hit very few of them, so elusive were they in woods combat. He knew it would be different fighting the British. They marched forward in a long thin line, closer and closer to the gunfire. Before they saw the British, they smelled the gunpowder. Suddenly the sparse woods was full of redcoats, firing in formation, throwing a lot of lead and hoping that the massed firepower would hit something. Trouble was, they were a good two hundred yards away and their muskets weren't good for the range.

It was perfect for Morgan's men, however. From behind the trees, they began to pepper the British troops. As more and more of the riflemen joined the fray, they spread out right and left, half surrounding the British. They waited hidden behind trees while the British companies fired their volleys, then they stepped out and poured their fire into the red-coated ranks. Now they could see men tumbling out of the ranks as the deadly fire found them. Morgan was behind his men, urging them forward, moving them close enough for their rifles to be even more deadly, but not close enough to get within range of the British musket fire.

The smell of the thick gunpowder smoke was like a hearty meal for Big Oak. Again and again he loaded and fired, and it seemed that every time he fired, another redcoat went down. At his side the next two generations of Watleys were doing similar deadly work with their rifles. Whoever was commanding the British troops on this field tried to maneuver them closer to their enemy, but all he succeeded in doing was to increase the rate at which Englishmen fell out of ranks with a wet red stain blooming on the front of their coats.

The heavy, accurate hail of gunfire halted the British advance as if they had hit a stone wall, but for a while the

British continued to hold their ground, taking casualties and giving few. Big Oak could hear the British officers through the rapid crackle of rifle shots, calling for a bayonet charge. And good soldiers that they were, they tried. But the lightly burdened riflemen merely fell back, loading on the run, then turned and fired at the closest gorgeous red target they could see. By now the screams and moans of fallen redcoats had added a chorus to the deadly symphony of gunfire, shouted orders, and battle cries.

The British were confused. Too many men were down. Already some of the reinforcements had been bloodied. If they kept trying to go forward, by the time they had conquered this little section of woods, none of them would be left.

The riflemen saw the British waver, saw some of them retreat, saw stranded pockets of worried redcoats. And then one of Morgan's men, not an officer, shouted, "Let's go get 'em, boys!" Suddenly the retreating riflemen were the shock troops, dashing forward, firing one well-aimed shot, then continuing the dash, waving hatchets and screaming the bloodcurdling cries they had first heard from their red enemies.

Big Oak and Thad were not about to be swept along by this outburst. They jogged forward at a sensible pace, watching carefully for a British counterattack. But Jinja had other ideas. As he had done the day before, he let out a wild screech and pursued his enemy. In fact his young, strong legs were so swift that he was threatening to outstrip the rest of the rebels. Thad dropped his rifle and sprinted headlong after Jinja, who had gained so much ground that Thad had lost sight of him among the trees. But unencumbered by his heavy rifle, Thad gained swiftly, until he had the boy in view. He then went into a full sprint, passing riflemen right and left, eating up the distance between himself and his son.

"Jinja, stop!" he shouted, but the boy continued on, not hearing or not heeding. Jinja was now within reach. In desperation, Thad reached out and caught his son by the shoulders and brought the boy to the forest floor.

Strangely, in the middle of this stampede, he could hear the strangled gobble of a wild turkey. That couldn't be, he thought, digging his knees into the back of his son, who tried to writhe his way free but could not get out from underneath Thad's powerful, solid frame.

Then the turkey surged past Thad and the mystery vanished. It was no turkey, it was Daniel Morgan, tooting his turkey lure, giving the signal to cease pursuit. The men ignored it until suddenly, up ahead, Thad heard several massed volleys from the retreating British army. That stopped Morgan's men. That and the turkey gobbler. Thad grabbed Jinja's hand and hoisted him to his feet. He now saw Morgan's men returning to their bird-calling leader. Let the main part of the army take over, he thought. Morgan's men had done their job by breaking the back of the sudden attack. Thad saw Morgan turn around and start walking away from the killing field. To his surprise, tears were flowing down the tough, craggy face of the commander.

Some of the bitterest action took place just a short distance from this little section of the woods. The British had found an open field about twelve acres in size, a good place for their formations and massed firepower. And because they were there, the rebels decided that they had to have the field. The rebels, under Benedict Arnold, chased the British off the field, then the British chased the rebels off, and so it went until nightfall. Big Oak and Paul Derontyan spent much of the day playing medic to Morgan's men, whose casualties had been a fraction of their mismatched British opposition.

Thad kept an eye on Jinja. He knew his son well. Whenever he saw the telltale signs of restlessness in the movements of his body, he grabbed Jinja and took him on a little mission, searching the bodies of British soldiers for papers, or carrying water to the wounded. There was no doubt in Thad's mind that as long as the guns were firing, he'd better keep an eye on his deranged son or the young man would be leading a charge into the teeth of the enemy. Thad could not understand. The ghastly wounds and the cries of the dying seemed to have little effect on Jinja, even though this was only the second day of warfare he had ever experienced.

As the day and the battle died, Thad studied his son while the young man cleaned his rifle in the fading daylight. There was no emotion, no sign that six hours earlier he had been engaged in life-or-death struggles. The arm that pushed the oily patch up and down inside the barrel might have been pushing a quill over the inventory books of Wendel and Watley. Who was this boy he had known since birth?

Jinja looked up and caught his father staring at him. He smiled. "I wish James was here to see this, Pa." James was Paul's son, a tough young warrior who worked for Wendel and Watley and was Jinja's best friend.

"Guess you wanted him to see you in action, hey?" Thad responded. "Why'd you go and try to whip Burgoyne all by yourself?"

Jinja shrugged, and clamped a new flint onto the hammer of his rifle. "I guess I thought I could," he said.

In the light of the campfires, Dan Morgan was making his way from group to group. Big Oak had heard much about the man, so he watched him with quiet curiosity as he dropped a word here and there. It didn't take words to tell how much the men respected him and how much he loved them. The tears, Big Oak realized, had been fear that his men might lose control of themselves and blunder into a British trap. These were woods fighters, not maneuver battalions. They were his men, handpicked for their skills and attitudes, and he could not stand the thought of losing them.

"Don't believe I know you men," he said as he appeared in the light of Big Oak's campfire.

"I'm Sam Watley," Big Oak said. "This is Paul Derontyan, my son Thad, and his son David."

"I don't know how you came to be with us, but you fight like the very demons of hell—especially that one."

"That one we're trying to keep alive till he gets some sense into him."

"Whose brigade are you with?"

"Nobody's."

"I'd be obliged if you'd like to join up with us. I could use more good men like you."

"Good of you to say so, General. But we're here by accident. We're traders, and these days we trade for guns and ammunition."

"Smugglers, you mean," the colonel responded, wrinkling his nose just a bit.

"Only for this war. Normally we're just reg'lar business folk. But war is a different time, and you have to do your business different, if you know what I mean."

Morgan nodded. "I guess we need your ammunition even more than we need you." Then he turned his head away and walked on to the next campfire.

❧ 6 ❧

"**WHAT WE HAVE TO DO**," BIG OAK EXPLAINED to Thad, "is get Cilla and the whelps down to Albany. Then we can do what we have to do, and not have to worry as much about them. That's what happens when you have a family, you worry about them."

Thad nodded but said nothing. He was pleased that his father had decided to take sides in this war. He might have known that a brawl or two would serve to knock the old man off his fence.

Very early the next morning, well before dawn, their long loping strides were taking them westward to Big Oak Pond. There were no good-byes. Big Oak and Paul, ever suspicious of authority, had no desire to deal with the entreaties and threats of officers to induce them to stay for the next battle. They had lent a hand, pulled an oar, put their life at risk voluntarily, and killed a few redcoats, without pay. They had even shot their own ammunition and eaten their own food, all in all a pretty good deal for the rebels. To Big Oak's way of thinking, they owed nobody and nobody owed them.

In northern New York, summer begins to fold its tent early. And although the day was warm long before noon, there was that feel of fall to come. Was it the slant of the sun? The smell of late summer wildflowers? The first faint

paling of the green canopy? All of them put together? Big
Oak and Paul didn't know. The senses were writing "fall"
ever so faintly in their minds. Time to do the things that
men do to tide them over through the winter.

And so they ran, Paul first, Big Oak last, Jinja and Thad
in the middle. Alert as the first and last were to the possibility of an encounter, they did not truly expect one. The
enemy was temporarily vanquished and sent fleeing to the
northeast, and as for hostile red men, both knew that their
time in this region was past. What were Paul's feelings
about that?

Paul did not know for certain. On one hand, he could
not bring himself to like most white men, in spite of the
love showered on him and other Oneidas by the Reverend
Samuel Kirkland. On the other hand, Kirkland had taken
him and others so far from the traditional ways of the Ganonsyoni that he felt little in common with the Mohawks
or Senecas.

It was on the trail, or on the river, where he felt whole.
Then he could behold earth, sky, and water, and feel that
the Christian God and the Holder of the Heavens were
one, and that therefore he could still serve both.

The way to Big Oak Pond was mostly uphill from the
Hudson, which made the way home long and hard for Big
Oak, but by the afternoon they found themselves close to
journey's end. As they cleared the final rise and he caught
his first glimpse of the cabin, Big Oak immediately grasped
that all was not as it should be. There were no boys wres-
tling on the porch and no fire in the chimney. With a
choking feeling rising to his throat, he made a quick check
of the outside of the cabin, perhaps too quick, then vaulted
through the front door, dreading what he might find.

Thad and Jinja were moving quickly from room to room,
and Paul was putting a sympathetic hand on Big Oak's
shoulder when the old trader let out a loud guffaw and held
up a wooden board that had been resting on the kitchen

table. Written on the board in brown ink were three simple words, lettered in large square characters: GUN FAR ALBANY.

"What does that mean?" Thad asked, looking over his father's shoulder.

"It means that we'd better head out for Albany as soon as possible," Big Oak told his son quickly. "She's fine in the woods, and the boys know how to hide like a cow hides her calf, but I'd much rather catch up to her as soon as possible before a bunch of redcoats, or rebels for that matter, find them in the woods and decide to make an enjoyable evening out their good fortune.

The footsteps they followed led unerringly to Albany, and when they arrived at Thad's house the following afternoon, they found Cilla and the three boys standing comfortably in front of the house, watching the heavy business traffic pass by on the hot, smelly, hard-rutted, dusty street. When the children caught sight of the four travelers through the dust-clouded snarl of wagons, carriages, horses, and foot traffic, they raced fearlessly among the horses and vehicles and assaulted, not their father, but Jinja, so that he arrived at the house wearing his uncles along with his rifle, shot pouch, pack, and powder horn.

Big Oak and Paul each approached a smiling Cilla and took a hand, while Thad headed directly for the entrance of the house. He found his wife Katherine standing in the doorway, having heard the screams of Big Oak's boys above the noise of the traffic. Although her mouth was smiling, the lines around her eyes suggested that the company did not altogether please her. Behind her was their daughter, Anne, who, Thad discovered for the fifteenth time that year, was no longer a child. Although Katherine was no small woman, Anne towered over her by a good three inches, and had the same lanky look and serene expression as her brother. It occurred to Thad that if her serenity hid the same fierceness as Jinja's, then he pitied any man unfortunate enough to choose her as a mate.

Anne ran to Thad, gave him a quick hug, then rushed

past him. This surprised Thad, because she had always adored her father. It was Paul she was wanting to see.

She stood before the Oneida, her hands clasped in front of her.

"Anne," he said, smiling, not knowing what else to say.

"How was your journey?" she asked.

"Fine." He waited, mystified. They eyed each other for a few long moments, while around them swirled the rush of excited family.

"How is James?" Paul and Thad had missed something that had probably been going on under their noses.

"He is well," Paul said, hiding his surprise. Thad smiled and glanced toward his wife to see if she had heard.

While the others continued to fuss over each other outside the house, Katherine took Thad's hand and led him out the back door, to a tree-shaded courtyard that seemed miles from the tumult on the street in front of the house. They sat down at a table, held hands and stared at each other in silence for several minutes, until Anne came out and broke the spell with a pitcher of lemonade and three glasses. She kissed her father and sat down, and neither of the parents thought it inappropriate for her to want to share the moment.

"The news we have is that General Arnold stopped the British," Katherine said at last.

"We stopped him all right," Thad replied.

"You were there?" Katherine asked, throwing Thad a startled look.

"We all were."

Now came more silence. Katherine had found in the past that when Thad fought a battle, if she asked him questions about it, he would just clam up, but that if she let him choose his own moment, he would eventually talk about it.

Thad took a deep pull on the lemonade. When he put the glass down, Anne refilled it. "It's delicious, baby," Thad said to Anne.

She smiled. "Mama baked some bread this morning," she

said. "We have fresh butter and we still have some plum preserves. Would you like me to go get some for you, Daddy?"

He shook his head. "Not just yet, Anne." He leaned back in his chair and looked from one face to the other. "When I come home, the first thing I love to do is stare at my two beautiful women."

"Where is David?" Katherine asked.

"He's still dusting little uncles off his back. He'll be out here shortly." He turned back to Anne. "You might want to bring out some food for him and your grandfather. They're always hungry."

Anne rose and headed for the house. Thad looked at Katherine but had no idea if she knew what was going through the mind of her daughter. Anne was more likely to share her thoughts with him than with Katherine.

After a few more moments of silence, Katherine raised her eyebrows at Thad. "Well?" she said.

"We fought the British at a little farm in the hills west of the Hudson," Thad said.

"Yes?"

"We bloodied them pretty good," he added.

Her eyebrows remained raised. "And our son?"

"Jinja behaved well," Thad responded, finally catching her drift.

A light breeze entered the courtyard and stirred the young maple that shaded them.

"Behaved well?"

"I mean he was cool under fire, kept under cover and shot well."

She stared at him. She's reading my thoughts, he thought, knowing that he must not say more or she would be certain that he was hiding something.

They stared at each other, or rather, he stared at her and she stared into him, with a look he had never recalled seeing on her face.

Anne looked out the kitchen window, watched them for

a moment, and decided not to hurry her preparation of the food.

"Thad," Katherine said. "When we were married, I had no idea what you had to face—out there. By the time I found out, it was too late to say no, and I had no say in what you did with your life. I was not foolish enough to think that I could change your nature. I was happy to see that you loved the woods less and the town more as the years went by. Even now, when you leave Albany and go west, every day is a fearful one for me. I could not bear to lose you.

"And yet, if one day you did not come home, I could find a way to go on. I could not say the same if I lost David. A mother cannot raise up a son, nurse him through the sicknesses and hurts of childhood, only to lose him when he is about to grow up. You must tell me now, what happened to David out there?"

Thad took her hand and looked toward the back door, as if he expected Jinja to appear at any moment. "He was too brave—too reckless," Thad said. "If I were a general, I would want to have a thousand just like him serving under me—a thousand who forget about their own lives once the battle has begun. But I would want none of them to be my son."

Suddenly Thad felt relieved. Having seen his son charge into the teeth of the enemy before his eyes, he was glad to have Katherine as an ally who would help to prevent a repetition of his recklessness under fire.

"Sometimes I think that we are not very good people," Thad said. "Fathers and sons who don't know how to fight enlist and serve in the ranks for the sake of their country. My father is a very brave man, but he taught me to believe that throwing your life away in battle was a waste and a sin. And you know something else? My grandfather, Kendee of the Western Door, taught me the same. These are the two people I admired most. How could I think differently? So Big Oak and I serve. But we serve on our own terms, in ways that keep our lives in *our* hands. We would no more put our lives in the hands of some stupid general than we would point a pistol between our eyes and pull the trigger. If we die serving as scouts, that is one thing. But to die marching into the mouth of a cannon—no, no, we cannot see the sense of that. Not for us.

"My first battle, I didn't give the Caughnawagas more than an inch of my head to shoot at, and not for very long either. It's a miracle I fought at all, that's how frightened I was. And I still don't like the feeling I get at the bottom of my belly when I go into a battle. I wish that Jinja felt those feelings, but he does not. Instead, the sound of guns makes him think he has wings that will send him soaring high above the battlefield. And now that he has had his first taste of battle and come out of it triumphant, it will be our battle to keep him away."

She nodded, but did not speak. Neither did she lift her cup to her lips.

"You know that next week is when our little trading expedition sets out down the Hudson. I want to take him with us."

A look of horror came over her. "You can't!" she said. "I want him here, with me, and I mean to have him here if I have to tie him up in the cellar."

"I must take him with us," Thad insisted. "The recruiters will be back, looking for boys to fight with General Gates. If he is here when they come, nothing you can do will make him stay. If he is with us, they won't get him."

"But your work is dangerous too."

"It is. There's even a chance we'll have to fight. But it'll be our fight, not some general's. We know when to fight, and when to run. He'll be safer with us than with General Gates."

He would have said more, but at that moment Jinja emerged from the back entrance, followed by a beaming Anne with a tray full of bread and fresh butter.

"We'll talk more about this another time," he murmured softly. "And I think you'll see the reason of it."

* * *

The night was clear but there was no moon. Silently, Big Oak turned the key to the big padlock protecting the old log warehouse just above the flood plain of the river. Only the four of them were there, plus Dieter, plus two of Dieter's most trusted employees, both Caughnawagas. None of them dared trust any of Dieter's other men. Misjudging just one man could cost them their lives.

The padlock opened with a loud metallic sound that took the breath out of everyone, sounding as it did like a rifle being cocked.

Quickly, quietly, they lifted bundles of beaver and otter pelts and hauled them from the warehouse down to the river, where three canoes were ready and waiting. It was an interesting trade, Dieter had told them the night before. Because of the war, furs were extremely scarce downriver, while weapons and ammunition were scarce upriver. On the other hand, American privateers were running the British blockade, so anyone who could take care of the river trade would have some pretty good commerce waiting for them down below.

"I can see," Thad said, "how easy it might be to run the river at night in swift silent canoes, but how," he asked, "would we get the furs past New York, out to the privateers?"

"We don't have to go that far," Dieter explained. "The ship sends up longboats to meet us just below Nyack. There is a creek there where we will exchange our furs for their ammunition and weapons."

"Why are the Caughnawagas coming?" Jinja asked.

Big Oak smiled. "The Caughnawagas have been in the smuggling business for many years," he said. "Nobody knows as much as they do about trade routes from the Saint Lawrence River down to New York Bay." It was Big Oak who selected Ooghnor and Gilles from among the Caughnawaga employees of the company. "I would trust my life with these men, not only because they are loyal, but because they are clever and careful."

In the deep dark they felt their way down the path to the canoes, stowed their load of furs carefully amidships, then returned to the warehouse for another load. They did not dare to light a lantern. Surely Burgoyne or Sir Henry Clinton had spies in Albany. The stakes were too high to take chances. Finally, when all the chosen furs had been loaded, they boarded their canoes, paddled out into the middle of the river and turned south. They traveled single file, connected by rope, Paul and Big Oak in the lead, Thad and Jinja in the middle, and the Caughnawagas bringing up the rear. Upon the keen eyesight of Paul in the bow of the first canoe, Ooghnor and Gilles in the rear rested their lives, while in the middle, Big Oak, Thad, and Jinja knew that their job was to listen for any sound that might mean danger.

Speed was not of the greatest importance. They had three full nights to get to the creek below Nyack, and the current was with them. Silently, the paddles dipped, leaving tiny luminescent eddies that vanished into the night. A soft breeze blew east to west, carrying the fresh scent of the river into their nostrils. Each man nursed his own thoughts as the long hours dragged by.

The paddles of Paul and Big Oak effortlessly steered a true course south, and the other two canoes followed their tow ropes. Heavily laden, the canoes rode low in the water, but on this late summer night the smooth waters of the upper Hudson promised little hindrance to the six men and their vital trading mission. And on they paddled through the night.

At the very first faint traces of dawn to the east, Paul turned his canoe toward the western shore until he could see the shoreline, then he steered the little convoy south again and looked for a break in the woods. Long before the first rays of the sun appeared, he found it, a creek just big enough to accommodate the canoes about two hundred feet upstream from the Hudson. They did not unload the canoes there, they simply lashed them securely to the closest trees and made camp on cold rations.

Thad, Jinja, and Paul curled up in their blankets, and the Caughnawagas and Big Oak stood first watch. They had a whole lot of daylight to kill, and since they had no idea who might be in the area, they had to kill it without a fire to warm their food.

Then the first shift slept four hours, woke up, ate, and let the others crawl under their blankets. Well after noon none of them had seen or heard a creature larger than a squirrel. Unconsciously they relaxed as the second guard shift went back to sleep and the first shift returned to their sentry positions around the camp. Neither Paul nor Jinja felt much like sleeping. They forced themselves to doze for a couple of hours in the afternoon heat, then gave up and settled for some whispered conversation.

"Was this all Iroquois country?" Jinja asked Paul.

"Is still Iroquois country," said Paul. "All of it is Iroquois country from the river to the north to the southern mountains of the Cherokee. But no, we did not live here. Here lived our children—Mohican, who we conquered more than one hundred summers ago.

"My grandfather once told me that the Mohican lived up and down this valley from the New York island to the Lac de Champlain. If you were to pick up your pack and follow this creek inland, you would find the farms of the white man, one after the other. But you would find no Mohican. They have gone, where, I do not know. Maybe west. I know they have not vanished. The spirit of the Mohican was too great for them to vanish. So said my grandfather. My grandfather was Mohican."

"The Mohican was an enemy to the Iroquois, is that not so?"

"This was true until we conquered them. We conquered everybody. Mohican, Delaware, Abnaki, Huron, Attiwonderonk, People of the Panther, all of them great warrior nations . . . everybody but the white men, though they were not great warriors. Them we made our allies."

"Do you wish the Mohican were still here?" Jinja asked.

Paul smiled. The boy did understand. His heart belonged to the Longhouse. "Ah," Paul said. "The Mohican made good enemies. Fine enemies. This my grandfather told me." Paul paused in his narrative and stared into Jinja's eyes. "Young Gingego, look at me and tell me if you still see a warrior of the Ganonsyoni."

Jinja looked at the broad, round face of the Oneida trader who was also a preacher. "You wear white man's clothes," Jinja said. "Breeches instead of breechcloth and leggings. No paint. No feathers. No scalp lock. But your eyes are the eyes of a Ganonsyoni warrior. They can see the enemy from afar."

"Not far enough, Jinja. I cannot see whether my enemy is the English, the Seneca, the Mohawks—or these rebels."

Jinja's eyes widened. "If you think we might be your enemies, then why do you fight for the rebels?"

"The white men are powerful. I do not know why, but they are—too powerful for the Longhouse to defeat. I have met few good white men. But those I have met—Reverend Kirkland, Big Oak, Little Oak, you—they are all rebels. So I am a rebel too. My people fight on the side of the rebels. That means that someday they may have to fight the Senecas and the Mohawks, the most powerful tribes of the Iroquois confederacy. They are fierce and cruel, my brothers who guard the Western and the Eastern Doors. I would not wish to fight them.

"And so you see, the Mohican made good enemies. I think back to the stories my grandfather told me, and I wish that once again the Mohican lived on the shores of the Hudson River, and the white man did not. I do not understand why my eyes can still focus on a distant animal and make out what it is, but my mind cannot seem to focus on the future. Perhaps I do not dream enough anymore. Yes, it is my Mohican enemies I wish were back on this shore, instead of my white man friends. Can you understand?"

The dark eyes of the Oneida met the dark eyes of Jinja.

"I understand," Jinja said. "It would be a pleasure to join you in roasting a Mohican."

Paul laughed, a short, bitter laugh.

"Jinja, it would be a pleasure for me too," he said. "Now if only we could find one."

Jinja took hold of his rifle and cleaned the old priming out of the pan, then began to take inventory of his powder and bullets. Paul, figuring the discussion was ended, reached into his pack and pulled out a small Bible, but before he could begin to read it, Jinja spoke again. "Does the land know the difference?" he asked.

"What?" Paul was such a courteous man that he was startled by his own abrupt response, but the question was an odd one, coming from a white boy.

"You said the Mohican were gone."

"Yes," Paul answered. "Their silent footsteps no longer cross these forests."

"And the white man covers the land?"

"As no red man ever did, or could have, or wanted to."

"Then does the land know the difference?"

Paul thought for a moment. Then his eyes widened with recollection and he nodded. "My grandfather told me a story of a white man who had a farm on the other side of the river—this river," he said.

"There was a beautiful field beside a creek that grew the biggest corn of all his fields, but there was a beaver dam that caused the creek to flood every spring. When it flooded it would cover the field with water, and the man grew impatient with the field because sometimes a flood would come after the corn had sprouted and then he would have to replant the field.

"There was an old Mohican who lived alone nearby, who sometimes would come by to share a deer kill with the white man. One day as he was passing through the field on the way to the man's cabin, he noticed that the man was out with an ax and a spade, breaking up the beaver dam.

" 'I see what you are doing, and I know why you are doing it,' said the Mohican. 'It is a white man thing to do, but are you sure you want to do that?'

" 'I am tired of losing my best corn crop every few years,' the farmer answered.

"The Mohican nodded his head. 'Mohican used to farm this field,' he said to the farmer. 'One of the women talked to the beaver and asked him if she could use the field. The beaver said that would be fine with him, he would make certain that the field had a fine crop of corn most years, but that if sometimes the field flooded, they must not get mad at the beavers, because if the beavers went away, the corn would no longer grow so tall and fine.'

"The farmer swung his ax and chopped into one of the main parts of the dam. It was a tree trunk so big that the farmer knew he could not have moved it himself, and he did not think the Mohican would help him. He told the Mohican that he was wasting his time with stories about beavers that talked to women, and would he go away because he had work to do.

"The Mohican was so hurt that he took the deer haunch he had prepared for the farmer and left, but first he said to the farmer, 'You will see, when the beaver are gone, this field will not grow corn like it used to.' And then he walked away.

"That summer the field grew its finest crop of corn ever. The farmer went to the Mohican's house and brought him to the field. 'Look at this corn,' he said. 'What of your beaver superstitions now?' The Mohican said only, 'You will see,' and he went back home.

"Over the next five summers the corn crops grew less and less, and the shorter grew the corn, the angrier grew the farmer. At the end of the fifth summer, he walked to the home of the Mohican and demanded that he take his spell off the cornfield. The Mohican looked at the farmer and said this: 'I am no medicine man. I am no priest. I can make no magic. Why is it that you cannot believe that a beaver would talk to a woman, and yet you would believe that I can talk to the gods and make the corn not grow? If I can do that, then maybe you should believe in me instead of the man on the cross.' "

"Then the land does know," Jinja said softly.

"Reverend Kirkland would say that the land does not know, that only God knows," Paul replied. "But I believe the land knows. I believe the land has told the animals to run and hide, the white man is coming and will kill them all."

"And the Ganonsyoni?"

Paul saw that Jinja was less of a child than he had thought.

"The land tells the Ganonsyoni. But the Ganonsyoni no longer understand. They think the land is telling them to stand and fight. They should know better. The Ganonsyoni always trained their warriors not to fight to the death, but to fight to live. And so we were always friends with the English, because a fight with the English is a fight to the death."

"But you are fighting against the English."

"There are two sides. To me they are both English. Reverend Kirkland has told me that the rebel side is the right side. And Reverend Kirkland is a great man. So I fight for the rebels. But like your father, and your grandfather, I do not intend to die fighting for the rebels. Now hear me, young Gingego. I saw you fight. You are a good fighter. But you have no respect for your own life. I want you to watch your father, and your grandfather. Be like them, not like the crazy Englishmen who die so easy sometimes when they are attacked."

Jinja looked at the Oneida with surprise. "I did not want to be afraid," he said.

"Better to be a little afraid than to be foolish. Do you understand what I am telling you?"

"I will be by myself and try to understand, Cansadeyo," Jinja answered.

"That is good," was Paul's reply.

❖7❖

THAD TAPPED HIS FATHER ON THE SHOULDERS and roused him. The sun had dipped well below the trees. The time had come to prepare for the second night's journey. Clouds scudding in from the west promised a dark night, with perhaps some wind and rain in the offing.

Just before they shoved off into the creek, Big Oak explained that they would be traveling close to shore most of the night. Jinja tried to argue that they had seen no river traffic the night before, so why not keep to the middle of the river? Big Oak replied that they would travel as if the whole British fleet were scheduled to sail up to Albany.

In the dregs of twilight they wound their way down the creek and into the Hudson, paddled about a hundred yards out, then headed south. Big Oak's wisdom was confirmed when, close to midnight, a two-masted schooner suddenly appeared, its white sails snapping in the fresh wind, tacking its way upstream. Big Oak stopped paddling, leaned forward and softly told Paul that the ship's pilot must have a very high opinion of his own eyesight to take a ship upriver on a night like this.

As the ship approached, they could see the lights on board and occasionally hear a word or two shouted. The ship worked its way upriver until it was nearly abreast of the canoe caravan. Although it was a good three hundred yards away and without any real lights, all the paddlers ducked down and hoped that heavily burdened canoes riding low in the water would be invisible to the passing ship.

Thad pulled on the cable until his canoe was within a few feet of Big Oak. "Can you see what flag she's flyin'?" he asked his father.

"Doesn't much matter," Big Oak responded. "I don't feel like being stopped by a Yankee ship either. We'd still have to do some fine talkin' to get back on our journey, and I'd just as soon we travel by our own time."

Thad could see the lighted windows of the stern cabin and the white froth boiling in the wake of the ship. They let themselves drift southward for a few more minutes before Thad felt a tug on the rope. He and Jinja dipped their paddles and they continued their journey south.

They must have been a bit groggy that second night out. The first light of dawn seemed to come upon them suddenly. They paddled swiftly toward the shore and turned southward, but they could find no creeks big enough to accommodate their craft. Finally, when daylight threatened to reveal them to chance enemies, they hurriedly beached their canoes, unloaded the furs, then carried the canoes far enough inland to hide them from sight.

Again they split themselves into two shifts, but Big Oak changed them so that Thad was up with Ooghnor and Gilles, while he shared his watch with Paul and Jinja. Big Oak wanted an opportunity to talk with his grandson alone, so that they could speak freely.

Toward the end of their second sleep shift, he arose, checked the priming in the pan of his fine Pennsylvania long rifle, and sat beside Jinja. To his surprise, Jinja's eyes were already wide open.

"You have always been a very good sleeper, my grandson," Big Oak said very softly. "Always have you slept with an easy conscience. Why then do I come to you and find your eyes already-bright?"

"I had dreams and I awoke," Jinja answered. "I could not

remember the dreams, but a question came to me as I lay here and I could not go back to sleep."

"Maybe I can help you answer the question."

"If you cannot, no one can, Grandpa. We have journeyed together many times and never have we been so cautious. I know we are in a war, but I have seen almost nobody on the river and nobody on the shore. My father has told me of all the times you and he fought together and all the people you defeated. And yet we hide like bats in the daytime and travel only in the dark. I do not understand."

Good, Big Oak told himself. At last, some thinking from the boy. "We do not know where the army of Sir Henry Clinton is," he replied. "Where the British go, they take their law. By their law we are smugglers and we are spies. If they catch us, they will stand us up against a tree and shoot us. All of us."

"And who has ever caught Big Oak before? Seldom the Indians, never the English. Look what we did to the English on the river above Albany."

"Do not overlook the English, Jinja. They may not look like much in the woods, but they are the most powerful nation in the world."

"But we are in the woods. This is *our* place."

"Jinja, when it was just me, I could be fearless. When it was me and Little Oak, I had to be more careful. But now that you are with us, I can take no chances at all. You have a mother who would never forgive me if you were harmed, nor could I forgive myself. She has always trusted me with you, and I cannot let her down. I tell you, boy, I can never remember being so frightened as I was when you broke from ambush and ran after the Tory."

"Did you think there were more of them hiding in ambush?" Jinja asked. "Were you afraid that without me you would be outnumbered?" Jinja smiled at the thought that he counted as a warrior on the warpath, but Big Oak looked at him in a stern way that Jinja had never seen before.

"It may be that you will never be killed by a tomahawk,

boy, for your skull is so thick, I fear there is no way of getting through to you. You are the bearer of my name, for many years the only one, and you are precious to me, so I will keep my patience. My life has been long and active and free and mostly happy. I could lose it today, and my only regret would be the children I leave behind. It was your life I feared for on that trail because you were so reckless and foolish.

"I fear that life in the stores and warehouses of Wendel and Watley has addled your brain. But you have a fine father, one of the finest men I know. Just a few more years of living will give you the wisdom that will lengthen your life, but until then you will be a danger to yourself and those around you when you are in battle. Do you understand me?"

To Jinja, danger was something you could see, hear, touch, or smell. He did not have enough experience to imagine what he could not sense. He had thought that he'd shined in battle, but his father, his grandfather, and Cansadeyo had all voiced their concern. Above all else he needed their respect.

He nodded his head but did not let his eyes meet those of Big Oak. His grandfather had never before criticized him so sternly. "I will be more careful from now on," he told Big Oak, and he meant it.

Paul's keen eyesight saved their mission late that night, and probably saved some lives as well. They were at the place where the river narrows, and the paddlers had their canoes gliding straight and swift when suddenly, for the first time in the course of their journey, he cried out and dug his paddle in hard against the current. Big Oak followed suit a split second later, and the paddlers in the other craft did the same, just in time.

The canoes came to a halt in a wreath of white froth.

Not ten feet from the bow of the canoe lay a great chain, stretched across the river. Paul turned his canoe to the right and made for the shore, and the other canoes followed easily.

"Who did this?" Jinja asked his grandfather when they had all brought their canoes to the shore and were unloading their furs.

"Had to be our boys," Big Oak responded. "They're the ones with the inland navy."

"That means the schooner we saw the other night had to be ours?"

"I would think so," Big Oak replied. "Come on, we've got some people to meet before the end of the night," he said, carrying another load of furs and dropping it on the shore. When the canoes had all been unloaded, the men carried them along the shore and launched them on the other side of the chain.

"Let's hurry and get them loaded," he said. "There might be some sentries down here guarding that chain. They might be away for just this moment." It was a matter of ten more minutes of swift, sweaty work to reload the canoes and move them back out to the middle of the river, which was so narrow at that point that they needed to get to the middle to be safe from witnesses on the shore.

"Why is he so worried about our own soldiers knowing what we're doing?" Jinja whispered to Thad in the second canoe.

"It's just easier to smuggle when no one else knows," Thad explained. "Otherwise everybody wants to be a part of it."

For another hour they paddled hard, veering toward the shore as the river got wider and wider. Now Paul brought the canoes close to shore. They paddled slowly for a considerable distance, until Big Oak spotted a peculiar clump of pine trees on a tiny peninsula. That was his landmark. That was why he had chosen this spot. The peninsula was a quarter of a mile away when he spotted it, but he had them back away another half mile and beach the canoes in a cove. There, Thad, Jinja, and the Caughnawagas waited, concealed, rifles at the ready, while Paul and Big Oak crept through the forest. Big Oak knew that the greatest danger to them would be at the time and place of the exchange. He would take no unnecessary risks.

Noiselessly they made their way through the trees, Paul in the lead, Big Oak guarding the rear. A bright half-moon cast shadows anywhere there was a clearing that let in the moonlight. They could hear careless voices by the river. Softly they slipped to the edge of the wood line and observed several longboats beached on the south side of the peninsula. They did not immediately make their presence known, but lay quietly behind a pair of large maples and listened.

"I don't want to wait too long for these red Indians," said a voice. "We 'ave to get down to the ship before first light. So if they don't show up in 'alf an hour, we'll leave you 'ere and—"

"We don't have to do that," said the other voice. "We've got men here. We've got muscle. If they don't come on time, we'll just hide the boats in the trees and wait. I do not intend to go back down empty-handed. The captain would not be pleased if we came back without those damned skins."

"You'll not have to wait," Big Oak said, stepping out from behind the trees. "I'm Sam Watley, of Wendel and Watley, and this is Paul Derontyan."

"Blue Douglass and Martin Horne," said Douglass, a man dressed half landlubber, half seafarer. They shook hands and the two men began to conduct Big Oak and Paul to the longboats to inspect the goods. But abruptly Douglass stopped and turned to Big Oak. "Where are your goods?"

"Down the river a piece," Big Oak lied.

"Down the river, you say." Douglass smiled.

Big Oak shrugged his shoulders. "Let's see what you've got."

There were four large boats with a half-dozen men lounging around them, smoking pipes and spitting. The men were a varied lot, Indians, blacks, whites, ranging from gaunt to burly, but all with bare, sinewy arms used to hard labor on the seas. Paul and Big Oak could make out their hard-bitten faces clearly in the light of a fire they had carelessly kindled to cook their food and warm their bones.

Three of the boats were half loaded with powder kegs and lead ingots. The fourth boat held an assortment of bullet molds, muskets, flints, spare parts, and bayonets. A simple cargo to be traded for a simple cargo.

Douglass leaned over Big Oak's shoulder as he took inventory. The man's breath had the kind of foul stench that comes with decaying teeth and rotting gums, but at least he remained silent as Big Oak examined the goods. The lead was lead. The powder kegs felt about as heavy as powder kegs should feel when they're full and dry. Powder from the one keg that he opened had just the right feel to his fingers and the right smell to his nostrils. The weapons were not exactly what he wanted, but in these times one had to take what one could get. He picked up several of the muskets and sighted along the barrels, examined some of the other items, then looked up at Douglass.

"Is this the best you could do for muskets?" he asked, looking around at the rest of the men as he spoke.

Douglass spread his palms upward. "I just 'auled the cargo, Captain," he replied. "To be honest, I hain't seen this lot except loadin' it on the ship and 'aulin' it up 'ere."

Big Oak nodded. "Well," he said, "I suppose we have to make do with this. We'll head on down and bring up the furs."

"Right, then, Captain."

Big Oak and Paul turned their backs and headed for the woods, listening carefully for any noise that promised danger, especially the cock of a pistol or any sudden movement indicating that a knife-wielding assassin had the veins in their necks on his mind. Hearing no such noise, they disappeared into the woods and headed south, first walking, then, when they were well away from their trading partners, shifting into a careful nighttime lope. After about three minutes of running they doubled back north in a wide circle that took them well west of the river until they judged that they were close to where their cohorts waited. Perhaps they were being followed. It was always best to be careful.

They turned east toward the river and easily found their people. In rapid Mohawk, Paul and Big Oak explained their situation and what they would have to do.

Within a few minutes Thad and Jinja were in the lead canoe, towing the other two canoes on very short leads, very slowly, keeping far out on the river until they saw the campfire. They would then drift below it and turn around so they would be coming from the south as Big Oak had said they would.

Meanwhile Big Oak, Paul, and the two Caughnawagas slunk back down toward the traders' camp and silently stationed themselves close enough to hear, far enough away to be unheard. What they saw confirmed Big Oak's suspicions. Douglass and Horne were walking back and forth along the shore with pistols in their belts, while in the half-light away from the fire their men were hidden away in ambush, or so they thought. The fire had been built into a bonfire so they could see their prey paddling their canoes ashore. No doubt they intended to fire just before the canoes grounded, while the men in the canoes still had paddles in their hands.

Big Oak was pleased to see Thad keeping the canoes well offshore, just close enough to be detected, but too far away to present a good nighttime target.

They waited at the edge of the forest, only about thirty yards from the camp, their rifles ready for bloody business. And Douglass and Horne continued to pace along the shore.

Out on the water there came a sudden shout. "Are you Douglass?"

"Aye," called the villain, the last syllable he ever uttered.

Big Oak fired and his ball took half the man's head off. The three Indians fired at the ill-concealed sailors, and at that close range they could not miss. The unwounded sailors turned and fired into the woods, but Big Oak and his fellow ambushers were no longer where the smoke from their rifles lingered in the trees.

In the meantime Thad and Jinja had picked up their rifles. The men on shore could barely see them, but in the light of the big campfire, the two Watleys could certainly make out several human figures, dead and alive. Thad fired first and left Horne wriggling in the dust with a bullet in his chest. Shrewdly, Jinja waited until he could make out a definite target, one of the sailors scurrying around in search of cover. Even as he reloaded, Thad watched Jinja while the young man calmly took aim on the moving target and squeezed the trigger. The pan flashed, the barrel roared, and the target spun to the ground. Jinja gave a satisfied grunt, like a carpenter pronouncing his work good, then he went into his reloading routine.

Ooghnor and Gilles were all for dashing in and finishing off the three surviving sailors, but Big Oak demurred. "They're done," he insisted, watching the longboats that the men were using for cover.

"Your leaders are dead!" he shouted into the night. "Drop your guns and come out with your hands on your heads, and I give you my word we won't harm you."

"Why should we take the word of a bloody colonial?" came a shaken voice from among the longboats.

"Why not? We can take you anytime."

"So you say, damn you!" In spite of the angry words, the man's voice quavered with fear, and neither of his mates spoke at all.

"So we say," said Paul, and he meant it, for he had made his way onto the peninsula and found a position above the boats and behind a tree.

"I could kill one of you now," said Paul. "Lay down your muskets."

Meekly, the men dropped their weapons.

"Now stand up and walk to the fire, where we can see you."

Two of them stood up and walked over to the fire. The third one lay still in the shadows. Paul laughed.

"We have a ghost here," he said to Big Oak, who was advancing into the clearing. "He thinks that we cannot see him."

With an angry toss of his shoulders the third man stood up and walked to the fire.

Paul found some stout rope in one of the longboats. By that time Thad and Jinja had beached their canoes and joined their business associates, who stood before the three captives, rifles trained on them.

"Jinja and Ooghnor, would you take a look at the others and see if they're as dead as they look?" Big Oak said.

They found Douglass and Horne deceased, but of the three who had been shot near the longboats, two were still breathing, barely.

"How bad are they?" Big Oak asked. Ooghnor shook his head. "That bad, eh?" he walked over to take a look himself. "Yeah, well, they might come around for a bit before they die, ought to finish them off now and save 'em the trouble."

And while the three surviving traders watched with widening eyes, Big Oak finished off one with a blow of his tomahawk and Ooghnor did in the other with a slash of his knife.

"Now, you three, believe it or not, you'll make it out of this alive if you'll tell me why your captain decided to sell us out."

There was a silence. Then the bolder one, the tallest, most scar-faced one; the one with the cruelest slant to his mouth, spoke. "What makes you think he was sellin' you out?"

Big Oak flicked his tomahawk and a few flecks of blood from his recent mercy-killing landed on the man's face and clung to his scraggly blond beard. "I know he was sellin' us out," the old woodsman said angrily. "The longboats are half empty. You could have made the trip with three or even two of them, unless you were meanin' to take back both the ammunition *and* the furs.

"Then there's the weapons. They weren't the weapons we'd asked for. Your captain would've known we'd never make the deal for old guns like those. Even Menominees wouldn't of dealt for guns like those. He didn't wanna go through the trouble and expense and risk of buying good weapons, since he never intended to trade them anyway.

"The only good weapons are the ones you men had. I don't know where you got 'em, but you men have more of a look of pirates than honest seamen. There's a difference, and I've been around the docks enough to know. And then that there Douglass. It's too bad his memory's not as good as mine. He come up the river about ten, twelve year back and stuck Warrighiyagey with a few hundred bottles of French wine that turned out to be French vinegar."

"What in hell is a Warriga—what you said?" asked the prisoner.

"That's Sir William Johnson, and if he were still alive, I'd bring him the head of this fool even though Sir William would have been on the other side of the war. At least it would have been worth a shared bottle of some real French wine."

The prisoner gave Big Oak the look of a man who might have just sampled some of Warrighiyagey's vinegar. "If you expect us to admit that—"

"I don't need you to admit. I'm telling you what I already know. I just haven't figured why. We trade with good furs. I'd have thought he'd want to keep the trading going."

In the course of this conversation he had led the three men to a clump of trees to which the two Caughnawagas, Paul, and Jinja were lashing them with the nautical rope.

"Owww! Damn your eyes! You right near broke me in half!" cried one of them as Jinja pulled his rope a little tighter than he needed to.

"I'd just like to know, and I thought you'd have an interest in telling us," Big Oak said, casting a meaningful glance at his still bloody hatchet.

"How do I know you won't do us in like you did those—if I answer your questions?"

"You don't. But if I want the information bad enough, these Caughnawagas would certainly know how to get it out of you. A little bit of cutting, a little burning, they'd have you telling us things we wouldn't even want to know. Now, I'm tellin' you they won't do that. They—Our—torturing days are over. And I've said we won't kill you. Now look over next to you at your friend who can hardly breathe because my grandson is so young and strong he sometimes overdoes things a little. If he were to tighten all your ropes, you'd never slip your bonds and you'd probably be in trouble with whoever found you, rebel or Tory.

"You just tell us why, and we'll give you knots you'll be able to slip before too long."

The man looked hard at Big Oak. In the light of the bonfire he could see the man's eyelids trembling with frustration.

He tried to shrug his shoulders. "There ain't that much to tell. He said it was gettin' too dangerous, too hard to run the blockades, so he was goin' to try his hand in the West Indies."

That sounded reasonable to Big Oak, but not to Thad, who had been hearing rumors of plots and counterplots all summer long in Albany. He nodded to Jinja, who pushed his rifle under the rope that held their informant and began to twist. The man grunted, then began to moan. The rope dug deeper.

"Stop!" he begged. Thad nodded. Jinja stopped. "I'm tellin' the truth, I swear on my mother's grave," said the man.

"I don't trust a man who'd swear on his mother's grave," Thad spat. Paul had stepped forward and pulled out his knife. He displayed the shiny blade about three inches from the man's eyes. Big Oak almost could not restrain a smile. Paul was wearing his grimmest warface. Their prisoners had heard much about the ferocity of Indians, but this must have been their first experience with them. Their fear was such that Paul and the two Caughnawagas could smell it.

"Cansadeyo, here, likes to slice up white men piece by piece," Big Oak told the man. The man said nothing. Paul placed the knife behind the man's ear and drew it downward. The man flinched but remained silent.

"Use the sharp side, Paul," Big Oak suggested. Paul did. The blood poured down the side of the man's face and the ear began to hang down a bit.

"My God—Bill, tell him or they'll cut us all up!" cried the man to his right.

But the man said nothing. He stood tall against the tree while the blood dripped down the side of his face.

"Tell us what?" Thad asked, moving toward the man at the next tree, a big, brawny fellow with a face that glowed chalk-white in the light of the fire.

"Let me see if he has swallowed his tongue," said Gilles. He tried to open the mouth of the first captive, but the man bit down hard. "Oh-ho, his jaws, they are locked together, poor fellow. I will help you open up," he said. He drew his knife and inserted it between the man's lips, but his teeth stopped the blade. "Here, I help you," murmured Gilles confidentially, and hammered hard, once, on the handle of the knife with the palm of his hand. The knife went in, half the length of the blade. The man's mouth opened and he let out a scream that bubbled with the blood that came surging out.

"Hold on, Gilles," said Thad. The Caughnawaga withdrew his knife and the scream subsided to a desperate moan, then strangled breathing. "Why should a man put up with this? What's he holding back?" He moved over to the second captive. Paul took his cue and followed. His blood-flecked knife held eye high, Gilles wiped his blade off on

the shirt of the man who had just received the tonsillec-
tomy, and followed.

"Your turn," Thad said, simply.

"B-But you're not finished with him yet," said the terrified
strong man, casting a glance at the first man, who was still
busy spitting out blood.

Thad and Jinja laughed, but Big Oak was beginning to
run out of patience. He stood nose to nose with the second
captive. "We are going to take you all apart until one of you
tells us what we want to know. It's simple, you see. If one of
you talks, we won't harm him. The others, ones who won't
talk, well, we won't like them very much."

That put a new slant on the interrogation. Did each of
the three men trust the other, and if one talked, what would
happen to the others? The strong man looked to his right,
then to his left, and decided he trusted the good faith of his
captors more than he trusted the steadfastness of his comrades.

"I'll tell you. Don't do anything else—please," he said, as
if he thought that a moment's delay would bring another
bloody act.

Thad waved Paul and Gilles back. "Talk to me," he said
confidentially. "Tell me."

" 'Ut up!" hollered the wounded captive through the
blood in his throat.

"Shut yourself up, damn you!" the strong man shot back.
"The British army knew about this right from the beginning. They—"

" 'Ut up!"

"You shut up! Sergeant!"

Big Oak and Tad riveted their eyes on the captive with
the half-severed ear and the bloody throat.

"A spy," Big Oak mused. "A rotten spy. You people shoot
spies, don't you?"

"Only him," said the strong man. "Him and that Horne.
Rest of us is just regular seamen, I swear it."

"How do we know you're tellin' the truth?" Big Oak asked.

"Truth? I'm tellin' you everything. Did you see that ship comin' up the river the other night? What flag was she flyin'?"

"We couldn't tell," Jinja said.

"Hit were a British ship, I'll tell you, and they dropped off a party of men on both sides of the river, I'll tell you, and another party in a longboat, comin' down the middle of the river, and they're all lookin' for you."

"Anything else?" Big Oak asked.

"That's all I know."

It was getting late. Not more than three hours of darkness remained. Quickly they hauled the longboats out onto the water, transferred the furs from the canoes to the boats, and chopped holes in and sank the canoes. Just before they shoved off, Big Oak came back to the man Jinja had nearly squeezed to death, and with some difficulty loosened the ropes that Jinja had tied.

"One of you is bound to get loose within an hour or two," he said. "We'll leave a little food for you. I would go south if I were you. You go north and you'll have to deal with Indians." He pointed a thumb over his shoulder to the two Caughnawagas, who with Jinja were putting the finishing touches on stowing the cargo. The Caughnawagas had scalps hanging from their belts, cut so quickly and quietly that nobody else had even noticed them doing it.

"One more thing," said Thad, who was looking at Big Oak but addressing the prisoners. "We don't like spies either." Big Oak gave a quick nod. Gilles held his knife before the suddenly widened eyes of the captive sergeant, then ran it across his throat, from one ear to another.

They extinguished the dying remains of the fire, shoved off with their cargo, rowed to the center of the river and set the sails. There was a useful breeze, and in no time they were heading upriver at a pretty fair clip.

❧ 8 ❧

DIETER WAS AT THE WAREHOUSE WHEN THE longboats appeared on the river below Albany. The afternoon was windless. The sails hung limp on their masts. Men were bending their backs rowing the heavy craft against the current, making slow headway but making it nevertheless. He squinted as he peered out at the boats, and was certain that the first boat was being rowed by his son-in-law. But where were the canoes?

He noticed that the boats rode low in the water. Maybe they had forged a better deal than he had expected. All six of the men were on board, and nobody seemed hurt. All in all, he thought, it looked like a good trading mission. But why the longboats? He couldn't help thinking that the boats appeared to be in fine shape, and that they would be of future use to the company.

Thad turned his boat sluggishly toward shore, then to the dock that protruded about seventy-five feet into the river. The other three boats followed. Two employees from the warehouse tied the boats to the dock. By the time Dieter had lumbered from the warehouse down to the dock, the goods were being unloaded onto little carts. To his disappointment, all he saw were furs.

"What is dis?" he asked. "Did they not come?"

Big Oak smiled. "They came, all right. They didn't come

to trade, they came to steal. But they were the ones that paid." It was then that Dieter saw the barrels of powder, the lead bars, and the weapons still sitting in the longboats.

Dieter did not smile but his eyes shined. Now *there* was profit. The company was paid not in worthless paper money, but in vouchers that would be redeemed at the end of the war if the rebels won. Unlike the Senecas, Dieter was betting on the rebels, not only with his heart, but with his pocketbook. "After all," he had told Big Oak cheerfully, "if the English win, they'll hang us anyway, den it won't matter that the verdammt politicians didn't pay me, yes?"

He took it for granted that the government would be broke at the end of the war. So how would they pay him? The only thing they had that was worth anything was the land. Indian land. Lots of Indian land once they threw the traitorous Mohawks and the rest of them off and kicked them across the St. Lawrence River, which is where they belonged anyway. Unless the Americans managed to conquer Canada, in which case there would be a whole lot of Indians to kick across the Ohio, and then there would be all sorts of land to be had by patriots like Dieter Wendel. As for the furs? Furs being as scarce as they were, they'd only be worth that much more the next time he smuggled them down the Hudson.

"You'll tell me about your adventure after we put away the goods," he said to Thad. "Make sure they put them there in the middle of the warehouse where it's dry. And put a big cloth over the powder just in case. Verdammt leaky roof! Oh, and by the way, your army beat the hell out of dat fancy General Burgoyne. They're all gone, except for the prisoners, and there was lots of them."

Big Oak was close enough to hear the news. "You don't say," he said simply. That was the full extent of their celebration.

"David," Dieter continued. "I want you should be out here early tomorrow morning. I need a new recount on the furs. I can't seem to keep track of their comings and go-ings."

Instead of nodding and going on with his work, Jinja walked over to Dieter and stared down at the stocky Dutchman.

"What?" the old trader asked impatiently. "What? Vat?"

"I won't be in the warehouse tomorrow, Grandpa."

"Zachariah!" Dieter shouted at one of the warehouse men. "I need for you to get that roof fixed quick. What do you mean you won't be in the warehouse tomorrow?" he added, turning toward his tall grandson.

"I'm gonna find me a militia unit to enlist with," Jinja said, attracting the immediate attention of Thad and Big Oak, who had had no prior warning of Jinja's decision.

"You are what?" Dieter spat back at his grandson. Thad and Big Oak said nothing, but closed in on Dieter and Jinja and stood on either side of them.

"Did you know about this?" Dieter asked them.

Thad and Big Oak both shook their heads. "What made you decide to join a militia?" Thad asked Jinja quietly, while at the same time he gave Dieter a look that told him to stay out of the dialogue.

"Because if we're to win this war, we have to have soldiers who will fight battles. I didn't think it was right that we go out and join those fellas in a fight, then the next day we go home, and they still have to fight," Jinja said.

"We fight the war in our own way, like the Indians do," Big Oak answered. "Which, by the way, you are one."

"No, I am me," Jinja insisted. "When you just talked about the victory up the river, I asked myself, what if all those men had decided to go home after the battle that we had fought in? That fancy general you always used to talk about until he got whipped would be in Albany now. And we would all be livin' in the woods."

"I thought you liked living in the woods," Thad re-marked.

"I don't like Mom and Anne living in the woods. I don't

like Dieter living in the woods. I don't like the English taking over the store and our houses. I am more of a white man than you or Big Oak. And I would rather be a soldier than a trader. Especially now."

"Why now?" Big Oak asked. "Why wait till we've driven the English away?"

"I have always believed everything you've told me," Jinja said, looking first at his father, then at his two grandfathers. "But I am older now, and I see things for myself. We were almost had by English spies. We had to hide like rats all the way home. We had to dodge that English ship three times. The English are *not* gone. I have listened to you. I have listened to Paul. I have listened to Louis, the son of the man you named me for. I know you think I don't listen. Sometimes you think I am a little feebleminded because I think of other things, but I listen too, and what you and Paul and Louis and the others have told me over the years is that the English never quit, no matter how many times they are beaten. I know they will be back."

Big Oak held up a hand, and Jinja went silent. His speech had come as a shock to the old woodsman. Big Oak loved his only grandson, and he was fiercely determined not to lose him.

"Jinja," he said. "We have taken you into battle with us. Your first warpath was the kind to make a legend of a Seneca warrior. But you were willing to sell your life too cheaply. That is not the Ganonsyoni way. The great warrior's life is too precious to sacrifice for a trifle.

"We are afraid that the next colonel you soldier for will sacrifice your life for nothing. That is what colonels and generals do. They lead their men into ambushes and then they ride away on their horses. *They* get to fight another day. Many of their men do not.

"And there is another thing. When you march with a regiment, it is more difficult to care for yourself. You cannot leave ranks and go and shoot a deer for a new pair of moccasins or fresh food. You cannot drop out just because

your rifle needs repair. Instead you take up a Brown Bess
that can't hit anything farther away than you can spit. The
officers like it that way, because the English officers believe
in those close tactics and they're the ones who know about
being a professional soldier.

"And then there are the camps, and the forts. I don't
know why it is, but in the camps and the forts there are
always plenty of sick soldiers. Men who are strong and
hardy in the field sicken and die behind walls. How well do
you feel you would be serving your country dying of the
bloody flux in some godforsaken fort?

"No, Jinja. You can serve your country here, with us, and
you'll do much more good than you would carrying a musket with a bunch of town boys who don't know an Indian
from the shadow of a tree stump."

Jinja looked around at his father and his grandfathers, his
gaze moving from face to face in silence until all three of
them thought Big Oak's words had won him over. When
Jinja spoke, he was brief.

"Well, I've made up my mind," he said, and this time he
did not wait for an answer. Without another word he
walked away.

❧9❧

THE SUSQUEHANNA RIVER WOUND LAZILY through the forest from New York to Pennsylvania, then back into New York, and then finally back into Pennsylvania on its long journey to Chesapeake Bay. On the upper reaches of the river, where the trees that overhung its banks turned the water green, a lone canoe drifted easily downstream. Its sole occupant let the current do most of the work, stroking only when necessary.

He wore the scalp lock of the Seneca nation, which meant he was a fair distance from the land of his fathers, but he felt at home anyway. He could hear the noise of activity downriver. The noise did not make him cautious. He had expected to hear these sounds, the sounds of his Seneca and Mohawk brothers preparing for war.

As the bow of his canoe appeared beyond a bend, chief Sayengaraghta raised himself from the rock on which he had been sitting, watching his braves patching up canoes and rafts for their journey downriver.

"Ah, Degata, I had thought that maybe your wife had taken hold of your spirit and bound it to your lodge poles," he said to the lone brave.

Degata beached his canoe, slung his rifle, his pack, his powder horn, and his bullet pouch over his shoulder, and leaped ashore.

"I would not miss this battle, Sayengaraghta," he said. A number of braves looked up from their work on the banks of the river, and several acknowledged their friend with a wave or a word.

"That is good," replied the chief. "Many moons have passed since we lost so many warriors to the rebels. I miss them still, and my thirst for revenge remains unquenched."

Degata dragged his canoe onto the bank and eyed the chief. "Then it is time we drew some blood, ten of them for every one of ours." He looked around him and was amazed at what he saw. There were scores of Ganonsyoni on the banks and in the woods, preparing themselves for the coming battle against the Yenkees from Connecticut who had long before settled down in Wyoming Valley. Nobody liked these people, not the Pennsylvanians who disputed Connecticut land claims, and certainly not the people of the Longhouse, who regarded the Connecticut claims as just another white man cheat. They were all rebels, fit objects of revenge, and the Senecas had been waiting the entire winter for this moment.

The following morning was a windless one. The heat came early and the sun shined upon an endless procession of craft descending the Susquehanna. Each craft was loaded with painted, angry warriors of the Longhouse, the Senecas of Sayengaraghta, and the Mohawks of Thayendanegea, whom the whites knew as Joseph Brant. The night before, they had danced, struck the war post, and sworn to each other that the rebels would forever remember the disaster that befell them the day they met the warriors of the Longhouse in Wyoming Valley.

Jinja was already down in Wyoming Valley. It was more or less an accident that thrust him in harm's way, the kind of accident his father and his grandfather had tried to avoid. He had found a small group of militia camped outside of Albany without a concrete mission. Since the defeat of Burgoyne the previous year, the citizens of Albany had been feeling very secure.

This little orphan militia group had no orders. The feeling among the men was that they should find a place where they were needed. They had decided to head south through New Jersey, traveling toward where the action was. Thad, Katherine, and Anne were out to see them off, and right to the end tried to persuade Jinja not to go. Thad in particular had a horrible feeling that nothing good could come from this ragtag expedition headed by a Captain Bonner, who had been a dairy farmer before a roving group of Mohawks had slaughtered all of his cows. Most of the militiamen were as young as Jinja, youngsters just becoming old enough to follow their older predecessors into the field.

Before the men marched off, Thad reminded Jinja that he possessed more woods experience than the rest of them combined. "If he leads you into danger, try to find your own way out, or he'll get you killed."

To Katherine, the scene had an air of unreality. She was close enough to her son to grab hold of him and lead him away, yet she could not do it. She held him for a moment and kissed him, dry-eyed, then walked back to their wagon and waited to be driven home. Then she would lock herself away in the attic room and cry her heart out where no one could hear her. "I love you, keep your head down," were the only things she said. The rest she kept to herself.

Thad looked at the group as they stood in uncertain formation before their captain. He felt that he ought to join up just so his experience might give them a better chance of survival. But he knew that if he joined, he would be under the command of Captain Bonner, and that loose-jointed misfit would never allow a woodsman's know-how to come between him and his command privileges.

"I'll keep my eyes open," Jinja said, and the simple way he said it made Thad believe the youngster had thought it out. Still, as the militia marched along the southbound road trailing a dust cloud behind them, Thad felt the same choking pain at the back of his throat as his wife and daughter.

Jinja felt the pain too, but it began to fade once the road

left the open plain outside the town and began to wind through the woods. These boys were longtime friends, but they were town boys and farm boys, not woodsmen. Adventure is nice, but many of the boys carried well-worn muskets that would not kill the way his father's and grandfather's rifles killed. They did not run the trail in swift silence either, the way his father and grandfather did. Their big feet seemed to find every dry twig in the forest, and their high spirits loosened their tongues.

"Shhh!" he hissed, drawing the attention of his comrades and the captain. The former were surprised to hear any kind of comment from their normally silent trail runner. The latter was annoyed because it was his job to keep the men quiet, and he didn't like some private reminding him of his duties. Albany was only five miles behind when Jinja, who marched near the head of the single file, stopped and put a finger to his mouth. His keen senses had detected something amiss in front of them.

From the woods came a runner three days out of the Wyoming Valley. A tall, gaunt youngster no more than sixteen years of age dressed in homespun, armed with an ancient fowling piece, frightened, hungry, and terribly relieved to find that he was not lost. His message was a panicked request for men to help fight off an invasion that was certain to come soon.

"The whole valley is in an uproar," he said, still gasping for breath. "Most of our men are with the army, fighting somewhere down south. There's nobody to protect the valley but militia and boys and old men."

The runner stood in his tracks, waiting for his breathing to slow down so that he would not have to talk in wheezes.

"What makes them so sure they're gonna be attacked?" Captain Bonner asked the runner.

"We've got scouts out. They've seen the Senecas coming south. They've seen the greens coming south. And the Tories in the valley—the ones that live there—talkin' mighty big. They'd been kind of 'fraid of us since we arrested a bunch of them back in January."

The captain thought for a moment. "Then I guess we oughta go and lend you a hand. Lead the way. We'll follow."

The runner shook his head. "You'll have to find your own way. I've got to find more people."

"Well I—I'm not sure I can figure—can you tell me—".

Jinja walked over to the runner and Bonner. "I know the way," he declared.

The features on the captain's face relaxed for just a moment, until he realized that an eighteen-year-old was relieving him of some of his hard-won authority.

"You been down that way before?" he asked skeptically.

"I wouldn't say I knew the way if I hadn't," Jinja replied.

"Don't get smart, boy," said the sergeant, a man not much older than Jinja, who had earned his position by sucking up to the captain.

Jinja knew better than to sass the sergeant. He just stood there, by the captain, and waited. He thought the sun would move in the sky before the captain made a decision. Finally, the dairy farmer sighed and nodded.

"If you're sure you know, then let's get started."

The runner nodded his thanks and continued his journey north, then stopped. "Please hurry, sir," he said, then turned and ran.

So Jinja led the way. He had taken so many trading trips with his father that he knew the trails to the Susquehanna Valley like he knew the streets of Albany. He knew the shortcuts. He knew the best places to ford the creeks. He knew the most dangerous places for an ambush, even though he and his father had never been ambushed. There wasn't much he didn't know about the way to the Susquehanna, but still the captain was not pleased, and neither were the men. Traveling at the head of the column, he was the one who set the pace, and, young though they were, none of his cohorts were in shape to keep up with him.

"Better slow down, Watley," puffed the captain after a while. "You've got 'em strung out over a quarter of a mile."

"Yes sir," Jinja said, and his loping trot subsided into a walk. But he was impatient to be where the fighting was going to be. Gradually his stride lengthened until he was just short of running.

"Watley!" It was the sergeant now, and his voice was hostile. "I can't keep up with you and neither can the rest of 'em, understand?"

"Yes, Sergeant, but the runner said—".

"Won't do no good if we get there and you've run all my boys into exhaustion," the captain insisted. "Slow down. If we don't get there in time, at least we'll get there alive."

Jinja might have been able to hurry the boys on the trail, but it was beyond his power to get them on their feet in the morning. Every night they quit well before sunset. Every morning they started out well after dawn. Eventually they found a good-sized stream that Jinja declared to be the Susquehanna. "So we just follow this river all the way," said the captain. "Good. I can take over from here, Watley."

Jinja shook his head. "We'll be following this river for a week, the way it winds, Captain. We better cross it and just head west." The captain grunted but didn't argue.

Later on in the day they arrived at another large stream. The captain looked across it and blew out his cheeks. "What's this one?" he asked.

"Susquehanna," Jinja replied, trying not to smile.

"But this river flows north," the captain insisted. "Doesn't the Susquehanna flow south?"

"Next time we see it," Jinja said, "it'll be goin' the right way again."

The sergeant swore under his breath.

They finally caught up to that part of the Susquehanna that plunged down into Pennsylvania for good, weary from all the hills and valleys they had crossed. The going south along the Susquehanna was easier, but Jinja was nervous because if every mile brought them closer to the Wyoming

Valley, every mile also brought them closer to battle. There was no Thad or Big Oak to read the winds and the woods for signs of the enemy. It was up to him to lead them safely to the forts he knew lay in the valley—that is, if Captain Bonner would let him. The closer they came to where they expected to find rebel forces, the more anxious Bonner was to take back all the reins of authority.

Late one sweaty afternoon they heard a cluster of rifle shots up ahead. Jinja gestured to them all to seek cover, and all did, including the captain and the sergeant. "I'll be right back," he whispered to the captain.

"Where do you think you're going?"

"You wanna know what's up ahead, don't you?"

"Don't let 'em see you," said the captain. Jinja wrinkled up his face with frustration, but before the sergeant had a chance to pass a remark about showing disrespect, he had disappeared down the trail.

Where the trail opened into a pasture, he dropped behind a tree and saw a handful of Indians racing for the woods on the other side of the field. Chasing them were a larger handful of militia. As soon as they saw that the Indians were certain to gain the woods safely, the militiamen stopped in their tracks and began to back off. Jinja emerged from the woods and gave a whistle. When some of the militiamen turned toward him, he waved his rifle, then retreated down the trail in search of his companions. There was no sense in roaming the valley hunting for rebel forts when he had guides at hand to bring them safely in.

With some difficulty, overcoming the objections of Captain Bonner, he brought the men out of the woods and into the field, where the members of the local militia awaited them hopefully. When he reached the little group, he could see the disappointment on their faces, which he supposed was because the group he brought was so small. "Where are the rest of you?" asked their commander, who was nearly as young as Jinja.

"We are all there is," Bonner responded. His tiny command looked even more insignificant to him than they had when they left Albany.

The young commander sized up the little group and turned toward Jinja.

"This is Captain Bonner," Jinja said quickly.

The young man nodded and saluted Bonner. "Sergeant Alan Beatty," he said. Bonner returned the salute. "Colonel Butler is gettin' all the fightin' men together at Forty Fort, and I'm sure he'd be pleased to see you when you come in."

Bonner recoiled at the mention of Butler's name. He chewed on his lip and tried to think of something to say, but his tongue was stuck to the roof of his mouth. Jinja sized up the situation quickly. "Colonel Butler?" he asked slowly. "Which Colonel Butler is that?"

Sergeant Beatty stared at the silent Bonner and finally caught on. "Not that filthy Tory John Butler," he said. "This is Colonel Zebulon Butler. He's real army and he knows how to fight. Will you come with us?"

The blood flowed back into Bonner's face. Without further discussion he followed Beatty and his men across the pasture, into the woods, through a cornfield, over a rocky hill, through another field, and into a small fort palisaded with stout logs but not particularly secure-looking. They entered through the front gate just as a tall, angular, gray-headed man in a blue Continental Army uniform was making himself comfortable standing before three loose ranks of local fighting men. He noted the new arrivals, smiled as if to say, "I'll be with you after I'm through up here," and began to speak.

"Men," he began, his honest face crinkling as he squinted in the sunshine. "Our scouts tell us John Butler is out there. He's got treasonous Tories and he's got savage Indians. He's got more of them than we do, and they can fight. What he doesn't have is our cause. We're fighting for our homes. We're fighting for our freedom. We're fighting for America. What's he fighting for? The blasted king and a few privileged bastards who love to wipe their feet on the likes of

you and me. Now there's gonna be some tough fightin'. The
Mohawks are coming down from Unadilla. The Senecas are
also comin' in on the Susquehanna. And you've seen how
cocky the Tories have been acting lately. But I'm telling you
we can lick 'em. Indians don't like to fight against folks who
can shoot. And we can shoot. We been doin' it all our lives.
In any event, we will never surrender to Tories and savages.
This is the valley of our families. We have cleared our forests and planted our corn and raised our children here. We
will never give it up."

Jinja studied the men in the ranks and was not encouraged. There were boys who should have still been in
school, and there were old men who should have been at
home with their pipe and slippers. There were very few
men of fighting age there, and none but Butler who looked
like veterans of recent campaigns. And they numbered only
a few hundred.

When Butler dismissed his men, Jinja noticed that several
officers were gathering around their commander. He
blended himself in with the men he had met in the pasture
and followed them to the ring of officers, then stood and
listened as the officers discussed their options.

Aside from Butler, he did not know the names of any of
the men who gathered in the informal group. There were
three others, none of whom had any sign of rank on their
uniforms. He identified one as being old, short, and stocky,
another as short, old, and skinny, and the third as tall,
young, and skinny.

The stocky one was doing most of the talking. "We can't
go out here and fight them," he was insisting. "There are
too many of them, and our men simply don't have battle
experience. But we can shoot, and if we stay behind these
walls, we can hold them off."

The thin old one shook his head. "If we can attack the
Tories at Wintermoot's Fort," he said, "we should be able to
lick 'em quick. It's not much of a fort, and if we hit 'em in a
hurry, there won't be but a few of them there."

Colonel Zebulon Butler looked at the three officers. The tall one did not care to venture an opinion. "We're alone out here, boys," he said. "If we hide behind these walls, they'll burn the whole valley while we're settin' here. That means our houses and our barns and our crops and our cattle and our families too." He turned to the thin old one. "Is tomorrow early enough to suit you, Harv?"

"*No!*" cried the stocky one.

"We have no choice," the thin old one called Harv said to the stocky one. "We can't protect the rest of the valley from behind these walls. And we can beat the Tories if we can somehow manage to surprise them at Wintermoot's Fort."

Degata had known of the Seneca named Cornplanter, but he had never spoken to him until a few nights before, when he had joined up with a small group of scouts led by Cornplanter. They had been assigned the task of watching Forty Fort, which they knew was where most of the rebel troops were holed up. With the patience of the great deer hunters from the old stone-arrow days, they lay in wait in the woods watching the fort, knowing that if the rebels came out, there was a chance for a great victory.

So far nobody in the fort seemed disposed to venture outside, but Cornplanter was ready to stay all summer if necessary, waiting. He knew that while he waited on the rebels, his Mohawk and Seneca brothers were waiting for word from him, their tomahawks sharp, their guns loaded and primed, and their hearts on fire to fight. Slowly came the twilight, and then the night, and still the gate of Forty Fort stood closed. Cornplanter took Degata and five more braves and stationed them in the tall grass of the field, closer to the fort, watching for the main gate to open. And still the gate remained closed.

As the moonless night closed in on the little fort like a shroud, most of the young rebels managed to sleep. The older ones found sleep much more difficult. And so did Jinja. As during the march down from Albany with Captain Bonner, he found himself lacking confidence in the men who would lead them into battle the following day. He lay by himself in a corner of one of the little buildings in the center of the fort and wondered what his obligations were. Marching in ranks and attacking a fort required a stubborn loyalty to the ranks in the face of death. In a woods battle, where each man is involved in a series of tiny wars with other individuals, a man is a bit freer to preserve his own life without compromising the lives of his cohorts.

Earlier in the evening he had become friendly with young Sergeant Beatty. Neither felt close to the men in his unit and each intuitively respected the other. They spent part of the night telling each other their life stories.

"My family moved into the valley about ten year ago," Beatty recalled. "My dad had broken land for a rich man outside of Philadelphia, and he wanted a place where he could work for himself. He built a cabin, cleared a few acres the first year, a few more the second, a few the third, until he had about forty acres under the plow. Then he died. I was fifteen years old and the oldest brother, so I took over." He showed Jinja a pair of large hands with an outsized set of calluses on each. "My family. My plow. My horse. Tell you, I grew up fast. They'll have to carry me out of this valley if they want me to leave."

Jinja decided that in the heat of battle this soldier might not be a bad one to be close to. The young sergeant seemed solid, honest, careful, the kind to watch the other man's back and not run out on a buddy.

Early in the morning Butler sent scouts into the field, and an hour later more than three hundred men marched out of Forty Fort, named for the forty families that had originally settled in the valley. Jinja felt out of place marching into battle in a troop formation, and he recalled how many times his father had told him that woodsmen tried to avoid getting themselves stuck in situations like that. And yet there he was, marching through the Wyoming Valley with boys who still wet their drawers and arthritic gray-hairs whose eyes and bodies had begun to fail long ago. The land was revealed in morning sunshine that turned the grass and woods a brilliant green but as yet revealed nothing of the enemy they were to fight on this day.

A shot rang out in the distance, followed by three more, and then one more, and then silence. The troops continued to march, and Jinja could not detect any response among either the men or the officers. But he knew what the shots meant. Their scouts had been seen. The enemy had been alerted. There was no longer a chance for a surprise attack.

Colonel Butler also knew what the shots meant. Beyond the woods a wide column of smoke sullied the morning air. Fields burning? Cabins burning? Zebulon Butler hurried the men on a run along the tree line until they spotted Wintermoot's Fort. To their surprise, it was the fort that was burning. "We've got 'em!" shouted one of the older officers. "They're retreating, burning the fort so we can't have it." The men were all excited as their officers ordered them into a long skirmish line in a thick stand of pine and brush. To their front, against the background of the burning fort, a line of local loyalists were firing and dropping back. On their flanks, stretched thin to the right and left, were Royal Greens and mixed Mohawks and Senecas. This was battle such as Jinja had never seen before, and it stirred his blood. Battle was battle. Let it happen. He was ready to feed the enemy a taste of his style of long range death.

As the rebels emerged from their pine forest, Jinja found himself in the center. In front of him an officer with a sword shouted something he could not hear above the excited shouts of the youngsters around him. The officer waved his sword and pointed toward the enemy. The rebels marched forward at a rapid pace, but the line stayed intact. So far so good. They stopped and fired a volley, loaded, and continued to march forward, while the Tories in front of them continued to retreat. The Americans picked up the pace, then stopped to fire another volley. Through the smoke Jinja noted that the Royal Greens and the Indians on the flanks were thinning out. He could not figure out what that meant, but it troubled him, even as he saw the figure in his sights fall to his knees, then pitch forward.

Now the rebels moved forward even faster, until their pace was just short of a run. They were closing the distance between themselves and the Tories, and they were confident that if it came down to a close-in fight, they could lick them. They stopped to fire one more time. Jinja drew a bead on a tall Tory officer through the gray smoke of the gunpowder and the black smoke of the blazing fort. There was a momentary silence as the rebels stopped their shrieking and took aim. The Wyoming Tories were still dropping back toward the fort. They were alone now, without the Royal Green forces and the Indians on their flanks. The rebels were sensing a sure kill. Not much more than a hundred yards from the enemy they took ruthless aim and pulled the triggers on their weapons.

Degata had fought white men before. He knew how much they loved to attack when they thought they had the advantage. They went crazy, he thought, lost all their sense when they sensed a quick conquest. As he looked ahead and to his left, he could see the rebels rushing forward, so certain of victory. They were so stupid that they had no business on the warpath. His mouth grew dry in anticipation as Sayengaraghta gave a whoop and brought his Senecas after the Mohawks onto the left flank of the rebels.

Degata had seldom had a chance to fight side by side with the vaunted Mohawk warriors, and he was impressed. Like a mighty wall of water from a broken dam they came down on the rebels and swept over them. Having just fired their weapons, the rebels had nothing with which to stave off their enemies except their empty rifles and muskets. Degata did not have to think about what to do. A lifetime of training as a warrior made him drop his rifle and draw his tomahawk from his belt. Along with more than a hundred other braves, he swooped down upon the rebels, picked one out, grabbed his shirt with one hand and with the other brought his tomahawk down on the militiaman's skull. The man's eyeballs rolled back in his head just before a wall of blood flowed down on them.

Not all that many rebels died with the first rush. Feeling the danger, many of them dropped their rifles and muskets and fled across the field, then through the brush and the pines toward the Susquehanna. Degata did not stop to take a scalp. While some of his fellow warriors chased the fleeing Americans toward the river, others rolled along the flanks toward the center of the rebel army. This was all happening in a very few moments, and the message was getting through too slowly to the rebels that they were being taken on both their left and their right.

The loyalists who had been acting their part as the bait had a good view of their enemies being smashed from both sides. Abruptly they stopped retreating and began to rush forward, just as the rebel center started to feel the crush of their own troops coming in from the flanks. Jinja was loading his rifle when he began to sense the disaster that was descending upon them. It was not what he saw, for his eyes were on his ramrod. It was the screams of fear and pain that were coming in from his left, men moving backward, getting in his way. As he was loading he moved back one, two, three steps. He looked to his left and could not believe what he was seeing. He moved back ten more steps and saw the panicked flood of rebels fleeing with hordes of tomahawk-swinging Iroquois in deadly pursuit.

"Pull back!" he screamed, but his voice was a hoarse croak and nobody heard him. He ran forward and grabbed Beatty and pulled him back to where the sergeant could see the left flank disintegrating. Beatty turned to move forward and pull all his men out of the struggle to the front, but the loyalists were now closing in, and Beatty's men no longer needed to be told.

Jinja had only a few steps on the rest of his cohorts as he began his flight from the field. The fear he felt was not the mindless terror that caused the others to run over their comrades as they gained the stand of pine trees and then the river. Jinja was still thinking. How do I survive? Can I hide? Must I swim for safety? For all his thinking, his solution for survival proved to be the same as that of the other men—drop everything, run like hell, hit the water, swim like hell and pray for a miracle.

All around him the swift, athletic Iroquois were overrunning the fleeing young militiamen, pulling them down and killing them quickly. His eyes were on the ground beneath him and the scene in front of him, but he could tell by the whoops and screeches that some of the Indians were stopping long enough to take scalps. He was still thinking that he ought to save his rifle if he could when a bullet entered his left shoulder and made his decision for him. His rifle spun away from him and he went down. He was up in an instant, his fear overcoming the pain, his moccasined feet driving him forward. Along with others, he had reached the bank of the Susquehanna. No need for him to keep his powder dry. Even as he bounded down the bank to the river he flung off his powder horn and his bullet pouch, then leaped from the bank in a long reaching dive into the swirling waters. Around him others were doing the same, turning the water white with their frenzied struggles.

His breath left his lungs when his chest hit the water, but he stroked nevertheless, and soon it came back, in great heaving gasps. Behind him he could hear Beatty splashing and crying again and again, "My God, my God, my God, my God!" He could feel pain where he had been shot, but his left arm still worked and his strength stayed with him, although he felt that his lungs would burst from his effort. To his left he saw a swimmer take a stroke then take a bullet in back of his head and disappear beneath the water, leaving a red, spreading pool on the river above him.

The river was not wide. He was on his feet now, in shallow water, when he heard a shout behind him and saw Beatty struggling with a Seneca who had grabbed his ankle and was pulling him back and lifting his knife for the kill. Jinja plunged back into deeper water, grabbed Beatty's arm and jerked him out of the grasp of the Seneca. Beatty and Jinja both reached for their knives, and the Seneca, seeing the danger, backed off into the river. Jinja and Beatty ran up the embankment on all fours, clawing at the mud for eternity until at last they stumbled into an overgrown field, then into the sheltering woods, where they turned northward.

Once they put a few trees between themselves and their foe, they lost their pursuers. The Indians had plenty of targets they could see without wasting their time rummaging through the forests in search of men they could not see. Behind Jinja and Beatty echoed the triumphant whoops of Senecas and their Mohawk brothers finally reaping their revenge tenfold for the losses they had sustained during their costly victory at Oriskany.

Jinja and Beatty ran for another mile, their breath coming in deep moaning gulps, their stamina spent, fueled only by their fear and their determination to survive.

For years the Mohawks had felt the hand of the Americans pushing on them, grabbing at their land piece by piece, humiliating them, making them feel small. Only then the Americans had been called Englishmen. Now that they were no longer Englishmen, it was open season on them, and the Mohawks hunted them down one by one without mercy. A number of them were making their way back to Forty Fort, but most of them had either been killed or were still out in the woods or in the river or hiding in the tall grass somewhere. Wherever the Indians found one running, they ran him down and killed him. Wherever they found one hiding, they pulled him out and killed him. Cries for mercy went unheeded. Some of the fleeing Americans were so thoroughly weakened by their exhaustion and fear that they gave up their lives gently to their remorseless Mohawk enemies.

Degata and the rest of Sayengaraghta's Senecas were equally merciless. There was no need to be cautious, these young white warriors were no warriors at all, more like the white man's cows, capable of feeling terror, incapable of fighting back, and so very easy to kill. There were few Americans left alive in the woods now. So many lay still, face down, the tops of their heads a mass of gore. Degata heard the sound of rapid footsteps approaching from his left, followed by shrieks and whoops. Coming toward him was a young blond-headed militiaman, his eyes so blinded by panic that he ran toward Degata without even seeing him. Degata cocked his tomahawk and swung it as the boy passed him, chopping deep into the side of the boy's neck. Blood gushed and the boy went down silently. Two Mohawks stopped and looked at Degata. Degata gave them a grim smile through his fierce war paint and walked away. The message: the scalp is yours, I have so many already. And he did, three, all of which hung from his belt.

Iroquois warriors continued to prowl through the woods, but now the chases were over. Bodies lay silent in the forest. Others bobbed against the rocks near the banks of the Susquehanna. The ones who had hidden in the brush or tall grass had died there. Here and there a prisoner had been taken, but none of them counted much on his chances for a long and happy life. The Mohawks and Senecas had won many honors for themselves that day, and as often happens in victory, the members of each tribe suddenly discovered great affection for the members of the other. At the end of the day they found themselves gathered together, and only then did they realize the magnitude of their victory. There were over two hundred scalps in camp, and yet only one of their number was missing and a small handful wounded.

That night they did not remain by the campfire, but went off into the night to spread their campaign of fire and death across the Wyoming Valley, to the undefended homes of widows and children. This valley, the Ganonsyoni said, would never again be home to those who had stolen it from them.

❖10❖

THEY LAY DOWN IN A FIELD OF TALL GRASS and young scrub a only a few hundred yards east of the Susquehanna River, but more than two miles upriver from the battle. Before the war it had been a cornfield, perhaps belonging to a Tory who had moved east to New York City after the war had begun.

Beatty raised his head carefully above the level of the grass and looked around. He saw nothing. Both could still hear the faint sounds of hunting and killing up the river. By now their breathing had calmed down to the point where they could listen carefully. They did, and the sounds did not seem to be coming any closer to them.

"We have to keep moving," Jinja said. "Get as far away from here as we can." He moved his left arm and gave a grunt as a wave of pain rolled through it.

Gently Beatty took hold of Jinja's arm and slashed the linen with his knife. There was blood, of course, but not a great amount, it seemed to the sergeant. The exit wound was not much bigger than the entry wound, and looked clean. "Could be all right if we can wash it out," Beatty said.

Jinja thought for a moment. "I'd feel a lot better if we could put some more distance between us and . . . that." He tilted his head south, toward the thin sounds of Iroquois celebration that carried far from the scene of the battle.

"Tell you what," said Beatty. "Let me fill my canteen in the river, then we can travel."

Jinja agreed, then lay down, and promptly passed out, while Beatty crawled through the grass toward the Susquehanna. The sounds of battle and massacre were fading almost to silence as the young sergeant made his patient way toward the river. He thought about the many youngsters that had marched into battle with him, and wondered if any others had managed to make their way from the battlefield. Ahead of him, through the brush, he could see the thin line of trees along the riverbank. He was very thirsty. The water would taste good.

Slowly he slid down the bank to a rock shelf. Just beneath, the water swirled slowly. He pulled the canteen strap over his arm and lowered his canteen toward the water. Did he imagine blood swirling around in the muddy water? He stirred the water with his hand. There was no blood, just mud. And a little mud in the water couldn't hurt anybody. He bent down and plunged his canteen into the water.

His scream pierced the eerie silence of the Susquehanna Valley, followed by the victorious whoop of the solitary Mohawk who had been stalking the young sergeant from the time he had first seen the grass move in a way that it shouldn't have.

Jinja jerked awake with Beatty's scream and understood his situation as soon as he heard the whoop split the air. How many were there? Did they know Beatty had a companion? He pulled his knife from his belt and lay still, listening to the silence.

He heard the splash as the Indian dumped Beatty's scalped body into the river. Then he heard nothing. He turned his head so that his left ear, his best ear, faced the river. He held his breath. There! He heard it, the soft sound of grass blades rubbing up against each other. Then again. The Indian was close by, and he was still searching. Jinja did not dare to climb to his feet, or even his knees, for fear that his foe would hear his clothes moving against his skin, but he put himself into position to spring.

He heard the grass again, and turned his eyes in that direction. There, a bristled Mohawk scalp lock appeared above the tops of the long grass. He sprang to his feet, knife cocked low in his right hand, and as the Mohawk turned toward him, tomahawk held high, Jinja thrust his knife deep into the Mohawk's side.

"Ahhh!" the Indian moaned, his breath leaving his body in a surprised gasp. Jinja reached up with his left hand and grabbed the Mohawk's raised right arm, while with his right he pulled his knife out and plunged it again, into the underbelly of the warrior, who groaned and pitched forward. For good measure Jinja slashed downward as he freed the blade. A horrid mixture of blood and innards flooded from the abdomen as the warrior fell. He twitched once and lay still.

Jinja would not have bothered further with the dead Mohawk had he not noticed the fresh, bloody scalp tucked into his waistband. He recognized it as the scalp of the man who a moment before had headed for the river for some water to wash out his wounds. Jinja's hands began to tremble with anger and hatred. He dug his bloody knife into the dead Mohawk's scalp. The knife hit bone but would not cut. He pulled on the scalp lock to raise the scalp, to ease his task. That didn't work either. He made a circle with the knife around the Mohawk's scalp then pulled, but the scalp would not come free. He tugged at the scalp lock with all his strength, but he might as well have been pulling on Plymouth Rock for all the progress he made. He was dizzy. He was tired. He was very thirsty. Did he want to scalp an Indian or did he want to save his life? Slowly, painfully, he crawled to the river. On the rock where Sergeant Beatty had drawn his last earthly breath Jinja lay prone, stuck his head toward the water and drank. Then he looked downriver and spotted the scalped body of Beatty stuck in the branches of a fallen tree limb, the strap of his canteen still wound tightly around his hand.

Jinja waded into the water and took the canteen from the dead man. It was half full. He then pulled the body onto the bank, but did not have the strength to do anything else with it.

He knew he was vulnerable. If one Mohawk was scouting the area for bodies, more would come soon. Weak and dizzy as he was, he finished filling the canteen, climbed up the bank and headed northeast, away from the Susquehanna, away from the Wyoming Valley. On this day he had drunk more than his fill from the cup of strife. He was ready for peace, if the Lord was ready to spare him for the journey home.

Degata stood among a group of Senecas and Mohawks in the middle of a cow pasture. Wherever he turned he could see columns of black smoke on the horizon. Standing among the Indians were a score of terrified civilians and a handful of equally frightened young soldiers. The Indians were awaiting the pleasure of a green-coated loyalist captain who stood a hundred yards away, conferring with other officers. The sun was setting on the end of a long, triumphant day. It was surely one of the great days in the history of the Keepers of the Western Door. The old men would talk about this day when the men of the east and west, who for so long had been rivals in the Longhouse, had fought side by side and annihilated a rebel army with virtually no losses to themselves. He looked at the three scalps that hung from his belt and had to admit that virtually all the warriors had similar prizes adorning their persons. He also conceded that the Mohawks were the best of all allies, and that never again should these two greatest peoples of the Longhouse let jealousy come between them.

In the west he saw the sun burning the horizon blood-red. To the east the darkness was laying its blanket over the horrors that had happened on this day. The tall green-coated captain turned away from his men and began to walk toward the Indians. With him was an Onondaga who could speak the white tongue and the tongues of all the Longhouse. They stopped in front of Sayengaraghta, and the captain began to speak, while Senecas and Mohawks gathered around them.

"We are fighting a war," the captain told Sayengaraghta. "It is important that the king not think we are fighting like savages." The Onondaga paused while he searched for a Seneca word that meant something like "savages." He settled on the phrase "bad men," although he knew that it did not convey the precise meaning the captain was seeking.

"You must let us take the civilians and soldiers back with us to Fort Niagara. The king will not allow his children to torture prisoners," the captain continued.

"My brother," Sayengaraghta replied. "Many of the prisoners are ours. We did so much of the fighting today. And we lost so many of our warriors near Fort Stanwix that we must have our revenge."

The captain knew he could not risk the displeasure of his Iroquois allies. He also knew what Sayengaraghta did not, that Forty Fort had surrendered earlier in the day and that the men taken prisoner there were already under way to the northwest in the custody of Tory militia.

"You have taken more than two hundred scalps, my brother," the captain told Sayengaraghta. "That is revenge enough. But the king loves you and cares for you. We must have the civilians," he said, waving his arm toward the old men, women, and children who stood huddled in a pathetic group near the green-coated soldiers.

"We will give you these rebels," the captain said, pointing to the captured militiamen. "But your father the king would urge you to treat them with kindness. The king believes that prisoners taken in battle are not to be tortured and slaughtered."

"The king is wise," said Sayengaraghta as if in agreement. But both the chief and the captain knew that they were playing a part. And if the prisoners didn't know, then surely they had their suspicions. The captain walked over to the half-dozen captured Americans.

"We are handing you over to the Senecas," he said. "Their homes are near Fort Niagara. They will deliver you to the commander there. I advise you not to try to escape from them."

"My God, Captain," said the oldest of them, a sergeant. "You can't give us over to them. Don't you know what they'll do to us when they're out of your sight?"

"Do what they tell you to do and you'll be all right," the captain answered, disgusted with himself. The soldiers began to complain and the two youngest began to cry. The captain turned his back and walked away with an ache in his throat. Life had been so good before this hellish war, he thought. Why had people like this been so determined to throw off the monarchy? Everybody had to pay taxes. Why should these people have been the exception? All of this could have been avoided had it not been for those arrant, traitorous fools in Boston. Damn them, damn them, damn them!

As night closed in, the Royal Greens marched away with their civilian prisoners, many of them weeping over the loss of loved ones on that day. In the meantime, Sayengaraghta gestured to his prisoners and spoke in fragmented English. "We go now," he said. "Nort'," he added. "Niagara." And then he laughed, and two Senecas near him also laughed. "Niagara," they echoed. And then they laughed again.

❧11❧

BIG OAK WATCHED HIS THREE BOYS AS THEY thrashed around in the pond. They were all good swimmers and were bound to do as they pleased whether he was present or not. He knew this, but when he was present and they were swimming, he found himself watching them carefully, anxiously, especially the youngest.

Over the years Big Oak had seen many people die, including a fairly large number whose deaths he had caused. One moment you see a man, strong, healthy, full of spirit, deadly and dangerous. The next moment he lies still on the earth, or worse, he is down, painfully maimed, pleading for someone to put an end to his suffering. Unless he is an Indian, in which case he glares back defiantly, daring you to do your worst. In his time of life, Big Oak took nothing for granted, and so he watched his children as they paddled around the pond, splashing and ducking each other, crying out in English and Tuscarora.

Just a week before, he had come back from a visit to the village of Louis, the son of Gingego. Gingego was an old Mohawk chief, and had been Big Oak's best friend among the Mohawks. Gingego had died more than twenty years before, fighting the French at Lac St. Sacrement, which the great trader Sir William Johnson had seen fit to rename Lake George. Cilla had begged Big Oak not to go, but he was determined, so she insisted on going with him, and taking the children along.

The reason Cilla did not want Big Oak to go was because the war had made enemies of Louis and Big Oak. The Mohawks, like the Senecas, had chosen to fight for the British, which was a surprise to no one, considering the Mohawks had always been more closely allied to them than any of the other tribes of the Longhouse. Cilla could only hope that Louis's village had not suffered too much from the war, and that he therefore would not have too much hatred for his father's old friend.

The boys had done Big Oak proud, keeping up with him and Cilla all the way. It was Big Oak who in the end had slowed them down. In recent years his left knee had showed signs of protest during his long lopes through the woods. He had ignored the little pains, but on the last day of the journey to Louis's village, on a brisk downhill walk, his moccasined foot slipped on a rock and his right knee popped.

A stab of pain shot down his leg. Suddenly he found himself leaning against a tree, squeezing his knee, surprised more than anything else. He caught his breath and gingerly put some weight on his aching leg. The test added no more pain, and he limped with his family the rest of the way to the village, with Cilla watching him carefully.

He had journeyed to the village to mourn the death of Gingego's widow, Louis's mother, White Bird. She had been Big Oak's friend for many years, a leader of the women in the village and therefore a leader of the village in this matriarchal society. Over the years, Louis too had become Big Oak's friend, and Big Oak wished to show his respect for both Louis and his mother.

Big Oak, like Cilla, was concerned that Louis would have figured that his father's friend was siding with the rebels, and that he would therefore not be welcome at the village. Yet when they arrived and tasted the hospitality of Louis and his family in his mother's Wolf clan longhouse, it was not Big Oak but Cilla who drew the wrath of Louis.

"How could you bring this woman into my house?" he asked. "She is a traitor to the Longhouse, and I cannot bear to see her here."

"If she is a traitor to the Longhouse," Big Oak replied without heat, through the smoke that hovered over Louis's hearth fire, "then so am I."

"Paugh, you are a white man, I always knew that, and I liked you anyway. You were so much better than all the other white men. The white men of the Longhouse can leave the Longhouse and the Ganonsyoni are still the Ganonsyoni, but when the Oneidas and the Tuscaroras leave the Longhouse to fight for the rebels, then the Longhouse cannot stand."

He glared at Cilla. "When you came up from the country of the misty mountains, we took you in and made you our own. You are the *only* tribe we ever took in. We did not put petticoats on you like we did to the Lenni Lenape, who were willing to be our women as the price of peace. We brought you in as our brothers. And this is how you show your loyalty? By fighting for the rebels against the people who took you in?"

Cilla did not back away from Louis's challenge. "We are not like the Lenni Lenape," she said. "We are your brother tribe. We speak a tongue like yours. But, wise Louis, the Mohawk did not take in the Tuscaroras, although in those days you had plenty of land to share. The Oneidas gave the Tuscaroras land to live on, and the Onondagas did not object if a few of our people found our way onto a corner of their domain. But not the Mohawks. The Tuscarora did not want to fight for the rebels or the Englees. It was the Mohawks who ignored us and the Oneida, and split apart the Longhouse."

"Ah, that is what you say to undermine our spirit," Louis retorted. "The covenant chain is an old and honored treaty between the king and his Iroquois children. Our mighty brothers to the west, the Senecas, have sometimes held loosely to their end of the chain. So have a few of the Cayugas who live too close to the Senecas to think right. Now it is the Oneidas, and the Tuscaroras, and even some of the Keepers of the Council Fire, the Onondagas, who have loosened their hold on the chain."

Louis stood straight and tall. "Only the Ganiengehaka, the mighty Keepers of the Eastern Door, have held fast to the covenant chain through all the generations. Without us, there is no honor left in the Longhouse."

"Louis, son of my greatest friend, and for many years my friend," Big Oak said, "what is the use of holding fast to a chain when there is no one to hold fast to the other end? It is like shooting a gun with gunpowder but no bullets—there is a big noise, but there is no food to put in the kettle. Do not blame Cilla. She was not at the council fire when the Tuscaroras agreed to fight for freedom from the king."

Louis growled softly.

"My brother," Big Oak continued. "My heart is like a stone because the great heart of your mother is still. I never knew another like her. When I think of Gingego, my heart soars because he had the good fortune to love your mother for so long, and then died like a warrior at an age when most men love the home fire. But when I think of your mother, my heart aches because I fear that only death awaits even the greatest of us."

"I thought that your faith, like ours, teaches that the souls of the just live forever."

"That is so, but there have been times, after a hard winter or a bitter battle, when I am certain that the Holder of the Heavens could not possibly love children such as us. And then I tremble for my immortal soul. And I say to my God, Lord, I will never cause another empty lodge. I will still my rifle forever, if only you will grant me a contentment that endures long enough not to seem like a foolish dream from the night before."

Louis took a drag on his pipe and let loose a great cloud

of smoke. "I too have thought of such things, Big Oak. My mother was so strong for so long. And then, just during the last snow, she became ill. Day after day she lay quiet and moved only to take a few sips of broth or tea. As her last sun rose she took my hand and whispered for me and George to take her from the longhouse into the little hut across the creek.

"When we laid her down gently on a soft bed of boughs and blankets, we asked her why she did not want her grandchildren and her daughters with her. She looked at us and told us that the pain was so great she could no longer stand it, that we must hold her hands and not mind if she cries out. And then for the only time in her life I heard her moan. I heard her whimper. I heard her beg for her death. She chewed her blanket. She cried like a child, this woman who had never complained her whole life, and then, when her pain would become less, she would apologize to us for her tears. Once she asked for you.

"Just before she died, she smiled and said she felt so much better now. I asked her if the pain was gone. She said it is still there, it just doesn't seem to matter as much anymore. And then her eyes closed, and she didn't see us anymore. She was dreaming, and speaking to her dream. She smiled in her dream and said, 'Do not worry, my husband, it is just a small pain from when the hot water spilled on my arm. After a moment it will be gone, and then I will serve your dinner.'

"And then her smile went away and slowly we could see her spirit leave her."

Big Oak listened to Louis, and his chest felt as if a great weight were pressing down on it. During the winter he had expressed a wish to Cilla that they go and visit White Bird when the snow was melted. Cilla agreed, and Big Oak looked forward to the visit. He did not wish to admit it, but the death of White Bird hit him harder than the death of Gingego had. The reason for this was that when Gingego died, White Bird still lived, and in her lived the spirit of

Gingego and all the other great Mohawks Big Oak had known over the years. Now nearly all of them were gone, and so was White Bird. It struck Big Oak that with White Bird gone, he would be far less likely to visit the Mohawks in the future.

And now they stood at the gate of the stockade, saying their good-byes to Louis and his brother George. Big Oak noticed that the stockade surrounding the village, which long ago had crumbled into disrepair, had been considerably refurbished. The militia was on the loose. They had some victories under their belts. They felt confident. And if most of them were not very good fighters, they were still capable of trying something foolish like attacking a Mohawk village. Wisely, Louis had chosen to make the village more secure. Big Oak noticed that there were even posted guards.

"Son of my friend—my friend—my heart aches so now that your mother is no longer with us. But there is something else. You and I walked the warpath together almost as much as your father and I did. I never dreamed that we would become enemies, and in my heart we never can be. I promise you that whatever I do, I will never fight against you."

Louis's eyes bored hard into the face of Big Oak. "That is easy for you, my brother. Not so for me. When we walked the trail together, we fought for the life of the Longhouse. Now you see the Longhouse in great danger. The people of the great rock, and their little brothers the Tuscaroras, fight against us. The English demand our help and send Thayendanegea against the settlements, but the English have gone away and left us to fight against armies. My brother, I fear for the future. Not so many moons ago the council fire went out in Onondaga, and I do not believe we will see it rekindled in my lifetime. This summer the fighting will be desperate, and we cannot afford friends who will not stand with us. You have said that today you go west to visit the Oneidas and the Tuscaroras. I must tell you, do not come back this way, for you will not be welcome."

"I will do as you say, my brother," Big Oak responded sadly. "And yet, there is always change. This war will not last forever. If the English win, I will have to go west like a Mingo to escape the anger of the king's men. If the English lose, it will go hard with the Ganiengehaka, who are so loyal to the king. But you will always be welcome at my house."

There were no more words. Louis did not want to hear about friendship. He did not understand how a man like Big Oak, who had fought so long and so hard for the king, could now fight against him with a bunch of other Englishmen who now called each other Americans. White men were impossible to understand, he concluded. There was no sense trying to understand them, because they had no sense.

Sad, but also angry, feeling betrayed by a man he respected, he stood at the gate watching Big Oak and his family until the forest swallowed them.

As Big Oak and his family left the Mohawk village behind, the old trader found his beloved woods dark and gloomy. The death of one friend, and the knowledge that the fortunes of war might soon have him fighting another, squeezed tears from his heart until they were almost too many for his eyes to contain. Sadly he turned to Cilla.

"I wish we could go back home now and try to forget about everybody but our own," he said. "Life would be so simple. Hunt a little. Fish a little. Plant a little. Go to Albany once a year and buy a little."

Cilla smiled with understanding. "If we did not have the children, we could do that. Live out our lives together." The five of them walked on in a gaggle, as if war were a million miles away, the children chattering to each other, the parents silent. It was their oldest son, Caleb, who brought them back to reality, pointing his scattergun at a bush and dipping into a crouch. Parents and children all dropped down and waited to see what Caleb had seen or heard.

It was nothing, but it was enough to bring Big Oak back to this world. What he had was more important than what he'd lost. On the frontier, loss of friends was a common occurrence, and a man had to cut his losses. Now he walked at the head of a single file, and the redoubtable Cilla, who had fought a battle or two in her lifetime, brought up the rear. Like tall brown ducklings, the three boys walked between them, having no trouble keeping up with the pace Big Oak set.

There was not just one trail here in the western end of the Mohawk Valley, but a series of trails and traces winding in and out, crossing and recrossing each other, the trails of that day, clear and worn, and other, rarely used trails from an earlier time, perhaps even before the people of the Longhouse had first set foot in the valley of the Te-non-an-at-che. Big Oak knew most of them. He liked the familiar scenes of the usual trails, but he also enjoyed some of the older trails and the surprises they held. On this day he was in a hurry to make it to Paul's village, Canowaraghere, so he took the shortest, quickest trails. He wanted to see Paul's family, but he also wanted to know what the Oneidas were doing to protect themselves. Their attitude, he knew, had wavered between neutrality and support for the rebels' cause, and he wondered if they understood just how much anger they were stirring up in the hearts of their Mohawk brothers. He did not wish to lose any more friends.

Big Oak could not be downhearted for long on the trail. His knees were whispering to him that they would not carry him forever, but that for now they would not trouble him. The weather was clear, he loved his wife, and his three sons by her were so much more than he had ever expected to receive from this life that as the miles between them and the Mohawk village grew, so did the mist that was gathering around his heartache. There were things to do now.

There was no time for the luxury of feelings for departed friends. Not now.

His spirit rose as the miles loosened up his joints. His eyes focused on the sunlight and shadows that played in never-ending changes wherever the woodlands thinned. There were the smells of the forest too, the wildflowers, and the dust and soils and decaying trees in intricate patterns. And the sounds—the noises and the silences that told a woodsman so much about who was prowling where. Afternoons fishing on the pond, Big Oak was only half alive. It was the long trails that brought him the full, sweet measure of existence.

He listened to his children behind him. Only the youngest, Joshua, occasionally spoke. The older two boys walked silently, looking left and right, their keen eyes missing nothing, their ears alive to every sound. Behind them walked Cilla, armed only with a knife, watching her men.

A day later they walked into Canowaraghere and began their search for Paul. They found him easily enough, sitting astride the roof of his cabin, trying to figure out a way to keep the shakes from coming off his roof in the next high wind that blew eastward from the lake country. He had a hammer in his hand and some big old nails, but the wood seemed to split wherever he hammered a nail.

"Come on down from there," Big Oak shouted.

From his perch Paul smiled and waved his arms. "Can't, until I fix this roof. Next rain'll ruin my chair!" he shouted. A rebel lieutenant had liberated the chair from the home of a fleeing Tory and brought it to Fort Stanwix. When he was sent west to do a little more Tory harassment, he had lashed the chair to the back of a spare horse because he couldn't bear to part with it. The spare horse broke down just outside of Canowaraghere. The lieutenant left the chair at Paul's house because he trusted Paul, and his house seemed more substantial than many of the others.

"Hold my chair for me will you, Paul?" he'd asked the Oneida preacher, and Paul said he would. "I'll pick it up when I come back," the lieutenant said. Paul kept it in his big room, determined to preserve it until the lieutenant came through the village. It was his most prized possession, even if it was not his. Normally, a leaky roof would not have troubled him, but no, he must keep the chair dry, and so he was on the roof scratching his head and wondering what to do.

"Why don't you just move the chair to where the roof doesn't leak?" Big Oak asked.

"Wherever I move the chair, that's where the roof starts leaking," the Oneida replied.

"Well, come on down anyway. It ain't about to rain, and I'll help you once we get through talking."

Paul slid down the roof by the seat of his britches, then jumped down into the dust. "I sure am glad to see you," he said. "All of you," he added, casting a look at Joshua.

"Paul, I hear the English plan to have Thayendanegea come down on this village for sidin' with the rebels. And I don't see a lot of your young warriors. Where are they?" Big Oak asked suspiciously.

Paul beckoned Big Oak into his house. For the moment, Cilla and the children stayed outside.

"Hello, Lizabet," Big Oak said to Paul's wife. She nodded, smiled, and said something in Oneida as she rushed past him.

"Tend the squash?" said Big Oak, who did not speak the Oneida dialect but knew the Mohawk tongue well enough to get by among the Oneidas.

Paul nodded. "My brother, the young warriors are not here because they are down south on the Unadilla."

"What are they doing down there?" Big Oak asked, astonished.

"Burning out Tories," the Oneida responded. "They will be back before long."

"They'd better. Your village is not safe."

Paul sighed. "I don't know why we didn't just stay neutral," he said.

"Doesn't matter, Iron Arm," Big Oak said, using one of the names given to Paul in recognition of his short, thick arms, which could turn man's work into child's play. "There is no neutral in this war. 'Neutral' means you're an enemy to the Tories and an Indian to the rebels." Paul understood what Big Oak meant. "Besides," Big Oak continued, "I have a message to your son James from my granddaughter Anne."

James's day was not going well. He and a dozen Oneidas were pinned down by a company of Tory greens. They were too few to fight their way out, and in no position to slip away by stealth. All that kept them alive was that the Tories did not have the stomach for charging the Oneidas' position and finishing them off.

It was one of those battles, fought by well-covered men who cared to keep their lives, in which a whole lot of shots were fired and the only injuries were a Tory's sprained ankle and a rock chip from a ricochet that found its way into the cheek of an Oneida. The leader of this expedition gone awry was Plenty Beaver, and Plenty Beaver was now plenty sorry for leaving his home in search of glory.

"If we can only hold out till dark. Not so long," he said to James. "In the dark we can slip past them, I don't care how many of them there are."

Several bullets whistled over their heads, and the two pressed themselves that much closer to the earth as they lay behind a long pile of rocks. James agreed that the key was surviving for just a little while longer. White men could not see very well in the dark, they both knew. But these white men were good shooters, and there were a lot of them. Plenty Beaver poked his head up, fired a quick shot toward the Tories, then ducked behind the stone fence that served as their cover.

James, unlike his father, was above six feet tall, and lanky, but very solid. His dark face and handsome features made him attractive to the white girls of the settlements. James generally was not interested in them. His dreams were peopled by girl children of the Longhouse, except for one girl, young Anne Watley of Albany.

They had met the previous fall on a hill that overlooked the Hudson and the Wendel and Watley warehouse. James had just helped his father unload some beaver pelts and was preparing to head for home when he ran into Thad. "Fine furs," Thad observed. James usually enjoyed compliments from Thad, whom he respected, but on this day he scarcely heard him, so strongly was he attracted to the young teenager who stood beside the half-breed trader.

"Yes I am," James said, in perfect nonresponse. Anne started to laugh, then stopped. "Who is this?" he asked Thad.

"This is my daughter Anne," Thad responded. "You've seen her many times before. You just never paid attention."

James thought he could see in the girl's face the look he had seen so often when he'd visited the villages of the Genesee Seneca, even though he knew the girl was mostly white. "She is very pretty," James declared.

"Then why don't you turn around and tell *her?*" Thad replied.

"I must find my father," he said instead. "I know he will be impatient to get started for Oneida."

"She won't bite you, I promise," Thad said, but James was already on his way down the hill, heading for the warehouse. Thad glanced at Anne, whose face had taken on a look of red distress.

"Means he likes you," Thad started to say, but Anne was headed down the other side of the hill, her feet pointed homeward.

Thad shook his head and walked over to where his father was standing, arms folded, with a little smile on his face. "Did you see—"

"Don't say no more, you said too much already."

"I didn't say—"

"Too much, Little Oak."

Thad shrugged his shoulders, looked down the hill at

James and tried to imagine what was going on in the young man's mind. James was standing in a daze by the warehouse, waiting for his father to finish his business with the Dutch trader. Would he ever see the girl again? Of course. Would he speak to her next time? He didn't know. His father had brought him to the white people, all the while reminding him that white people thought red ones were savages. Why ask for trouble?

Now, months later, James was having nothing but trouble on the Unadilla. The bullets were whistling, and James was praying to his father's Jesus that one of those blind lead balls would not somehow find him and tear the top of his head off. At his back he could feel the sun dipping behind the hills. Somehow he choked down his panic, loaded his rifle while lying on his stomach, dumped too much powder in the pan, flicked a little out with his finger, and lifted his head just enough to point the rifle into the near darkness.

He pulled the trigger. His rifle bucked and spat lead. Quickly he reloaded. It had to be his imagination, but wasn't the firing from the Tory side beginning to die down? He waited until he was sure he was right, then hazarded a peek over the rock pile behind which he lay concealed. In the gloom, along the tree line, he could see movement. Automatically he brought his rifle up, pointed it toward the movement and tightened his finger on the trigger. Then he stopped. Why make 'em mad? he thought. A little more darkness and he was certain that Plenty Beaver would find a way to outsmart the whites who were making it so hot for them.

He felt a tap on his foot, turned around and found himself staring into the calm eyes of his leader. "You," Plenty Beaver whispered, "and the other young ones, as soon as it is all dark, the five of you will slip out toward the south, circle around behind us, and head for home while we keep their thoughts on us. Once you are in the woods, don't stop running until you are back in Oneida. Do you understand? The others know, now get on back with them."

James crawled over to their southernmost flank, to where four other young warriors his age waited, shaken and anxious to free themselves from their trap. Plenty Beaver moved over to them and began to speak.

"When you hear me give my war cry, I want you to wait until we have got the white men stirred up, which should take no more time than it takes for a small cloud to blow past the moon." The five young braves all said they understood. They waited in a group and watched the older braves fuss a bit with their war paint. They watched Plenty Beaver as he led his veterans into place behind the stone fence. He then gave a high-pitched ululating yell.

The older Oneidas screeched out their war cries, vaulted over the stone embankment and began to run *toward* the hundred or so unseen enemy, firing their rifles and waving their tomahawks. That woke up the enemy, who fired back wildly. It was a well-calculated risk. The ground between them and the enemy was rolling, with plenty of cover and no background against which the Tories could see the silhouettes of their enemies. They were firing strictly at sound.

The young braves knew that this was the time to go. Silently but swiftly their legs carried them south on the first leg of a long U pattern that would take them out of danger. They did not remain long enough to see the others suddenly halt their charge, steal back to the stone embankment, then follow the creek bed north, intending to find their young brothers in the forest before the night was over.

"Come on!" a brave named Runs the River hissed as he took the lead into the shelter of the forest. Ahead of him James could see the shadows of his cohorts flitting through the woods, first south, then westward. He hoped they would continue in that direction for a good while, but then Runs the River tripped and sprawled on his face. Barely slowing down in the process, he regained his feet, found himself pointed north, and immediately headed in that direction. In the distance, James could hear firing, probably Tory muskets and rifles firing into an empty Indian position. They'd get suspicious quickly once they realized that nobody was returning their fire, he thought.

"Hurry, hurry!" Runs the River cried as they sprinted through the woods, desperate to put distance between themselves and the scores of Tories who were keen to kill them. "We must—"

The woods exploded all around them, in angry booms and violent orange flashes. James dove to the ground and Runs the River dove on top of him, not to protect him, but because when he dove, that's where he landed. For about a minute the firing continued. The Oneidas fired back, but half of them had been wounded on the first volley. They worked their rifles and muskets bravely, but the enemy was too numerous, and too close, and one by one, in a very short time, they fell.

The breath had been knocked out of James when Runs the River dove on top of him, but he wasn't about to draw a breath anyway. The firing continued from every direction, even though the Oneidas were no longer firing back.

Finally a voice arose among the firing. "Cease fire! Cease fire! Stop your shooting, you blithering idiots!" And slowly the shooting died down. James felt something warm running down his ribs—a lot of something.

"Okay, any of you Indians still have any life left in you?" said the voice. Someone gave a snort and someone else laughed maliciously.

James held his breath and lay quietly beneath Runs the River while the Tory soldiers walked from body to body and kicked at them.

"This one's alive," said a Tory private to the officer.

"Run a knife through him and make him dead," the officer replied.

The private followed orders, three times. The first thrust produced a harsh grunt. The next two thrusts elicited no response. Someone put his boot against the body of Runs the River and rolled him over. James could not decide whether to stay put or rise with his hands up. Either way he was probably a dead man. He continued to hold his breath and hope that Runs the River's blood, which covered much of James's upper body, would save his life.

He was being prodded with a bayonet. One of the Reverend Kirkland's prayers was finding its way to his lips when a shot rang out from five feet away.

"What in hell did you do?" cried the officer, shaken.

"Put a bullet in the head of a breathin' heathen is all," came the answer. The rest of the men laughed as if the shooter had said something very funny. A little farther away came the noise of something very hard shattering a skull.

"Brained 'im with 'is own war club," spoke the voice of a very young man.

The officer was impatient to be gone. "Well, are they all dead or aren't they?" he asked.

"Dead as Guy Fawkes," said a voice right over James's head.

"Well, let's get the hell out of here, then."

He had to take a breath. Slowly he let just a little air out of his lungs and took a little in. No good. He tried again, too much this time. If anybody had been watching him, his life would have ended. The crackling of boots on old leaves told him that he had a chance. And then all the footsteps were far enough away for him to take a real breath. He nearly passed out as the fresh air came roaring into his lungs again and again, as if he had been running uphill full speed for an hour.

He opened his eyes and lifted his head just enough to look around. All that was left was him and a half-dozen bodies that used to be his friends. He was certain they were all dead, but felt that he had to look at each of them to make sure. He went from one to another. Nearly all had been mutilated in one way or another. He'd had such a narrow escape that he had no emotion left with which to mourn his cohorts. Afraid there might still be enemy lingering, he loaded his rifle and lay flattened against the ground, listening. Finally satisfied that he was alone, James climbed to his feet and started loping north.

Big Oak, Cilla, and the three boys left Canowaraghere, heading for the small Tuscarora enclave where Cilla's family lived. The Tuscaroras had once been a mighty southern tribe, one of several, including the Cherokees, that spoke an Iroquois dialect. In the beginning they had befriended the English. In return for the friendship, English settlers not only seized Tuscarora lands, but seized Tuscarora people to enslave.

The result was a series of wars that nearly wrecked the Tuscarora nation. Desperate, they sent emissaries to their brothers far to the north. The Iroquois were pleased to give the Tuscaroras a refuge. A large part of the nation headed north, where the Oneidas took them in and gave them land from among their portion. Then, in 1722, the council did something unheard of. They granted the Tuscaroras status as the sixth nation in the Longhouse.

Only a day away from the Oneida village lay the village of Cilla's family. They had once lived farther to the south, but during the long years when Cilla was a captive of the Hurons, a land speculator had somehow turned up with an animal skin with writing and signatures that cost the Tuscaroras their village. So they moved northwest, to a less desirable piece of Oneida territory.

The children could barely contain themselves as they emerged from the woods and headed for the familiar lodge that belonged to their aunt Louise Makesplenty. The children did not notice the poverty of the village or the gauntness of many of the inhabitants. They did not feel the melancholy that hung over the village like a ragged, dirty old blanket. They saw only the smile of their aunt Louise and the eager faces of their cousins as they spotted each other.

The three boys dashed across the open field between the woods and the village. Big Oak and Cilla followed at a more leisurely pace, each one taking in the details as they approached.

"It goes hard with them," Cilla said with an edge to her voice. "At the old village, where you dropped a seed, the corn grew tall. Here there is little bottomland. The hillsides are dry and rocky. Their life is hard."

Big Oak nodded. Cilla came here often when Big Oak was away on business. She knew how it was, and it saddened her.

By this time they had nearly reached the lodge of Cilla's sister. Cilla threw her arms around Louise, who was a hefty, strong woman with a round face and a big smile. At this moment, however, she was not smiling; tears were coursing down her cheeks. "I cannot help it," she said to Big Oak. "When she was gone for so long, I thought I would never see her again, and now everytime I see her I feel like she has come back from the dead people." Louise stepped over to the fire and stirred a large iron kettle. "Marie, will you get the bowls out?" She wiped the tears from her face with the back of her hand and smiled. Cilla reached into her pack and brought out a large piece of dried venison. Louise started to shake her head, but Cilla placed the meat in her hands.

"Walk with me, my sister," Cilla said softly. The two women walked away from the lodge. "You must let me help you. I look around and I see how little you have. We have so much." They continued to walk until they were near the edge of the woods.

Louise's eyes again filled with tears, but she would not let them flow. "He is a white man," she said, softly and sadly, "and your children are white men. Is that the way it must be to survive? That men like my husband cannot find meat for the kettle of his family? Where are the deer? Where are the beavers to trade? And why does my husband care only for rum and brandy? Do you know that he killed Frenchmen during the last war? Their scalps hang in our lodge. He was a man then. Now he is nothing. Does a man have to be a white man to be a man? I look around me and see nothing but changed things. And it is always worse for our people. What will become of the Tuscarora?"

Cilla looked into the eyes of her sister and her heart ached for her. Louise had once had the same staunch spirit as Cilla. She never complained no matter how bad her fortune. And she never gave up. Not until now.

"One day the Mohawks come to our village. 'If your men fight for the rebels, we will come and burn your villages,' they say. 'We will first burn the Oneida villages, then yours.'

"One moon after, the Senecas come to our village. 'We know your men scout for the rebels,' they say. 'We know that your warriors, and the Oneida warriors, fight against the king. They must leave the rebels and fight on the side of the king or we will scatter to the winds the ashes of your villages and the blood of your men.'

"Do you know what I told them? I told them that we are children of the Longhouse and that the Holder of the Heavens would not forgive them if they make war on their brothers and sisters. How they frightened us! They were painted and they threatened us. There was a white man in the village, a church man sent by Reverend Kirkland. They took him away and we never saw him again. My sister, will they do what they have threatened to do to us?"

"I do not know the answer," Cilla replied. "Will you let us take you with us? We live north of Albany, not near anybody. We always have enough. My husband has gold. He can take care of us all. He will build a house for you, a good house that does not fill with smoke and wind in the winter."

Louise shook her head. "We cannot do this, my sister. Would you have us give up our people and become red white men? We cannot follow the white road. It is the wrong path for us."

"But if the Mohawks come, if the Senecas come—"

"Then our men will protect us. They are men. They will be here when we are in danger."

"Do you really believe this?"

"There is nothing else left for us to believe," Louise answered.

❈12❈

Jinja took a deep swig from his canteen and struggled back up the bank into the tall grass. He decided to travel eastward first, to get as far away from this part of the Susquehanna as possible. But he hadn't traveled a quarter of a mile when he realized that, unequipped as he was, he would die of starvation. Reluctantly, he returned to the dead Mohawk.

As bad as he felt, he was not sure at first that he would be able to find the place in the grass where the struggle had taken place, but the scavenging birds showed him the way. The Mohawk proved to be well-equipped with powder and ball, a small pouch of dried deer meat and corn, a good blanket, and a sharp-bladed tomahawk. Only his firearm was a disappointment, an old, worn musket with a filthy barrel.

Jinja was most pleased with the food, because it was what his body craved most, but he could not stop to eat. Quickly he slung the powder horn, food pouch, and bullet pouch over his shoulders, slipped the tomahawk into his belt, lifted the musket and headed eastward with a piece of dried deer meat in his hand. He tore off a morsel with his teeth, chewed, and sucked the juices out. Just knowing that there was food in his mouth made him feel stronger. He left the tall grass of the open meadow for the shadows of the forest.

He chewed some more, then drank deeply from the canteen. All this time he did not stop walking, and gradually, as he felt his strength flow back into him, his steps got faster and his stride got longer. He listened carefully and heard nothing that would alarm him. The distant sounds of battle had ceased. The birds around him were doing what birds do when they do not feel the threat of humans. The woods felt like home, and home was where he was headed, maybe forever.

His bleeding had stopped. He had poured water and nourishment into his body. His youth and his strength did the rest to make him fit to travel. He had not yet tried to slip into the familiar long-legged lope that made the miles fly by, but his walk was a rapid gait. For a while the trail he followed was fairly level, but halfway through the afternoon it began to climb toward a ridge line to the northeast. It was then that he realized his body was not all that he wanted it to be. He began to labor, and then to lag. He remembered the morning slaughter, and he felt compelled to put more miles between himself and that horrible massacre, but by the time the sun was red and huge on the horizon behind him, he knew that he must stop.

When he found a cool, tiny creek pouring off a rock shelf, he felt he should go no farther. He had to make do with little. He ate much of the corn left in the dead Mohawk's pouch, and drank freely from the cold water in the stream. Leaves from last fall became his bed, but the ground was hard in spite of them. The events of the day, however, had left him so tired that he was asleep before the gray twilight had faded to black.

Jinja awoke not because his body clock had told him to, but because someone had seized him by the shoulders and was shaking him, hard. He found himself staring into the dark eyes of a ferociously painted Mohawk warrior. He'd been sleeping for many hours. The high, late morning sun sneaked through the trees and glistened off the Mohawk's shaven crown.

Jinja reached for his knife, but it was not in his belt. The Mohawk caught Jinja's right arm in his left and held it.

"Stay," the Mohawk said in his native tongue.

"Who are you?" Jinja asked in the Mohawk dialect, not because he cared who the man was, but because he had to say something. This Mohawk was a big man, although not nearly as big as Jinja. He was in the prime of life and strength, with rippling muscles and no fat around his middle.

"Ahhh," the Mohawk said, pleased, and wagged a finger at Jinja. "And why do you sleep so late? Sleep late, you could get killed."

"Then why didn't you kill me?" Jinja asked, sitting up and flexing his stiff shoulder. He winced in pain.

The Mohawk observed the bloodstains from the wound. "You escaped from the battle?" he asked.

"I thought I had," Jinja replied. "Until now."

"Some did not escape." The Mohawk reached into a pouch and pulled out a handful of scalps. "You were lucky."

"Are you going to kill me?"

The Mohawk looked straight into Jinja's eyes. "My time for killing is past. That is what I dreamed last night. How do you come to speak the Mohawk tongue?"

"My grandmother was a Seneca. My grandfather is a trader. He took me to your villages and I learned more Mohawk tongue than Seneca. Would you kill me if I was not of the Longhouse?"

"I said, my time for killing is past." He smiled. "That is so for today. Who knows what I might dream tonight."

Jinja nodded. He felt pleased that he had not been able to scalp the Mohawk he'd killed the day before. How long, he thought, would he have lived if this Mohawk had found him with Mohawk hair in his belt? That made an impression on him. Never in his life would he take a scalp.

"Where are you going?" the Mohawk asked.

"Back to my father's house in Albany."

"You mean you came all the way from there to fight the Mohawk here?"

"I did not come to fight the Ganiengehaka. I do not wish to fight the Ganiengehaka. They are the brothers of my father and grandfather. It makes me sad that we must fight each other. I came, like you, to kill white men. Only I came to kill different white men."

The Mohawk laughed at Jinja's wry joke. "I should kill you now," he said. "There are too many white men. And they want so much of what belongs to the Ganiengehaka."

"I hope you will not kill me. I long to go home to see your brothers, my grandfather Big Oak, and Little Oak."

"What is your name?"

"In English my name is David. But I have a Longhouse name too. In the Longhouse I am called Gingego."

The Mohawk smiled with his eyes, though his mouth kept a straight, taut line across his face. "I am Tekarihoga," he said to Jinja. "You must cover your trail better. I followed it from the Susquehanna. I will leave you. Do not stay here. Tomorrow my time to kill may come again."

Jinja heeded Tekarihoga's warning. As soon as the Mohawk had vanished, Jinja slung his equipment over his shoulders, filled his canteen, picked up his knife and musket, and headed up the bed of the creek so as not to leave a trail. Twelve hours of sleep had done wonders for his young body. He found a rock shelf and left the creek without leaving tracks, climbed to the ridge and then over, heading down toward the next valley. He rummaged through his food pouch and found a little corn, ate it, and then poured half a canteen of water down his throat. His shoulder was beginning to ache again, and he still tired quickly. He was hungry, but he dared not hunt with his musket.

There were some wild blueberries to be found, but they were not yet ripe enough to eat. As hungry as he was, he could not chance a case of what the Indians called "devil in the belly." He walked east until he struck a northerly trail, which he followed silently, carefully, hungrily.

* * *

The next morning Jinja awoke with a fever. He was not frightened or angry, just disappointed that his wound had not simply healed the way he imagined a wound should heal. Now his musket was a walking stick and he shook like a leaf in a summer rain with every step. To make things worse, the sky opened up on him. He wanted desperately to find shelter in a cave and curl up in a ball until the fever subsided, but was afraid that if he did that, the fever might never go away. He did not want to admit it, but what he needed was his room and his bed. As he struggled east and north, he imagined himself struggling through the doorway of his home, and his mother burying him under a goose-down quilt. He imagined the warmth of the familiar quilt, and the feeling of a hot tea, perhaps laced with brandy. He feared the night, the cold, and the need to stop moving because his body craved rest. To make things worse, there were signs of war parties passing through. Signs of warriors ahead of him on the trail he walked. Signs of warriors on the trails that crossed the trail he traveled. He knew they were grown men by the size of the print and the length of the stride, and he knew they were warriors, not hunters, because the Iroquois he knew did not go deer hunting in packs.

But he felt too sick to play hide and seek. He would plod homeward and look to the Lord to rain on the Indians and keep them off his back.

He slogged through the mud with his head down. One thing he had learned from his father and grandfather was that on the trail, if you didn't stop, no matter how tough the going or how slow the pace, every step brought you nearer to where you needed to go. A spell of dizziness made him stumble and nearly fall. In spite of his determination, he had to pause and lean against a tree until his sense of balance returned. He was certain that if he laid down to rest, he would never again see home.

And yet, as the first shades of darkness began to creep in

on that part of the earth where he walked, he knew he
would have to stop. He was so weak that in order to climb
a hill he needed to rest at every tree. Finally he found a
great hollowed-out beech tree, a tree so big that he could
lay down in the big chamber just above the root line. Dripping wet, aching and shaky, he curled up against the inner
walls of the beech tree and slept.

All night long Mohawks loped through his dreams as
monstrous painted demons. Wherever he ran, he kept running into Mohawks—shrieking, whooping Mohawks exactly like those whose villages he used to visit in the
peaceful days. Except that these Mohawks were looking for
him, had followed him all the way up from the Wyoming
Valley, would follow him to the gates of Albany, and when
they caught him, they would surely kill him and scalp him
and dispatch an Oneida messenger to carry his scalp home
to his mother. In his dream his breathing was rapid and
shallow and frightened. He awoke three times during the
night, breathing just that way, then relapsed into his fitful
sleep. He was surprised, then, to awaken at first light
breathing normally, his body steady, his stomach feeling as
cavernous as the beech tree that sheltered him. He also
saw, to his amazement, a rabbit sitting in plain sight outside
the entrance to his beech tree.

Slowly he turned the barrel of his old trade musket till it
was pointed at the rabbit. The range could not have been
more than six feet, too close to miss *if* the priming was dry.
Jinja found that he could not even remember if he had
taken care to shelter the pan from the rain during his long
wet trek the day before. He would have to take a chance
now.

The flint sparked and the primer flashed and the musket
roared. Confined within the beech tree, Jinja nearly lost his
hearing. The little room was filled with choking smoke, and
the rabbit had disappeared. Disgusted, he crawled out of
the tree and looked across the trail. He spotted what was
left of the rabbit immediately. The musket ball had hurled

the animal up against a tree and made a great hole in its middle, but it was a big enough critter to provide substantial nourishment if he could find some dry wood to cook it over.

His hunger and his illness made it difficult for him to walk around. He reached out and grabbed the rabbit. Hungry as he was, he could not bring himself to take a bite of raw meat. He began to crawl around on the forest floor, looking for dry deadwood. But the rain had been a thorough, soaking one. Everything was wet. The wood that had been protected from the rain by other wood was on the ground, which had soaked up moisture and given it over to the wood that lay on it.

After about five minutes of grubbing in vain for dry wood, Jinja was beginning to feel discouraged, when he found several large dead tree limbs tumbled over each other, some of them a foot or two off the ground, resting on others. He felt the underside of these limbs and found them dry. With his knife he started shaving pieces off them, thin slivers for kindling, large chunks for the fire. He paused, took a deep breath to ward off a spell of dizziness, and continued to slice, piling the wood on a slab of dry rock that lay next to him. The limb was large and he soon had enough wood for his fire. He made a pile of kindling shavings, sprinkled a little gunpowder on top, pulled the hammer back on his musket, pulled the trigger and released a shower of sparks into the powder. The powder flashed and the wood shavings caught.

He ignored the pain from the powder flash that had leaped toward his hands, laid the musket down, cupped his hands around the shavings and blew gently until he had a flame going. Then he piled the dry wood chunks around the flame. Now he had a good-sized fire warming his face and his still damp clothes, but he continued piling wood on until all the wood he had cut was burning, and then he started to cut some more.

He cut two green sticks. Then he skinned the rabbit. He

cut out the liver, put it on one stick, and skewered the rabbit on the other. He held both sticks over the fire. The rabbit would take a while to cook, but the liver would cook quickly and he would eat it first.

The liver sizzled and turned black in the open flame. He didn't care. He just wanted to get it cooked as quickly as possible. It seemed to take forever, but finally it was done, so he took the stick and whirled it around in the air to cool it off, then took a bite. It was the best bite he had ever taken. He took two more bites and the liver was gone.

The edge was off his appetite. Now he could be more patient with the rabbit. And yet he wasn't. Five minutes later he was slicing strips off the animal and putting them in his mouth. As he ate, his thoughts wandered back to the battle and he began to wonder about his part in it. If he had held his ground, would that have turned the tide? Had he let his mates down? Did any of them survive? He thought of Beatty, his scalped body floating in the Susquehanna. His shoulder was aching again, reminding him that Sergeant Beatty had died going to the river to get water for him.

Jinja's thoughts did not turn into feelings. He wondered, but he did not feel great pangs of sorrow. He sliced another chunk of meat and nibbled on it. He thought about his first battles with his father and grandfather and Paul Derontyan, first the ambush, then the fight at the farm, where he was not expected to march with other men and stand still in the open while people were firing at him. Indians had the right idea about fighting, he thought. And they had proved it in the Wyoming Valley. They were the ones who had turned a rebel victory into a rout.

It occurred to Jinja that he had seen considerable action over the past year, and that he would be pleased to preserve his scalp awhile longer, if only he could manage to find his way home before his wound became infected or he caught pneumonia, or one of the Mohawk war parties spotted him and made his dream come true.

* * *

James's clothes felt stiff on his body and were disheveled even for a trail costume. He thought about Anne and her pretty dresses, and about Jinja and his fine, tailored attire. His heart sank. He was a poor Indian, he thought. All Indians were poor Indians, except maybe for Thayendanegea—Joseph Brant. His father was a poor Indian, for all the money he earned working for Thad and Thad's wife's father. Only white men got rich. Only white men were greedy enough to hold on to their money, as if just having it kept their bodies warm and their stomachs full.

He was thinking all these things because he was crossing the long clearing just outside of Albany. Anne was in Albany. James wanted to see Anne, but he was just a poor Indian, so why would Anne want to see him? She liked him, he was sure of that. Yet could she take him seriously as a man? The thought made him angry once again. How was it that these soft white men had a way of being able to make him feel as if he was less of a man? Not just him, many, even in the Longhouse. Why do we call the white men our fathers? he wondered. They wouldn't even call us their brothers.

Down the streets of Albany he walked, his rifle cradled carelessly in one arm. It was morning and there were a number of people on the street. Each one he passed made him angry. If one looked at him, James imagined that the person was staring. If one did not look at him, James imagined that the person was avoiding him, out of insolence. Why, he asked himself, did he so want this white woman when whites are such cruel people? And why were his moccasins leading him through the streets toward Anne's house just as certainly as if he were being pulled there on the end of a stout rope?

It had rained in Albany the day before, just as it had rained on Jinja. The streets were so muddy that it seemed to James his moccasins could not find firm bottom beneath the mud. Around him everyone walking in the street appeared to have this problem, and yet he felt muddier than the rest. He had acquired the habit of gripping his moccasins with his toes so the mud would not suck them off his feet. Instead, huge, heavy gobs of mud clung to the footwear, making his feet look like the huge hoofs of a plow horse. He didn't care anymore. He just wanted to see Anne and tell her about his adventures.

He walked down the busy street past her grandfather's big store, past a tavern and several houses, before he arrived at her house, her father's house. He paused for several moments. He could not picture himself calling on her. He looked at the mudballs on his feet and his awkward dirty linsey-woolsey shirt, and he almost turned around and walked out of Albany. But he had a stubborn persistence that had served him well in this life, and he was determined to see Anne. His jaw went rigid as he walked up the stairs to the front door and knocked.

Anne answered the door looking brokenhearted, but when she saw James her features lit up. "Oh, my lord, it's James!" she yelled toward the interior of the house. "Oh, James, I'm so glad you came. Where have you been?" She stood before him trying to do things with her hands that would make her feel more comfortable. "James, James, where have you been, and have you seen Jinja?"

"I've been off to the war," he said, "and I haven't seen Jinja."

He looked closely at the girl who had been the object of so many of his dreams in recent months. She obviously had not been getting a lot of sleep lately. Her mouth was drawn in a tense line, and her hair was carelessly done. In short, her appearance was not that much better than his.

"Were you down in Wyoming Valley?" she asked.

"No, we were—someplace else. Why? What happened in Wyoming Valley?"

"Oh, you don't know, you don't know. There's been a massacre down there, and there were boys from here caught in it. Hundreds of soldiers were killed by the Indians!"

Her tone when she said the word "Indians" chilled him. What did she think he was? What did she think part of her was? But he kept his face a mask and said nothing.

"They killed our boys like they were animals! Butchered them. Joseph Brant was there, killing his old friends! My God, James, Jinja was there and—*he was there!*"

At that moment Katherine walked to the doorway, very polite, very correct, very cold.

"You can see that Anne is upset now," she said. "I think you should leave, James." She did not add, "Come back another time, when she's feeling more herself."

Sad for Jinja, but also hurt and confused for himself, James turned away from the door and stepped back into the muddy streets of Albany.

❧13❧

GEORGE HAYES LEANED BACK AGAINST THE
reins and pulled a huge piece of cloth from his belt. It was
summertime, and cultivating between the rows of corn was
even hotter work for him than for his mule. He didn't know
why he loved doing it, especially at this late stage of his
life. What were all those sons good for if not to do his
plowing for him?

Every square inch of his huge bandanna was so wet that
there was no use trying to wipe his face with it. His eyes
stung and his back ached and there was no way he was
going to finish this field before the gray cloud over the hill
was going to rain on him. So he clucked to the mule, untan-
gled himself from the harness leather and began to lead the
animal down the hill toward the barn. He loved moments
like this, when needed rain came flying in on the wings of a
summer wind. His wife Rachel would be waiting, and together they would listen to the wind rattle the windows,
watch the rain come in waves across the yard and observe
the chickens heading for cover.

There'd be grandchildren too. Always when the rains
came some of them would be sure to be closer to Grandpa's
home than to the homes of their parents down the valley.
They knew that if they wound up in Grandpa's home,
Grandma Rachel would have time for them. There would

be sweets and games and all sorts of good things that they never got from their mothers and fathers, or so it seemed.

From the hill he'd been plowing he looked around the valley and the surrounding slopes and could see his sons and sons-in-law similarly making haste to get their mules in their barns and themselves in their houses before the rains soaked them. All except George, Jr., or Jughead, as his old friend Sam Watley still called him. Jughead was stubborn. He'd keep his animals working until the first drops hit, and then go a little farther down the row until he was sure that this was going to be a real gully-washer. Well, you can't fault a boy for bein' a hard worker, reflected George the father.

As George and his mule got halfway down the hill, he spotted a familiar horse kicking up clods along the road and turning into the barnyard. The rider dismounted and banged on the back door with a great urgency.

"Wonder what that damned Onondaga wants from me today," George muttered. But he began to hurry the mule down the path to the barn. Rachel was at the door listening to the man, who was Rachel's brother. The rain was beginning to fall in earnest now. He could see Rachel waving to him and shouting, but he could not hear her words through the clatter of the rain on the barn roof. He led the mule into the barn and quickly, nimbly, separated the animal from the cultivator. There was hay and water ready for her.

"They're here," said Peter Littletree to George as he clomped through the back doorway into the kitchen.

"Who's here?"

"The Senecas. They're in the village recruiting our boys. All the women and most of the older men are arguing with them, trying to get them to leave, but some of the boys— you know boys."

Peter was long-legged and fine-featured, like his sister, who had married George more than fifteen years ago and borne him three children to go with the eleven by his first wife before she had died. And then there were the three children they had adopted, William, Richard, and Barbara, sad specimens—the boys at least—that their friend Sam Watley had rescued from renegade Senecas more than a decade ago. They had come around nicely, those children, and were taking their first steps into adulthood. All in all, George had populated the valley with about fifty descendants. So when he found Peter Littletree at his back door telling him that the Senecas were recruiting Onondagas in the nearby village for a war party, George was very interested.

"Will they be coming here?"

"I'm sure they might."

"Damn redskins!" George snarled. "What are the people in the village gonna do?"

"Nothing until they see what the Senecas want to do. If they don't tell them you're here, they might go in another direction. But it's hard to miss a valley like this."

Peter ignored the "redskin" comment. George had been fulminating against Indians for years, but his comments were always directed against all those "other" Indians that he didn't know. In the meantime, the whites in Hayes's valley and the Onondagas in the next valley over had lived together in peace. George had even come up with a scheme to protect the Onondagas from white land encroachments on nearby Onondaga land. He had gone through great pains to get some papers made that gave him ownership of that land, then he had conveyed the property to his brother-in-law, who was in line to become a village chief. Anytime a squatter showed up on the land, he and about twenty sons, sons-in-law, and grandsons, along with some of the more white-cultured Onondagas, would make an appearance at the half-built log cabin and wave papers in the face of the squatter. However ready he may have been to face off an Indian village, the trespasser generally would not want to buck a local country squire, and the next day his wagon would be packed and he would be off looking for another valley.

It wasn't that George was so partial to Onondagas—he would never admit to such a thing. He was just basically a conservative man, and the predictable world he had enjoyed for thirty years happened to include a village full of Onondaga people he had grown to like, or at least tolerate.

"If it looks like the Senecas are heading in your direction," Peter said, "some of our people will come among them and try to talk them out of attacking you."

"How many of them are there?"

"Maybe . . . thirty—maybe more."

George's fighting spirit, once ample, had been cooled by thirty years of settled life and good eating that had fattened him considerably since his scouting days with Sam Watley. "Will your people come and help us?"

"I will stay and help you, but the rest will not. They say they cannot afford to fight their brothers, that the confederation is too important to them. But they say they love you and your family and they will give you a nice burial when the Senecas get through with you."

George smiled grimly. "Very loyal of them," he observed sarcastically. "When do you think they might be here?"

"I think they'll visit in our village until it stops raining. They'll be here tomorrow morning, I believe."

"I don't think you can afford to fight against your brothers either. But I know you'll want to help your sister. Our house is big and strong and built to hold out against . . . enemies. If you'll stay for the night, you and Richard and William can go out on an early morning scout and give us an idea of when they'll be comin'."

But neither one of them was about to rely on the Senecas staying away until morning. Hayes bellowed for his oldest adopted boy, and Richard came in, a tall, thin wisp of a young man without the bulk of George's natural progeny but with a look of energetic intelligence.

"Richard," he said, "the Senecas are coming." The young

man's face tightened around his mouth, but he said nothing. "I want you and Peter to take a ride through the valley and get everybody in here. I think we're about to fight our own little war."

Within two minutes Peter and Richard were mounted up and riding in opposite directions. Peter had six homes to alert, and Richard five. Richard found himself muttering aloud as his horse splashed through the muddy course that led him to George's daughter Sarah and her husband Lawrence. Memories long suppressed flooded back to him: the quick death and scalping of his father at the doorway of their house, the killing of his hysterical mother two miles along the trail of the house. The efforts of his sister Barbara to keep the boys from angering their captors by whimpering too much, and their subsequent rescue by Big Oak Sam and some coolly efficient Mohawk warriors.

In the years that followed, he came to realize how fortunate they were that a band of Mohawks would actually fight Senecas to rescue them, and he never probed into the complex politics behind that little skirmish, which left four Seneca bodies twitching on the forest floor.

And now, what was that behind the big elm just off the road there? Nothing. Damn. Seeing things. Quickly he dismounted and pounded hard on the door of the house, delivered his message, and remounted, leaving in his wake a rush of feverish activity.

"Don't try and take everything with you!" he shouted back at Sarah through the pouring rain as his horse descended to the main road in the valley.

Twice more he stopped, pounded on the door and gave the alert, then continued onward. At the fourth house he knocked and knocked on the front door, then went around to the back and did the same, with no response. He noticed fresh wagon tracks leading to or from the barn, along with the tracks of an outriding horse. To make sure, he opened the door of the barn and looked in. No wagon. They must have gotten the word somehow, but Richard's gut was tight nevertheless as he climbed on the back of his shiny, dancing, restless wet horse and headed for the last house. This was the house of Walter Hayes, George's third son.

As he rode he saw apparitions behind every tree close to the road. He saw armies of phantom red men rising from the cornfields, seeking to cut him off as the road wound around a bend. Years of doing man's work on the farm had made Richard believe that he had grown up, but his knees were feeling as weak as those of a child. One more house, then he could ride back home and take refuge behind those solid stone walls. His horse topped a rise, and through the deluge he could see a neat white farmhouse. The animal slid to a halt in front of the porch. Richard kicked out of the stirrups, dropped his boots into the mud, stepped onto the porch and knocked on the door. The rain was pelting so hard off the roof of the porch that he could barely hear the noise he made as he knocked again, harder.

Now the door opened, quickly, and standing before him was a near naked Seneca warrior painted in red and black, tomahawk raised above his head. Richard raised his arm to defend himself, too late. The last thing he saw before he died was either a fierce grimace or a smile on the face of his executioner.

In the Onondaga village over the hill from Hayes's valley, Degata stood before the man called John Justice, an Onondaga dressed in a shirt and breeches even in the summertime.

"What are you anyway?" Degata asked, as puzzled as he was angry.

"I am Ganonsyoni," the Onondaga man responded mildly.

"You look like a white man, are you proud of that?"

"Here, where it counts, I am Ganonsyoni," said John Justice, patting his heart with his right hand. "I do not do the bidding of English masters."

"You . . ." The Seneca pointed an accusing finger, his

face now twisted with scorn. "You side with these rebels who would have all our land."

"I side with no white man," Justice answered. "You are the one on the warpath. You are the one wasting the best blood of the Seneca nation. And when this war is over, who will there be left to resist the white man? There were not so many of us to start with. The more you fight, the less you survive. And for what? For the English, who cut off our gunpowder and bullets after we helped them beat the French. No rebel has yet asked that we shed our blood for them. They ask only that we stand aside and not fight for the English."

The Seneca felt himself being defeated in debate. But he had the weapons in his hands and in his belt. He and seven other braves crowded around Justice and several others, brandishing their tomahawks and knives.

"You will guide us to the white men here, and then you will help us to slay them or we will have a fight right now."

Now Justice stood tall and let his contempt rain down upon the bullying Senecas around him.

"What! You dare walk into a village of the keepers of the council fire and threaten them? This is how you respect the Longhouse and the Great Peace? We welcome you to our village as brothers and feed you. And you threaten us. I may be dressed in white man's clothes, but I have fought the Abnaki and the Cherokee, and we will fight you if you threaten us. Look around you and see if you think you could win such a fight.

"But for the sake of our brotherhood I will tell you, first, that there are whites close by and that you will have to find them yourself if you want to fight them, and second, even now they are being warned that you are near. You see, they are our brothers too. They took one valley, and only one valley, and they have helped us to keep what belongs to us. We cannot kill you for the sake of them, but neither will we kill them for the sake of you."

Degata spoke slowly, ominously. "You have warned

white men about us? You are not Ganonsyoni. You are nothing. You would kill your own brothers."

Justice was not daunted. "Am I pointing a gun at you and making you attack the white men? What are you doing here? This is not Seneca land. This is Onondaga land."

"It is our time to attack the rebels. We have—"

"Ah, the English have given you a job to do. Then go do your job. But we warn you as brothers. Those white men, should you find them, will not be easy. And if you lose precious warriors for no good reason, do not blame us, for we have warned you."

Up to this point the Onondagas had been passive, but now a number of them emerged from their log homes with weapons.

Rising to the challenge, the Seneca braves were about to swing into action when one of their scouts came running in through the downpour.

"I have found them," he said excitedly, for he was brand new on the warpath. "Ashes Rising has already killed one and we have captured one family." He was pointing due south.

Degata looked at John Justice with death in his eyes. "Do not attempt to help the white men any more than you have or there will be a fight between us," Degata warned.

"Onondaga words are not smoke," Justice said.

"Haya!" Degata cried. "Take us to them, Tsitsa."

More than thirty years had passed since George Hayes had scouted for the English during one of their long series of wars against the French. For many years he had lived in peace in this valley and raised a huge family. Incredibly, the cemetery he had fenced off when his first wife had died fifteen years before still contained only a solitary grave. It was inconceivable that so many babies could be born in that valley without death paying him a visit. And yet it had happened.

Until now. In the rain, they stood in front of the big stone house and stared at a solitary pillar of smoke across the valley. Walter's house. Richard had not returned. And Walter's house had been Richard's last scheduled stop.

"It could only have been a few of them. The others were still in our village, trying to force our men to go with them," Peter said.

George would have noticed that Peter did not say braves or warriors. He would have wondered if the Onondaga village near his valley had become too white for their own good. But his mind was working too hard on the survival of his family.

"We could stay in the stone house and fight it like a fort," he said, "but they would burn all the houses in the valley and maybe burn us out too."

"Then why don't we just take our families and leave this valley to the Indians?" The voice was that of Ezra, one of his younger sons. Ezra the peacemaker. George wondered about Ezra.

"You can't run from Indians when you're loaded down with women and children," George replied. "Besides, I'm damned if I'll give up this valley without a fight. We're not gonna stay cooped up in that house and let them roast us all together. Ezra, you get them all together down in the basement. Walk 'em through the tunnel underneath the barn. Meanwhile, Peter, we're gonna set up a neat little surprise for them."

The rain had stopped, leaving a warm mist throughout most of the valley. Quietly, eleven men plus five boys fourteen or older followed Peter to a wooded draw along the only path that came down the valley from the north. George and Peter agreed that the Senecas would take the quickest route in, expecting the people of the valley to fight out of their houses, as folks were doing all that summer in the upper half of New York.

Quietly they hid themselves in the long wet grass above the path. George went from man to man to check their weapons and remind them of what they were supposed to do. It might be a long wait, he added, and when the Senecas appeared, it was important that they not fire until they were all within the killing area. He would fire the first shot, and the rest would fire immediately after. "You are all good hunters," he said, "so take aim and make your shots count. Your lives depend on it."

They all understood, and they waited wet and uncomfortable in the tall grass while the mosquitoes bit their backs and arms right through their shirts. They were armed with rifles that they had been taught how to use. They had hunted with them, fired at targets, and even, as children, played frontiersmen with them. But they had never killed men with them, and now as they waited, guts clenched, it was only their desperation that gave them the determination to see the job through.

When the Senecas came over the rise, they came single file, on the run. Before them lay the beautiful valley, so lush and green on this rainy day, the houses well spread out. They knew how the whites defended their homes, shooting from the windows and hoping for rescue. Well, Degata thought, they'd have the whole valley up in flames before nightfall. Down the road they ran, into the valley. Off to their right they could see a column of smoke where Ashes Rising and Tsitsa had struck the first blow. If the other whites had not yet fled, there would be some bloody work before the end of the day.

Degata thought he felt a mosquito bite him on the leg. Then he heard the shot and he dove to the ground. Around him seventeen rifles fired and at least six of his braves followed him down. The rest of them—and there were two dozen still unscathed—fired at the smoke that rose from the grass on either side of the road.

They did not stay on the road, but ran for the tall grass and hid there. The Hayeses continued to fire at where they imagined the Senecas would be, and the Senecas fired back wherever they saw smoke rising from the tall grass. For a long half hour the battle continued in the wet grass, the blind shooting at the blind, with very little damage being done.

George Hayes was a very tough old bird who had long ago been Big Oak's trailmate through two wars against the French. But he had been at peace for many years and seen his children all grow to adulthood. Except for his first wife, he was accustomed to life, not death, in this beautiful valley community that he had created through the force of his will. Now his thoughts were on how to keep his sons, daughters, and grandchildren alive. When a lull in the firing occurred, he shouted, "Keep pourin' lead into them, boys!" and the shooting resumed.

If only he could keep the Senecas pinned down long enough, he thought, the Onondagas might come down the road and envelop the Senecas. After a while he realized that they would not war on their brothers. Well then, they were known as great compromisers. Maybe they would come down and work out a ceasefire. But as the sky cleared and the day got hotter and the firing continued, he knew they could expect no help at all from the village to their north.

Damn them, he muttered through his dark beard as he cocked his rifle and aimed where he hoped a Seneca might be skulking. Living side by side for thirty years, helping each other, taking care of each other, and now that he finally needs them in a matter of life or death, they're in their houses quaking beneath their blankets.

He thought about that and rejected the image. No, he thought, as he loaded, primed, and cocked again. They told the Senecas where we were. Just dirty, no good sneaking Indians. They expect to have our fields and homes after the Senecas wipe us out and go away. Now he was no longer annoyed. He was furious. When we finish with these Senecas, we'll come down on those Onondagas like the ten plagues. We'll see who takes whose fields.

But they couldn't stay where they were all day. He'd hate to have to fight a band of Indians in the tall grass once the sun had gone down. Both sides were still pouring grazing gunfire into the tall grass, but nobody was hitting anything.

"Okay boys, listen up!" he hollered. "We're gonna duck on outta here, head south and form up around Charlie's barn!" Charlie was one of his older sons. His house was only about a half mile down the road. When the war had begun, Charlie built a wooden barricade about four feet high around his barn and house. He had been grazing his cows in the fields around the barn all summer long. There were good long fields of fire if the Senecas wanted to rush them. "Anybody hurt?" he asked.

One by one the boys called out that they were fine. The Senecas fired at where they thought the voices were, but the Hayeses all had the sense to move as soon as they spoke. Only Charlie, it turned out, was hurt, though not seriously.

"Okay boys, let's do it quietly, first pull back, then move on south!" He knew they all understood that they would find each other when they'd made it out of the tall grass into the open. He could only hope that none of the Senecas spoke English well enough to understand what he was saying.

They renewed their fire. One of them was fortunate enough to wound a Seneca, not fatally, but painfully. When the Indian let loose a howl, his angered cohorts fired a ragged volley and continued the fire for several minutes. The silence of the Hayeses' guns was covered by the shooting of the Senecas. They all retreated in a wide circle away from the Senecas and down into the valley. Once they were out of the tall grass, into the grazed field, they broke into a run down both sides of the road and made for the barn, which they could see more than a quarter of a mile distant. Uncertain that the Senecas did not know of their trick, they sprinted full speed and did not stop until they vaulted the wall of the little stockade around the barn and stood there panting, watching for Indians and grateful that everybody who had been in on the ambush had survived.

George Hayes leaned forward against the stockade wall and looked out across his beautiful valley. This was the first time in years he'd had to run this hard, and he could not seem to catch his breath. No question about it, he was too old for war. Aside from the one wisp of smoke from the cabin of his son Walter, the valley seemed quiet. And Walter was here. All the men and boys who had gone with him on the ambush had made it behind these walls. Charlie's wound was so trifling that he was still ready for action. As anxious as George was about the safety of his family, he had to be satisfied so far. They had bloodied the nose of the Senecas, the women and children were hidden away, and they had a good position if the Senecas should attack. Let them come. His boys would give them a hot time.

The men were preparing for a siege, filling their canteens with water from the pump by the house and carrying from the house everything that might be of conceivable use to them. The house was on a rise, so anybody trying to enter the house might be exposed to fire from the Senecas if they attempted to enter it once the siege began.

He was proud of his boys as they waited by the low walls, calmly checking the priming of their rifles and keeping a sharp eye out for snakes in the long grass. They had sharp eyes, all of them. And steady hands, Hayes thought to himself. He was hoping the Senecas *would* attack. He would teach them a lesson, as well as his Onondaga neighbors. He was breathing easier now, finally.

For half an hour they sat behind their low wooden walls and waited for the Senecas to come, but all was still in the tall grass that surrounded the grazed pastures. It was Charlie, peering out the second-story window of the house, who first spotted the Senecas, or at least their works. "Smoke in the west, over at Lawrence's house," he shouted down to his father. A moment later two others watching from the walls spotted smoke coming from two other homes in other directions of the valley.

George's son Ezra looked at George. "We're in for it now," he said.

But George smiled. "No, son. They're in for it. They've split up their forces. See where Lawrence's house is burning? Rob's place is the next one over, but I believe we can make it there before they do. We'll outnumber them, and I think we can make them regret the day they decided to come after us. Let's go!"

They were on the run again, headed straight for a large flat rock that overlooked the path between Lawrence's and Rob's houses. It took them ten minutes to get there, but as George had suspected, the Senecas were too busy looting and destroying Lawrence's place to be quick about going on to the next. All through the run out from the little stockade in the valley, George could hear Lawrence cursing the Senecas for destroying his homestead. Good, thought the old man. Lawrence was one of the boys closest to the Onondagas, always insisting that George be a little kinder to them. Let's see how he feels when it's time to rebuild his pile of ashes and he reflects that the village didn't lift a finger to avert the catastrophe.

They made it to the rock in plenty of time. The four best shooters found positions on the rock and the rest of them scattered in the woods along the trail. George found a position with a good field of fire, and Charlie laid down next to him. To their left they could see the smoke rising from Lawrence's house.

They could hear whooping and screeching, and there was no doubt it was coming closer to them. This was going to be a turkey shoot, he thought, as the first two braves rounded a bend and came on with the colorful curtains of Lawrence's wife's kitchen streaming from their bodies. The men on the rock fired and both braves went down. Then came a whoop from behind George, and a shot, and George saw Charlie's body flinch and go limp. George turned quickly and spotted a single flanker. He fired at him, then in rage charged him, rifle in the air. The Seneca pulled his tomahawk and hurled it at the old scout. George pulled his head sideways and heard the weapon go whirling past him. The Seneca pulled his knife from his belt. The two charged each other, both on a dead run. As the Seneca raised his knife, George struck him a glancing blow at the side of his head with the butt of his rifle. The knife went flying off into the tall grass, and the Seneca, now weaponless, fled. George returned to where Charlie lay unmoving, unbreathing.

The firing around the path was loud and heavy. The remaining Senecas had found positions in the woods. Once again the two sides fired at each other for a few minutes, and then it occurred to George that the other groups of Senecas might stop their burning and looting long enough to join the fight. He passed the word around to reassemble at Charlie's house. They withdrew into the woods and headed eastward. This time the going was slower because George and Lawrence had to carry Charlie's body home. He sent half of the men ahead to occupy the little stockade just in case the Senecas spotted it and had a similar thought. George's idea, like most of his on that day, proved to be a good one.

They toiled through the woods, then down a grazed slope and across the cornfield. Lawrence was in tears, but George had no time for that now. They were still in the middle of a battle, and the life of one son was cheap if the rest of the family could somehow be saved. They had made it to the middle of the cornfield when they heard the gunfire commence at Charlie's place.

"Put Charlie down," George told Lawrence. "We've got some more fightin' to do."

"We can't just leave—"

"Do you want more brothers dead like him? Put him down and check to see that your rifle is loaded!"

They began to run again, George and Lawrence and young Ezra and four more sons and grandsons. Through the cornstalks they could see several Senecas firing at the low log wall. If they could sneak a little closer and get good shots, they might bag a bunch of them. His boys inside the stockade were taking fire from all directions. George could see his stalwart son Jughead directing the defense of the stockade.

Lawrence didn't wait for any orders to fire. He pulled his rifle to his shoulder and squeezed off a quick shot that hit nobody, but flushed the Senecas and sent them fleeing out of range in a hurry.

"Damn it!" George hollered. There was no sense trying to run them down, and a quick look around revealed that the Indians attacking from the other sides had decided to pull back.

One of his grandsons, a boy of sixteen named Tom, gave a whoop and fired a long shot toward the back of the last fleeing Seneca. His bullet kicked up a little dirt well short of his target.

"Weren't many of them left," he said to his grandfather. "Did we kill all that many?"

"I don't think so," George answered wearily. "I think some of them just took their loot and went home." There must have been a lot of loot to carry off, he thought. Drifting toward the sky was smoke from at least seven burning buildings. How many houses lost, how many barns burned, how many livestock slaughtered, and how many—how many of his children and grandchildren dead? He felt his throat constrict. The battle was over, of that he was fairly certain. But now, what was the cost?

❖14❖

JINJA HAD EATEN TOO MUCH. HIS STOMACH felt as if he had swallowed a swarm of bees. His shoulder still ached and his body was shaking again. And that was only the half of it. Ahead of him a Mohawk raiding party was dragging an unhappy family from their cabin, one at a time. The father was already standing by the steps, hands bound behind him, head hanging low. Next to him was his wife, silent, holding a baby in one arm and with her free hand clutching the hand of her son.

A painted warrior was leading an older daughter out of the house roughly but doing no damage. From inside the house came angry screeches, and then another girl, older than the last, pitched headlong down the stairs onto the hard-packed dirt in front of the cabin. The last Mohawk to emerge from the cabin showed bloody red welts across his cheek in addition to the smeared white and vermilion streaks of paint.

Two of the Mohawks threw firebrands through the windows. The curtains caught immediately. The oldest daughter and the mother wept piteously. The younger daughter and the son were too frightened to take a breath, much less make a sound. The father stood in silence because he was afraid that anything he said might make somebody mad.

So far, so good, the father thought. They haven't hurt us

yet. If they had intended to hurt us, they would have done
so already. Keep your mouth shut. Don't even look into the
eyes of one of them. Don't give them a reason to get mad.
And pray, silently pray, because, my God, if ever we
needed help, this is the time.

The farmer was not the only one praying. Jinja lay in the
woods about fifty yards from the cabin. The Mohawks were
obviously obeying orders to be civil to civilians. If they
caught him lurking in the woods, they would surely inflict
on him what they would have enjoyed inflicting on this
family, which had cleared twenty or thirty acres right in the
middle of what had once been prime Mohawk forest.

His stomach cramps had reached a point where they
were demanding that he give up his roasted rabbit. He
wanted to, but he had never been taught how to throw up
in silence. With all the power he could generate with his
jaw muscles, he kept his mouth clamped shut and watched
the family watch their cabin burn to the ground. Please, he
begged silently, take them wherever, but take them, so I
can empty my stomach and head for home.

Now the Mohawks shoved the family into line and
pointed them along a trail on the opposite side of the clearing from where Jinja lay. They pushed the family into a
swift lope down the trail. The man turned to ask one of his
captors to cut him free so he could carry the baby. He
received a butt stroke in the back that made him stumble,
but somehow he kept going. Long after the family disappeared down the trail, Jinja could hear the sounds of weeping from the mother and her children. "Good," he said,
"they won't hear me."

The rabbit came up quickly, followed by more. He felt
better now, but not as good as he needed to feel. His body
weaved a bit as he grabbed a tree trunk and boosted himself
to his feet. He cradled his captured musket and lurched
down the trail in the opposite direction from that taken by
the Mohawks. Even feeling as bad as he did, he knew that
Albany was only a day away. Were things so bad that

Mohawks could burn out settlers within thirty miles of Albany?

He tripped over a rock and went sprawling. Now he had a few more bruises to go with the wound, the chill, and the bellyache. All in all, he figured, his trip south had been a failure. Everything had gone wrong, and now, as he thought about the events that had transpired, he found himself near tears for his newfound, newly lost pal, Sergeant Beatty.

Jinja noticed that when his mind wandered, he stopped walking. That was odd. It seemed that he could only do one thing at a time. If that was the case, he had to stop thinking. He could think later. One foot in front of the other. Again and again. It was tedious, but if he daydreamed, he might waste precious time and energy standing in one place, using his brain instead of his feet.

So he put one foot in front of the other until late afternoon, when he found that he could go no farther. He drained the last drops from his canteen, found a crevasse between two huge rocks, laid down—and discovered that he was looking into the eyes of a copperhead snake.

The spark of alarm that leaped through his chest was very feeble. He stared heavy-lidded at the copperhead and didn't move a muscle. The snake stared back. This went on for eternal minutes. Lazily, as if he were watching someone else undergoing this trial, he wondered what would happen next. He supposed it was possible that the snake might strike and sink his fangs into his neck, but he didn't think so. Why should the snake bother? he thought. What good would it do the snake? The snake couldn't eat him. He couldn't eat the snake, or anything else. It was sort of like the war, he thought. The minutes slid by and Jinja and the snake just stared. It was the snake that finally gave in and slithered away. Jinja couldn't have. His eyelids closed and he slept.

It was raining on him again toward the end of the following day, when Jinja emerged from the forest. Across the clearing Albany glittered like crystal to the half-dead, half-starved young revolutionary. The previous night's sleep had brought him back to the point where he could think and walk at the same time, but he had weakened with each hour of daylight. Only the stubborn spark of survival had kept him going. Now that home was in view, his pain and his illness seemed a light burden. Nevertheless, crossing the clearing was a major effort.

The muddy streets were empty. The last gray light of day's end cast a layer of gloom over the town's houses of wood and brick which the feeble candle glow from within did little to lift. Jinja clutched at his nearly useless Indian trade musket as if it were one of his grandfather's prize Pennsylvania long rifles, though his weakness and fatigue told him that the time had come to let it go. No, he would return home with a conquered weapon, as if it somehow made up for his frightened flight from the scene of the massacre down in Wyoming Valley.

He turned a corner and labored through the muck, downhill past his grandfather's store. There was no light from within. The hour was late enough that even the old man had closed his ledgers and gone home. Just a few doors down was the house where he was born. There were candles burning on the bottom floor. He could see their glow faintly through the curtains that covered the windows.

He tried the door latch. It was locked. He grabbed the brass door knocker and pounded three times. A voice from within said, "Oh my God!" A wave of dizziness washed over him and he leaned against the door for support. The door opened, a little at first, then wider, and he forced himself to stand alone.

His dad reached under his arm, too near to his wound. Jinja sucked in a sharp breath. His mother took his hand, kissed him and said nothing. Her tears did the talking for her, but she did not carry on. His mother never carried on, and that pleased him. His knees buckled. His father had to help him to a couch in the sitting room, his boots trailing the fetid brown mud of Albany's streets across the expensive rug.

"I wish Cilla were here," he heard his father say. "Katherine, please bring a cup of water. And make some tea, and heat up some broth. I'm gonna get this boy to bed."

"Pa, there was this copperhead—" Jinja was not completely out of his head. He knew what was going on around him, he just didn't know what was important to say, so he let out random thoughts. "Pa, did you know how hard it is to scalp a Mohawk?"

"I never wanted to scalp a Mohawk," Thad muttered as he nearly carried his son up the stairs to his bed. "I knew better than to make an enemy of a Mohawk . . . except one Mohawk," he added, taking a candle from a table and heading downstairs to light it.

His mother brought Jinja a cup of water. He drank some, carefully, and held it down, gripping the cup with both hands, like a child. He sipped again, while his father removed his moccasins and then the rest of his clothes. His head cleared a bit. He could smell the sweet, freshly laundered sheets and feel the softness of his bed and his pillow. "Ooh," he sighed, letting his head fall back. "Pa, you won't believe what happened down in Wyoming Valley," he whispered.

His father let some air out of his lungs, a gesture of exasperation and relief. "The news got back here a couple of days before you did, son. We were afraid that we'd lost you."

"Well, you ain't." Jinja smiled.

"You sure?" his father asked him.

"Ahhh," he responded. "I hope Mom comes up with the food pretty quick. I'm empty. And then I hope I can keep it in my stomach."

"I don't doubt you will," Thad said. "You always—" He stopped. "There's someone here who's awful worried about you."

In the doorway, dressed in a nightgown and robe, stood

his sister, hands clasped in front of her, peering through the gloom. Like his mother, she didn't want to make a fuss, but even in the dim candlelight Jinja could see the glint in her eyes.

She stood silently for a while, waiting for her emotions to come under control. "How is he?" she asked, finally walking toward him.

"I think he'll be right in a day or two if your mother can get some good Dutch food into him."

"That's fine," Anne said, smiling, stopping at her brother's bed and sitting in the chair closest to him. He was sleeping now, and breathing easily, while his father was inspecting his wound, which in spite of Jinja's ordeal seemed to be free of infection.

Katherine walked in with some steaming broth. "Might as well leave it on the fire," Thad said. "He needs his sleep as much as he needs his food."

Katherine nodded, but before she left the room, she put her tray down and looked at her son's face. "My husband," she said. "I don't care if you have to lock him up, I don't want him running off with any militia, ever again."

Thad looked at his wife. "I know. You put young boys out in the woods against a bunch of Mohawks and they won't stand a chance. There's a whole lot of mothers in this town with their hearts broken. We're very lucky to get our boy back. I'll not let him out of my sight again."

The leaves were colored like Joseph's coat down on Big Oak's pond. He threw in a line, took a puff on his pipe, leaned back against a tree trunk and allowed himself some satisfaction. His grandson was up and about, in fact he was staying with him and Cilla for a while. His health had been restored, but a muscle under his left shoulder had not yet come around. Try as he might to resist the pain, he still could not raise his arm above his head.

Peace had not yet come to central New York. The Senecas and Mohawks were still rampaging, but there were rumors that come spring the rebels would mount a mighty offensive that would drive the Longhouse completely out of New York. Big Oak accepted the news with mixed feelings. On one hand, if the Mohawks were pushed out, he could count on peace at last on the Te-non-an-at-che, the River Flowing Through Mountains. On the other hand, the Te-non-an-at-che was the Mohawk River. The Mohawks were his brothers. The land was theirs. Before the war he had felt good knowing that not far to the west lay the village of White Bird and her sons, Louis and George. These were high-born Mohawks, quality people. But now White Bird was dead and Louis and George followed Joseph Brant around New York burning farmhouses and scalping their neighbors.

He turned to Jinja to ask him about the Mohawks. "Are they still mighty warriors in battle?" he asked.

"Grandfather, I must tell you what I have not wanted to tell you," Jinja said. It was his grandfather, not his parents, who would hear his confession. "When the Mohawks and the Senecas came down our flanks, I could not stay. Their cries chilled my blood. I had thought that I had courage. And yet on that day I had none. I ran, and I saved myself without thinking what would happen to the others."

Big Oak's sharp gray eyes fastened on Jinja's deep brown ones. "I know what happened to the others. They ran too." He took a puff on his pipe. A great puff of smoke rose into the brisk autumn air. "There is an old Mohawk story about two hunters who were in camp when they saw a great bear approaching. They tried to hide, but the bear was coming closer. Suddenly the bear broke into a dead run. The older hunter kicked off his moccasins.

"The younger one laughed. 'You think you can run faster than that bear?' he asked.

"'Don't have to,' said the older one. 'Just have to run faster than you.'"

Thad thought about the old Mohawk joke and laughed. "What does that have to do with me?" he asked.

"I have been on the trail with you many times. I have been in battle with you twice, my boy. You are no coward. The Indians know it is no disgrace to run away from battle to save your life. There are not so many Indians. When a village loses a great warrior, it is a tragedy for that village. You will fight again, but in the woods, with other woodsmen, never in the ranks of an army. We tried to tell you. I think that now you know."

"Know what?" said a new voice that nearly made Big Oak jump out of his skin.

"I did not hear you come, Paul, my brother. My ears no longer hear like they should. I am not such a good man to walk the trail with."

"Have you some tobacco, my brother Big Oak? It has been a long journey without the comfort of smoke."

"Have you eaten?" Big Oak asked.

"Cilla fed me well before I came down to join you."

"Why are you here? I thought you had goods to deliver to Canowaraghere."

"I delivered the goods and a war party went south. James went with the war party. And then Lizabet called me into the house and screamed at me for letting the raiding party go. 'The Mohawks will come and kill us all!' she shouted. 'Don't you care about your own village? You have no sense. You must keep our warriors here, where they can defend us against our brothers the Mohawks, and our brothers the Onondagas, and our brothers the Cayugas.' Oh yes, she screamed at me and would not let me answer with a single word. And then she threw me out of her lodge. She screamed loud enough for the whole village to hear, and the women from the next lodge made faces at me and acted as if they had just caught me beating my wife."

Big Oak shook his head in sympathy. "So you left."

"My village don't need me. They have my wife. I pity the Mohawk that sets foot in my village when my wife is there. I'll go home in a few days, when she has a better temper. Tonight I will sleep in the loft with your boys." He was so absorbed in his narrative that only after he had gotten it all out did he pack his pipe with Big Oak's fine trade tobacco and borrow some glowing ash from Big Oak's pipe to light his.

"Aren't you worried about the Mohawks?" Jinja asked.

"Not so worried. I think they will leave the people of the boulder alone, unless our young braves kill one or two of theirs, and then there will be a bad time. But," he added, leaning back and puffing with contentment, "right now I do not think the Mohawks will bother with the Oneidas."

"Why not?"

Paul shrugged his shoulders. His lips moved but no sound came out. How could he tell a young white warrior what was in the hearts of the old ones?

"Before I came here, I stopped to visit the Mohawks."

"You visited the Mohawks?" Jinja, who had nearly lost his life to them, was astonished. Even Big Oak took his eyes off his bobber and looked at his Oneida friend.

"My wife is of the Bear clan," he said. "I went to them. While I was there, I went to see my friend, Old Nickus, the chief of the village. Old Nickus is a fine man, a great man. I came to him, and his wife fed me and I listened while he told me what was in his heart."

Big Oak laid his fishing pole down. He had only once met Old Nickus, but he knew that the Mohawk chief was one of the wiser sachems of the Longhouse.

" 'My father,' I said to the chief," Paul went on, " 'what will happen to the Longhouse if the Ganiengehaka attack the Oneida, like some of the young warriors have threatened?' His answer was that the young warriors talk much but that they would much rather attack the white settlers, because the rich white settlers have more to take, and because the white settlers will not know how to seek revenge. 'We will not support them if they attack our little brothers, and they know that.' That is what Old Nickus said."

"Then the sachems still dream of holding the Longhouse together?" Big Oak asked.

"But he also said this," Paul continued. " 'It is my fear that the Longhouse is falling apart. In the west those who once called themselves Ganonsyoni now live among Shawnees and Delawares and no longer honor the council, nor do they mourn that the council fire in Onondaga has gone out. They are for themselves only, not for the Longhouse. In the north, men who were once Mohawks mourn the passing of the French and worship Jesus nailed to the stake, like their fathers the French do. They say they are part of the seven nations, and call the Abnakis their brothers. They speak the same language as we, and yet they no longer honor the Longhouse.

" 'Is it any surprise that our own children go raiding where they want, no matter what harm they do to the Longhouse, and no longer honor the sachems? My heart is cold,' he told me. 'And yet I have hope. If the young ones do not make war on our brothers, then maybe the Longhouse will survive, after *this* war between white men is over. If that happens, then there is still hope.' "

Big Oak seized his pole, hooked a piece of salt pork and flung his line out into the pond. He puffed hard on his pipe, just in time to keep it lit. Paul had seated himself next to Jinja and found a tree trunk to prop his back against. His wife loved life in the village, among her family and friends. Otherwise he would have a place like Big Oak's, in the woods, away from strife between whites and Indians, and whites and whites, and Indians and Indians.

He released an angry cloud of smoke, and the cool autumn wind carried it past his face, into the woods. If he were to do such a thing, how long could he last? Until some white man made an animal skin with a mark scratched by some drunken Mohican? Or he could ask Big Oak for a corner of his land that he and his family could dwell upon while the red man faded from New York. No, that was too much, to beg for a little piece of his people's land from the race that had stolen it from them. He did not hate Big Oak. Big Oak was his friend. Big Oak would give him anything.

But Big Oak was a fake. He was not Big Oak of the Seneca nation, hadn't really been Big Oak for years. He was Sam Watley. When the red man was forgotten in New York, the Indian strain in the Watley descendants, whether Seneca or Tuscarora, would also be forgotten.

Paul had known whites all his life. He had taken a white name. He had taken a white job. He had taken a white God. But he had never taken a white skin. And may God have mercy on my son James, he thought, because I have tried to raise up a white son. He had failed, of course.

"Big Oak," he said. "Look across this land, this land of yours, once the land of the Longhouse."

"And before that it was the land of the Mohicans, and way before that, who knows whose moccasins trod its forests?" Big Oak interjected.

"Still, it was once the land of the Mohawks, at a time when all the Ganonsyoni were honored by all other Ganonsyoni."

"It is a beautiful land."

"This is your pond, my brother, but it is full of my tears. I am a fool to live in a land that holds so much sadness, but I cannot leave it. I am bound to it. When the war is over, what will happen to my people?"

"If the rebels are victorious, your people will be victorious."

"But—"

"But after a while the whites will forget and take your land from you, just as your people took from your cousins the Wendot, and the Tionantot, and the People of the Panther. My brother, I wish that the Mohawks and the Oneidas could be my neighbors forever, but it is not to be. The thought that they will soon be gone puts tears in my heart, and yet I must live."

"Easy for you, you are a white man."

"Hard for you, and yet you must. It is *your* children that matter, not the children of the other lodges in the Longhouse."

"The Longhouse *does* matter," Paul insisted.

"Tell me, my brother, would you trade your rifle for stone-headed arrows?"

"I would not."

"Would you trade your iron kettles for baskets heated by hot stones?"

"Never."

"This wool blanket you wear, would you trade it for a stiff old bearskin?"

"No one with sense would make such a trade."

"And yet these are white things. Why, my brother, will the Ganonsyoni not send a young boy to Albany to learn to be a gunsmith so you would not need a white man to repair your rifles?"

"Our boys would not learn such a trade."

"And yet someone must, for you have learned what a curse it is to depend on the white man."

"Our children do not desire a shed to work inside all the time, taking rifles apart, putting them together, taking them apart, putting them——"

"The white man believes a man must work," Big Oak explained. "And he must often do things he does not want to do."

"Indians believe they should do things they do want to do." Paul smiled. "It is what free men do."

"Cansadeyo, will you be an Indian or a white man?"

"You ask me to make a choice that I do not have, my brother." They sat by the pond, silent now, Big Oak wishing that he knew the answer to Paul's problem, and Paul, knowing there were no answers, wishing he had a jug so he would not have to think at all.

James had had more than enough fighting for a while. The day after his cold reception from Katherine, he had walked down to the warehouse and told Thad that a few Caughnawagas he knew had some prime pelts they had somehow secured from the Crees in northern Quebec. Re-

trieving those pelts from the Caughnawagas meant a journey up the Hudson to Canada via Lake George and Lake
Champlain. It was a grueling trip involving a couple of long
portages, and involved quantities of rum. Rum was a powerful force in James's trade. He did not have the scruples
about it that Big Oak had. Almost no traders did, but James
certainly did not, because he thought of rum as good, not
bad. He did not crave it every day of his life, and therefore
did not misuse it as badly as others, but he thought it was
the most wonderful stuff ever created. The Caughnawagas
loved it. They were used to brandy, which was potent but
did not get them as drunk as quickly as the darling water of
the English.

Thad had agreed to the trip. Within a few weeks James
and Ooghnor had begun their journey, and now they were
on their way home.

They had a big canoeload of prime furs coursing along
the western shore of the Hudson. James felt wonderfully at
ease, for he had not seen a single hostile soul during the
entire journey to and from Caughnawaga. It was just the
right time to be on the river. The green hemlocks formed a
perfect complement to the oranges of the maples, the yellows of the birches, and the reds of the oaks. The geese
were flying too, in slow, graceful strokes, their necks
stretched straight out in a southward vee.

Fall should have been a time of caution or fear for the
Indians. Have they laid by enough corn to last the winter?
Have they dried enough meat? Have they enough ammunition for the winter hunt? Are their homes sheathed tight
against the north winds that would soon be howling
through their valleys? How about their bearskins and wool
blankets?

James was like most of the young men. His thoughts
were on happier things. Mainly, his thoughts were on
Anne. He had not seen her since Jinja had come home,
mostly because of this trip. Now that Jinja was home, and
safe, he felt that the time had come to call again. He was

certain that her grandfather, his boss, would be generous with him when he saw what he and Ooghnor had brought with them back to Albany.

There was very little money in Albany, and most of that was continental paper and therefore worthless. So Dieter kept a running tab on his employees, which was, in a sense, an internal barter system. He thought he drove a fairly hard bargain with them, but they thought he was pretty generous compared to the rotten traders they were used to dealing with. Neither Dieter nor his employees made known their satisfaction, so no one thought they were giving away too much and everybody was happy.

Ooghnor was perched in the bow of the canoe. He was the first one to spot the town through the autumn haze. The early afternoon sunshine slanted down on the roofs of the houses of the town. Ahead was the dock and the big Wendel and Watley warehouse. With the end of their journey in sight, Ooghnor and James eased up on their paddling routine. James dipped his paddle to starboard and let the current and their momentum take them down to the dock. By the time they closed in on the dock, they were in a slow, comfortable drift. One quick stroke by Ooghnor brought the canoe parallel to the dock, where the Caughnawaga Gilles was waiting to secure the canoe fore and aft.

He had brought a wagon out to the dock, and the three of them began to pile furs on it. Ooghnor and James had been very careful with the way they packed the skins, which had weathered the trip in fine shape. Having emptied the canoe of its cargo, they lifted the canoe out of the water and left it on the dock. Then the three of them pulled the wagon up the path to the warehouse through the large, double front doors, past quantities of hoes, shovels, kettles, lead bars, blankets, woolen apparel, boots and shoes, nails, hatchets, knives, construction tools and supplies, lengths of fabric, and other goods for trade both red and white, frontier and town. The furs were stored in a special area on shelves raised well above the floor, and it was here that they found Dieter, walking around with a ledger under his arm, looking at some of his rougher fur stock.

"Wait till you see these skins, Dieter," James said, smiling. "These are special. Soft, beautiful color. And we got a lot for the goods we had. Look."

Dieter reached for a few skins and brought them away from the shelves. The men walked toward the front doors and the sunlight for a better look.

"You had a good journey?" the old Dutchman asked, without interest.

"Good journey," said Ooghnor.

"Some Caughnawagas nearly skinned us, but we talked them into giving us these skins instead. They saw your goods and thought they were the best they'd ever seen, then thought it might be nice to see how tough Ganonsyoni are these days. When it looked like we might have to be tough against about a dozen of them, we told them that if they ever wanted to see goods this good again they—"

"It is good you are back. I will put you down on the books as usual, yah?"

James looked carefully at Dieter. "These are mighty good pelts," he said. "I've never seen any like them in this warehouse."

"Good pelts, yah, we do a little better for you then," he said, and made some marks in his book that were Greek to Ooghnor but looked satisfactory to the more learned James. "I am very busy now. You tell me when you are ready to go out again. Anudder time." He dismissed them by turning his back on them and walking back through the doors into the warehouse. The two Caughnawagas and the young Oneida trader looked at each other, puzzled. Dieter was usually careful with Indian sensibilities. When a trading mission returned, he would compliment the men on their trip, point out one or two items they had acquired that particularly delighted him, and hand them a little off-the-books hard cash to spend at the Musket and Arrow Tavern on a good meal and a little rum. Both Ooghnor and James had gotten to the point where they enjoyed the well-prepared food as much as the rum, and they were disappointed that the old man had not opened his little cash drawer for them. Never mind, James thought, he had intended to pay Anne a visit on this night anyway. Her mother and father always invited him to stay for dinner.

So he said good-bye to his Caughnawaga associates, slung his rifle and blanket over his shoulder, and headed toward the big house near the store.

The weather around Albany had been dry for some time. Consequently, every step raised its own cloud of dust as James made his way from the waterfront to the neat row of houses on the street where Thad had first met Katherine more than twenty years before. James was looking forward to seeing not only Anne, but also her brother, whom he had not seen since Jinja returned half dead from the battle in the Wyoming Valley. He was anxious to swap war stories with Jinja, not so much for the fun of it, but to gain a sense of just what was happening in the war. James wanted the war to be over so he could pursue his profession without having to risk his life every day he was on the trail. This last trip up to Canada had gone so well, he had the feeling, as his moccasins settled at the door of the Watleys, that his life was heading in the right direction.

He gave the door two sharp, confident raps and waited with a rare smile for the door to open. After a minute or so he knocked again, just as hard. This time he paced back and forth a time or two. Again there was no answer. He waited awhile longer. He was afraid to knock again, thinking that whoever was inside making his or her way to the door eternally slowly would be angry with him for his impatience. If he was going to live in a white world, he would have to master the subtleties of white behavior.

He knocked a third time. Was nobody at home? They had a house servant. Surely she would be answering the door. The Watleys did not stand on ceremony. If their servant was busy, any one of them might take it upon themselves to open the front door and welcome a guest. Was it possible they knew who it was and did not want to see him? They weren't too friendly to him the last time he had come by. But no, last time they had been worried about Jinja.

He pulled his fist back to knock a fourth time when the door swung open. It was Anne. James stood there, not knowing what to say, and almost moaned with relief when she took his hand and led him in. "I'm so glad to see you," she said. "I was worried because Father said you had been gone so long."

There was nobody in the big foyer, but he could hear conversation out back in the courtyard. He was hoping that Anne would take him to the sitting room so the two of them could be alone. Instead she led him to the courtyard, where her parents were entertaining guests.

A large table stood under an awning surrounded by small trees that were molting their red and yellow leaves. A swirling breeze in the courtyard was blowing the leaves around in circles, but the day was mild. There were nearly a dozen people at the table, drinking wine and eating fruits and nuts. Most of them stopped eating and stared when they saw who, or what, Anne had in tow.

One of the guests was wearing a blue Continental Army uniform with light blue facings and high rank insignia on his shoulders, though James did not quite know how high. Thad, sitting next to this major or colonel, sized up the situation and stepped forward to meet James.

"Colonel Denniston," Thad said. "This is James Derontyan. He works for us, and we have been waiting for him to come back from a trading voyage to Canada." He looked at James. "It went well?"

James did not trust his voice. He nodded.

"James is an Oneida. He knows your part of New York. If we could spare him, you would do well to hire him on as a scout for next spring."

James saw the man scowl at Thad, as if Thad had said too

much. Thad caught the scowl too, but he was not about to
let it pass unchallenged.

"Colonel, I wouldn't worry about James. The Oneidas
have sided openly with us for more than a year. They've
been more loyal than a lot of colonials you and I could
both name. Tell me, James," Thad added, turning away
from his uniformed guests, "how do you feel about the
Mohawks these days?"

James was ready to head for the house, Anne or no Anne.
This flabby, puffed-up colonel wouldn't last a minute alone
in a room with him, and yet he felt too intimidated to open
his mouth. But when he saw the familiar, suspicious,
"What's he hiding?" look in the colonel's eyes, his voice
came out strong and clear. "The Mohawks are our brothers," he said. "But they are very stubborn. They are fighting
on the wrong side, and they will someday regret their
choice."

Thad smiled. "They say the Mohawks are terrifying
fighters. What do you think, James?"

James shrugged. "I say the Oneidas are terrifying fighters.
Let the Mohawks fear us. We do not fear their idle threats."

"Have they threatened you?" The questioner wore civilian clothes, but James did not know him. James knew very
few Albany civilians.

"They have threatened to attack our villages," James replied.

"I think we should tell him," Thad said.

"I don't—" the colonel began, but Thad cut him off. "I
have trusted this man and his father with the goods of this
company for years, and they have never failed to be honest
and faithful employees. James, next spring there's going to
be a big expedition against the Mohawks and the others
who are supporting the king."

"Better be very big," James answered.

"Big," Thad repeated with a knowing look. "I would sure
hate to lose you, but they need some good Indian scouts.
Would you hire on?"

James thought silently, for just a moment. Scouting for arrogant white rebel officers was not his choice for military action, but it occurred to him that he might be in a position to keep these fools from attacking the wrong people. Like his people.

"I'd sign right now," he answered. He saw a tall figure rise from the end of the table and walk toward him with a big grin on his face.

"Me too," said the tall man, and only when he spoke did James realize it was Jinja, returned from his sojourn at Big Oak Pond, but still looking gaunt. "You and me, James, in the woods like when I was a boy and we used to hunt together."

Thad laughed. "See, Colonel, it so happens I'd trust him with my only son too." The colonel nodded politely.

At this point Anne took his hand again. "If you will excuse us," she said. "I believe that James came to see me." The look she caught in his eyes told her that she was correct. She began to lead him back into the house when a voice from the courtyard stopped her in her tracks.

"Just a minute!" It was not an angry voice, but urgent, nevertheless. It was Katherine, and she was insisting that James join them at the table. Anne was not fooled.

"Mother, these are your friends. James is my friend. Let me have him."

Katherine rose from the table and walked toward them. Out of earshot of the other guests, Katherine did not seem to care whether or not James heard what she was about to say.

"I would like you to go inside now, Anne," she said. "The colonel doubtless would like to talk to James."

"Then I will have him after the colonel is through with him," Anne replied, without disguising the anger in her voice.

Katherine seemed on the verge of disputing the issue with her, but apparently changed her mind. "You may have him—for a few moments—when the colonel is through with him," Katherine told Anne.

Katherine had always been kind to James, but there was no kindness in her voice now. He found himself disliking her for the first time. Who did she think she was? The blood of the Longhouse flowed strong through the veins of her husband and through the veins of her two children.

"Won't you sit down, James?" Katherine said.

The colonel was sitting at the end of one of the tables. Katherine gestured to an empty chair on his left.

"Would you like a glass of wine, James?" Thad asked.

Katherine threw a quick glance at Thad. "Are you sure that—"

Thad gave a snort and poured a glass of wine for James. "I've seen your—" He stopped himself just before he was about to deliver a lecture on her father's tippling, which always grew extreme right around Christmas, when the days were short, business was quiet, and Dieter always wondered if he'd be a pauper before spring. Thad then poured a glass for himself and resumed his seat across from James, which put him to the colonel's right.

The colonel drained his glass and Thad poured him another. "Let me understand, Thad. This 'John,' here—"

"It's 'James,'" prompted Thad. Both Thad and James knew that to some whites all Indians were named John. "And you can ask him the questions. His English is as good as most." He meant most white men, but the colonel assumed he meant most Indians, so he spoke slowly, distinctly, as if he were speaking to an idiot.

"You know land south of Mohawk River?" he asked.

"That, and the lakes too."

"What about the Mohawks?" The question wasn't clear and drew a puzzled look from James, but the colonel assumed it was James's Indian stupidity that made for the confusion. "The Mohawks, man, the Mohawks."

Thad stifled a snicker. "He means will you fight the

Mohawks if it becomes necessary . . . I guess," he added in a low tone.

"I know my job," James replied. "I will do my job."

"If he says he'll do his job, you can count on him," Thad added. Katherine's face showed her displeasure. She respected rank considerably more than Thad, or James, or Big Oak or Jinja, for that matter. Maybe it was the effects of the wine, but the colonel seemed satisfied by the responses he was receiving from Thad and James. He grew a bit friendlier and more expansive.

"I have been corresponding with General Washington," he said, puffing up. "And General Sullivan. We have been planning the expedition for next spring. It is very important to General Washington. He wants to know when will the rivers be low enough to ford, and when will the grass be high enough for the packhorses. How many men? What routes will they travel? How much artillery? It is as if he were leading it himself. I am sure that he will be keeping a close eye on it. It is very important that we wipe out the settlements," he said. Both Thad and James were well aware that he meant not only loyalist settlements, but Iroquois villages.

James knew that he was addressing rank, but he could not keep silent. "And what about Oneida villages?" he asked.

"The Oneida are our allies," the colonel answered.

"And the Tuscaroras?" The questioner was Thad, thinking of his father's wife's people.

"What about the Tuscaroras?"

"They are our allies too," Thad said.

"Yes," the colonel remembered. "But as for the Mohawks, and the Onondagas, and the Senecas—we will drive them out of New York." His face grew dark as he spoke, his eyes fastened on James. Thad stifled a laugh. "He's one of *us*, Colonel," he said. James gave Thad a grateful look. "One of us" sounded much better than "one of ours." This stout man in the blue uniform made him uncomfortable. There were few white men James trusted, but this one was worse than most. James would see to it that he never found himself in this man's camp, or for that matter, on his battlefield, if he could help it. It was going to be a very complicated campaign.

"James!"

He turned around in time to see Anne stamping her foot by the back door to the house. "If you will excuse me," he said, making a bow that fairly stunned the colonel.

The colonel nodded, and the corners of Thad's mouth twitched. James took in all the reactions around the table, and he did not miss the look of annoyance on the face of Katherine as she rose from her chair and prepared to follow him to the house.

❧15❧

THIS WAS NOT THE WAY HE WANTED TO BE with Anne. He was having enough problems dealing with the war and his place in the Longhouse without having to romance Anne in the presence of her angry mother. What was she so angry about? What had he done?

James found himself sitting in a straight-back chair about six feet from Anne, who was seated in a similar chair. In a more comfortable chair between them sat Katherine, hands clasped on her lap. For a few moments James stared at Anne, with her wavy yellow hair, her tiny nose, and her clear complexion. She was the most beautiful thing he had ever seen, and he did not understand why he felt that way. He certainly was not trying to be a white man. Or was he? He was a Christian, he could read and write and speak English. He had long ago shed his earrings and let his hair grow in.

And yet, he kept telling himself, he was a warrior of the Longhouse, and he would prove it when the time came for him to fight Mohawks.

Anne stared at her mother for a minute, as if she could drive her out of the room with her eyes. But her mother only glowered back. Anne now looked at James, rolled her eyes in exasperation and smiled. Like her mother, she had her hands folded on her lap. James did the same, in mimicry. Anne got it. She chuckled. Her mother did not, and James observed that Katherine's mouth had acquired a mean look over the years.

Finally James spoke. "Your father has not yet looked at the furs we just brought in. They are the finest I have ever seen."

"My father says you are very good at getting good value for your trade goods."

"I know the men I am dealing with," he said simply. "I . . . thought of you much on the way home."

The scowl on Katherine's face deepened, but Anne giggled. "Only on the way home? Who were you thinking about on the way to Canada?"

"Me, mostly. There could still be war in the northern woods. Life is good. I want to keep mine, so I look much and think little. I brought something back for you," he said.

The sudden switch in topic from gloom to gifts delighted her. From his pack he took the prettiest beadworked pouch either of them had ever seen. He stood up and brought it to her. She reached for it, and as she took hold of it, their fingers touched just long enough for both of them to know the other's feelings. If Katherine noticed, she did not let on.

Anne studied the pouch and almost grew dizzy. A gift from the handsomest young man she knew. She was at an age when girls became serious objects of affection, and yet she had had few suitors because so many young men in her class were either Tories or had marched off to fight in the war. They looked at each other in a way that Katherine could not miss, or even pretend to miss.

"Anne, my darling," she said. "I must talk to James, could you help Lucy tend to the guests?"

Anne did not object. She was feeling too giddy. The last few moments would be enough to keep her going for many nights. She floated out the door and left James staring benignly at Katherine, who was actually wringing her hands.

"James," she said, "Thad and I have always been good to you. You have been our guest so many times. You and Jinja have hunted together. You have been treated more than fairly in business by Thad and my father. I want to know where you have picked up the notion that you can marry into this family?"

There it was, in hurtful, unminced words. Here, James called on memories of his father bearing a thousand indignities at the hands of lesser white men, and yet somehow managing to preserve his own sense of pride. There would be no arguing, no quarrel with him asserting his fitness and her assailing his presumption.

He was still standing. Solemnly, he walked over to Katherine and looked down at her, serenely. She flinched ever so slightly, but he ignored the reaction. "I have known you since I was a little child," he said, and then nothing more. He turned around and walked out the door.

Katherine knew what he meant. She had disappointed him. She had betrayed him. He had expected more human decency from her.

She had lived too long with Thad and been friends too long with Cilla not to know how easily bruised were the feelings of an Indian. She noticed how straight his back was as he let himself out of the house and closed the door behind him.

Times were changing fast, she knew. The Indian was going, only he didn't know it. As she watched James leave, it seemed she was watching the last Iroquois warrior duck out the door of his stinking, smoking, crumbling longhouse for the last time. On the walls of the sitting room were individual paintings of each member of the family. She studied the dark features of her husband and her son, then looked at the picture of her daughter. Anne's hair was blond, as hers had been the day Thad had waved good-bye to her on the trail to Lake George more than twenty years before. But in the corners of Anne's eyes, and the corners of her mouth, dwelt an Indianness that Katherine could not deny. But her daughter would not grow up to be an Indian, nor would her son.

One Indian in this family was enough, she thought, and she meant every word.

These years, winter made Big Oak's bones ache. The only way he knew to feel better was to get his blood up, and the only way to do that was to get out in the woods. So he and his rifle snowshoed their way over the east trail, toward the Hudson River valley in search of deer or bear. Not that he expected to get within a mile of any animal, what with his three boys cavorting through the woods like a pack of hungry pups.

The snow was coming down silently, windlessly, sending the boys into noisy high spirits. He told the boys to hush because he'd come across some deer sign and there was a chance he might bring one down if only they'd act quiet like real Ganonsyoni.

The sign was fresh. His senses warmed to the chase and he could feel them closing in on the deer as surely as if he had one in his rifle sights. Deer had been scarce this year. Ice fishing on the pond and eggs from Cilla's hens had been their main winter source of fresh food. A deer would have Cilla dancing. She had said she wouldn't dump another chunk of salt pork into the pot no matter how hungry her men got.

It turned out to be a short chase with a young buck on the end of it. Ken saw the deer first and proudly pointed it out to his father. Big Oak put his sights on the animal and downed it with one clear shot. In half a minute's time he was standing over it, field dressing it, as steam rose from the deer's abdominal cavity.

He butchered the deer into several large portions, wrapped them in skins or blankets, and divided them among himself and the boys. As they were about to head for home, a shout from the east reached their ears and froze them. Big Oak spotted some movement through the trees, dropped his load of deer meat and faded behind a tree. His boys did likewise.

"Big Oak!" This time the voice was clear, conveying not only the message, but the messenger. Big Oak's eyes may not have been quite what they had been, but his ears were still keen, and he recognized the sound of an old friend, John Jamison, formerly of Rogers's Rangers.

He stepped into the opening, wondering if Jamison was still loyal to the king. Big Oak had kept a low profile throughout the hostilities. His smuggling and scouting activities were discreet. Dwelling as he did in the fastness of the forests well north of Albany, he had no idea whether his politics were known to the outside world. If so, this encounter was bound to be uncomfortable. Big Oak checked the priming of his rifle and slid his right hand into firing position, thumb on the hammer, forefinger on the trigger.

He need not have worried. Jamison was wearing the woods garb of the ranger, but his two companions wore ragged remnants of continental blue uniforms.

"Sam, you old catamount!" Jamison shouted, even though he and his men were within twenty feet of Big Oak and his boys.

"Hello, John," Big Oak said, extending his hand. They slapped each other on the back so hard that it knocked the snow off each other's deerskin jackets. Sam looked at John through the falling snowflakes and his eyes narrowed. "Why do I have this feeling that you are not here by chance?" he asked.

Jamison did not smile, at least not outwardly. "Because you know me, and you know I don't do things by accident. I do not have to ask you whose side you have chosen." It was a question spoken in the guise of a statement.

Big Oak laughed into the big man's face. "You don't, but you oughtn't be so smug. It wasn't such an easy decision. On one side the king's mincing minions, looking down their long noses on anybody without a coat of arms on their wall. On the other hand, Washington's greedy rebels, longing to get their hands on Iroquois land and kick the

Ganonsyoni clear out to Michilimackinack if they get the chance. I tell you, John, it was no easy matter. Most of me wanted to sit the whole war out, warmin' my bones by the fire with my woman."

"With your—the devil you—you mean these are yours?" he asked, seemingly noticing the three boys for the first time.

"Best bunch of boys a father could ever hope for."

"Look too dark to be on our side of the blanket," Jamison replied good-naturedly, though his face still refused to smile.

"No darker than my first get, and you liked him well enough," Big Oak said, scowling.

"Well," Jamison smiled, finally, "you've got your own ways, and you're the best man I ever knew. That's why I need you. Need you bad. This is the summer we're gonna kick the Tories clear across the Saint Lawrence, and with God's grace, we won't stop there. But we need the best scouts we can get so there won't be any surprises. What kinda Indian is your woman?"

"Tuscarora, John."

"Fine, then. That's just fine, Sam. What about it?"

Big Oak had picked up his deer meat and begun his trek westward. The boys followed, and so did Jamison's two young continental soldiers. "I don't think so, John. Look at me. I can barely straighten my back in the morning. My knees hurt every night. My eyes couldn't even make you out when you first hollered. I'm not surprised that it finally happened, John. I've become an old man and there's no denyin' it."

"None of us is all that young anymore, old friend," Jamison answered. Only then did Big Oak notice that Jamison was heavier than he had remembered, and that the walk up the trail was making him gasp for breath. Big Oak slowed his pace and Jamison was grateful. "But there's gonna be a powerful push this spring and summer, and I can't believe you'd want to miss out on the fun."

Big Oak had been thinking that he would love to miss
out on the last battles of the struggle for New York. He had
fought too many battles for New York, and nothing ever
seemed to change except that whoever won, the Indians
wound up with less land and the whites wound up with
more. He did not have a strong sense of injustice about
that. It was the way of the world, and if the Iroquois were
getting a raw deal, well, a century or so before, the Iroquois
had given the Lenni Lenape a raw deal. But he did regret
the passing of the red man in his part of the world, because
he liked his Iroquois brothers. He liked their way of life,
and he liked what was in their hearts. His skills were red
man skills: woodland skills, hunting skills, trapping skills.
Of what use would all his hard-won skills be when the plow
had replaced the forest?

And yet he felt a duty to help his friend Jamison, and his
country. But he would do it his own way, on his own time.

He knew how to handle Jamison. Big Oak and his boys
snowshoed a fine path through the forest for the three
soldiers to follow in their boots, and finally, at the top of
the next hill, in the twilight of the short day, Big Oak could
see the glow of the hearth fire burning in the windows of
his log house.

"There she is, John. It's my home, and you are the highest ranking gentlemen to ever set foot inside it, if you will
accept our hospitality."

Jamison peered through the tumbling snowflakes at the
smoke rising from the chimney. "We could spend the night
here and go back to the ship tomorrow."

"I wouldn't accept any other answer," Big Oak responded
heartily. "Come on, you must meet the best wife a man ever
bedded on a cold winter night."

Big Oak and the boys stopped by the stairs below the
porch, removed their snowshoes, climbed the steps and
leaned the snowshoes against the wall of the house. Jamison
and his two men followed them onto the porch. "I'm sorry I
forgot to introduce Sergeants Ames and Small."

"Pleased to meet the both of you," Big Oak said, shaking their hands. "Get ready for some of the best food you ever put away." He started to knock on the door, but Cilla, who had heard them coming when they were still half a mile away, was already opening it. Big Oak laid his load of meat down by the fireplace and told the boys to leave their meat out on the porch, where it would quickly freeze. Then he swept Cilla into his arms, gave her a great big kiss, and began to make a speech. Meanwhile the three continentals had stripped off their gloves and walked over to the fireplace, where they stood absorbing the glorious warmth of the huge fire.

"You remember me talking to you about Captain Jamison, now, don't you?" he asked, and by the tone of his voice Cilla knew that the game was on. "Captain Jamison is now —what are you now, John?"

"Colonel," Jamison said laconically.

"Colonel Jamison he is now, and a rebel colonel to boot. And guess what he wants out of me?"

She shrugged her shoulders, because that is what her husband wanted her to do.

"He wants me to spy, and he wants me to scout, and he wants me to fight. Imagine, a man my age and he's—"

"No!" she cried out. She turned to Jamison and stuck her face out so far that her nose nearly touched Jamison's.

"He's an old man, my Semm Watley! You get your face outta this house or you change your words." She took a step forward, and Jamison took two steps back. "Enough battles. Enough scars all over his body. You tell him no, Semm!"

Big Oak had found a warm spot in front of the big fireplace, where he sat packing his pipe with tobacco. "I think you already told him, Cilla," he said, smiling.

"And I tell him more, you see." She walked over to the table, picked up a huge kettle and strode angrily toward the fireplace. For a moment Jamison thought the woman was about to break his skull with the thing, but she continued on out the front door. She came back in more slowly, struggling with a kettle full of snow, which she hung over the fire. Then she started tossing pieces of deer into the kettle —meat, organs, bones, more meat—at first the pieces merely sank into the snow, but soon the fire had turned the snow to liquid. Before long the smell of boiling meat had begun to color the room. Now she flung dried vegetables into the kettle, and some herbs, onions, and dried mushrooms, and finally a small piece of salt pork, just for the flavoring. She swung the kettle away from the fire to lower the heat to a simmer, and left it there.

She looked hard at the gaunt, hungry faces of the two sergeants and the round, hungry face of Colonel Jamison. "Hah, you'll be lucky if I let you have any of that food, then you'll remember my Semm is not your soldier but my husband."

Jamison puffed his cheeks up in exasperation and let the breath blow out his mouth.

"You *better* blow out your face," she said. She looked at Big Oak. "Your friend here is a smart man," she said. "Keep his big fat face shut 'cause he knows who's the boss, right?"

Big Oak blew a cloud of smoke and offered his tobacco pouch to Jamison and his men. All of them reached for their pipes. The fire was so big that it warmed most of the room. All the men felt their eyelids closing down as their bodies took in the warmth of the fireplace. Even the boys were drowsing. Only Cilla was still in motion as she did her domestic chores, all the while shooting vicious looks in the direction of Colonel Jamison, who would, if he could, take her husband away from her.

⊰16⊱

YESTERDAY HAD DAWNED WITH A BITTER cool edge to it, but this early summer afternoon, the sweat flowed freely as the troops trudged north into the Wyoming Valley. The horses of the officers were prancing nervously. Did they sense the mayhem that had overtaken the valley the previous year, or did they feel the tension of the men around them?

There were more than two thousand men in this army. They were a bold force who believed that their numbers could overwhelm the puny groups the Tories and Iroquois could put in the field against them. But the ghastly emptiness of the valley chilled them. Tall grass was growing among the ashes of burned cornfields. Fence lines and tree rows that should have led to houses led instead to black and gray ash heaps with stark black timbers lying in rows like charred bones. The hundreds of people that had settled this valley and turned it into a gorgeous garden had fled—if they had survived.

Up ahead were Big Oak, James, and Jinja, who along with other scouts were prowling along the front and flanks of General Sullivan's army, looking to flush out skulking brothers of the Longhouse. Jamison had agreed to allow Big Oak and his men to act independently, reporting only to him. Some of the other officers resented the arrangement, but Big Oak won their respect soon enough.

James and Big Oak cast anxious glances at Jinja. They knew they were close to the site of the great battle, and they were wondering what effect it would have on Jinja when they arrived at the battle site.

And then they were there, walking through the tall grass.

"Here is where we stood and watched them burning the fort," Jinja observed. "We thought we had them that day. Who would have believed they'd burn down a fort just to make us believe they were retreating? And we bit. Like a big ol' bass, we bit."

He pointed off to his left. "There is where they came from," he said to James and Big Oak. "And you know what scared me? It wasn't seein' them Mohawks. I've seen Mohawks before."

"You played with them when you were a whelp," Big Oak reminded him.

"No, it wasn't the Mohawks. It was seein' our boys runnin'. They turned their backs to them and started climbin' all over each other tryin' to get away. I could smell the fear in them. Lord, they were the boys I had to depend on for my own life. And suddenly I got so scared I knew that I had to start runnin' sooner and get there faster or I'd be the only one left. What was I gonna do, face five hundred Mohawks and Senecas by myself? 'Course I ran."

"I've run away from a fight or two myself, Jinja," Big Oak said. "And so has James. I wouldn't fret too much over it. Fact is, me and your father was afraid you wouldn't run when you should. That's why we didn't want you goin' out with no militia."

They spread out and walked northward, their eyes on the tree lines ahead and to the right, and the bare slope on the left. There was no evidence that anybody had visited this part of the valley in months. It had been a dry spring. The tall grass was already burned brown.

They walked among the ruins of what had been a pair of

prosperous Yankee homesteads. Now there was not one stick of wood left standing on another. Only the stone chimneys stood, like crippled craggy old men. There were no signs left there either of a fight or of bodies. "I believe you'll find this is pretty much the way the whole valley looks," Big Oak said, studying the horizon. "Let's go back and report to Jamison."

Quietly, eyes and ears ever on the alert, they retraced their steps down the valley to the battlefield. By the time they arrived there, members of the lead company were walking around the field, studying the ground, kicking at the tall brown grass. One of them grunted, reached down and picked up a skull, the top of which had been smashed.

Others were picking up bones and pieces of bones, some stray bits of clothing, and an occasional bullet pouch or canteen. There were no rifles to be seen, or boots or moccasins. But one private stumbled and nearly fell as he tripped over a heavy object of some sort. He reached down and lifted a huge Mohawk war club. The end of the club was stained with blood, and the stem of the club was cracked.

"What did you find, Watley?" The questioner was Colonel Jamison.

"Sir, this valley is empty. Should we go north, we will have our fill of them, that I'll wager."

"Look at this, Colonel," hollered a young private standing about a hundred yards to the rear. The colonel walked over to the private, by the tree line at the edge of the field. Big Oak, Jinja, and James followed. The remains of five bodies lay in a tangle, picked clean by the wolves and vultures. Near them were the remains of more men, all lying facedown, where their bodies had been allowed to settle after they'd been stripped of their equipment, their clothes, and their scalps.

The colonel looked around him and saw the bones of other men lying across tree roots, or in gullies, or in the tall grass. "Poor devils," he said. "Poor cowardly devils. They were all running away, tripping all over each other. The Indians must have had a regular party taking these boys like they were so many goats. If only they'd had more spine."

Jinja could not tell one stripped skeleton from another, but he knew that some of these remains belonged to men he knew.

"Colonel, if I may say something." Big Oak looked at Jinja as if to silence him, but it was too late.

"What is it, son?" Jamison said evenly.

"Sir, I wouldn't judge these boys. You wasn't there. You don't know what went on here."

Jamison's eyes narrowed. "You were here, Watley?"

"Right here," Jinja said, pointing to a moccasin print. "That mighta been my footprint, outrunnin' the rest of 'em."

"Uh-huh, and just what were you runnin' from?"

"The Mohawks 'n' Senecas had turned our flank about there," he said, pointing to a small hill to the right.

"Why didn't they stand and fight?"

"I guess the Mohawks killed the officers real quick, and these boys hadn't fought much before, and when you see a bunch of men runnin', you figure you better start runnin' too or you'll be the only one left against five hundred Ganonsyoni."

"And you ran."

"Fast as I could," Jinja answered.

Big Oak guffawed sympathetically. "Colonel, I think you ought to let it alone, don't you think? We've all done a bit of runnin' somewhere in our lives, haven't we?"

"Not me," Jamison snorted. "I'm not the runnin' kind."

"Long as you've lived, I'm sure that sometimes in your life the urge has come over you to disappear."

"An army survives by staying together and supporting each other."

"Sure, Colonel. And sometimes it survives by retreating and finding themselves another place to go."

The colonel scowled and was about to turn on his heel and walk away when a faded old memory struck him and made him smile. "My first battle, I was seventeen, you never saw a boy run so far so fast. I guess anybody is entitled to run—once." he thought about that, and smiled again. "Maybe twice."

The army camped in the valley and waited for General Sullivan and the rest of the troops to come up and join them. The scouts reported no enemy in the immediate area, and Jamison was satisfied that this was so. Day after day soldiers were trickling in, in units small and large, sometimes in tens and sometimes in hundreds, sometimes overland and sometimes down the Susquehanna via canoe. Equally important, Big Oak noticed, were the supplies: food, ammunition, shoes and clothes. Somebody in this army knew his job, that was for sure. And then one day an artillery battalion moved in, complete with horses, wagons, ammunition, and cannons, and men who knew how to work them. There was a Major Stevens commanding the battalion. The day after they arrived, he picked out a hill and began to use it as a target zone for his cannoneers.

The soldiers in camp complained that they couldn't get any sleep with those blasted cannon firing every morning, but Major Stevens insisted that artillery might well mean the difference against the Indians. Big Oak had seen Indians react to cannon. He agreed with the major.

Colonel Jamison kept a clean, orderly camp and had the horses watered downstream. Consequently, it was a healthy, fairly happy camp, as Sullivan's army prepared for what had been planned as a spring campaign but now was scheduled for the summer. When the sun disappeared behind the western hills, and the soldiers gathered around a hundred campfires, the talk sometimes grew morbid. When they weren't out scouting for security, Jinja and James would drop in on one of the campfires and listen.

"What went on last year," said a short wiry private, "down in this valley, was bloody murder. Tell you what I heard. That the bloody Mohawks would shut a family up in their home and set it ablaze and dance around the fire while little children inside got all burned up."

"You know who it was? It was that damned Joseph Brant, is who it was," a stout soldier in clothes that were barely military added. "He's got a white name, but he's a Mohawk and he hates patriots. He's king through and through, and meaner'n even an Injun oughta be. Took an old man, they say, out of his house, dragged him out by his hair and tied him by his legs to two saplings that were all bent over, and then when they cut the saplings loose, one flew one way and one the other and near tore the old guy in half. They say when Brant heard him scream, he laughed like it was the funniest thing he'd ever heard."

"Tell you one thing," said a corporal who still had a mouthful of corn. "If I ever meet this Brant, I'll rip his eyes out with my bare hands."

"Hell, him and every other Mohawk too!" They were beginning to build up a head of passion on the subject.

"Damned Injuns!"

"Wait a minute," Jinja found himself saying. "We got Indians fighting on our side too."

"Well, I don't mean them, I mean—"

"Hell, I do," said the scrawny private. "I mean every damn lazy thievin' heathen redskin in New York, what do you think about that?" He shoved his knifelike nose toward Jinja and dared him to argue.

"Look at me," Jinja replied, taking a step toward the private, who was a head shorter and then some. "I got the blood of Seneca chiefs in me, you see?"

"I don't see." The private laughed. "You look like a dumb ol' Dutchman, if you ask me. And I got nothin' against dumb old Dutchmen." The rest of the men around the campfire laughed, and so did Jinja. That's what one of his grandfathers called his other grandfather. And he thought the same, sometimes, about old Dieter.

"Well, what about my friend James, here? He's Oneida, and he's a better man than any—"

"Aw, shut up, dumb ol' Dutchman. None of us is gonna harm ol' James, here. But as for his Mohawk friends . . ."

"They ain't my friends," James said from the shadows beyond the campfire.

"Friends, cousins, whatever they are, if I see a Mohawk, I'll roast him," said the corporal.

"Do what you please with the Mohawks, you just leave the Oneidas alone."

"Sure, sure," muttered the corporal, holding his hands up defensively. "Before I pull the trigger I'll say, 'Mr. Savage, which tribe do you come from?' And he'll say, 'Why, Mohawk, sir.' Then I'll say, 'Thank you, Mr. Mohawk,' and then I'll shoot him, if the hellion ain't shot me in the meantime. By the way, James, do you still worship rocks?"

"I'm a Congregationalist," James responded, refusing to be baited.

"That's what I thought," came the answer, and that put an end to the conversation, because nobody sitting around that campfire had the slightest notion what the corporal meant by that last remark.

At noon the following day the camp was suddenly in an uproar. A dozen canoes lashed together and paddled by only five men had found their way down the Susquehanna, into the camp, and the bosses of this convoy were none other than Thad and Paul. Among the cargo were a hundred and fifty brand new muskets and cartridges to go with them. All the soldiers in camp had experience with rifles and muskets, but many of them were not woods fighters experienced at measuring the right amount of powder out of a powder horn in the midst of a fight and squeezing off a shot.

Colonel Jamison was ecstatic. "Where did you get all this?" he asked as Gilles, Ooghnor, and a big old Frenchman named Henri brought up box after box of the cartridges. "Will they work with what we've got?"

"They'll work with most of your weapons, and as for

where we got it, I guess you might say that sometimes pirates are a general's best friend." Thad laughed.

"You mean privateers?"

"These characters were no American privateers. More like Spanish or Portuguese or I-don't-know-what. They took an English ship off New England and somehow made it up the Hudson with a cargo of guns and ammunition and rum. I expect they kept the rum. Hello, Pa."

Big Oak walked into the little knot of people above the riverbank and he and Thad gave each other a big hug.

"Who in—" said Jamison, but Thad interrupted.

"Where's Jinja?"

"He and James are up in those woods somewhere. The colonel here wants people out there all the time. Says he doesn't trust the Mohawks."

"I'd say the colonel has the right idea," Thad replied just as the colonel's face lit up.

"I knew I'd seen you before," he said. "You're the boy I tried to recruit for Colonel Rogers, my God, more than twenty years ago, it was. You didn't wanna go then, and I see you're still not wearin' a uniform."

"I remember you" Thad answered, unruffled. "I'm glad you wound up on the right side."

The colonel laughed. "Well, now that you're here, why don't you stick around and help us win the war? Gonna be a busy summer."

Thad looked around at the valley full of soldiers. He thought about his wild son. "I think I will come along," he said.

Thad was especially glad to stay when Gilles and Ooghnor told him they had heard there was going to be a big party. They had thought it might be a white man's version of the big feast Indians often arrange before they go off to war. But what it was, they were informed, was a celebration of the third anniversary of America's independence.

When Big Oak heard about it, he was surprised. He had known about the Declaration of Independence, but didn't think it would be a very big thing until they finally kicked the English off the continent. It hadn't really dawned on him that independence meant allegiance to a country. When you live on the frontier, you learn to rely on yourself and your friends, rather than your government. Big Oak had spent most of his years in the forests, far away from any government: Government politics was something he seldom thought about.

The valley had not been completely deserted by its former occupants. There were still some cattle roaming through the fields and woods. Former property of rebel and loyalist alike, they were now rounded up, butchered, and barbecued over huge fires. While the beef sizzled over the flames, a sort of a parade took place, not a very long one, but a colorful one featuring unit colors and new state flags, plus the stars and stripes, which Big Oak, Jinja, James, and Paul had never seen before. There was music too, a fife and drum marching band that played a few tunes Big Oak had heard from British bands, and a few that were strange to his ears. A platform was erected in the middle of a field and several hundred men gathered round to listen to the first Independence Day speech they had ever heard.

The speaker was General Sullivan, who looked tall and handsome in the finest uniform on the field that day.

He held up his hands for silence, and almost didn't get it. The men were hungry, but mostly they were thirsty, and they knew that a celebration like this meant more than a normal ration of rum. General Sullivan was understanding, and he was patient, but he was determined to deliver his speech, which he felt was an important way to start off the campaign.

He kept his hands raised. Some of the officers began walking among the soldiers urging them to silence, and gradually the men got it into their heads that the sooner they quieted down, the sooner they'd get to feast.

In the silence, those who were paying attention could feel a breeze blowing across the field. The noon sun was hot, but not unbearably so. Hungry and thirsty as they were, most of the men were ready to listen, to the point of telling the others to shut their mouths and let the general speak.

"Thank you," he began, sincerely, for he had not been sure that they would ever be quiet.

"We have been at war for four years now, and there is no end in sight. The big battles are going on in the south. Here in the north the noble art of war has reduced itself to the cowardly acts of massacre on our farmers and their wives and children." Here he swept his arm around the field, to take in the blackened patches of earth and timber that all knew existed beyond this wood or that mountain.

"This cowardly way of making war exists because less than two years ago the men of New York and New Jersey and New England beat the backsides of the British army bloody!" He delivered this statement with spirit, and his audience responded with applause, whistles, and a few war whoops.

"But it does exist. Throughout the northern part of New York the Mohawks and Senecas and Onondagas and Cayugas are burning our homes, murdering our families, trying to break us in a most craven fashion because they could not best us on the battlefield. Well, we're gonna put an end to that!"

"When?" came a voice from the crowd to the front.

"Damn soon!" he shouted. "In just a few weeks we will march west. We will find the villages of these miscreants, and wherever we do, we will leave nothing. We will burn their houses, burn their crops, kill their livestock, and when we are through, they will have nothing left in New York to remind them that they were once the mighty Iroquois.

"If their warriors are foolish enough to want to fight us, we will drive them from the field. They will disappear into the woods and we will not see them again this year. But— and here's the best news of all—what we begin, the winter will finish. Because when we are finished with them, they will not have their storehouses full of corn, and beans, and squash, and watermelons, and dried meat. They will have nothing but their old empty muskets and the clothes on their back. We will have destroyed the rest.

"Lest you underestimate the importance of this campaign, which General Washington and his staff planned very thoroughly—when we are through with our campaign, two months from now, the Iroquois menace will be gone from our lives. Forever!"

There was a great cheer. The men thought the speech was over, but they were just a bit premature.

"Last thing, gentlemen. When this war began, many of us had our doubts that we could win it. Just a bunch of poor Americans up against the finest army in the world. But we have seen that every year the English grow weaker. They are gone from New England. They are gone from most of New York. They've left the Indians and a few Tories to burn our homes. But this summer we're gonna drive them all away. Three armies stand ready to do that. Us, General Clinton to the north—"

"Clinton? Has he gone over to our side?" came a voice from the rear. The men laughed, and so did General Sullivan. "Not Sir Henry, my friend, but our own General James Clinton, a much better fighting man. And in the west there is another army, led by Colonel Brodhead. The Iroquois have never seen so many men fighting in New York under the flag of the United States. When they see forces like this, well-armed, well-supplied, Indians usually run, for they are intelligent fighters. But they are fighting for their lives. If they know that, let them attack. We shall smite them hip and thigh and clear them from our midst forever. What we are about to do, gentlemen, is the beginning of the end of the English in our country! Jamison, these men have been very patient. Let's celebrate."

Long boards had been set up on barrels or rocks for makeshift tables. There was an officer's table, a sort of dais, that actually had chairs, but the enlisted men had to make do with packs, rocks, planks, or whatever. Their drinking glasses were their canteens, and their plates were just about anything they could make serve. But when General Sullivan walked over to the nearest fire and with his sword carved a huge slice of beef, a thrill of anticipation went through the soldiers as they stood patiently in the several lines that formed around the barbecue pits.

"You'd have thought they hadn't eaten in weeks," Big Oak said to Thad.

"Well, you know, that hard bread they have to eat isn't really food, not really."

Big Oak laughed. "Jamison thinks you're too used to good livin'. Maybe he's right."

Thad smiled. "I intend to stay used to it," he said. "Do you blame me?"

Big Oak shook his head. "I don't believe the Lord ever put out a commandment that said, 'Thou shalt starve thyself on wormy food and not enough of it.'"

As the beef was dispensed, so was the rum, enough to please most of the soldiers, and enough to get them into the spirit of the day. Once the men had sat down with their food and their drink, the buzz of conversation grew into a roar, and then, gradually, out of that roar, arose the sound of singing, in the form of a hymn. Soon a competing sound rose from a nearby table, no hymn this, but a bawdy drinking song about a wench and her many lovers from the town of Kidderminster.

There were singers at several other tables too, weighing in with any other songs that came to mind. Religious, lullaby, alehouse songs, they clashed with each other in dissonant disarray, competing in volume, emotion, and occasionally, sweetness of tone.

And then, from the center of this cacophony, came the sound of a half-dozen strong, melodious voices. The song they sang contained no inspirational message. It did not urge men into battle, nor did it urge men to a closer relationship with their creator. In fact, it said nothing very flattering, written as it had been to mock the fathers of the men who were singing it.

> Father and I went down to camp
> Along with Captain Goodwin
> And there we saw the men and boys
> As thick as hasty puddin'.

A lyric written by snobs to mock the pretensions of their inferiors. The Americans had hurled it back at the British in vicious ridicule as they gunned them down during the British retreat from Concord.

> Yankee Doodle keep it up
> Yankee Doodle dandy
> Mind the music and the step
> And with the girls be handy.

One table after another dropped the song they were singing and picked up "Yankee Doodle" wherever it was. They all knew the words, enlisted and officer alike.

> And there was Captain Washington
> Upon a slapping stallion
> And giving orders to his men
> I guess there was a million.

By the second chorus the entire camp had signed onto the song. Less than a year after the horrible massacre of American troops in Wyoming Valley, five times as many of their brothers were there, armed and ready, their voices echoing impudently off the hillsides, daring the fates.

> And then the feathers on his hat
> They looked so 'tarnal finy
> I wanted peskely to get
> To give to my Jeminy.

Another chorus, another verse. The soldiers were on their feet now, in full voice, their canteens raised, facing their officers, who raised their glasses back and sang the words back at their troops. There were no social distinctions at this place, on this day. And then, as the fourth chorus died down, a captain with a large frame and a larger voice vaulted onto the dais with such force that the board bent, but it held. The captain raised his rich baritone voice and stretched it across the valley.

> And when the war is at an end
> The lobsters will be leavin'
> We'll send a message to the king
> A king can't beat a free man.

Now every soldier in the valley raised his voice for the final chorus:

> Yankee Doodle keep it up
> Yankee Doodle dandy
> Mind the music and the step
> And with the girls be handy.

Some of the soldiers attempted to repeat the final chorus, or maybe they'd had so much rum that they had forgotten where they were in the song. Most of the soldiers simply broke out into a roaring cheer, then threw their heads back and poured down the rum.

The huge captain called for quiet, and after about two minutes of confused singing and cheering, the rest of the men quieted down long enough to hear the captain raise his glass and announce the following:

"To New York, may she lead the way to independence."

To which some soldiers tried to respond by repeating the toast while others erupted into raucous noise.

Now General Sullivan stood up, and he got the attention of the troops fairly quickly:

"To New Hampshire and the beautiful White Mountains."

Simple and modest. The soldiers liked that, and many of them managed to repeat it, though not quite in unison. After that, one toast after another was drunk to the various states, until all thirteen had been covered. Someone made a toast to the king and queen of France, which the soldiers repeated with enthusiasm. "To the United States!" came next, and the cheers of the soldiers drowned out whatever was said about their brand new nation.

Now a sergeant jumped on top of his table and almost fell off. His mates steadied him while he collected his thoughts. "To civilization—or death to the savages!" he cried. Thad looked at Paul and turned a palm upward. Paul said nothing and revealed nothing of his thoughts.

"To George Washington and the army!" came from a private bellowing from atop a table near them, and abruptly the savages were forgotten.

❧17❧

AT THE END OF JULY THE ARMY OF GENERAL
Sullivan finally began to move up the Susquehanna River,
toward the state of New York. The men were not sorry to
leave the Wyoming Valley. More than a few of them
thought it was bad luck to linger there. They called it the
"place of skulls."

Slowly the troops wound their way north, moving no
faster than their artillery and supplies, which moved slowly.
Ahead of them, making their way back and forth along
their front and flanks, were the scouts, who now included
Big Oak, Jinja, James, Paul, and Thad. Gilles, Ooghnor, and
Henri, deciding that it was safer for them to make their way
homeward by land, left the canoes hidden in a grass-
shrouded hollow along the Susquehanna. With so many
men on the move, Big Oak knew that this army was no
secret to the Mohawks and Senecas who had spent the past
two winters marauding back and forth across central New
York. There was no absence of sign to show that the army
had been seen. And yet, neither was there any indication
that the Indians were ready for a fight. The river wound
northwesterly now, and so did the men who followed it.
Sometimes they sang, and sometimes they complained
about the food, or their shoes, or their powder. But Big Oak
noticed that no matter how many days passed without

them sighting the enemy, nobody complained about being sent on a wild goose chase.

One afternoon, as their trail topped a hill at a clearing, Big Oak looked through a thin shield of trees at the beautiful valley below. Contented, he stretched his legs and arms and bared his grizzled face to the hot summer sun. In the summertime his bones seldom bothered him.

He thought that this summer might be his last scout. For years he had felt that his senses had been losing their edge, but forty years of experience in the woods more than compensated for the physical loss. Over the past two winters he had noticed how much easier it was for him to stay close to the fire. On this journey his muscles were protesting during the endless loping that took the scouts back and forth across the route that the army was taking.

That evening he felt Thad's hand on his shoulder. Their eyes met, and he knew that Thad had noticed the heavy breathing, and the shambling gait into which his tired legs had degenerated near the end of the day's march.

"How's it going?" his son asked as they waited in a clearing for the rest of the scouts to come in.

"Fine," Big Oak answered.

"Mmm." Thad looked at his proud father and swallowed hard. Big Oak was so much stronger and more vigorous than any of the men his age Thad knew in Albany that Thad had been slow to realize that his father was not the man he'd been. "We've got a scout late tonight. I think we can handle it without you."

"I'll be ready tonight," huffed Big Oak, wiping perspiration off his face with the sleeve of his woolen hunting shirt.

"We're gonna need you a lot more come tomorrow," Thad responded. "We'll be comin' up on Chemung."

Big Oak nodded. He had dreaded this day. Chemung was a large Seneca community. The people of the great hill were bound to make a defense here, and Big Oak hated the thought of fighting against those who had once called him brother, and meant it. It was his job to find the village, and when he did, Sullivan's army would sweep down on it and destroy it. He thought about a time more than twenty years ago when the French had set an ambush for the English near Lake George. In those days, it was still called Lac St. Sacrement. The ambushers were largely Caughnawagas, and the men to be ambushed were mostly Mohawks. The Caughnawagas came from the same grandparents as the Mohawks did, and so Iptowee, the Caughnawaga chief, rose from his hiding place and tried to persuade the Mohawks to go home. A hotheaded Mohawk brave shot and killed Iptowee, and only then did the Caughnawagas proceed with their ambush.

Big Oak did not feel that kind of loyalty to the people of Chemung. The village was far from Big Oak's old Seneca village on the Genesee, and anyway, he and Thad had been cast out of the Seneca lodges long ago. Still, Thad's mother, Big Oak's beloved first wife Willow, was a Seneca who slept by the banks of the Genesee. He would not enjoy the coming night's work.

But neither would he shirk it. He ate sparingly, drank only water, stretched himself out, wrapped his blanket around him and caught four restorative hours of sleep before Paul Derontyan tapped him on the shoulder and awakened him. Standing with Paul was James. He would be their messenger and guide. When the scouts found the village, they would send him running back to where the army waited. He would then guide the leading units to the village, and the bulk of the army would follow.

Noiselessly they slipped through the moonlit darkness, Paul, Big Oak, James, Jinja, and Thad. They pretty well knew where the village was, so they did not spread out but loped down the trail in a group until they came to a rock outcropping that Big Oak remembered as a landmark. They ran due west from the outcropping. The woods thinned out and the three-quarter moon threw blue shadows on the forest floor. The trees spaced farther and farther apart and then stopped altogether. Beyond the tree line was the most beautiful stand of corn plants Jinja had ever seen. Bent low to blend in with the cornstalks, they ran across the field, only to find more fields—squash, pumpkins, beans, and one field of something Jinja could not even identify.

Big Oak sent Jinja back with James. Once the two younger men were gone, Big Oak decided that they should draw closer to the village to get a glimpse of what was going on inside. But when they arrived at the site of the lower village, they found houses and nothing else. The campfires were stone cold. Enough was missing from the houses to indicate that the people had taken their belongings and run away. Fine, Big Oak thought. At least we will not have to fight them.

Once they were certain nobody was there, they walked through the village. Big Oak had visited this village once, more than ten years before. He had put his considerable gun repair skills to use then, and serviced many of the weapons in the village. The residents of the village had rewarded him with an ox. Big Oak had been touched. He could not very well herd the ox himself to his home north of Albany, so he butchered it instead and threw a feast for the warriors.

A year later he and Thad came back with several canoes full of trade goods and had a glorious two days of trading with these Senecas. He remembered the hospitality, the kindness, the welcome he had received from the villagers. Every villager wanted them to linger in their lodge and eat from their kettle. The villagers had sung the familiar songs and danced the familiar dances and consumed their food so prodigally that they would have to work harder through the summer and fall to store away enough food to get them through the winter.

Now the memories followed each other down the still paths of the Seneca village. Big Oak did not remember the name of the village chief. No matter, the chief was dead anyway. Still, he found it eerie to walk through the deserted village and imagine the sounds when it had been full of life.

Common sense told them to race back to the trail and wait near it for the soldiers to come along. Time was important. They did not want to be caught in front of the village, their bodies silhouettes for the soldiers to use as target practice.

Paul was even more dubious. "Unless James and Jinja are leading them, they will be itchy to open fire on anything that moves," he said. "Like a hungry Shawnee who thinks he sees a deer in every shifting shadow." Big Oak and Thad understood what Paul was saying. And they understood what Paul was feeling. Like Paul, they knew the feelings of many of the soldiers toward the Iroquois. Senecas, Cayugas, Mohawks, and many of the Onondagas had joined in a year of laying waste to the rebel settlements of New York. Camping among the death and ruins of Wyoming Valley had simply been the final chapter in their book of hate. Paul did not want to be the one to test Sullivan's army on their ability to tell a Christian Oneida from a heathen Seneca.

So they decided to lie quietly away from the trail, at the edge of the woods, and wait. For an hour they sat without a word, listening to the night sounds. There was no need for these old comrades to pass the time in idle chatter. Often in the past, when danger was near, the forests had been their shelter. They knew that although the villagers had fled, there remained the possibility that a party of warriors remained behind, ready to hit and run in the night, not stopping their enemy but bloodying them nevertheless. The Senecas were not used to leaving their villages to the mercies of their enemy. They would be angry, anxious to strike a vengeful blow. So Big Oak, Paul, and Thad lay silently among the trees and clumps of underbrush.

Normally a woodsman can feel the change in the sounds of the forest before he can hear the approach of the intruder, but on this night the lead elements of Sullivan's army were crunching every twig to fall on the trail in the past month, and telling each other about it. They tore past Paul, Thad, and Big Oak without looking right or left, and didn't quiet down until an officer commanded them to in a voice loud enough to be heard in the village, had there been anyone left in the village to hear them. The three woodsmen waited a few minutes longer before the main body of soldiers came up, silent of mouth but clumsy of foot. They easily followed a path of trampled corn plants toward the village. They took quite a while to pass, and by the time they had, flames were beginning to leap into the sky on the other side of the fields, where the advance party was burning the houses in the village. A few minutes more and Big Oak could see torches emerging from the village.

"James! Jinja!" Thad half whispered, half shouted as two figures approached on the trail. The five met at the edge of the forest and watched the fields bloom into flame until the smoke blowing toward them made them retreat along the trail. They decided to make their way around to the other side of the village, upwind from all the smoke. Their route took them up into the hills, from which they could witness the appalling sight of a prosperous Seneca village disappearing before their eyes.

Thad and his father looked at each other. Both of them knew that what Sullivan was doing was exactly the right thing to win a war and exactly the wrong thing to do to other human beings. Both had lived through years in a Seneca village when the harvest had not been plentiful enough to carry the people through the winter. Both had heard the cries of hungry children and seen the helpless looks on the faces of braves coming home empty-handed after days of searching the snow in vain for deer tracks. What would happen to the people of this village come winter?

A few miles up the Cohocton River, Degata and a small band of Senecas watched the orange glow on the horizon, and they knew what was happening. Camped along the river were a few hundred warriors from the Seneca and Cayuga nations, but they could only look on while the rebels laid waste to their valley. Where were the rest of the Ganonsyoni? Why would they not come? Did they not know that if they did not stop the rebels, their towns would be next?

The night before, he and two others had sneaked across the valley to spy on the rebels. Their campfires had stretched far along the river. Even if every Seneca, Cayuga, and Mohawk warrior were to assemble in this one place, they would be outnumbered. To their shame, his two friends told him that they were going west to their village because they would be needed there. Degata was angry at them because they were needed here, to help stop the rebel army before they could go any farther. And yet he was now asking himself if he was better off going back to his village, to his family, in case the enemy showed up there.

No! he thought. The rebels would not get so far. Sayengaraghta and his braves would be here soon, and Major Butler had promised that his rangers would not let them down. And so he sat quietly in the cold summer night, with only his blanket for comfort, waiting.

The following morning a young chief called Yellow Eyes went looking for volunteers to do a little skirmishing. Most of the men turned him down. They were waiting for more warriors to come. They would not get themselves killed in a fight where they were outnumbered a hundred to one. But Degata and a dozen more liked the idea. So that morning they attached themselves to the left flank of the lumbering rebel army and followed them as they marched west. The men they were watching had not had much rest. By the late afternoon they were stumbling over each other as they continued their search for Seneca warriors to kill and villages to burn. Toward the end of the day, just before it was time for the men to fall out and make camp, the Senecas found a lovely little knoll with good fields of fire, and there they settled down.

They watched the troops marching by until they found a small group straggling a hundred yards behind the main body of soldiers. There might have been twenty-five of them, more or less. When the soldiers were as close as the trail would allow them to get, Yellow Eyes fired, and then the rest of the men followed suit. Degata took a lot of pride in his marksmanship. His rifle felt good against his cheek. He did not jerk his trigger, he squeezed it. His pan flashed and so did his barrel, and a young rebel private lay squirming on the forest floor with a bullet in his hip. Seven men fell at the first volley, three of them screaming from the horrible wounds they had received. The Senecas reloaded, and when they saw that the soldiers were confused and exposed, they fired again, wounding two more, then retreated into the depths of the forest. Two or three of the soldiers fired wildly after them, their bullets clipping some leaves above the heads of the fleeing Senecas. About fifty men who had already passed retraced their steps to help their comrades, but in classic Indian style, the Senecas were gone, leaving three dead and six painfully wounded American soldiers.

Yellow Eyes had calculated his ambush well. The entire army stopped in its tracks so General Sullivan could send an aide back to investigate the gunfire they had heard. What the young war leader failed to calculate was the presence of two scouts on his flank, who happened to be Big Oak and Jinja. When they heard the shots, they guessed right away what had happened. They dropped down behind trees and listened, and soon they heard the soft sounds of Indians coming their way.

Big Oak first saw them about a hundred yards up the trail. He didn't hesitate. He raised his rifle, pulled his trigger and buried a bullet in the chest of Yellow Eyes. The young chief fell backward, dead before he hit the ground, with bright red blood gushing all over his upper body. The other Senecas in the ambush party saw Big Oak and Jinja vault from their place of concealment and go careening down the trail. They let out a chorus of whoops and started to go after the two white traders, but then behind them they heard shouts and screeches as a large gaggle of soldiers who had passed earlier now heedlessly pursued the Indian band. The Senecas broke off their pursuit and headed for the river.

When Jinja saw the Senecas veer off from their pursuit of him and his grandfather, he ceased being the prey and became the hunter. At least fifty yards ahead of the soldiers, he sprinted hard after the Indians. He was fresher than the soldiers or the Senecas. His long legs ate up the ground beneath them, putting more distance between himself and the soldiers, and less distance between himself and the enemies he pursued. Big Oak sized up the situation and sprinted after him. He was not the runner he had been, but he was still good enough to outrun the heavily burdened infantrymen.

Jinja, on the other hand, was gaining so swiftly that he was soon nearly out of view. Here we go again, Big Oak thought. Will he ever learn? He took a turn in the trail and leaped onto a rock that looked downhill, and what he saw nearly made him despair. Three of the warriors, realizing that only one man was in close pursuit, turned to face Jinja. Two of them cocked their weapons while the third finished loading his. Big Oak had no time to think, only to react. Throwing himself against a tree trunk to steady his heaving body, he pulled back the hammer, raised the barrel and fired, nearly in one motion. The man he fired at was either very lucky or very unlucky, depending upon one's point of view. Big Oak's bullet carried away the ear of his target and startled Degata into firing too quickly. That shot splintered a tree trunk close to Jinja, driving a splinter into his forehead. Finally perceiving the danger he had put himself in, Jinja dove behind a large maple tree and wiped the blood from his eye. The one-eared warrior had had enough.

Without pausing to fire his weapon, he hurriedly retreated in the direction of his cohorts.

The third warrior had finished loading. He was young, barely fifteen, and too inexperienced to react well when he saw Big Oak charging down the hill, whooping and loading in flight as he zigzagged in and out of the trees. Shaken by the confident moves of the veteran, the young warrior fired in haste, too high, then fled frightened down the side of the hill. Now Big Oak and Jinja had only Degata to contend with. Degata might have hung around awhile longer, for he was a bold, confident warrior and he was not afraid to do battle with two white men in his native woodlands, but he knew that the American soldiers would be arriving at any moment. While Big Oak tended to Jinja, Degata vanished like a spirit.

As the soldiers boiled down the trail, Big Oak pointed with his rifle toward where he had last seen Degata and the young warrior before they disappeared. Worried, he took a look at the left side of Jinja's face, which carried a fresh red coat of blood from his forehead to his chin.

Big Oak used his sleeve to wipe the blood away, and was relieved to see what was causing the gore. Without hesitation he pulled out the two-inch-long sliver that had ripped a shallow gash in Jinja's forehead just below his hairline. "My boy, my boy, I thought you'd learned," he said. "That was so foolish, runnin' after them wolves like you did. What would I have told your father if those Seneca brothers of mine had managed to lift your hair before I could get to you?"

"I knew you'd be there," Jinja said. "You never let me down your whole life."

"So *you* say," the old trader responded. "But there's somethin' you should know. There's an Indian wanderin' around out there without an ear."

"And he's gonna be real mad, I know. Don't worry, I'll keep an eye out for—"

"I'm not worried about how mad he is. I'm worried about

how close I came to missin' him altogether. Now Jinja, my eyes are not what they used to be. When I fired at him, I was firin' at what I thought was the dead center of him. I sure as hell was not trying to pick an ear off, not with your life in danger. I fired at what I thought was dead center of what I thought was a man at fifty yards, and if I didn't catch a piece of ear, I don't think your life would have lasted another minute."

"Grandpa, I—"

"Listen to me, boy, I can still follow a trail for days. I can still read sign. I can still make a good trade. But don't ever again rely on me to save your life with a rifle. Those days are over. They ended today."

❊18❊

DEGATA CAUGHT UP WITH HIS TWO CO-
horts and together they fled from the white soldiers. They
lost them when the officer in charge sensibly realized that
he might be leading his men into an ambush.

The Seneca who had lost his ear to Big Oak's bullet was
in pain, but it was his vanity that suffered most. By the time
they had caught up to the rest of their band, he was afraid
that someone would try to rename him One-Ear, or Ear-
Shot-Off. Instead, the rest of the men were properly sympathetic, or at least as sympathetic as men can be who are
concerned about their own lives. Aside from Yellow Eyes's
death and the injury to this one brave, their little sortie had
been a success, and they were feeling good about themselves for having executed it.

They loped up the valley of the Chemung River until
they arrived at a small village called Chucknut. Looking
back, they could see a gray haze drifting above the forest
canopy, which told them the whites had found more crops
to burn. At Chucknut there was good news. Major John
Butler had arrived with a couple of hundred loyalists, regulars, and rangers. And Sayengaraghta was there too, together with four hundred Senecas and Cayugas. Degata's
spirits rose immediately. Here was an army big enough to
whip those fool rebels, who were not very good fighters

anyway. He began to hunger for a major battle. Come on, he thought. Come on, and we'll give you war.

The rebels were coming on, marching up the Chemung River in generally good order, stopping here and there to burn a few more houses or a few crop fields. There were Iroquois scouts along their flanks, managing to dodge Big Oak's and Paul's scouting patrols, reporting every move. And back around Newtown, near Chucknut, Major Butler deployed his men on a ridge, waiting in ambush for the rebels.

Butler's force was a badly mixed bunch of Senecas, Mohawks, rangers, and regulars who did not necessarily get along with each other, but they had found a fine place from which to do a little killing. They knew the rebels would be marching along the river trail, their right flank laid bare to the rifles and muskets of Butler's little army. But they did not know when the rebels would get there. So Major Butler and his Indians and Tories sat still and waited.

After about five hours on the hot ridge, waiting and swatting at mosquitoes, they heard a couple of gunshots echoing on the mountaintop behind the hill on which they were perched. Degata turned around for a moment and watched a group of rangers toil up the mountain in the direction of the shots. He then turned his gaze back to the river trail below. Next to him was the fifteen-year-old who had been with him when Big Oak had shot the ear off their companion. The boy was called Otter because he had been the best swimmer of all the children in the village. He had come south with three older braves who, like Degata's cohorts, had developed a bad feeling about the campaign and gone home. Major Butler had raged at and cajoled many of these Senecas, but to no avail. Some of them went home to defend their villages from attacks they knew would come, and some of them went home to pack their families and move them west to where the Mingoes did not have to think every day about how the white men were closing in on them. Some of them probably just wanted to hang around Fort Niagara and be fed.

Otter did not follow the other braves home because he believed he was now a real man, and he wanted to strike a heroic blow against the hated rebels. So he managed a sickly grin when he heard Degata snort after the gunshots.

Degata and Otter did not like the Tories, partly because the Tories were just Englishmen who wore green uniforms, and the Senecas, unlike their Mohawk brothers, had never particularly liked the English, or any other white men. Also, they disliked many of the Tories because the Tories so obviously hated them. The day before, while they were lining up for rations, two of the loyalists were giving each other their opinions about Indians.

The biscuits, they agreed, were inedible, but they were still too good for Indians because the maggots in them had not yet putrefied.

"I have heard," said one of the Tories, "that the damned Indians eat their own children."

"My Gawd," replied his messmate. "Who would be so disgusting as to eat an Indian child?"

They were saying these things because they were surrounded by Senecas, who, they were sure, did not understand a syllable of English. They were almost right. Actually, one of them understood every syllable. In the Seneca dialect, which the Tories did not understand, he translated each line to his cohorts as the two Tories spoke.

"Look at them," one of the Tories said. "Nary a stitch of clothes on the beggars. And you can smell them five miles downwind."

"They're not a damned bit of use to us. They just eat up our rations and I'll wager they'll run at the first shot, the dirty cowards. And can you believe how infernally ugly their women are? Why, their camp dogs are—" He was stopped, mid-sentence, by the vicious look being directed at them by the Seneca who knew English.

"Oh dear," said the Tory with the biggest mouth. "I be-

lieve one of the buggers has been listening. Didn't mean it,"
he said. "Not a blasted word of it." He walked away with his
rations. "Yes I did," he said softly to his messmate. "Yes I
did, every blasted word, you ugly red devils."

About an hour or two later the Senecas manning the
breastwork of logs and cut brush spotted the rangers creep-
ing back down the hill toward their spot on the ambush
line. "Hya! Hya!" cried one of the Senecas derisively. "You
find an army on the mountain?" Others took up the game. "I
saw some women with kettle spoons up on the mountain.
Did they drive you back down here? Look at that one! Got
a face like a false face," said one, referring to the grotesque
ceremonial masks carved by Iroquois from time immemo-
rial. "Great Tahiawaghi, why did you make these men so
ugly?"

The Senecas continued to make rude noises at the rangers even after they were all back on line. When one of the
officers took a hand and tried to get the Senecas to quiet
down, the Senecas just turned their venom on him, mostly
in the Seneca tongue. He may not have understood the
text, but the tone of their voices was hard to miss. Few of
the Tory officers awed the Senecas in any way. This one
decided that if he ignored them, they would finally get
tired and bored and stop. He was right, but only after five
more unbearable minutes for the proud Tories, who needed
their Indian allies so much more than they ever wanted.

The next day Butler paid a visit to Sayengaraghta on the
left flank. "Our scouts found a much better ambush position
three miles upstream," he told the chief. Would he help him
move his Indians?

"This ambush place is a fine ambush place," the chief
insisted to Butler. "Would be very bad to move now." Butler
looked squarely into the face of Sayengaraghta. And he
looked at the faces of the warriors manning the breastworks. Many of them were close enough to have heard and
seen the discussion, which was carried on in that curious

patchwork of sign language, flawed interpretation, Seneca expressions, and English phrases that so often passed for conversation in this patchwork army.

Butler sighed. He knew he could not demand that they shift positions. If he ordered them, Sayengaraghta and his men might pick up and go home. Better they stay where they were than get into a fight about where they should be. But his thoughts turned to divine providence, and he asked why, in His wisdom, God had chosen to bedevil them with these stiff-necked Iroquois allies. As long as he had known these people he could not understand them. Did they not realize that their future was at stake? Did they not realize that if they lost the war they would lose everything? Did they not realize that the English could lose the war? What is it with these people? Butler asked himself.

And yet he knew, when the shooting started, they could fight like the very devil himself. The trick was to have them there when the battle began, and make sure the battle was set up so as to make them feel they had an advantage. They didn't mind fighting, they just didn't want to die. Butler thought that was a fairly sensible way of thinking. It was the ones who wouldn't come and fight that really drove him crazy. There were also plenty of loyalists who had run off to New York or Canada instead of fighting for their homes.

But what of these rebels, these lowest and laziest of people? There were said to be six thousand of them under arms marching around New York. Were they good soldiers? Maybe not, but they weren't quitters either, and Butler had a bad feeling in the pit of his stomach about the way this whole thing would come out. He'd felt that way ever since the rebels had licked Burgoyne at Saratoga. Well, he and his army had an appointment to meet with that rabble in a day or two, and he knew that he had better find a way to lick them or he might as well say good-bye to New York.

The rebel army stayed on the old river path because they had no choice. They were supposed to have a dozen

Oneida scouts. The only Oneidas who remained with them were Paul and James. The excuses of the ones who had gone were virtually the same as those of the Senecas. They needed to go back to their villages to protect their loved ones from their enemies. The Mohawks hated the Oneidas for siding with the rebels, and would soon be down on them like God on Sodom. Besides, they said to themselves, they were never really keen about taking orders from anybody, much less white officers, who were mostly fools to boot. But even rebel officers who did not like Indians—and that meant most of them—had a sort of reverence for the ability of Indians to track the enemy in the woods. Paul and James were woods Indians, therefore they could scout. Unfortunately, they were not familiar with this particular neck of the woods.

Nevertheless, their skills were up to the challenge. Well ahead of the army, they ranged their way through the woods and fields on one side of the river, while Jinja, Big Oak, and Thad covered the other side. In the quiet of the morning they made their way through the woods with their eyes and ears on full alert, for they knew the enemy was near.

"We'd better get into the open, closer to the river, if we're going to see anything," Paul told James.

James nodded. "The enemy will see our army when it approaches, there is no doubt of that. But we must find them, and that won't be easy. We'll stay close to the tree line if we can, but we must be where we can see."

They moved closer to the river, till they were walking along the bottomland where the crops grew best. There were some overgrown fields along the flood plain of the river. The two Oneidas' senses bore a keen edge. They knew that a moment's relaxation could easily cost them their lives. Paul studied the sky for a moment. The morning had dawned clear, but now white puffy clouds were scudding across the summer-blue heavens, casting their own shadows to mingle with the shadows of trees below. Paul climbed the tallest tree close to them, climbed it as high as it would safely allow him, and looked across the valley.

He allowed himself a little smile and motioned his son to join him in the tree. He looked straight ahead at a hill in front of a higher mountain. "Do you see?" he asked.

His son looked but he did not see. "I did not raise you right," said the older scout. "Too much book, too little woods. You see about halfway up that hill?" James stood behind his father and aligned his view to follow Paul's finger. Now James saw. On the hill were the purples and whites of Longhouse war paint. They could see the wooden breastworks in front of the painted Cayugas and Senecas. "A good place for an ambush, but maybe not such a good place to defend against an enemy that knows you are there. James, get on down and bring the army up. I'll get Big Oak and Thad over to this side of the river where they can be useful. I think we've got them, but get the army up fast!"

Major Butler was taking a morning walk around his hillside stronghold when he noticed that a pair of Cayuga warriors had moved portions of the breastwork down the hill from where they had been. He said something to the two Cayugas, but they both stared back at him blankly. The major wondered briefly if it mattered all that much, decided that it did, and knew that he could not let this pass. It was compromising the entire plan. He looked at the two Cayugas, who were glaring back at him defiantly. My God, he thought, one of them is a baby and he's ruining the whole position and I will not stand for it. He stomped off to find Sayengaraghta.

The chief was busy talking to one of his warriors, a tall bull of a man with a long red scar running down his left arm. As Butler approached, the two men ended their conversation and began applying brilliant war paints to all exposed parts of their bodies, and it being a warm day, nearly all parts of their bodies were exposed. Butler knew better than to interrupt them in the midst of their ritual, but he stewed inside as he walked away and waited. When he returned, he found the chief ready to listen to what he had to say.

Butler pointed to the Cayugas up the slope at the end of the Indian position. "My friend," said Butler through clenched teeth, "I need to get those men back on the line we have prepared."

"I cannot tell the Cayuga what to do," came the reply. "You must talk to Sacangherada."

Butler had been afraid of that. He had never gotten along with the Cayuga chief Sacangherada. He spotted the Mohawk Joseph Brant and told him the situation. Brant understood things like this, and accompanied Butler to where Sacangherada stood staring down at the river.

"They are coming," he said to Butler and Brant in an angry tone that made it sound as if it was Butler's fault that they were coming.

"I know they're coming," Butler said through Brant. "Would you please tell your men over there"—he pointed toward the flank—"to get back to where they're supposed to be?"

"Where *you* say they're supposed to be," he said to Brant, who relayed the message faithfully to Butler. Butler looked to Brant for sympathy and took a deep breath. Brant turned to the Cayuga chief and tried to explain why Butler's concern was justified. The Cayuga responded with a short list of grievances and then repeated the obvious, that the rebels would be here soon, his scouts had told him so, and the major had better be ready when they arrived. Butler knew enough of the language he was hearing to understand the gist, and he had to clamp his jaws together tightly to keep from giving the chief hell in front of his braves.

Patiently, carefully, Brant told the chief how mighty were the Cayugas, what a bulwark they had been in the long, honored history of the Longhouse, and how important it was that a certain two Cayugas conform to the plan of defense so the history of the Longhouse could continue to be honored. The Cayuga cast a cold look at Butler, but squeezed Brant's arm with a powerful, gnarled hand, and together the three leaders walked over to where the two Cayugas peered over their logs toward a woods line that held no threat to anybody.

One of them had a dream, they told the Cayuga chief, who turned around and told Brant. The dreamer had said that the attack would come from above, and that if he, Tagleehta, would be ready for it, then he would win a victory for the Longhouse and the English. The Cayuga chief tried to explain, and Brant tried to persuade, and Butler glared down at the two Cayugas in a vain effort to display authority. The two Cayugas refused to budge. The Cayuga chief would not insist, and anyway, he said, they would not listen, for Tagleehta's dream had been very powerful.

James climbed down from the tree, hit the ground running and headed back to where he knew he would find General Sullivan. Paul, meanwhile, lingered at the tree line and looked across the river, hoping to see some sign of Big Oak. He stood still for five solid minutes, but there was woodland hiding them from his view, and him from them. He decided that his cover was good and that he might wait for the army.

It was the worst decision he ever made.

The woods had been so quiet. Suddenly it exploded into sound and he was nearly surrounded by a scouting party of Senecas.

Paul reacted quickly, but again his decision was not the best. Relying on his strong legs, he vaulted from the woods into the flood plain and sprinted along the tree line with five Senecas in pursuit. Two of them fired their muskets at him, but though the distance was only about thirty yards, they missed, and the shots alerted Big Oak, Thad, and Jinja in the woods on the other side of the river. It was Thad, peering through the woods and across the river and flood plain, who first observed the chase. He pointed and the three raced toward the river, intending to bring down Paul's pursuers and save their friend.

If Paul had known, or guessed, he might have run toward the river. Instead he ran along the open space beside the tree line, using his swiftness to widen the distance between himself and the five Senecas. Once the gap had become fifty yards, he ducked back into the woods, hoping to lose his pursuers in the trees and brush. The Senecas likewise disappeared into the forest. Frustrated, Big Oak and Thad could only stand at the edge of the river and hope that Paul might reemerge from the forest, followed by his enemy. Big Oak fired a shot into the woods where the Senecas had disappeared, not expecting to hit any of them but hoping that it might serve as a signal. Jinja, meanwhile, ran frantically along the riverbank, looking for a place to cross. As a child he had traveled many miles on the trails with Paul, and was determined to do something to save him. Galvanized by his action, the cooler, more calculating Big Oak and Thad ran after him. But just as they started to cross the river they heard two shots, followed by a single shot, followed by three more shots, then silence.

Jinja was three steps into the river when the shots came. Determined as he was to save his grandfather's friend, the shots halted him. Big Oak and Thad reached a spot on the river's edge near where Jinja stood crouched in the shallow water. Together they waited for more shots or noises that would indicate their friend was still at large. They heard nothing.

"We have to do something!" Jinja insisted.

Thad and Big Oak looked at each other, silent for several moments. They knew that the battle was imminent. They did not know whether or not Paul and James had located the enemy. In fact, they had no idea what might have happened to James.

"What's the matter with you?" Jinja cried. "If it was you, Paul would be trying to save you."

"It's too late," Big Oak said. "The enemy is close and it's our job to find him. The army is depending on us."

Jinja threw his grandfather a look of wrath. "And would you do that if it were me instead of Paul?"

Big Oak had been ready with an answer, but not to this question. His mouth opened but no sound came out. He tried again and found his tongue. "All right, you and your father go and find yourself a Tory army, and I'll bring back Paul one way or another. But for heaven's sake do what he tells you to do or you'll get yourself killed, and maybe him too."

Thad gave him a look as if to say, I'll kill him myself if he steps out of line.

Abruptly, Big Oak stepped into the river and began to cross it. Thad and Jinja followed. All three crossed the flood plain, but while Big Oak plunged into the woods where he had last seen Paul, Thad and Jinja moved along the tree line, parallel to the river, toward the place where Paul had climbed the tree and found the enemy position. They moved slowly, carefully. It was possible that the Seneca scouting party had dispatched Paul and were now in the woods searching for more rebel scouts. Thad was determined not to fall into their bag the way Paul had.

Big Oak, meanwhile, had no problem discovering the spot where Paul and the Senecas had had their little shootout, but there were no bodies to be found. He did pick up a bullet pouch from the floor of the forest, Paul's, he was certain, and found the scuff marks and broken branches that indicated a fight. He saw some drag marks too. Paul was alive. Senecas don't drag bodies around with them, especially before a big battle. If they had killed him, they would have scalped him and maybe further mutilated him, leaving his body or pieces of it where they'd killed him. He was alive, and they had left an easy trail for him to follow.

* * *

Paul had discovered the Tory defensive position more or less by chance. Thad and Jinja might never have found it, but they didn't need to. While examining some moccasin tracks, Jinja's acute hearing picked up faint noises well behind them.

He tugged at his father's hunting shirt and pointed to his ear. Thad stopped moving, listened, and heard the same faint sounds. Both of them knelt on one knee, completely still, listening until they were certain that the sounds were getting louder. Before they could tell who or what was making the sound, they heard another sound, more distinct, coming on quickly. Then around a bend came the figures of James and about twenty lightly equipped troops, a forward party, including Colonel Jamison. James saw Thad and Jinja, gave them a quick wave, but sailed right past them with the vanguard. Thad and Jinja fell in behind them and saw James give a signal to stop. He stepped farther out into the flood plain and pointed toward a hill. Jamison shook his head, pulled out a little telescope, peered through it, then nodded.

They were still well out of range of the Tories on the hill, though they had no doubt that the Tories could see them. Jamison led his men into the woods, where half of them waited for the main body and the other half prowled around in search of any ambushes or harassing parties. There were none. Major Butler was relying upon the defensive position of his men and his belief in their superiority as fighters to steal a victory from a numerically superior American army.

What he did not count on was Major Stevens's artillery. One of his young officers found a little swell of ground, barely a hill, but it was high enough to give him a clear look at Major Butler's defense line. On his black charger, requisitioned from a Tory in Schenectady, he galloped back to Stevens and led him to the hill. One by one the horse teams galloped into position. In swirling clouds of gray dust the sweating, swearing cannoneers unlimbered their guns and pointed them toward the British barricades on the other side of a stretch of forest. As if their lives depended on it, they raced to the wagons, brought out the iron and gunpowder, and laid it out in perfect order. The gunners then sighted the weapons and awaited orders. There were eight guns on that little hill that day, and they were enough to make a difference.

⫸19⫷

PAUL WAS BARELY CONSCIOUS WHEN THEY dropped him to the floor of the forest clearing. They had dragged him less than a mile before they found the clearing. With their moccasined feet they beat a tattoo on his ribs for a minute or so before the oldest stopped them and told them that Seneca men back in the days when they did not fight for English money had fine ways of honoring their prisoners. They understood. Through a red haze of pain and grogginess, Paul felt himself being dragged roughly over the ground, hoisted to his feet, and tied to the trunk of a straight young oak tree. At first his eyes did not want to open, but after a while he began to smell smoke and then his eyes opened wide. All he could see was darkness. Had they blinded him? As his senses returned, he felt warm stickiness covering his face. He shook his head to rid his eyes of the blood that covered them. One of the Senecas, seeing what Paul was trying to do, walked up to him and wiped the blood away. He didn't want Paul to miss a thing that was about to happen to him.

The Senecas were coaxing a fire from a pile of deadwood that lay five feet away from him. While the leader of the group looked on, two of them piled on more deadwood, while the other two prowled about the immediate vicinity in search of large pieces that they could build up into a proper inferno. Paul waited patiently for his head to clear, and when it did, he knew well what was in store for him. His hosts were preparing a slow roast, one that would not suffocate him with smoke, but would bake his skin until he was writhing in exquisite agony; then they would reach for him with long sticks and peel the crisp skin from his body. He would scream and beg, and they would taunt him for being a woman and allow the fire to cook the next layer.

In the old days warriors had been trained to withstand torture, the idea being that the tormenters would respect their captive for his fortitude. Perhaps they would then kill him quickly to spare him further pain. They might even eat a morsel or two of him after he was dead in order to acquire his courage and fortitude. The tradition fostered a strange relationship between the captive and his captors. The victim attempted to assert his superiority by insulting his tormenters and daring them to do their worst. The captors, whose role was considerably more fortunate, would do their best to break their victim's spirit, but if the victim demonstrated enough fortitude, then they would show respect and perhaps even give him time and refreshment to prepare him for his next round of torment. It was a ritual familiar to Paul by virtue of story and song, but he had lived many years among men like Reverend Kirkland. Many of the old traditions no longer made sense to him.

The days of ritual torture were over, he had thought. Nobody had told these Senecas about it.

Paul watched the implacable painted faces as the Senecas made their preparations, and he saw no hope for himself. His thoughts, strangely enough, turned not to his Oneida heritage nor to Jesus, but to the Reverend Kirkland. How would that worthy man suggest he stand up to the horrible fate that awaited him? Paul was a brave man. He had withstood many tribulations in his life, but he could not withstand this. Nobody could withstand this.

One of the Senecas, a young man with a badly pockmarked face beneath the paint, approached him and cut a great gash in his left side, long and fairly deep. With his knife he carved a large pocket in the muscle tissue. Then, spreading the muscle tissue with his fingers, he plunged a flaming stick deep into the wound.

Above the forest canopy dingy gray clouds were beginning to darken the sky, throwing the forest floor into a deep gloom. Big Oak lost the trail on a creek bed and a rock shelf, but by that time his senses had caught a whiff of the smoke and that drew him. Then the wind shifted, and he was moving by guesswork when he heard an unearthly screech that sounded nothing like Paul but had to be him. The scream was close, and therefore he had to be careful even as he hurried. Now he saw the smoke again, and fire, and Senecas, and Paul, his body bloody and twisted and taut against the oak tree, as if he were trying to wring the pain out of it. His mouth was wide open and the screams that came breath after breath were involuntary and inhuman. In spite of his need to control his emotions, Big Oak's heart nearly crumbled before the horrible agony of his friend.

How could he free Paul, with one gun and one bullet against five armed Senecas? Perhaps the one bullet should be for his friend, to end his agony. But no, his life could still be saved, and Big Oak knew how much Paul loved life. There was no time to think it over. They were piling the wood on, good, dry, hot-burning wood that would cook him quickly. Big Oak leveled his rifle and fired at the nearest Seneca. The Indian's knee fairly exploded and he fell to the ground screaming and rolling. Three of the Senecas turned and headed for the sound, while a fourth bent over his fallen friend. Good, at least there was no one left to stoke the fire any higher. But now he had to shake his pursuit and figure out a way to double back and free Paul before the fire cooked him beyond hope.

Big Oak zigzagged through the woods, loading as he ran. One of his pursuers fired. The ball thudded into a tree by Big Oak's head. He tried to put more trees between him and the Senecas, but they were young and agile, and he could feel them gaining on him. A strange feeling that wasn't quite fear but was more than discomfort crept into his stomach. They were closing in and no amount of determination could make his legs move faster. He did not know how he was going to save himself, much less his friend.

It was then that the artillery began to fire.

The woods muffled the roar of the cannon, but they failed to mask the horrifying sound of the iron roaring overhead. Long on gunpowder, short on balls, the artillerymen were firing a horrifying miscellany of ordnance—grape, chain links, spikes, pieces of old kettles, harrow teeth—they flew through the air in deadly constellations, directly overhead. Nothing terrified warriors like artillery did. They had seen men blown apart by cannon fire. One moment they would be whole and full of life. The next moment their pieces would be scattered all over the landscape.

Big Oak's pursuers would have no part of artillery. They scattered like dandelion seeds, vanished so quickly and completely that Big Oak merely retraced his steps to the clearing. The only ones left were Paul, who was suffering from the wound and the fire, and the Seneca with the shattered knee.

Big Oak cut his friend free from the oak tree. Paul's screams had subsided to a succession of hoarse groans. His eyes were wide open but they did not focus on Big Oak. His skin was hot, but not yet seriously burned. His right side was a singed, bloody mess. The artillery continued to roar overhead as Big Oak left the wounded Seneca in the clearing and carried Paul away from the fire, to a nearby creek. There he began to do what he could to ease Paul's torment.

The Americans may not have been very good soldiers when it came to marching in straight ranks and doing musket drill by the numbers, but they were experienced troops who knew how to fight. The English lines were well within range of their rifles, and the rebels used every tree, every creek bank, every depression for cover. But it was the artillery, with its bizarre assortment of metal garbage, that terrified the Indians into impotence. First they huddled behind their breastworks, pressed against the logs and the earth, awaiting their own destruction. That gave the artillerymen time to adjust their weapons, and soon enough of their fire was finding flesh to fill the air with screams and panic. An explosive shell crashed into the breastworks and threw large pieces of earth and wood high into the air. A Cayuga warrior glanced to his right and saw that the lifelong friend next to him no longer had a midsection. The survivor was not curious about where the next rounds would land, but jumped up and headed for the mountain that loomed behind the hill, looking wooded, covered, safe. Others followed him.

Farther along the British defense line, Degata swallowed his terror and stayed put, loading and firing down at the Americans, but then something fell out of the sky and turned the head of the brave to his right into pulp, part of which spattered onto the head and shoulders of Degata. The veteran Seneca warrior waited no longer, and neither did Otter. They fled up the hill, down the reverse slope, onto the wooded mountain, and did not slow down until the roar of the battle, and especially the artillery, had dimmed in their ears. And then they only slackened into a lope, their toes pointed toward their home village. In the woods, marching toward the left flank of the British and their Indian allies, was the bulk of the American army. They were not about to charge the enemy while their own artillery was raining mayhem on the barricades, so they waited, and watched, until most of the Indians guarding the flank had gone.

There was no way to communicate quickly with the guns. The attack had to be made now, before the enemy could form again on the flank. Sullivan ordered the attack, with a huge private carrying the biggest stars and stripes they had. Major Stevens caught on quickly and stopped the bombardment, though he continued to fire a few more salvos of powder and wadding to keep the defenders on the center and right occupied.

The Americans charged from the woods into an almost deserted flank. At the last moment an alert Tory sergeant spotted the charge and tried to shift some of his greens and Mohawks to cover the decimated line. But there were hundreds of Americans rolling forward, screaming their battle cries. In the close-quartered trenches and behind the barricades, huge numbers of American tomahawks overwhelmed British bayonets with ease. The struggle on the left was bloody, nasty, and short. The Mohawks fought with pride and skill, but once they had sized up their situation, they pulled back without orders. Some of the Tories stayed and died, but many followed the Mohawk example.

Feeling the disaster rolling up his left flank, there was nothing for Major Butler to do now but save his army. As rebels came flooding across his flank from the woods, Butler began pulling his men back across the river. There he finally caught a lucky break, when the clouds that had been gathering suddenly erupted into a downpour. The rebels, fleet shadows in overwhelming numbers, through water falling in sheets, chased remnants of a once proud loyalist army. Fleeing but not surrendering, hungry, weary, demoralized at the prospect of defeat by rabble, the loyalists ran over trails that churned to mud.

Somehow they managed to find each other in a rendezvous five miles away from the battlefield, soaked and exhausted, some of the men shaking with fever. Butler was satisfied to discover that casualties had not been heavy, and that his little army would live to fight another day. On the minus side, his Indians were gone. Having lived close to the Longhouse for many years, he had entered this war feeling that the Mohawks and Senecas would be the margin of victory in New York. Now he realized that had never been the case, that when the crisis came, the Mohawks and the Senecas would be for the Mohawks and the Senecas. He did not think beyond that, for the next question would have been, Isn't that the way it should be? Were the English for anybody but the English? Butler's thoughts at the end of the day were purely tactical. He posted guards, doled out rations where needed and where possible, and told his officers that they would be moving out at dawn. The goal, he told them, was to save the army.

Thad and Jinja had spent the afternoon tucked into a creek bank sniping at the enemy's breastworks. When the Indians fled and the rebel army overwhelmed the Tory positions, the two scouts faded into the woods. It was always a concern that there might be a British army roaming the forests that Sullivan was not aware of. Although Jamison had not assigned them the task, Thad and Jinja considered it their spare-time duty to discover hidden enemies. When the rains came, they gave up that mission and returned to the battlefield.

Big Oak was not far away. After he had cut Paul free, he tried to shake a little sense into his friend, but the ordeal had turned Paul into a heavy-lidded babbling idiot. "The sky is turned upside down," he said in English, followed by a rapid ramble in the Oneida dialect. Big Oak stopped trying to follow his gibberings and instead threw him over his shoulder and carried him toward a creek he'd seen earlier in the day. He paid little attention to the clamor of battle that was occurring on a hill beyond their piece of woodland. Sullivan's got the guns and he's got the men, Big Oak thought. He sure doesn't need me to mop up this mess.

At the creek he gave Paul water to drink, and poured water on his face and body to cool his skin. Then it began to rain, and that was too much water. Big Oak cut large branches and quickly formed them into a domed wigwam shape, tying them together with leather strips he cut from the remains of Paul's shirt. He cut big sheets of bark from several elm trees and covered the frame. The night would be cool. There would be no dry wood, so Big Oak unrolled his blanket and covered Paul with it.

He probed Paul's skull with his fingers and found several big lumps but no fractures, as far as he could tell. Paul began to cough, and each time he coughed, he groaned. Big Oak could see bruises in his rib area. Mostly he attended to the cruel wound in his side, washing the ashes and dirt out of the gash and binding it shut as best he could.

He took a piece of dried deer meat out of his pack, bit it, and began to chew. He then put the pack under Paul's head as a pillow. The day had been long, and he was very tired. But the Senecas might still be in the area. He sat in the doorway of the little wigwam with his knife on his lap and his rifle charged and in his hands, waiting. Not until nightfall did he allow himself a dark corner of the wigwam, and even then he did not lie down, but slept sitting up, his ears tuned to the night noises of the woods and the breathing of his friend.

Degata and Otter knew where they were going. Their muscled legs were tireless as they carried the two Senecas northwest along a ridge line parallel to the river. The trail was one Degata had traveled many times over the years. Even in the dark, with the trees still dripping from the downpour earlier in the day, Degata's feet were sure. Did he feel angry? Did he feel frustrated? Was he worried about the future of his people? Mostly, he was relieved to have escaped with his life. He wondered what had become of Sayengaraghta. He felt no shame at having left the battle at a crucial time. As an experienced warrior, he had no doubt that defeat was inevitable, and he saw no need to stick around to see it happen. Such was the stamina of Degata and Otter that they far outstripped Butler's army in the length of their retreat that night. Nevertheless, within two hours of sunset they were spent. Without any conversation, they took some corn out of their pack and nibbled on it, washed it down with water, then wrapped themselves in blankets to catch some sleep. Tomorrow they would continue the journey toward the Genesee River, and they probably would not stop there.

The following day, Sullivan's army spread all over the countryside in search of their foe. They were never going to catch the Senecas and the Cayugas, who had traveled fast and far and wanted no part of a war that had them facing cannon raining rusty iron down on them. The Americans did pick up the trail of Butler's army. Without artillery and wagons to slow them down, the Tories could easily outpace their pursuers. Veteran campaigner that he was, Sullivan was not about to get careless and race into an ambush. Now it was the Tories who were forced into fighting hit-and-run Indian style, if they were to fight at all. Well, let them. Butler's army was not Sullivan's first priority. It wasn't big enough to do anything but harass a careless, overconfident, scattered mob, and Sullivan's army was no mob. It was the farms and villages of the Senecas that Sullivan wanted to destroy. If in the process they also managed to bag a tiny Tory army, that was just so much gravy.

Two days after the battle, when it became clear that the chase would be long and hard, Sullivan stood before the troops. Standing on an ammunition wagon, with much of his army in formation before him and the rest patrolling that portion of the Chemung River valley, he let his army know what was on his mind.

"Men," he began, "we have been fighting this war for four years now. At the beginning we fought it because we had no choice, either we had to die on our feet or live on our knees. But if you look overhead at the sun, and then down at the earth, you will note that the sun is today shining on free land, and that every step you take forward gives the sun that much more free land to shine down on."

As he spoke he could feel a sort of tension in his men,

not fear, but anticipation, as if every one of them were feeling his words.

"Now, I am not saying that this war is over. I'm saying that from where I'm standing, I believe we are winning it. Where we stand today, never again will a Tory traitor praise the king, and never again will an Iroquois warrior menace our husbandmen."

Alongside of the assembled troops stood Jinja, Thad, and James, listening to the oration. As James listened, he could not help but ask himself, Why are we fighting for the Americans? What will become of us?

"Our job is to see to it that wherever we set foot, we will put an end to the enemy's presence on the land. Wherever we go, the Indians will never return. Think of it. No more Mohawks. No more Senecas. No more Cayugas. No more Onondagas. No more Delawares. Wherever we go, American farms and towns will spring up behind us. With our weapons, and with our feet, we are creating a new nation, a free nation, such as the world has never seen before, for ordinary men like you and me. It is great work that we do. It will be hard work. And because we must travel farther than we had ever thought, we will have to do the job on half rations."

Sullivan paused for a moment, because at the mention of half rations, the quiet tension broke into a roar from the men. His first impression was that the men were angry, but then the roar coalesced into cheers—hip, hip, hooray—as if he had announced that he was doubling the rum ration. Under the cheers he could hear the faint echoes of a song he had heard weeks ago. "My father and I went down to camp . . ."

That evening, when Thad, Jinja, and James camped by a gently flowing creek made wider by the recent rains, Thad caught the despair on James's face. "I heard the words of the general," Thad said.

"What have we done?" James asked. "Have the people of the great stone made the death song of the Ganonsyoni?"

"The death song of the Ganonsyoni was made the day the white men set foot in Virginia," Thad replied. "Once word of this beautiful land with so few people, and none of them Christians, returned to England, there was no chance." They were sitting cross-legged beside a small fire, taking hypnotic pleasure from staring at the dancing flames. "My brother, your father saw this years ago. He decided that the Ganonsyoni may be at risk, but that somehow he and his family would survive."

"And where is he now?"

Thad said nothing. They had not heard from either Paul or Big Oak since the battle. Only their faith in the skills of these two old veterans had prevented them from taking leave of the army to search for them.

The way was slow for Sullivan's army. There were too many rivers, too many hills, too much territory to cover, even with all the men he had. It did not take them long after the battle to discover that their chase would be a grueling one. They became engineers. Their path became a road, with brand new bridges to take the wagons and guns across deep rivers and ravines. Where the path climbed a hill, so did they; the trail had been made for the feet of men only, but now they were using oxen and horses to haul heavy equipment. Often the animals were not enough. Men by the score pulled on long ropes to drag the guns and wagons up the rocky trail.

When they were not scouting, Thad and Jinja were beasts of burden. They could have stayed on the perimeters at all times if they'd wanted, but they had caught the spirit that already inflicted the rest of the men. They were Americans doing hard things out of a strange new pride called patriotism, a love for a country barely born. The men who labored beside them did not hold James in the same low regard as they held the Senecas and Mohawks. He had been with them throughout the march. They knew that James and his father had been the ones who discovered

Butler's army on the hill. He spoke their language and he dressed like any woodsman and he was a bear for work. He was almost one of them.

He did not complain when they were waist deep in the swamps. Bears and snakes were grist for his mill. His tracking was flawless. Most of all, he had a good word for any man who had a good word for him. But they never knew how he hurt inside at the thought that every step forward by this army was one step backward for the Ganonsyoni. And they never noticed that he vanished anytime there was a field or village to be burned, or an orchard to be girdled.

As they marched west it became obvious that Butler's army was slipping from their grasp. This troubled Sullivan not at all. With all military threat to them removed, Sullivan spread his army farther and farther across the land. Now they were not only looking for the big towns they knew about, they had men out to find the small towns and farms they did not know about, and the ones they found were reduced to ashes. They found no Cayugas, and they found no Senecas, but they found their homes and their fields, and Sullivan was determined that when his army had gone home, and the Senecas and Cayugas returned, they would find nothing left to sustain them through the winter. Then they would go back to Fort Niagara, back to the Tories who despised them, and the fort would feed them, reluctantly, while the Tory officers and men cursed the lazy good-for-nothings who always ran from a good fight and were always begging the white man for food.

James occasionally found signs that Mohawks were dogging the army's flanks. Sometimes he found signs of stragglers here and there. And then one day, while the army was destroying a village in the valley below, he stumbled upon an assemblage of Seneca witnesses, high on a mountain, in a clearing that looked down upon their village.

They were the stranded ones of the village: old men, old women, women with young children, young children who had been orphaned, huddled together in misery, leaderless, hopeless. Many were in tears.

One of the women turned her head away from the smoke and fire and saw him. He walked toward them, his heart like a fist. An old man pointed his ancient musket at James. James caught the fear in the old man's eyes. "No," James said, but the old man struggled to pull the hammer back. The hammer was rusty and hard to operate. The musket trembled in the old man's grasp, but he seemed determined to cock it. With a flick of his wrist James swung the barrel of his rifle at the old man's hands and the musket dropped to the grass in front of him.

Now an old woman walked up to James. "You must not tell them that we are here," she said softly, "or they will kill us." She spoke in the Seneca tongue, but she seemed to think she was addressing a white man. Her face did not expect a response.

"They would not kill you," said James in fluent Seneca. "But I would not tell them you are here. Are you hungry? Do you need food?"

The astonished woman showed him open hands to indicate that they had taken nothing when they fled the village. He opened his pack and took out a pouch of parched corn. "I will leave this with you," he said.

"Then what will you eat?" the woman asked.

"I have friends," he answered in a voice that implied, And you have none.

The children and some of the women were now crying out loud. Mothers were hugging their children, using their bodies to give them the security denied by the flaming, smoking walls in the valley below. The old men stood wrapped in their blankets, their faces expressionless but their eyes betraying their pain. These men could still remember a time when white men worried enough about the Longhouse to care how its warriors felt. These men had fought in battles and emerged alive and triumphant. These men were too spent and powerless to try and defend their village. All they were still able to do was hide. Like rabbits.

James's face hurt him as he watched the people huddled in a clearing on a mountain, determined to stay and watch their village and their winter food supply go up in flames.

"Where will you go now?" he asked the woman who was face-to-face with him.

"Many of us have family on the Genesee River," she answered. "We will go to them."

"As soon as you reach their village," he said, "tell them to pack and leave. This army will not stop until they have burned up every Seneca village in New York."

Several women who heard what James said put their hands to their mouths in astonishment and fear. "Then where can we go that the army will not touch us?" she asked.

"The Spay-Lay-Wi-Theepi," he answered, using the name by which they called the Ohio River.

Now there was more weeping. One woman replied, "That is too far. Tell us a place that is not so far."

"You can go to Niagara, then to Canada, but Spay-Lay-Wi-Theepi will not be so cold in the winter." He had seen the signs that told him the coming winter would be a very cold one. He looked at the old men and young children and wondered if their spirits had a slippery hold on this world. Would winter be their executioner?

❧20❧

PAUL DERONTYAN WAS A VERY TOUGH MAN. The day after one of his Seneca brothers ripped him open and tried to fry his innards, he and Big Oak were in the woods looking for his rifle. His long association with Big Oak had made him very particular about his rifle. They found it in the clearing where the Seneca warriors had taken Paul to torture him. They took it apart, cleaned the mud out, wiped off the water, applied oil where oil was needed, and put it back together.

Paul loaded the weapon, leaned forward, fired, and clipped a branch off a tree fifty yards away.

"Good enough," Big Oak said.

"Mmmph," Paul grunted. "I feel awful."

It was still early in the morning, and both were feeling better about life, Big Oak because it was one of those rare mornings when he felt twenty years younger, and Paul because the Senecas had failed by minutes to grill him like a deer haunch. The torch his tormenters had thrust under his skin had cauterized his wound and prevented infection. There was pain, but Paul was a Ganonsyoni, so he did not complain much, though he moved more slowly than usual, and his breath sometimes came in gasps. Earlier they had run across a lagging teamster they knew. He had agreed to find Thad and James and tell them their fathers were well.

"My brother," Big Oak said. "I have a friend who lives not far from here in the most beautiful valley you have ever seen. He has an Onondaga wife whose grandfather knew the healing arts. We will spend a few days there while you regain your strength."

Paul nodded. They crossed the river and headed northeast, single file, along a narrow path, while Big Oak told Paul about his friend.

"George Hayes hates Indians, all of them, except the ones he's met. He has a tribe of sons so big and strong that together they have cleared the valley and the lower hillsides and planted them in corn and wheat. They supplied the English army for years. I don't know who they supply today. George and I scouted together back in the forties when he and I were still young, but he has never answered the call since, nor would he let his sons. They all have families now. They and the Onondaga village live in peace. This is his second wife. She will take care of you."

Paul walked faster, until he had nearly caught up with Big Oak. "I am anxious to get back to my village. I am worried about the Mohawks."

"Look at you," Big Oak said, raising his voice a little. Paul had slipped back. He was obviously not able to keep up. "You better sit down."

Paul sat down. The walk had made the wound begin to bleed. He had a nasty headache from the pounding the Senecas had given him with their rifle butts. His ribs ached from the kicks they had given him. His bones ached all over. Perhaps while he was unconscious they had beaten him elsewhere on his body.

"I just want us to stay there for a day or two. You'll feel a whole lot better, and it's not out of our way."

"Let's go, then," Paul said, using his rifle as a crutch to push himself onto his feet.

As they walked across the land, passing the southern end of Cayuga Lake, they saw what war does to good growing country. Here had been a Cayuga village. Now there was ashes. Here was a white farm. Now there was nothing. The rain had washed the ashes away and the summer had brought new growth to cover the atrocities. The bleaching skeletons of cattle grazed in formerly cultivated fields bleak with weeds; buildings were falling in on themselves.

Big Oak did not feel any satisfaction that the land was returning to the state of nature that he preferred. Land, once tamed to the hand of the farmer, should remain that way. He had seen the backbreaking effort necessary to carve a farm out of wilderness. It pained him to imagine the disaster and heartache it took to separate a farmer from his land.

Big Oak had fought in enough wars to understand that losers suffer consequences. Early in this war he had heard Tories talk about hanging rebels, confiscating their lands and deporting their families. Then the war had taken a sharp turn and it was time for the loyalists and their allies to suffer. Big Oak's heart was no longer joined to his adopted brothers, the Genesee Senecas. They had cast him out long ago. But he still loved his friends of the Ganiengehaka, and the Oneidas, and his wife's people, the Tuscaroras. When the war was over, he did not doubt that the Mohawks would be driven from their lands forever. But what of the Oneidas and Tuscaroras, who fought beside the Americans in their war of independence? Big Oak knew how the whites were. Would they seize the moment to get rid of all Indians, including their allies?

Over the next hill was Hayes's valley. Big Oak had his arm around Paul, helping him up the rise to the top of the hill. The going would be much easier after that. The lines of strain from the pain and exertion were carved deeply into the face of the Oneida.

He was not surprised at what he found when he looked down into the valley. The roofless stone houses, the black-charred barns, the deserted fields, were just a continuation of what they had seen since they left the Chemung River valley. But this was different. He *knew* the people who had lived in these houses and labored in these fields. With a toughness that came only from many years of warfare experience, Big Oak subdued his emotions. "Let's go," he said to Paul, and the two descended into the valley. "North is an Onondaga village. If they are still there, they will welcome us."

"Onondagas? I don't know," said Paul, who, after all, had just barely survived the love of his Seneca brothers and had no desire to try the affections of these British allies.

"They will welcome us," Big Oak insisted, but he began to wonder himself. In wartime there were always young warriors who resisted the common sense of their elders, and sometimes won the battle of wills between themselves and their fathers. Halfway down the hill, where the land was better and the weed-choked cornfields began, the path became a wagon road that had been vastly improved by the labor of George and his sons. The going was easy now for Paul. Big Oak resisted the impulse to see what had happened inside the burned-out houses. It was enough to know that no one had come back to make them whole again. Had the attack been repulsed, the fields would be tall and neat with corn plants, and smoke would be rising from the cooking fires of neatly roofed stone houses.

All that remained to be seen was the cemetery, George Hayes's pride and joy, the mowed field that held only one grave, that of his first wife. Old George had been in awe of this valley, especially the last time Big Oak had visited it five years before. In a day when baby deaths were as common as a cold, Hayes's valley had resisted the death of human beings year after year; the population had grown, and George deemed this phenomenon to be a sign that the Lord approved of the life he and his family led. Big Oak was not a skeptic by nature, nor did he dispute with George on the subject. He was so amazed himself, that his only question was why, of all the souls of the valley, the Lord had chosen to take Ida, George's first wife, the finest of them all.

Ten minutes into the valley he found the area where he knew the cemetery was located. The spot was surrounded by tall weeds. Big Oak pointed to a lone poplar tree, and Paul sat down in its shade. Big Oak then waded through the weeds and was surprised to see that the cemetery was still neatly mowed. Instead of a lone grave, the field held a half-dozen headstones. Whereas Ida's stone was chipped and shaped as if by a stonemason, the other stones were not stones at all, but large wooden planks. This told Big Oak that among the victims must have been Martin, the gentlest of the brothers, who had the skills of the stone cutter.

He walked up to the line of headboards. They might not have been stone, but they were neatly aligned, and beautifully carved and painted. Something sank deep into the pit of his stomach as he read: Charles Hayes, 1754–1778. He was buried on the left next to Ida. To the right of Ida was Martin. These were the center graves, with two more on the right, Martin's wife Ruth, and their son Jonathan. On the other side was Richard, the boy Big Oak had saved from the Senecas thirteen years before.

Big Oak walked over to Ida's grave, listened to the wind for a while and thought about George who was so confident of his righteousness, so strong in his abstract hates and his personal loves. He was a man who could pick your pocket then turn around and give back twice as much because you needed it. A man who raised children like himself, children who could not stand to be idle for a moment, patient, plodding children who loved that valley so much that not a one thought to leave it. And Big Oak was certain that until the day the raiders came, George was a happy man because wherever he looked in the valley, he could see a home where one of his children lived, or a furrow being plowed straight and deep by one of his progeny.

He looked around the valley. From the open ground of the cemetery he could see most of the homes of the community, built on the hillsides where the land was less valuable for planting, among the orchards. Not a single house showed a sign of life.

Except one.

It was Jughead's house, the house closest to the cemetery, a house he called the apple house because he had planted apple trees so close that in September you could lean out the loft window and pick the fruit off the nearest tree. There was the place to go.

Paul was lying under the poplar tree, his pack for a pillow, asleep. Paul rarely slept in the daytime. He must have exhausted his last reserves on this second day of the journey. Big Oak did not want to awaken his friend. The rest would do him good. Shouldering his rifle, Big Oak shuffled up the road to see the son of his old friend.

Off the road was a narrow path that led to Jughead's house. Big Oak's eyes may not have been what they used to be, but he could see eyes peering through the window next to the door as he walked toward the house.

"George!" Big Oak shouted when he had come within thirty feet of the porch. Jughead's real name was George Hayes, Jr., and Big Oak felt certain that the nickname was no longer appropriate.

The door opened and a once young farmer walked from the house. Big Oak remembered the many visits he and Thad had made in this hospitable valley, and the laughter of the man once he had gotten over his initial suspicions. English-speaking visitors were rare in this part of the country. Young George came to view the visits of the Watleys as special events, moments that brought joy to the usually stern New England face of his father. When Big Oak and Thad were around, his father always seemed to loosen up. Then George Jr. could loosen up.

"Big Oak, isn't it?" he asked, without much enthusiasm.

"What happened, George?"

The oldest son of Big Oak's old friend stood tall and gaunt before Big Oak, his face skull-like in its ascetic leanness. "When an army fights and loses a battle to the Indians, there is disappointment and sadness. When a family fights and loses a battle to the Indians, it breaks hearts and makes people want to not go on living."

"Senecas?"

"Your brothers, Big Oak. Your cruel, savage, miserable brothers, may they all rot in hell. We were bothering no one. Our corn fed them as well as us through the winter months. When the war began, we were selling thousands of bushels of corn to the British army at Fort Niagara."

"Did you defend your father's house?"

"Our people took the tunnel from the house to the shelter under the barn. The Senecas burned the house. They burned the barn. If the smoke from the barn had ever gone underground, we would have lost the women and children."

"Where is everybody?"

"Over at the Onondaga town."

"Why have they not come back?"

"They are afraid the Senecas will return. I have to say that I am too. But I stay down here to show them that we have the valley back, and that if they go back to their houses, then all will be well. But they won't go. Pa wants them to go back, but they won't till the war is over. So he stays with them."

"Is your family well?" Big Oak asked.

"They are well, but they would like to live somewhere else. They still see scalp locks in the bushes. I keep hoping that time will change their feelings."

By now Big Oak realized that young George was not about to invite him into his home. He remembered the hospitality of his father and the openhanded generosity of the entire family. He did not blame George for his insecure behavior. He had seen it many times on the frontier. Maybe it was because of fear of hostile Indians, or maybe it was a case of people simply being where they no longer belonged. Big Oak had given up trying to separate the tormenters from the victims on the frontier. The chain of history was too confused.

"How does it go at the Onondaga village?" Big Oak asked.

"What do you mean?" George had cocked his head aggressively, remembering his father's speeches about Big Oak's partiality to Indians.

"How are your father and the rest faring there?"

"The Onondagas have taken good care of them," George admitted. "Maybe they are afraid of what the whites might do to them when the war is over."

There was the Hayes suspicion, always there hidden behind their close relations with the Onondagas.

"We have just come from the war around the Chemung Valley. I am with an Oneida who was wounded. I remember that Rachel knew the healing arts. Would you like to go with us to the village?"

"No," young George answered quickly. "I don't go there much anymore." He looked across the valley, which must have once seemed so beautiful to him and now must appear so desolate.

Big Oak understood. He stuck out his hand and young George took it. "If there is anything I can ever do for you, send a message to me through Wendel and Watley in Albany."

George bowed his head, said nothing, and after a perfunctory shake, released Big Oak's hand. The old trader walked down the path, onto the main road and up toward the poplar tree where Paul was still resting.

On the north side of the valley Big Oak led the way along the wagon road, and was surprised to see that it did not diminish to a bare footpath as it did on the other side of the valley. Apparently there had been a considerable amount of traffic between the valley and the Onondaga village before the Seneca raid had decimated the valley. The way out of the valley was hard for Paul, but he never faltered. Up and over the hill they went, then down the long slope to the Onondaga village five miles away.

Big Oak noticed that along the way were bridges over

creeks and places where the road was cut into the hillside to reduce the steepness of the slope. There were some places where the road had been corduroyed with logs, and others where drainage ditches had been dug. It was the finest stretch of road Big Oak had seen since he had left the vicinity of Albany. The final mile wound through a sloping hillside of ash trees that led to the summit of a low hill, then down into the village, which consisted of more than three dozen cabins ranged along the wagon road and two narrow paths that crossed it. Beyond the last Indian cabin the wagon road narrowed. Fifty yards down that path stood a small cluster of newer, smaller cabins, temporary shelters for the refugees from Hayes's valley.

Of the six nations, Big Oak had spent the least time among the Onondagas. They were the keystone of the Iroquois. Centrally located, they had been the keepers of the council fire until January of 1777, when a disease epidemic in Onondaga had so weakened the village that the council fire had been allowed to go out. They had refused to side with the rebels, but neither had they sent braves to Niagara in large numbers to fight for the king. It seemed to Big Oak that the Onondagas pretty much went their own way.

There were few people in the village on the afternoon that Big Oak and Paul walked down the wagon road into the center. The women, he thought, would be tending the crops, the men fishing, more likely than hunting. But there was a familiar figure standing in the doorway of one of the cabins. Peter Littletree.

Big Oak could feel Peter's eyes on him as he approached the house along the wagon road. He met Peter's eyes with his own, and when he came within a few feet of the Onondaga, he stopped. "I know you," he said. "You are Rachel's brother."

Peter nodded. "I know who you are," he said.

"I must see Rachel. My friend is hurt," Big Oak explained.

He led them into what he called the lower village. There, many of the people were hanging about: women, a very few men, quite a few children, thin-looking, anxious-looking people. Big Oak recognized the tall, dignified Onondaga figure of Rachel as soon as she opened the door of her little home.

"Look at them," Peter said with an edge to his voice, his arm sweeping around the lower village. "They depend on her for everything, and they have no heart left in them."

She smiled when she saw Big Oak. "Hello, Sam," she said, extending her hand in greeting.

Big Oak took it. "You look well," he replied.

"Thank you. And how is your wife?" Big Oak had no desire for small talk. He wanted her to help Paul, and he wanted to see his old friend George.

Quickly he introduced her to Paul, explained what had happened, and had Paul remove his shirt. She did not flinch when she saw his grotesque wound. "The Senecas," she said, "have not been kind to you and me."

"The Senecas are being punished," Paul replied. "This winter they will feel the cold in their bones. They will know what it means to fear for their children." Big Oak listened and thought sadly of the tricks time has a way of playing on people. Twenty years ago Big Oak thought the Senecas were the finest people on the face of the earth. And now to hear what their brother and sister of the Longhouse had to say about them—well, the Senecas hadn't changed, it was just that a little history had happened.

Rachel had a lot more to say about the battle than Jughead had told him. "When the men went out to make their ambush," she began, "we hid in a tunnel under our barn. We were nearly smothered when they set fire to the barn. Lucky it was a long enough cave that if we crowded far enough in we were beyond the smoke. There we stayed in the dark for almost the whole day, until young George and several of the others came back and led us out. How good the night air felt, and how we cried when they told us who was dead. It was then, as we looked around, that we realized people were missing.

"Young George, my brother, and Simon, the third oldest"
—Big Oak nodded to show that he remembered Simon—
"said that the Senecas must have taken prisoners. Martha,
whose husband Alexander was missing, squeezed her hands
together and began to cry, and other people started to cry,
and young George, he said that they would go after the
Senecas and get the prisoners back. I told them I thought
we would only lose more people and they would kill their
prisoners. Some of the women who had men missing got
angry at me, and George said it was something he had to
do, that his father would want him to do it. I told him that
was true, but that when they find them, they must decide
whether it is possible to rescue them. One of the women
became angry with me and began to hit me. She said that
we must rescue her husband, and I knew that nothing I said
would make any difference, so from then on I was silent.

"They did not wait, they took supplies and left that
night, seven, eight of them. The second day out they
walked right into an ambush. Three were killed right there,
and two more were taken prisoner. Only young George,
Peter, and Bob, one of the grandchildren, ran away.

"Peter told me all this. George would never tell anybody
anything. They found a spot on a hill where they could see
into the Seneca camp. That night the Senecas must have
decided that the traveling was too slow with their prisoners.
While my stepson and my brother watched, the Senecas
took the prisoners out, and killed them suddenly—cut their
throats or tomahawked them. There was no thought of taking any home with them, no thought of spending time
torturing them, they just killed them, scalped them,
stripped off their clothes, and threw them in a big fire." As
she spoke, a dark shadow of sadness passed across her face.

"When they got back and told the women what had
happened, Martha cried out and promised that she for one
would not spend another moment in this valley without her
man. There was all sorts of mourning and shrieking and
blaming, and the rest were so frightened and sad that they

all agreed they would spend no more nights in Hayes's valley.

"Then Judith, you know Judith." Big Oak recalled another of George Hayes's daughters-in-law. "Judith said she was frightened to live in this valley but she did not know where she and her children could go. It was then I suggested that we go to my village."

" 'You think we should go to the Indians so they will kill our children while they are sleeping?' Judith asked. I just told them they can either stay in this valley and try to fight off the Senecas alone next time, or they can come to the Onondagas. They will protect you, I told them."

All the time she was talking she had been working on Paul, packing herbs and other substances into the wound. "It looks good in there, but this will draw the poison out, if there is any left in there," she told Paul.

"Tell me, Rachel," Big Oak said. "While all this talk was going on, what was George doing?"

"George?" Her dark eyes regarded the old trader. "My George said nothing. Until that day he was the big, strong leader in our valley. You know how he was, a man with a will to get things done, and so powerful that the boys did his will. He was so sure he knew the right things to do. Until the battle was over and we buried our dead. Buried his children. And then there were the ones we never did find."

She continued to work on Paul as she spoke. "When we decided to move to the village, I thought he would refuse. He had spent half his life building up the valley. But he said nothing. He just followed us quietly to the village. When John Justice tried to talk to him about arranging our stay, he would not talk to him. 'Talk to Rachel,' he said to John Justice.

"My people treated them kindly. Ten different families made room in their homes for the Hayeses. And then they helped them to build these little houses."

"Don't they want to go back to their homes in the valley?" Big Oak asked.

"We are afraid the Senecas will return. We have stores of food that the Senecas did not touch when they destroyed the valley. And my people have taught the older boys much about hunting and fishing. So we have all made out all right. Many of the women say they will never go back to the valley. When the war is over, they will go back to their families, or back to Albany."

"And where is George?"

"Either he is out fishing with the men in the village," she replied, "or he is out walking in the hills. He does that a lot. Sometimes he walks back to the valley to visit the graves, but not lately.

"There," she said as she finished winding a clean strip of linen carefully around Paul's body, trying to cause as little pain as possible. Paul did not cry out, but Big Oak could see that her attentions had been very painful to him.

Paul thanked her. "And what about you? What will you do?" he asked. Rachel was surprised at the question. She had addressed none of her commentary toward Paul and hadn't noticed any interest from him in her dialogue with Big Oak.

"Why do you ask?"

"You are a leader among these people now," he said, but she shook her head.

"George is the leader. He will get over this. He is still a strong man. He is hurt, but not dead. One day he will walk through this door, pull me by the hand and say, 'Enough! We are going back to the valley. We will make it even better than it was, and this time no one will dare set foot in it without us allowing them to!' That's what he'll say."

Peter looked at Big Oak and gave the slightest shake of his head.

"Do you think that George would like to see me?" Big Oak asked with great delicacy.

She smiled gently, and Big Oak decided that not once,

but twice, his friend George, like himself, had been extremely fortunate in his choice of mates. "He will want very much to see you," she said, "when he is George again. Now? I don't know."

❖21❖

TWO MONTHS HAD PASSED SINCE SULLIVAN
and his army had set out from the Wyoming Valley. The
way home was much easier than the way out. The footpath
west had become a highway east. All the battles had been
fought. There simply were no Indians left skulking in the
woods. No Senecas, no Cayugas, no Mohawks.

Thad wondered at the changes that had occurred in such
a short time. Although he, James, and Jinja continued to
roam the flanks, the front, and the rear of their army, they
could tell that it was all over. Forests have their ways of
forgetting the men who once used them. Old tracks get
obliterated by the rain or obscured by new growth. Bent
twigs and grass blades straighten out. The wind scatters
yesterday's campfires.

All the way west they had seen signs of crafty Ganonsyoni watching, always watching, the marching continentals.
Now, on the way back, there was no one left to watch. The
Senecas and the Mohawks of Major Butler had been swept
westward by an army of patriots. Thad believed those Senecas and Mohawks would not be back. Ever.

James knew what Thad knew. He wondered what that
meant for his people, and his father, and himself.

The men had left a wide trail of burnt fields and destroyed Seneca and Cayuga towns on the way west. After

the battle that had nearly cost Paul his life, Butler had turned only one more time on Sullivan's army, by now estimated at close to five thousand men. Butler had attempted one last ambush, of an advance party of scouts and skirmishers.

Maybe Paul would have figured it out. Paul had an uncanny sense of where to look and what to look for. James was good, but not good enough, while Thad and Jinja were much better fighters than they were scouts. So the first clue that they were in trouble occurred at dusk when pinpoints of fire licked at them from three sides in a field of tall grass.

The Americans did what they should have done. They turned tail and ran back toward the main army with about fifty Senecas and Mohawks in frenzied pursuit. James, Jinja, and Thad were swift afoot. They outran their pursuers. Behind them they could hear the screams of several soldiers who had been brought down and were about to lose their scalps and their lives. There were about five others with them in the advance party, and on command they stopped, turned around, and fired a volley into their enemies. A few bodies tumbled and the rest faltered long enough to allow the fortunate few to make their getaway. By that time elements of the main body of the American army were coming up at the double-quick. Abruptly the fleeing scouts turned around and became the battle guides leading lethal, superior forces against their tormenters.

Like a snow flurry on a spring day, the Senecas and Mohawks melted into the surrounding forests with a couple of unfortunate prisoners. Butler, meanwhile, pulled his little army back and continued his retreat to Fort Niagara.

For a moment James had felt a joyous pride at being followed by a battalion of American soldiers screaming like eagles, scattering the enemy to the winds. This was his army and on this day he was one of them, rushing forward toward where he had first seen rifle flashes, with the confident power of seasoned soldiers at his back. Through the long grass and up the hill they ran, and when they reached the top, they found the body of a green-suited Tory. His comrades had left in too much of a hurry to take his body with them.

They never stopped as they swept over the hill. They ran down the other side and were rewarded when they overtook a pair of limping stragglers. The Americans beat them to the ground with their rifle butts, and five stayed with them while the multitudes rushed on after James, who had a clear trail of fleeing loyalist troops to follow. Only the darkness prevented the excited Americans from overtaking Butler's men and wiping them out. Butler had escaped again, and in the process his Indians had bloodied the soldiers a bit, but it was a final, futile gesture. After the battle, James searched for and found Thad and Jinja.

"Where were you?" James asked, laughing. "I thought at least Jinja would be runnin' on ahead, trying to catch the whole Tory army."

Thad looked at Jinja, who was leaning calmly on his long rifle. "I think my son is finally about ready to go home," Thad said.

Two days later Sullivan decided that his men had done the job they had set out to do, and turned them eastward. Like old plow horses who knew that they were finally headed for the barn after a hard day's work, their backs straightened and their pace picked up. There were smiles all around. On the way home, Sullivan occasionally sent Colonel Jamison and his men on a side foray to burn another Seneca or Cayuga town, and the fields around them. It was sweaty but easy work. There were no Indians dogging their steps. Thad found himself shaking his head. There are no more Indians here, he kept thinking over and over. They're gone, they're really gone. Remembering the happy days he had passed among the Senecas as a child, and among the Mohawks as an adult, he knew that his heart would ache with loneliness once the war was over and the loss hit home.

The way back east was a pleasant one, except for the

poor teamsters handling half-starved horses pulling guns and baggage. It took about two weeks to get back to where they started. The men were hungry, but there were few desertions because they were so filled with a sense of victory and achievement. The officers had to ply them with vague, good-natured threats to keep them from making the forests ring with song on the long march home. They were like children on the night before Christmas, warmed not only by their sense of victory, but by their discovery of what sterling human beings their comrades in the ranks were, and that they were all Americans. The song they kept wanting to sing was "Yankee Doodle." Like many a later anthem, it was the spirit of the song, not its grand lyric content, that made them love it so; a song they could shove in the face of their enemy and say, "How do you like it? What do you think of us now? Do you still think that you are our betters? Too bad, because we just beat on your hind end till you can't even sit down on your fine horses."

The starting point for many of them had been tiny Fort Tioga. Now they were only a day away when Colonel Jamison summoned Thad, Jinja, and James, and sent them ahead to the fort on the run. The colors had been stowed at the fort and the band had been left there with the garrison troops. The following day around noon, the army marched out of the woods, across an overgrown field, and over a rise. The road veered to the right about a quarter mile ahead, so they could see nothing when they first heard the distant sound of approaching drums.

Sullivan drew his army up in a parade formation, with companies side by side across the crest of the hill, and there they stood at attention, awaiting their blue-clad fife and drum band.

What they saw first, rounding the bend a quarter mile away, were three small figures, their rifles at right shoulder arms, marching side by side in step with the drums. They were puzzled at first. This was no color guard, nor were they officers, lacking both swords and, for that matter, uniforms. The three marched another hundred yards before the soldiers finally realized that they were their three most trusted scouts, for these men were usually swift shadows guarding their flanks, and never had they been seen marching to the beat of a drum. Somehow the sight of the three free-ranging woodsmen marching in step to the cadence caught the imagination of the ranks, so that when the adjutant put them at ease, they broke into a long, roaring cheer. As the three men marched closer, the cheers got louder.

Then from around the bend came the colors, the unit flags and the state flags, and in the center, the American flag itself. The cheers grew louder still when the band appeared. They were the showpiece, with their fine blue uniforms and their shiny brass buttons and their polished black boots, in tight formation, to a stirring drumbeat, with all other instruments still silent. The three scouts approached the army from the right flank, executed a smart right turn, and began to parade past the cheering company formations. They had passed halfway down the line when the general called his army to attention, an order relayed down the officer chain to company level, at which time each company snapped to stiff attention and then presented arms as the flag bearers did their turn and began to parade before the troops. Thad could not help but note the pride and sharpness of the formations, and if the uniforms were not uniform, and the boots and rifles did not shine, the men were nevertheless an army of disciplined fighters.

Now the band commenced, and of course the tune was "Yankee Doodle." The men in the ranks did not join in. They were in formation, and orders were to be obeyed. But their eyes moved with the colors until they were out of their view, and then the eyes of the troops moved with the band. More than a few of them felt their eyes sting with emotion and their chests heave with pride, and sometimes their weapons trembled, because the arms that held them were trembling. General Sullivan's throat ached him. He could scarcely believe what his army had accomplished in the past two months. If other armies farther south could do as well, another year or two could bring victory to the thirteen united states.

Now the three scouts dropped out of the parade. The colors wheeled and headed back down the road toward the fort, followed by the band and then the army, formation by formation. They marched around the bend, over another rise, and down the last stretch before reaching the fort. The guns boomed from the fort in salute. The gates, which had stayed closed against surprise attack throughout the summer, now opened wide for the returning army. In addition to the hundreds of garrison troops, there were many civilians in and around the fort, cheering madly as the army marched into the fort and formed on the parade ground within. Never had the civilians seen so many men under arms at one time. Never had they seen an American army so certain of its worth and accomplishments.

And when the last ammunition wagon creaked through the gates, three dusty figures walked the last hundred yards into the fort, and even after they entered, the gates remained open. There were no warriors left outside to fill the hearts of the civilians with terror.

General Sullivan stood on a catwalk overlooking the parade ground.

"Men," he shouted when the civilians had ceased their uproar and the soldiers had moved into formation on the parade ground of the fort. "I have had much to say to you before and during our march across New York. I need say no more. You know what you have done, and I know what you have done, and we can all be proud. I will say no more to you for now. You have earned your rest. Officers major and higher will meet in my quarters after dismissal, and now I give leave for all commanders to dismiss their units."

And they did.

Soldiers mingled with their wives and civilians. There was rum and there was beer, and there were more questions than there were answers. But as Thad, Jinja, and James walked among them, each with an iron cup in his hand, what they heard most about was the countryside that these men had seen and conquered.

"And once we had beaten them bloody," cried one, his mouth wearing a beard of beer foam, "we found ourselves chasing them across the finest farmland you'd ever want to see!"

"I hear that when the war is over soldiers might be paid in grants of land," a gray-headed trader said, ladling out rum for one of the scouts but talking to an artilleryman who lacked two fingers on his left hand.

"I'll take a few acres of land over a million dollars continental!" exclaimed the artilleryman. "I tell you, the land is ours. I do not believe we'll ever again see a Seneca skulking around our cabins again."

"There you have the nub of it," responded an infantryman in a dirty linen hunting shirt. "The land is ours."

Degata and Otter had little left to them but the clothes on their backs when they finally struggled in through the gates of Fort Niagara. The interior of the fort was a madhouse of desperate red men from a dozen tribes. They spilled through the gates to the fields outside the fort, where hundreds were clustered in makeshift wigwams and huts. They came from many tribes, from many places. In addition to the Senecas and Mohawks there were Onondagas, Lenni Lenape, Conoys, Nanticokes, even some Oneidas and Tuscaroras, and a few Shawnees from the banks of the Allegheny River. What they all had in common was a war that had stripped them of their land, their possessions, and many of their best people.

Degata saw the fear on the faces of the women and children who had recently arrived from their decimated villages. Some of them walked around from point to point in the fort, looking for a familiar face or someone who might say something to them that might be helpful, but afraid to touch a stranger. Others sat huddled together, waiting.

He had known women and children like this before. He had even helped them get that way, during his younger years when Seneca braves still raided west. What he had never seen before were the scores of warrior-age men milling around, looking for someone who would help them. He had seen handfuls of loafabouts before, but never in such numbers, from tribes who only months before would have cheerfully killed each other on sight, now thrown together in a pitiful stew of lost hopes and dreams.

In the office of Colonel Guy Johnson, his commissary officer was asking him how he could be expected to feed all these people.

"We have food. We have to feed them or we will lose them," Johnson answered.

"But they keep coming, every day."

"In a few weeks we'll have the men out hunting," he said.

There was an older man in woodsman's garb standing by the doorway, watching the confused, unhappy mob of people and listening to the cries of hundreds of babies and young children. His name was Kirby and he had been trading with the Cayugas and Delawares for almost as long as Big Oak had been dealing with the Senecas and Mohawks.

"I'm not so sure you'll be able to get many of them to go out huntin', sir," Kirby said to the Colonel. "I seen defeat in the eyes of people before, and it makes 'em not good for much. They went to war for us, and we promised we'd help them drive the rebels out of this colony. We told them there was only a few rebels, and we told them the rebels weren't no account. I'll never know why them poor devils keep believin' us year after year, no matter what we tell 'em. They seen more men with guns runnin' through the hills and burnin' up their country this year than they ever seen before in their whole lives. I think maybe they don't believe us anymore. But they're a little late in findin' out."

"Kirby," Johnson said, "I suggest you get back into the woods and see if you can find out where the rebels are."

"I know where they are all right, sir. They're back home and feelin' like they just whipped the whole world."

"Well, they didn't whip a damn thing," Johnson growled.

"Maybe not," Kirby agreed. "But they drove the Indians out of their villages and into the fort, and now we'd better find a way to feed 'em or it's gonna be a long cold winter for all of us."

Degata and Otter somehow found a quiet corner of the fort, and there they consumed their last handfuls of corn, undisturbed. "Do you think our families have made it up here?" Otter asked Degata.

"Maybe not yet," Degata answered. "We must look for them." They closed their pouches and returned to where soldiers were handing out bowls of soup to the people who over the past few days had learned to queue up.

Otter's eyes scanned the sea of dark faces. "I know none of these," he said. "When will we go back and fight the bad white men again?"

Degata studied the inquiring coal-black eyes. "Someday," he said. "Maybe."

❧22❧

BIG OAK AND PAUL HAD EARNED THEIR RIGHT
to relax, or so they thought. That was part of the illusion
cast through the magic of Big Oak Pond amidst the colors
of fall.

When Big Oak had returned from Paul's village, he decided that he needed a project. He called the boys together
and told them he wanted to build a little guest house. Naturally they thought that was a great idea. They spent an
afternoon sharpening tools, then the next day they began
leveling trees on a piece of land down the hill south of the
house. Three weeks later they had the house built, complete with a stone fireplace and chimney that drew a fine
draft. While the boys spent the next couple of days carefully chinking the logs, Big Oak took a run west to Paul's
village and talked Paul and Lizabet into spending a week
with them.

It pleased him that they needed no persuading. Further-
more, Paul's wound had healed so well that they made great
time back to Big Oak Pond. The boys had done a satisfactory job on the cabin, and Cilla had managed to take a stick
of furniture from here and a stick from there, to make the
cabin look a bit like a home.

"Sorry about the shutters," Big Oak told them. "Next time

I go to Albany I'll bring back some window glass and someone who knows how to put it in."

"Fine cabin," Paul said as he looked around. "Let's fish."

The women walked over to the main house, which was about eighty feet from the new guest house. Big Oak and Paul followed them as far as the front porch. Big Oak reached under the porch for a pair of fishing poles and the two walked down to the pond. On the way, Big Oak spotted Joshua and promised him a penny if he would catch them some crickets. The boy smiled, nodded, and headed for the house to find a container.

The two men each found his favorite tree, leaned back and lit up. The fall colors were at their height. The two studied them on the mountain that formed the backdrop to the pond, the green of the pines and hemlocks and the blue of the spruce contrasting in color and texture to the reds, oranges, and yellows of the oaks, maples, and elms.

They puffed and blew smoke and watched the wind carry the fragrance away, and felt contentment. It was not just the colors and the tobacco, it was not just the feeling that the war in their part of the country was over and that their children would be all right, at least for now. Most of all it was the realization of the rarity of perfect friendship. For Big Oak it was the horror of nearly losing a friend followed by the relief that comes from saving him. For Paul it was the fact that a friend had put his life in peril to save him. So there was an additional exquisite richness in this ritual, which they had performed so many times before.

They had had hundreds of conversations over the years, first short ones, feeling each other out, then gradually, as they had learned to trust each other, discussions that revealed their deepest thoughts. They never burdened each other with the meaningless conversation that provides mere rhythm to companionship, and they seldom spoke sentiments that they had told each other before, for they knew each other's thoughts, and each knew what the other knew about him. In short, they shared a lot of silent moments, and rarely failed to enjoy them.

Joshua returned with a wooden box. Inside were a score of crickets crawling over each other. Each hooked a cricket and tossed a line into the water. They sat back, puffing on their pipes just enough to keep them lit, their eyes sometimes on the water, sometimes on the mountain, sometimes on the sky, and sometimes nearly closed. What did they think about? Did they think about their battles and their triumphs? Their loves? Their children? Did they think about the changes over the land? Perhaps they thought about the eternal God's cruelest trick, the trick He played on all those fortunate to live a full life, the trick whereby a man blinks his eyes just once and his youth is gone, never to return. It's such a cruel trick that it leaves a man blaming himself. Why didn't I stop time when I could? Why did I let myself get this old?

On the final warm fall day of 1779 these two great friends let their pipes go out as they nodded off into a hazy snooze. The fish did not bite. No woodpecker went rat-tat-tat on a bug-ridden old beech tree. No rabbit exploded out of a thicket. Their chins sank into their chests. And their cold pipes dropped from their mouths.

The sun had moved halfway across the heavens when Paul's chin rose from his chest. He had heard something that stirred him from his nap. His eyes opened. Suddenly he was awake. The mountain was the same, and so was the pond. There was no movement in the brush. Still, something had awakened him. And now it came again: "Cansadeyo!"

He looked toward the sound, up the hill to their right, where the house was, and smiled to see the tall, strong figure of his son silhouetted against the sky. James called him Cansadeyo, his Oneida name, usually when he was excited about something.

Paul picked up his fishing pole and waved it. He could not hear the laughter, but he could see it in the motion of

James's body as he half walked, half ran down the hill to shake his father's hand. Big Oak was taking all this in. He had awakened to the same sound as Paul had. And now he was surprised to see that as James approached, he had a great big smile on his face. At first Big Oak wondered if the young man was grimacing with pain, for he had never seen James with such a huge grin.

"What is it?" Paul asked as his son stood before him, continuing to grin like a fool. "There is a reason why you're here instead of making a pest of yourself around this man's granddaughter in Albany."

"I *have* been making a pest of myself with this man's granddaughter in Albany," James replied. "At last I made such a pest of myself that to get rid of me she agreed to marry me."

Paul looked at his son with his best hide-your-feelings-from-the-white-man look. There was a long silence. "And this is what you want to do?" he asked finally.

James wished to be polite. His father seldom asked stupid questions. "Yes," he answered.

Paul turned his eyes toward Big Oak, who stroked his beard thoughtfully.

James looked at the two men, puzzled. He had not expected this reaction and did not understand it.

"Did you talk to Thad about this?" Big Oak asked.

"Thad is in Schenectady on business," James replied.

"What about Katherine?"

"What about her? Why should I talk to them?"

"Because that's what people do," said Big Oak. "That's what English people do . . . American people," he added, confused.

James looked into Big Oak's eyes. "You don't want me to marry her, do you?" he asked.

"Want you to—of course I want you to," Big Oak responded peevishly. "I think the two of you—"

"Would you go with me back to Albany?"

Big Oak folded his arms in front of him and started to

laugh, but James's face was so serious that the old trader choked off his chuckle. "I think that's a very good idea, don't you, Paul?"

"Better than sittin' around here waiting for the fish to bite on a dead cricket," Paul said.

"Guess we'd better get ready to go, then," Big Oak suggested.

The three men walked into the great room of the house and announced to Cilla and Lizabet that they were going to Albany. The women asked why, and the men told them that it seemed there was a wedding coming up in the near future and that therefore some discussions were in order. As good Longhouse wives, Cilla and Lizabet were certainly not going to be left out of that, so they immediately began packing. "Call the boys," Cilla told Big Oak. "We'll be ready quickly."

It was only a day's walk for the little group, nothing special, so in fifteen minutes they were about ready to go. Cilla made certain the fire was out. Then they stepped off down the trail, with Caleb proudly in the lead, his keen eyes taking in every detail in front of him, as if the woods were still alive with Abnakis and Mohicans. Joshua walked in the footsteps of his big brother, watching their flanks.

Then came the two older couples, in a gay mood, chattering like squirrels. James followed, silent, watching the tree lines but mostly thinking about the step he had taken three days before. Suddenly, with all these people making a journey on his account, it seemed so much bigger than it had when he and Anne went for a walk and she seemed so happy to be with him that the question just popped out of him, unplanned, unrehearsed, natural and charming. Anne had been used to the pompous attentions of the wealthier boys in town. They were fun, but James was more like her father, and that was real stuff. James made her feel grown-up, and she liked feeling that way.

Bringing up the rear was Big Oak's reliable boy Ken, and Ken knew that the last man on a trail party was critical. He stuck close to James but did not speak to him. Like the boys up front, his ears and eyes were on notice for dangers. The trees and the rocks were his enemies. They concealed deadly things. He wanted to tell his parents and James's parents to be quiet, but adults knew best, there must be no danger out there.

They made it to Albany late the following afternoon. The dusty streets were deep in shadow by the time they arrived at Thad's house. Big Oak took hold of the new heavy brass door knocker and let it fall on the door, which it did with a bang. Then he did it again. The door was opened by a black male servant he had never seen before, tall, regal, unsmiling.

"Yes?" said the servant, who refused to be disconcerted by the eight unexpected persons who stood on the porch of his house.

Big Oak was surprised. "Would you tell Mr. Watley that his father has arrived?" he said.

His father and half the Iroquois nation, thought the servant, but he just bowed and closed the door.

A few moments later the door opened and there stood Thad, still clad in the suit he wore on his journey back from Schenectady. He gave a chuckle but did not invite them in. Instead he walked out on the porch and started to hug each of them. The boys returned his hugs noisily and wanted to know who was the man with the dark skin who opened the door. Cilla thought Thad looked fine, and said so, and Big Oak told him he needed to eat less.

"How did you know they were coming down?" he asked James after he had lavished the proper affection on each member of the group.

"Know? He fetched us," Big Oak interjected.

"Oh," Thad replied. The group grew silent while behind them a carriage pulled by an unmatched team rumbled by.

James looked into Thad's face. "I must talk to you," he said.

"Later," Thad said, a little grin on his face. "Let's go inside."

Thad opened the door and walked in, followed, single file, by his father, Paul, the women, the boys, and James. It took only a moment for Big Oak to figure out why his son was behaving so strangely. The chandeliers in the big front room had been lowered and four workers were installing dozens of new candles. People were scurrying around bringing in food and bottles of wine. In the middle of all the activity stood Katherine, hands on hips, giving orders, waving her arms, and almost running her hand through her hair, but always stopping short of doing so, because somebody had done it up in the latest fashion.

Her face turned from the wine bottles to Big Oak and his Indians, and froze with her mouth open just short of giving an order. "Thad!" she shouted above the noise of a chandelier being raised, fully lit, to the ceiling.

She backed off to the far end of the room. Thad followed her until he was close enough to hear her shouted, sibilant whispers. Big Oak and his party were treated to the sight of watching his son's wife launching a hissing, arm-waving tirade. He stood two feet away from her, his hands clasped behind his back, one ear turned toward her, listening as if her every word were gold to him. Big Oak looked at his family and friends. "Looks like we picked a bad time to visit," he said unnecessarily. "Let's go out and wait on the porch. Thad'll be out directly."

James put a hand on Big Oak's arm. "Not yet," he said. By now half the workers had stopped what they were doing and the room had grown quiet enough for the visitors to hear Thad say in a soft voice, "They are my family. I will take care of them. You may take care of your party."

He beckoned his father to follow him, and he began to climb the stairs, two at a time, with Big Oak, Paul, the women, the boys, and James trooping up after him. At the top of the stairs he turned left down the hall and threw open the door to a large room with a bed and several stuffed chairs in it.

"Make yourselves comfortable," he said. "James, would you care to come with me?"

James followed Thad out the door. The boys started jumping up and down on the bed, a bit of business that Cilla stopped quietly but immediately. Big Oak looked at Paul and shook his head.

"What are they doing?" Paul asked, referring not to the jumping boys, but to the activity going on downstairs.

"The war has made my son and his father-in-law a lot of money. In big cities, white people who get rich throw big parties for their friends."

Paul brightened. "They do the same in the Iroquois villages, don't you agree?"

"It is the same," Big Oak agreed.

Thad had taken James down a back stairway, through the kitchen, into a small library off the back porch that served as Thad's office at home. He pointed to a stuffed chair. James sat.

"Would you like a glass of wine?" Thad asked, pointing to a crystal decanter that stood with a pair of glasses on a tray.

James declined the wine. He needed to be at his best on this night.

Thad looked longingly at the decanter, then looked away. "Why did you bring all these folks down here?" he asked.

"Anne did not tell you?"

"No. You tell me." Thad's tone of voice was not hostile, but neither was it pleasant.

Things were beginning to happen that James did not anticipate or understand. But James felt he had done right, and did not procrastinate. "Four days ago I asked Anne to marry me."

Thad said nothing. His neutral expression did not change.

"She said yes."

Thad scratched at the back of his neck. "Why did you not come to me first? That is what boys do, you know. They ask the father first."

"I am a woodsman, Thad. Like you. Many customs were taught to me in my village. Some were not. I thought that if she said no, I wouldn't have to bother you. She said yes, but then she said she wanted to talk to you herself before I talked to you. I thought that by the time I came back, everything would be settled. I wanted to bring your father, and mine, to meet my future wife."

Thad laughed. "My father has known his only grand-daughter all her life."

"But not as a grown-up woman. I do not understand what is happening here, Thad."

Thad sighed deeply. "James, my boy, are you sure you want to marry into such a family? Are you sure you want to live your life in Albany?"

"In the Longhouse a man comes into the house of his wife."

"The Longhouse is gone from this place. You know that. You saw it go. You helped it go."

"Do you not want me to marry Anne? Say so."

"You are a woodsman. You are an Indian. A man needs education."

James stared at Thad, not believing the words he was hearing. "You were a woodsman," he said. "You were an Indian. You were educated in the west by a minister. So was I. You married Katherine. How am I different?"

"It is not you who are different. It is not me who is different, no matter what you may think. It is the times that have changed."

"The times? What has—"

Thad waved away his words. "But I would like to have you as a son-in-law. It is Anne's mother who would not want it."

"Do you think Anne has told her?"

"I do not think Anne has told her. I do not think that Anne knows her own mind."

"She said she loves me. She said she wants to marry me."

"She is younger than most girls her age. If she knew what she wanted, we would not be having this party tonight. There are several boys home on leave from the army. Her mother has arranged this party to give her the chance to meet them. Remember, Anne has grown up in the middle of a war which has taken many of the best boys away from Albany. This is what her mother wanted, and Anne does what her mother asks her to do. So she consented to this party. She is directly upstairs from where you are sitting now. I suppose she may be brushing her hair, tying a ribbon, doing things that girls like to do before parties. It's her first chance to do this since she became—more a woman than a little girl. But in some ways she is still like a little girl. Still, she likes you very much. She might have you, but her mother won't."

"Her mother had you!" James insisted with some heat.

"Those were days when an Indian was still a common sight in Albany. But the Indians are gone; cheated and defeated. Maybe men don't want to be reminded."

"Where is Jinja?" James asked.

"He is on the Mohawk River with Ooghnor and several canoes filled with trade goods."

"The Mohawk River?"

"What we—you and I—have always called the Te-non-an-at-che. The people call it the Mohawk River."

"So that people may remember the Mohawks?"

"In the minds of many, the Mohawks are gone. They certainly hope the Mohawks are gone. Never mind the Te-non-an-at-che. Why did you suddenly want to know about Jinja?"

"He is about my size. I want to go to the party tonight."

"You what?" Thad was dumbfounded. "You don't just go to a party. You have to be invited."

"Then invite me. Can't *you* invite me?"

Thad smiled. Then he laughed, a quick chuckle. "Hell, yes, I can invite you. And so you are invited, on one condition, that if she smiles at a young gentleman, you don't pull out your knife and cut his throat."

"Done," James agreed, as if he had just concluded a trade deal with the Lenni Lenape down on the Susquehanna.

"Come with me," Thad said, leaving the room and clumping up the back stairs. James followed him to the upstairs hallway, then to Jinja's room. "I don't think Jinja will mind you borrowing his suit for the night. It will serve a good purpose." He pulled out a fine dark blue suit of clothes with a buff vest and white stockings. "I'll have one of the servants—no, I'd better do it myself—I'll bring up a basin of water so you can clean yourself up a bit. You've still got trail dust on you. Then you can try to put these things on. After a while I'll come back up and see how you're makin' out."

Thad went downstairs, fetched a water basin, walked outside and pumped it full of water, then brought it up to James. From Jinja's room he walked over to the spare room where his friends and relatives waited patiently. "I'm sorry for what's happening tonight. Pa, would you take everybody out to the courtyard? There are torches up around the tables. Just light them and I'll be out in a few minutes with some food for you. You must be very hungry."

Big Oak knew the way. He led everybody down the back stairs into the courtyard. Thad, meanwhile, walked into the big front room, kissed his wife, told her how beautiful everything looked, what a fine party it was going to be, and not to worry about his family, that he would be taking care of them and they would be no bother to her.

"Thank you, dear," she said hurriedly, worried about the preparations for the party, but also worried about the Indians in her house. At that point Dieter walked through the front door.

"Hello, Father," Katherine said, quickly presenting a

cheek. "Here's Thad." She withdrew the cheek and went on supervising.

"Come on into the kitchen with me," Thad said. The old man followed him and watched him grab two large fresh loaves of bread and a huge sausage and haul it out the back door to where Big Oak was lighting the torches.

Dieter smiled to see his old friend and partner Sam, and he was not displeased to see Paul, who was one of his best employees and had made him a lot of money during this war.

"And the ladies," he said, bending over and touching the hands of Cilla and Lizabet. "Und the kinder!" he exclaimed. "Grown too big to carry around on my back anymore, how are my wild Indians?" he asked.

"Uncle Dieter!" they all cried and pushed him and pulled him around with an affection that nearly disjointed the big old fellow.

"You are not going into the party?" Dieter asked with alarm.

"Not on your life," Big Oak said. "Not our kind of party." Through the door they could hear instruments being tuned inside. "If we had known this was happening, we wouldn'ta come, of course," Big Oak declared.

"But of course you would not have come," the old Dutchman agreed. "You could not have known. To tell the truth, I am not such a man for parties either. I come for the food."

And the wine, Big Oak thought to himself.

"Of course," Dieter added, "This food looks good too. You will not mind if I join you for some sausage?"

"A pleasure," Big Oak replied, taking a chair from another table and making a place for Dieter. "Let me do some slicing here," he said, pulling his knife from his belt and grabbing hold of the sausage.

The musicians were warmed up and playing by the time James had made himself comfortable in Jinja's suit. Thad was downstairs helping his wife welcome guests. James could hear carriages and wagons and an occasional rider clattering up to the door. He could also hear the buzz of conversation below becoming louder and louder. For a few moments his courage failed him, especially when he thought that Jinja's shoes were so narrow that he would never get his feet into them.

But then Thad entered, grinned, and told James that he was by far the handsomest lad there.

"Are you sure this is the right thing to do?" James asked.

Thad laughed. "Of course I'm not sure. What do I know? But it's what you want to do, and I think you oughta do it. We'll find out how right it is after it's done. Anne just came down. We'll give her some time to get settled down there, then you can make your appearance. She still doesn't know you're in the house. Can you beat that?"

"I'm not sure I ought to do this. If she truly wanted me, she would not be having this party."

"I told you," Thad insisted, "that Anne still lets her mother run her life. Maybe tonight, when she sees you looking like the noblest gentleman in the house, maybe then she'll let go of her mama. I'll go downstairs for a while, and when the time is right, I'll come and get you myself."

James nodded and sat down on Jinja's bed. Alone now, he felt a wave of sickness washing over the pit of his stomach. He did not belong here. This was for white people. He was not a white man. He began to sweat, and it occurred to him that he was feeling as he felt before a big battle. That was absurd. Men got killed in battles. No matter what happened this night, he could walk out of the house a free man, and go back to his people if he so chose.

Then he took a deep breath and felt better. He had walked the streets of Albany dozens of times, dealt in trade and made money. Why should he worry about the white men downstairs and what they thought? And as for Anne, did she not have the blood of his Seneca brothers flowing through her veins? He could not completely reason away his nervousness. Maybe it would have been better, he thought, had the Reverend Kirkland never taught him the English things.

And then the door opened and Thad was standing in the light of the sconce outside.

"Let's meet the fine folks of Albany," he said.

James stood up and followed Thad into the hallway, then down the stairs. "Stand up straight," Thad said over his shoulder out of the side of his mouth.

James did not have to be told. When he was not crouching in the woods, his bearing was always straight and dignified. Halfway down the stairs he stopped to take in the tableau. There were tables with white cloths on them and glittering glasses on the white cloth. People were picking up the glasses and sipping the contents. Young people were dancing in couples while older people looked on. The fireplaces at either end of the room were ablaze with great fires, as the fall evening cooled down. The candlelight from the big chandeliers gleamed off the polished wood floors.

He looked around for Anne and found her earnestly paying attention to a thin, pale young man who seemed to be saying terribly important things. Instinctively, James did the right thing. He did not shrink into a corner and he did not walk over to the table to hug a glass of wine as he had seen officers do at such parties. He stood by himself on the staircase and waited to be noticed.

Unfortunately, the first person to notice him was Katherine. James was watching her inspecting her party, her eyes taking in the room one area at a time, then freezing when they found him on the staircase. Her mouth opened for just a moment, then angry lines formed on her face as she strode over to Thad, who *was* at the table pouring himself a glass of wine. She got very close to him and her head began to move from side to side as she gave him what for. Thad's expression did not change, and his mouth did not move while he listened to her. When he was certain she was through, he said something very short which made her turn away and head for her daughter. She said something to

Anne that made her turn toward James. The young man she had been talking to looked where she looked, and for a moment both of them stared at James. He stood straight up on the staircase, his arms at his sides, looking for all the world like a tolerant lord waiting for some minor disturbance to die down so he could go on with his business.

Katherine stepped apart from the young man, and Anne followed her example. The young man, socially aware, walked away. Katherine was now talking to her daughter almost as animatedly as she had addressed Thad. Anne listened, obviously distressed, nodding repeatedly.

She said something to her mother, but Katherine gave her a gentle push in James's direction. He walked to the bottom of the stairs to meet her. On Anne's face was a frozen smile. On his was no expression whatever. It seemed to him that it took her all night to cross the floor to meet him, by which time everybody in the room but the musicians and some of the servants were watching her.

She stopped in front of him.

"Hello," he said.

"My mother asked me to talk to you."

"There are many eyes upon us. Maybe we should go out on the porch," he said.

"Maybe we should."

He let her lead him onto the porch. All eyes followed.

"My mother said you should not be here."

"Do you think I should be here?"

Anne did not answer.

"Did I not ask you to marry me?"

She bowed her head and stared at the wooden floor of the porch.

"Did you not say yes?"

More silence.

"You didn't mean it, did you?"

"I did mean it, yes, I did."

"But not now."

"After you left, I wanted to tell my mother about us. But

before I could, she started talking to me about marriage. We had never had a talk like that before. It was as if—she knew. She said that I should marry somebody more—like us."

"Did she make such a marriage for herself?" he asked, feeling as if the porch had suddenly gone askew.

"That's what I asked. She said that when she married my father, Albany was still a frontier village, with Indians still close by to help us or kill us. That's what she said."

"And now?"

"She said that in a new nation, fine social relationships make life more honorable."

"I don't understand a word of what she has told you."

"What who has told who?" came a voice from the steps that led onto the porch. James's spirit took a leap as he saw his friend Jinja standing in the dust.

"Your sister is telling me why your mother thinks she should have nothing to do with me."

Jinja walked up the stairs, over to James, and put a finger in a buttonhole. "You look a hell of a lot better in this suit than I do. Would you like to have it?"

"Doesn't feel comfortable. Too many clothes," James said sarcastically, and Jinja laughed, but Anne started to cry. Jinja studied her as she dabbed her eyes with a handkerchief. He heard the music drifting through the brightly lit windows and looked up to see the formally dressed party-goers who were once again dancing. It did not take long for Jinja to imagine the scenario.

"Why would anyone want to get into this?" Jinja asked, pointing through a window at the dancers. "Annie . . ." Jinja shook his head for a few moments. "James is my brother and my friend. If you care for someone, you don't let your mother tell you what to do. Go inside."

"No," she said. "I don't want to."

"Yes you do. In there is what you want. If you wanted my friend, you'd be in there with him now trying to teach him to dance."

"In front of all those people?" She was aghast.

"You couldn't hide him from them forever. Go inside."

She obeyed. Jinja sat on the steps, and James sat on the porch rail above him.

"You know, James, she may wake up tomorrow morning and change her mind. And then Ma will talk her out of it, if you're lucky. She's a pretty bit of fluff, but that's all she is, yet. I think she'll wind up doing what my ma wants her to do. She always has. And I guess you can see that lets you out."

Jinja saw the stricken look on his friend's face, more emotion than he had ever seen James display.

"I am her brother. I have known her all her life. She holds no mysteries for me, and none for you."

James stared hard at his friend, and listened.

"It is not Anne who has hurt you. It's her mother."

"Not her either," James replied. "It's the truth that has hurt me. And it has not hurt me much. I am Ganonsyoni. A woman should not mean so much to a warrior."

"That is what my father has told me."

"Your father? I thought he loved your mother."

"He does, but he does not always want to be near her. Why do you think he has gone on so many trading trips over the years? He does not need to. Not for the company. But for him. I don't think they could stay together if he didn't spend three months a year out on the trails and the rivers. He says the best times of his life are the three or four days after he gets home from a trip. Once she gets used to him being home, she forgets who he is and starts to treat him like a servant."

"How did your ma ever marry your father?"

Jinja turned around and looked up at James, and James thought about the kid who only a year ago still chased his enemies down as if it were a ball game.

"If it were today, I'm not sure she would," he said.

"But I always thought she loved him so much."

"He has had twenty years to grow with Albany. She is

not the same as she was when they first met. And neither is
this town, or the people. You don't want to be what this
town is becoming. And neither do I."

James's spirit plummeted again. He had seen Jinja as an
ally against Katherine, but he feared that Jinja, his friend,
was right. He was alone, too white for his village, too Indian for Albany.

❧23❧

Big Oak had never remembered the colors being brighter than in October of 1782, exactly one year after the British surrender at Yorktown. There were seven men with him, more than the mission called for, but this trip was half trade mission and half outing. After more than six years of hazardous trade that amounted to smuggling, many of Dieter's employees longed to be on the first peacetime trade mission north, and the old merchant had relented.

Big Oak's legs were feeling young and strong on their first portage north, as they struggled beneath the weight of the canoes and goods they were carrying. Perhaps this was his last long distance trading trip. At his time of life, you never knew, he thought. The only thing to do was pretend you'll live forever. On days like this, pretending was easy.

Big Oak had repeatedly told Dieter that he did not trust the British, and that until the day they were thrown out of North America they would be scheming to get the colonies back somehow. Dieter waved his hand airily and reminded him that the first ones to make the trip up Lake Champlain would be the ones to capture much of the trade with Montreal. "Don't the French live in Montreal?" he said. "And hadn't the French helped us to defeat the English? Don't worry, the French in Canada will be happy to deal with us."

It had taken nearly a year to find the right people to deal with, but Dieter had friends who had friends and the deal was made.

Besides Big Oak, the eight included Thad, Jinja, Paul, James, Ooghnor, and Gilles. At the last minute Peter Little-tree arrived in town, broke and lonesome. Big Oak and Paul talked Dieter into adding another load of goods and putting Peter on the payroll.

They would have loved to load their cargo on a couple of large bateaux, but there were portages, so the eight men paddled a train of canoes up the Hudson River. The woods along the river were glowing gold. The day was mild but windy. Occasional gusts blowing along the ridges sometimes released leaves like showers of gold coins from the birch limbs that held them so tenuously.

Paddling in the lead canoe was James. Three years had woven their magic on his heart. The first year he had watched his Anne become somebody else's Anne, and then an Anne that had little to do with the Anne he'd thought he loved. There had almost been a war in the house over wedding invitations. Katherine insisted that James not be invited, but both Thad and Jinja had been so infuriated over the slight that Katherine consented to ask the silent Anne how she felt about it. It seemed she had measured her father's and her brother's emotions against those of her mother before finally surprising Katherine by inviting James.

Naturally, James wanted nothing to do with going. After consulting with Jinja, he settled on a note that said he'd be away on business and would not be able to return on time, but that a gift would be forthcoming.

The second year, while on a trading mission at Fort Stanwix, James had met a young white girl, the daughter of a deceased British captain. They spent a long evening at a community social event, and he was drawn to her. The girl's charms matched those of Anne, and she saw James not only as exotic, but as a young man with a future. But the moment he met her mother and saw the corners of the woman's mouth turn down at the sight of him, he switched his conversation with her from words of love to words of friendship. And the next day, when he left, he was pleased to see that she did not appear at the fort's gate to see him off.

Then, three months ago, he'd met a girl down at a Tuscarora village who felt like such a good fit that he inquired about her clan and was pleased to hear that it was not the same as his. His travels between Albany and the village had been frequent since then. She was not shy.

There was a long portage from the river to Lake George that would take days to negotiate. They had planned on it, but they weren't the only ones. On the hills overlooking the north bank of the river stood a half-dozen delighted Senecas. They were far from their usual haunts, but then, their usual haunts were not theirs anymore. Having fled to Canada to escape the wrath of the victorious rebels, this particular party had decided to do a little fall hunting to the south. Imagine their excitement when down below they saw a string of canoes loaded with trade goods.

"But there are more of them than us, and they have fine rifles," said an older brave, called Canawiyando.

"They can only be going north to Montreal or someplace in that direction," Degata replied. "They must carry their canoes and goods a great distance to reach Lac Saint Sacrement. We will follow them and watch them while they wear themselves down, for the labor will be hard. When they have carried everything to the shore of Lac Saint Sacrement, and their arms have no feeling left in them, that is when we will strike."

By this time Otter was with them, listening. "Is it right that we attack them?" he asked. "We are not at war with them."

"Are we not? See the one in the bow of the lead canoe? I saw him in the battle on the Chemung River. And the one behind him? I have seen him trading at our villages."

"They are dressed like white men."

"They are Oneidas. It is the Oneidas who betrayed the Longhouse," Degata exclaimed. "They are the white men's pets. They dress like white men and they believe in the gods of the white men and they think that they are very high and mighty now that they have taken the white path and the Longhouse is no more. But we shall teach them a thing or two, and those things will be the last things they will ever know."

Otter felt his war spirit rising within him. When he had gone on his first warpath with Degata, he had expected victory. Wasn't the Longhouse always victorious in battle? Instead he had witnessed a long series of retreats punctuated by occasional battles that were defeats or little victories, but always there was more retreat. "It was not the way Iroquois were meant to fight," Degata had explained. Someday they would get their chance to fight again like real Ganonsyoni. And now, here it was, beneath them, riding along the ripples of the upper Hudson River.

"But Otter," Degata explained, not only to Otter but to Canawiyando and the three other warriors who walked the trail with them. "If we are to be successful, they must not know we are here."

As was usual with Degata, his reasoning was good and so was his planning. He and his men watched as the traders hauled their goods from their canoes, brought them ashore, then dragged the canoes from the water. Patiently, each trader took a load and began the trek over the hills to Lake George. The journey was not long, perhaps ten miles, but the loads were heavy, and when they were through they had to go back down the trail for another load.

The Senecas stood on their hill snickering to themselves while the traders carefully hid their goods and headed back to the beginning of the portage. When they were gone, Otter turned to Degata. "Why don't we just take the goods and go home with them?" he asked. "Whatever they are, our people can use them, and it will be a good joke that when the red white men return, they will find that their goods have walked away."

"On another day, yes, little brother," Degata responded. "But these men have cost us much. They have cost us everything we loved—our villages, our fields, our hunting grounds, and our Longhouse. Tomorrow we will make them pay."

The eight men walked back up the trail, then broke into a lope, realizing that they had only so much time to bring their second load of goods to Lake George before nightfall. None of them relished hauling heavy loads over steep trails in the dark of night, and anyway, they wanted a little time to relax by a fire, light their pipes and tell each other a few stories before sleep overtook them.

On a plain there would have been an hour of sunlight left, but in this land of hills and valleys, the sun had nearly disappeared by the time the traders had returned to Lake George with their second load. The bundles were large sacks loaded with farm tools—hoes, shovels, mattocks— and kettles, hatchets, blankets, rifles, flints, shirts, dresses, the kinds of goods their customers' ancestors had not known two hundred years before, but were now necessities in their daily lives. The sight of the traders hauling valuable goods whetted the appetites of the Senecas for action. Three of them sought out Degata in a clearing on the reverse slope from where the traders were securing their goods and making camp for the night.

"Come and look at them, Degata," said one of the Senecas. "Their day has been long, they have no strength. Tonight should be our night. Their sleep will be deep. We have their goods. Let us have them tonight."

"My brothers," he replied. "We will have them all. But we must have all the goods too. They have one more load to get, and then they must bring their canoes. We must have their canoes or we will have to leave goods here when we go back to Canada."

The men did not want to leave most of the goods cached in a forest by Lake George, or Lac St. Sacrement, as many of them still called it. Neither did they want to carry heavy loads all the way to Canada if they could paddle most of the way. They bowed to his wisdom and stayed with him to smoke and eat some corn.

But Otter was not with them. He was high in the branches of a tall elm, studying the packages of goods that the traders had brought in. One of the packages was open, revealing four beautiful-looking rifles. Otter glanced at his own old, pathetic trade musket. Then he looked back down at the new rifles lying on the stroud that had served as their wrap. He coveted one, but knew the older warriors would covet them too, and take them. Otter was tired of being the youngest and least respected. He would have a fine rifle tonight, when both his enemies and his friends were asleep.

That night, he laid his blanket down fifty feet away from the rest of his trailmates. He waited until he was certain they were all asleep, then headed downhill, through the woods, bound for the spot where the goods had been hidden. There was not much of a moon, but his keen young eyes immediately spotted the thicket in which he had seen them conceal the packages.

The guns were on top, all in prime, well-oiled condition. They were the best firearms Otter had ever touched. They were not identical. He spent several minutes choosing one. Only when he heard a small animal stirring in the thicket did it occur to him that he might be in peril. For a moment he puzzled over what he should do next. He chose a rifle, refolded the stroud, and returned it to its place in the thicket. Now that he held the prize in his hand, he found that he was getting nervous. Quickly he took his old musket and hid it behind some rocks, climbed out of the valley and found his way back to his blanket. He was breathing heavily, not from the exertion, but from the tension that came with fear of discovery. He lay staring up at the sky, his hands sliding over the smooth metal of the new weapon that lay beside him. So excited was he with his new acquisition that it took an hour for sleep to overtake him.

But when he awoke the next morning, it occurred to him that Degata, at least, and maybe some of the others, would notice that he had a different weapon. It was early, still dark. Down he went to the site of his theft the night before, and when he returned to the hill he had with him his old musket. He hid the new rifle in a rocky crevasse on the hill and wondered what he was going to do about it. He would worry about that later. As long as nobody knew, that was all that mattered.

But shortly after dawn, somebody did know. Among the group of traders camped near the lake, Big Oak was the first to arise. Stretching, he left the clearing to check on the goods they had hidden. He wanted to get an early start because they had one more load of goods to bring up before beginning the long, grueling haul of the canoes. He was not certain how long it would take them to carry the canoes to the lake. There were some precarious hillsides along this trail, not that much of a challenge for strong men carrying loads, but an absolute chore for canoe bearers.

He knew immediately that somebody had been in the thicket. Otter had been careless about rearranging things, so anxious had he been to carry his new prize away. Big Oak saw which package had been disturbed. He opened it and was not surprised to find one rifle missing. There was a footprint or two, a broken branch or two, a few bent grass blades where there ought not have been, a clear trail toward the hill opposite the trail from the lake.

And yet he said nothing to the others, who were now up and getting ready for the day, which would be the toughest of the trip. He led them south at an easy lope for about a mile, then stopped them for a brief rest. Paul suggested that it was too early to rest, because there was so much work to do.

"Somebody stole a rifle last night," Big Oak announced when he had everybody's attention.

"Not me," said Gilles, who had in his many years of working for white men seen Indians accused of every crime imaginable. Big Oak made a sour face. "Somebody knows we're here. Maybe one man, but I don't think so."

"Then why are we not going after them?" Jinja asked.

"*You're* not going after them no matter what," the old woodsman said. "You think you're an army by yourself. James, could you and Thad go back and find out how many you think there are?"

James nodded. He and Thad trotted off. "I don't want to start a war out here," Big Oak told the rest. "If it's somebody who just stole a rifle and left, there's no sense wasting time by going after him. If it's a multitude, which I doubt, we have to figure out a way to get our business done without having to deal with them."

They waited in a hidden hollow off the trail, watching for any movement far or near that might indicate they were being observed. Nearly an hour passed, and all six of them were restless. They had been making great time on the trail until this new matter came up, and none of them welcomed the delay.

"Fsss!" Jinja whispered to the rest of them. His ears had picked up footfalls on the trail, which turned out to be James and Thad. They spotted Big Oak as he stepped from the hollow.

"Senecas!" James muttered. "Six of them. They've been following us on the trail, and it looks like they've camped in the hills overlooking the lake."

"Ah," Big Oak sighed. "I think the devils want us to do all the work for them. They won't attack us until we've brought the canoes up. Let's make 'em wait, bring the next load up, then instead of going back for the canoes right away, circle around and take 'em."

Paul looked sadly at Big Oak. "Wisest of all brothers, this time you are in error," he said. "What if while we're away they decide not to risk a battle but instead carry off what bundles of goods they can carry, then where are we?"

Big Oak agreed that his plan had less merit than he thought. "What do you suggest?"

"If we can sneak up on them now, or when the sun is almost overhead, we can wipe them out and then finish our job."

Big Oak looked at Paul, James, and Peter. "Are you sure it's such a good idea for Oneidas and an Onondaga to be fighting Senecas?" he asked.

Paul looked back at Big Oak, melancholy spread across his face like jam on toast. "Look at what they did to me," he said, pointing to the ugly scar on his torso. "And what they did to Peter's people. And what they tried to do to my village," he added, referring to an attack that failed to happen only because a large group of Oneida warriors coming in, unexpectedly stumbled upon the mixed Seneca and Mohawk war party and drove them away.

"The council fire is out. A cloud hangs over the house like a great black shadow. I do not believe the sun will shine down upon it in my lifetime," Paul said. "But we are Ganonsyoni. We are warriors. We must fight them or we are but women. And we must not take the chance that they might slip away with our goods."

So they decided to go back, then and there, while they knew where the Senecas were, and finish the business.

❧24❧

WHAT HAPPENED NEXT ASTONISHED THAD and Jinja, and even surprised Big Oak. James stripped off his shirt, took a small package from his pack and began applying paints to his face and body, in a time-honored Oneida manner. He handed his paints to Peter, and Peter began to do the same. Ooghnor and Gilles watched the proceedings with interest. It had been a long time since the men of their Caughnawaga village had painted themselves before battle. They were Catholics, and this was a heathenish practice. In fact, the entire art had been lost to the people of their village.

But Gilles said something to Ooghnor in French, and the two began to strip off their shirts. James had to explain the significance of the paints and shapes and how to do it. And they did it.

All this time, Paul had been hanging back, watching, but saying nothing. On one hand he was a Christian. One of Reverend Kirkland's most dedicated pupils, he had long ago put away from him the notion of traditional Longhouse war-making, with its zest for combat and all the ceremony that went with it. He had passed Kirkland's teachings on to the children of the village.

And yet now, as he watched the younger men solemnly applying their paints, it occurred to him that this little skirmish had a significance beyond being just a bloody little scuffle between some traders and some thieves, more like the closing chapter of a book in the Old Testament. He reached for, and was given, the paints. He did not have to be told what to do. It was he who had shown James, many years ago, when James was a child, and Paul was still an Oneida warrior.

Now it was Jinja's turn. As a child he had spent many days in the villages of the mighty Ganiengehaka, the people of the flint country, the Mohawks. He had learned all they had to teach him, and forgotten little of it. He threw his shirt on the ground, dug into the paints and began to work them with his fingers, to the admiration of James, who had no idea that his friend possessed this skill. The resulting effect on Jinja's lean face, with its thin nose and strong, bony chin, was nothing short of horrifying.

Finally Big Oak came forward. He did not strip off his shirt, but he did apply some white and vermilion streaks and circles in a pattern learned during his years with the Senecas. Only Thad stood aloof, refusing to participate in a ritual that his Seneca grandfather, Kendee, had shown him thirty years ago on the Genesee River. For him, the Longhouse had meant pain and sadness, while his life in Albany had been everything he could have asked for. First he had lost his mother after a brief illness. Then he had lost most of his friends, including his beloved grandfather, in a massacre of his village. Finally, some of the survivors blamed him and his father as the reason for the massacre. Even Kawia, the girl who had been his first love, turned her back on him. So the customs of the Longhouse held no lasting charms for Thad.

And yet he had no desire to do battle with the Senecas, the people of his mother. Only loyalty to his friends, and to the firm of Wendel and Watley, determined him to take part.

James had explained the nature of the terrain and the position of the Senecas to Paul and Big Oak. A half hour's observation had convinced James that the Senecas were bored and careless and completely oblivious to any danger.

They left the hollow by the trail and climbed a thickly wooded hill above the knob where the Senecas waited. From where they were, they could see through the thinly leafed trees, into the Seneca camp. As James had noted, the Senecas did not expect company. Two of them were lazing around, while others were in a thicket on a little bluff overlooking the spot where the traders had camped the night before.

None of them had their firearms handy. It was a fine time and place for an ambush. Big Oak had the men fan out across their hill and take aim on the figures below. The distance was less than seventy-five yards. Every one of the traders had made far more difficult shots than these in their lives. The battle would be quick. Death would be sudden for six warriors of the Western Door. And now they all sighted their targets, tightened their fingers on the triggers, and squeezed.

Sometimes it happens. A good shooter will sight an easy target, pull the trigger, and draw a complete miss. Maybe the powder was faulty and did not ignite right. Maybe the ball was flawed and swerved. Maybe the patch leaked. Maybe the barrel was too worn. Or maybe this one time the shooter forgot his technique and jerked the trigger.

Whatever the reasons, as the eight men fired they expected to see six men down when the smoke cleared. Instead they could hear whoops and through the smoke could see the Senecas dashing for their weapons. There was nothing for the traders to do but follow up on their surprise by charging down the hill and overwhelming their outnumbered enemies before they could gather their wits. Down they dashed, through the golden-leafed trees and over a dry creek bed, from three directions, their rifles at the ready. Big Oak and Thad were a shade slower. They were reloading as they ran, but Jinja had dropped his rifle and drawn his knife and tomahawk. Peter had let fall his firearm in favor of a big old war club that he brandished over his head as he charged in ahead of everybody, even Jinja, with an ear-piercing, ululating shriek.

As soon as they spotted the traders through the trees, four Senecas fired their rifles or muskets, but all they hit were the trees. Now, high in the wild fall-touched hills of northern New York, it was man on man, war clubs, tomahawks, knives, gun butts, fists, elbows, fingers and teeth, six on six with whoops and grunts, exclamations and epithets, and maybe the sound of the final crash as the Longhouse fell in on itself. There were thuds of weapon on weapon, and weapon on skull, while Big Oak and Thad strode into the melee fruitlessly looking for an open shot, fearing to injure their own.

Instinctively looking to protect his son, Thad stunned a Seneca with a blow to the skull with his rifle butt. The Seneca's knees folded. He dropped to the forest floor and lay still. Jinja spotted Otter fleeing in terror and did not try to stop him. Now there were eight against four, and the weight of numbers was telling on the four. Blood had been spilled, but all were still in the fight. Paul's man Degata was weakening beneath his onslaught, and when he saw why, the Oneida simply grabbed the man's tomahawk from his hand and flung it into the woods. Whoever had drawn Degata as a target had not missed. He had a gory wound in his thigh, and the loss of blood had sapped his strength. Paul saw his legs wobble, saw the glassy look in his eyes, gave him an easy push and watched him fall.

Now there were three. Paul, Big Oak, and Thad each picked out a man, bore him down from behind, and prevented further bloodshed. Big Oak shouted in the Seneca tongue that nobody would be harmed, and the Senecas ceased their struggle.

Except for Otter, who chose that moment to dash back onto the battlefield waving his brand new rifle and threatening to kill somebody if they did not let the Seneca braves go.

Ah, so here was the thief of the missing rifle. Big Oak and Thad both leveled their rifles at the young brave. Big Oak told Thad to hold his fire, then took a calculated risk. In Seneca he said, "What are you gonna shoot out of that weapon, boy?"

He was betting that all the young brave had were big old musket balls, nothing that would fit in the barrel of his beautiful new rifle without a mallet and rod to pound the ball into the grooves. Angrily, he pulled the hammer back, pointed it at Big Oak and pulled the trigger. The flint sparked, the pan flashed and the rifle belched flame, but Big Oak did not fall.

James walked over to the boy, blood dripping down his right temple from the glancing blow of a tomahawk, and gripped the rifle just in front of the trigger guard.

"The war is over, my brother," he said, and the boy gave up the rifle.

Of all the men Paul saw when he looked around, only the one he had been fighting was still down. Most were nursing wounds, but none looked to be gravely injured. One of the Senecas was patching up Degata, while another was trickling water down his throat. Soon it was clear that his wits were returning to him.

Big Oak looked around at the Senecas, his one-time brothers, at the Oneidas and Caughnawagas, at the lone Onondaga, at his son and his grandson. Then he laughed, leaned on his rifle, and began to address them in fluent Seneca.

"What a fine bunch of warriors we are! Sneak up on an enemy with our guns afire, and can't kill a one. Then there we are, a-cuttin' and slashin', doin' everything we can to beat each other's brains out, and not a one of us can kill our man. Where are the scalps we should have hanging on our belts? Where is the glory we should have to tell our children about? I think we have all seen too many days on this earth."

He walked over to the Seneca he had shot at from above

and missed. The man was nursing a huge red lump on his forehead and shaking a bloody finger that somebody had bitten in close combat.

"There was a time," he said to the brave, "when this rifle in my hands could take a pigeon from the sky every time. I was Big Oak in your villages. Everybody knew me. Did you hear my bullet?" he asked.

"No," said the surprised Seneca, and Big Oak laughed again. "I thought so. I did not even come close to you. When this business is over I will go back to my fire, my pond, and my pipe, and the only thing I will ever again kill is a fish that does not have the sense to know a hooked cricket from a free one."

Many of the others laughed at Big Oak's joke, including some of the Senecas, but his almost victim did not. "It is easy for you to laugh," he said. "You have beaten us now, and you won the war. We have no land left. We will spend our lives in the cold snow of Canada. I apologize that I cannot laugh at your joke."

Big Oak frowned. "Do you not know your own tribal legends?" he replied. "The Longhouse has lived in the north before. And the Longhouse has lived in the south too. Your brothers live by the Spay-Lay-Wi-Theepi. You are still free men. Go where you choose."

"Where can we go that the white men will not find us and do the same to us then as they do now?"

Big Oak thought. "By then maybe times will change. Maybe disease will wipe out the white men. Or the French may come back. Or the men of the Longhouse will learn to make better weapons than the whites."

"And maybe the sun will turn blue and the sky gold," said the old warrior, Canawiyando. "I have lived for many years, and always, always, it is the white men who somehow win in the end, with their tricks and cheats. The Longhouse is dead. Without the Longhouse, how will the people live on?"

Big Oak looked around at the surly but pathetic band of

Seneca warriors. He felt that he would never see these men again unless it was over a cup of rum in some Canadian fort. And yet at this moment he had to admit that they were still dangerous, and that if the traders dropped their guard, the Senecas would be all over them. So Big Oak conceived a plan that would finish their transport job and permit them to travel safely toward Montreal without having to kill their prisoners.

As bloodied and bruised as the men appeared, only Degata was seriously injured. The eight traders herded the Senecas up the trail toward their remaining canoes and bundles. Otter and one of the other young Senecas helped take Degata about two miles up the path, then Big Oak made him sit down, tied him to a tree, and left him there.

At the north end of the portage were the four canoes and several more bundles. Big Oak announced to the Senecas that they were to help them carry the bundles and the canoes, and that if they refused, they would be killed. If, on the other hand, they consented, they would be paid with the contents of the last bundle. When Canawiyando asked what was in the last bundle, Big Oak replied that he would not say, but that it was full of worthwhile trade goods, otherwise they would not be bringing it with them.

In quick time the thirteen men arrived at the north end of the portage. The four strongest Senecas carried two of the canoes, while Jinja, Thad, Gilles, and Peter carried the other two craft. Paul, James, and the Seneca who had been knocked silly by Big Oak's butt stroke carried bundles.

Big Oak and Ooghnor, who had borne the brunt of the damage on the trader side during the skirmish, walked behind the Senecas, with rifles leveled on them. The job took nearly the entire afternoon, for the path was sometimes so steep that it took four men to get a canoe over a ridge, and the Senecas did not have their hearts in their work. Despite the difficulties, there was still more than two hours of sunlight left when they neared the lake. They would pass Degata on the way back, but Big Oak would not allow the

Senecas to free him then. They would have to go back for
him after the traders were gone.

Shortly before they came to where the injured Seneca
lay, Big Oak decided their temporary help had become so
tired manhandling the canoes that he had better give them
a brief rest. It would be disastrous if their fatigue made
them stumble on a hill and lose a canoe into a ravine.

While the entire party was resting, James chose to run up
the trail to check on the condition of Degata. It would not
do, he thought, if the injury had been worse than they
thought. The Senecas were barely compliant anyway. If
they were to come upon a dead or dying Degata, their
desire for revenge might outstrip their desire to survive.

He found the Seneca warrior alive, in pain but not desperately uncomfortable. His attitude, however, was sour as
a September apple in July.

"What brings you here, betrayer of the Longhouse?" he
asked. "Are you afraid I might limp away and wait till night
and kill you in your sleep?"

"I wanted to see if you were still with us," James answered.

"I am not ready to go. I believe this leg will carry me
through many hunts yet."

"And warpaths, my brother?" The look on James's face
made the veteran warrior take the young man's thoughts
seriously.

"It looks as if the war is over and my people have lost
everything," Degata said. "And your people too, if you but
knew it."

James thought for a moment. "I know it," he said. "I believe we will meet someday on the Spay-Lay-Wi-Theepi.
Maybe we will walk the trail together then, far away from
the white man."

Degata looked at the young Oneida who seemed so
white under his war paint. "You could still walk that trail?"
he asked dubiously.

"It is the trail I would walk if I could choose," James answered earnestly.

A grim smile crossed Degata's face. "I will be there," he said. "And if you come, I will welcome you back into the Longhouse."

Degata's simple declaration touched James's heart. He read the face of the young Oneida and spoke again.

"Do not feel too bad," Degata said. "It was not only the Oneidas who betrayed the Longhouse. Many of the Senecas and the Cayugas and the Onondagas too betrayed the Longhouse by staying home when they should have been fighting."

"Big Oak says that nothing the Longhouse could have done would have changed our destiny. He says it didn't matter whether the English or the Americans had won. The white men were bound to have the land."

There was nothing more to say. James gave Degata a long drink from his canteen, then he returned to the portage party. When the party passed Degata on the trail, he and his Seneca brothers spoke briefly but nobody stopped for him.

The Senecas helped the traders load the canoes, then, to their consternation, Thad and James climbed the hill and brought back with them all the weapons that had been left up there during the fight. The Senecas begged for them back. Big Oak compromised. He gave them their firearms but took their powder and bullets. Then they demanded their tomahawks and knives. Big Oak said nothing. Three of the canoes pushed off. The paddlers waited thirty feet offshore, their rifles pointed at the Senecas to protect Big Oak and Paul as they shoved the unmanned canoes onto the lake, then launched their canoe. They fastened the tow ropes. A few quick strokes brought them well out from the shore.

"Give us our tomahawks and our knives!" shouted Canawiyando one more time. "We cannot hurt you any longer!"

Big Oak nodded, and began hurling tomahawks and knives toward the shore. At first the Senecas, fearing that the old trader was hurling their weapons *at* them, scattered, but once they realized that he was just giving them back, they simply moved away, waited for the hail of metal to stop, then gathered them up.

"Good-bye, my brothers," Big Oak shouted back at them. The Senecas glowered back and said nothing.

The first three canoes made the water hum as they headed north, but Big Oak let Paul paddle the last slowly while he looked back at the warriors on the shore. He remembered their fearsome raids on their western enemies, and the terror they inspired when they fought the French. He also remembered the long summer days on the Genesee River, when the men fished and the women gossiped as they farmed the fields and the children played all day long. The life of a Seneca was sweet in those days.

But now they had lost not only the war, but their homes, fields, and hunting grounds. Sadly he watched them as they began to make their way back up the trail, first to reclaim Degata, then to take possession of the bundle they had been given. Big Oak had no doubt they would be pleased with the goods they found inside, although the firm of Wendel and Watley had not had to give much to acquire them. He felt his heart go out to them as the last one disappeared into the endless forest.

The sun was slipping beneath the hemlocks on the horizon. A chill wind was blowing across the lake as he took his paddle and began to stroke in perfect cadence with Paul. He felt a rheumatic twinge in his shoulder, and longed to be by the fire on this night, with Cilla and the boys. The day of the Longhouse was just about over, and so, he observed, was the day of Big Oak.

THE FIRST FRONTIER SERIES
by Mike Roarke

At the dawn of the 18th century, while the French and English are locked in a battle for the northeast territory, the ancient Indian tribes begin a savage brother-against-brother conflict—forced to take sides in the white man's war—pushed into an era of great heroism and greater loss. In the tradition of *The Last of the Mohicans*, *The First Frontier Series* is a stunningly realistic adventure saga set on America's earliest battleground. Follow Sam Watley and his son Thad in their struggle to survive in a bold new land.

THUNDER IN THE EAST (Book #1)
_____ 95192-2 $4.50 U.S./$5.50 Can.
SILENT DRUMS (Book #2)
_____ 95224-4 $4.99 U.S./$5.99 Can.

TERRY C. JOHNSTON
THE PLAINSMEN

THE BOLD WESTERN SERIES FROM
ST. MARTIN'S PAPERBACKS

COLLECT THE ENTIRE SERIES!

SIOUX DAWN (Book 1)
92732-0 _____ $4.99 U.S. _____ $5.99 CAN.

RED CLOUD'S REVENGE (Book 2)
92733-9 _____ $4.99 U.S. _____ $5.99 CAN.

THE STALKERS (Book 3)
92963-3 _____ $4.99 U.S. _____ $5.99 CAN.

BLACK SUN (Book 4)
92465-8 _____ $4.99 U.S. _____ $5.99 CAN.

DEVIL'S BACKBONE (Book 5)
92574-3 _____ $4.99 U.S. _____ $5.99 CAN.

SHADOW RIDERS (Book 6)
92597-2 _____ $4.99 U.S. _____ $5.99 CAN.

DYING THUNDER (Book 7)
92834-3 _____ $4.99 U.S. _____ $5.99 CAN.

BLOOD SONG (Book 8)
92921-8 _____ $4.99 U.S. _____ $5.99 CAN.

DETECTIVE DEVENTER HAD A LOT OF QUESTIONS:

Who was the lovely young girl with the cumbersome portfolio? Were its startling contents the reason she had to die? What was her link to the bohemians at Poplar's Fen? To Roger, the captain of a very well kept sailboat? To Trudi, the second-rate artist with first-rate tastes? To Mrs. Vincent, owner of Moat's Cottage, who sold their work for a profit? To Sally, the sunny beauty who specialized in compositions of sea lavender?

AND HE NEEDED ANSWERS BEFORE A COLD-BLOODED KILLER STRUCK AGAIN. . . .

MURDER INK® MYSTERIES

SCENE OF THE CRIME™ MYSTERIES

A SPRIG
of
SEA LAVENDER

J.R.L. Anderson

'A DELL BOOK

For
Tom Matthews

Contents

I

The Girl with the Portfolio

That there should be a surviving railway station at the little Suffolk town of Sudbury in these days of axed branch lines seems improbable; that it should still actually have trains·seems next to unbelievable. Privately, Keith Tomlinson had doubted the accuracy of his aunt's information. Coming down from London on Friday to spend the weekend with her at Long Melford, she had met him at the main line station of Mark's Tey, near Colchester, and driven him the dozen miles or so through the pastel-coloured countryside of the Essex-Suffolk borders. On Sunday evening she had had a bad attack of migraine, and although she said that she would still be able to drive him to Mark's Tey on Monday morning, he wouldn't let her. She was close on seventy, and he didn't think she was up to it. He was persuading her to let him order a taxi for Mark's Tey when she said, "But you don't need to go all that way. It will be very expensive, and you can get the morning train in Sudbury, which connects with the London train at Mark's Tey."

Not wanting to argue with her he had agreed and ordered a car for Sudbury, reckoning that he could always tell the driver to go on to Mark's Tey. Of course there had once been trains at Sudbury, but he thought that his aunt's migraine-bemused mind had probably gone back thirty years.

To his surprise, the taxi-driver seemed to think it reasonable enough to be asked to go to Sudbury station, and when Keith got out in the yard of the Victorian country station he was encouraged to see two or three other people making for the entrance. "Could you please tell me which is the right platform for the Mark's Tey train?" he asked one man.

The man laughed. "You'll see," he said.

Keith soon saw. The entrance to the footbridge that once crossed the lines was boarded up, and the track itself that once served the Down Platform of the little station was gone. A single track came to the Up Platform—and stopped. Beyond the station, where the track had once gone on to Clare and Cambridge, was what looked now like an overgrown country lane.

"There is no booking office—you pay on the train," Keith's fellow-traveller explained.

Sharp on time, a diesel rail-bus drew up at the platform. Keith, savouring what he felt as a plunge into railway history, stood at the carriage door to watch the train pull out. It had actually started moving when a girl, carrying one of those huge black portfolios that hold pictures or large-scale architect's drawings, ran on to the platform. Keith opened the door for her, got an arm around her shoulders and hauled her in. The portfolio was a nuisance. It half-jammed in the doorway, but the girl clung to it, and with a considerable wrench Keith managed to drag it in.

"Thank you . . . thank you ever so much," the girl panted. "I don't know what I'd have done if I'd missed this train."

At Mark's Tey passengers for the London train had

to cross a bridge to get to the main line. The girl, who looked pale and far from well, was staggering with the huge portfolio, so Keith helped her with it. He himself had a return ticket from Mark's Tey to London, but the girl had to go to the booking office, having bought a ticket only to Mark's Tey on the Sudbury train. There were two or three people ahead of her at the booking office window, and she swayed unhappily as she stood in the queue. She looked so wretched that Keith offered to get her ticket for her. "Oh, if you would! You are very kind." She gave him a five-pound note, he got a single ticket to Liverpool Street, and gave her the change. When the London train came in he found her a seat. The portfolio was too wide to go on the luggage-rack, and as there were no spare seats in the compartment he stood it in the corridor just outside. The girl muttered thanks, but seemed to have lost interest in things. She sat back in her seat and closed her eyes.

When the train got to the London terminus at Liverpool Street she was still sitting with her eyes closed. The other passengers, hastening to start their week in offices and shops, left without taking any notice of her. Keith, who also wanted to get to his office, was irritated and perplexed. He knew nothing of the girl, but he couldn't help feeling a sort of half-responsibility for her. He watched to see that her portfolio was untouched, and when there was room in the compartment he brought it inside. Then he gave the girl a little shake. "Wake up, we've got to Liverpool Street," he said.

She took no notice. Deciding that she must be ill, he got out on the platform and was lucky to see a porter. "Can you help, please? There's a passenger in the train who's ill, I think," he said.

The porter was helpful, got into the train with Keith, and studied the girl. "Don't like the way she looks," he said. "I'll get the First Aid man. Can you stay with her?"

He didn't at all want to stay, but Keith felt unhappily that he couldn't now get out of it. He was wondering how much longer it would be before he could get to his office when the porter came back, with a man wearing an ambulance-corps armband. He felt the girl's pulse, and gently lifted one of her eyelids. "Nothing I can do," he said. "I think she's dead."

The next couple of hours—for Keith was kept for all of two hours—were a nightmare. Doctor, ambulance and a railway policeman arrived almost together. Keith asked if he could go but the railway policeman said, "If you don't mind, sir, we'd like a statement from you. I'll take it as soon as I can, but we must let the doctor see what he can do first."

The doctor examined the girl carefully, feeling her scalp, studying her eyes, lips and fingernails. Then, "Where is her handbag? I'd like to have a look at her handbag," he said.

There was no handbag on the seat beside her. The railway policeman looked under the seat, and under the seat opposite—nothing. "I don't remember seeing her with a handbag," Keith said. "She had her hands full with that big portfolio."

"How did she get her ticket?" the policeman asked.

"She bought a ticket on the train from Sudbury, but only to Mark's Tey," Keith said. "I suppose she took some money from a pocket—I didn't notice. She had to book again at Mark's Tey. I'd helped her with her portfolio because I thought she looked rather ill, and I got her ticket for her at Mark's Tey—a single to Liverpool Street. She gave me a five-pound note, and I gave her the change with the ticket. Again I didn't notice where she took the money from."

"She's wearing a coat and skirt and there are two small pockets in the coat. I expect the ticket and her

money will be in one of them," the policeman said.
They were, but she didn't seem to have much
money—only the change from buying her ticket, and
a few odd pence. There was nothing else in either
pocket.

"Rather looks as if she was expecting to be met,"
the policeman said. "I wonder if there's anyone hanging around at the barrier. I'd better go and see."

There was no one obviously waiting at the barrier.
The policeman had a word with the ticket-collector.
"No, no one's asked about anyone off this train," the
ticket-collector said. The policeman called out, "Is
anyone waiting to meet a young lady off the Colchester train?" People standing about on the concourse
glanced at him, but no one came up to him. He
waited a minute or so, then walked back to the compartment.

"Doesn't seem anyone meeting her, or if there was
he's given up and gone away," he said.

"Well, I can't do any more here," the doctor said.
"There'll have to be an autopsy, and the sooner we
get her to hospital the better." He told the ambulance men to take her to the City Hospital, adding,
"I'll have a word with the pathologist on the phone."

The men took a stretcher from the ambulance and
laid it on the platform. Then they lifted the girl
gently, carried her from the compartment and laid
her on the stretcher, covering her with a blanket. She
seemed pathetically small. As the ambulance drove off
the doctor beckoned to the policeman, took him away
from where Keith was standing around unhappily,
and had a brief conversation in a low voice. The
policeman nodded, and the doctor went off.

The policeman then went back to Keith. "Sorry to
keep you waiting like this," he said. "We've got to get
the train away now, and I think I'd better have this
carriage uncoupled and shunted off where it can be
examined. Give me a few minutes to make arrange-

ments, and then perhaps you'd be good enough to come to the police office. I'll look after that portfolio—no point in sending it to the hospital after her. Perhaps we can identify her from it. Unless you can give us a line on who she is."

"I don't know her from Adam—I mean Eve," Keith said miserably. He was thinking of all the work piling up in his office, particularly of a conveyance to be completed for a young couple buying their first house. As a solicitor, though, he was also conscious of his duty to make statements if they were required from him.

The railway police go back to the very early days of railways, when they were originally recruited as signalmen. Before fixed semaphore signals came into existence, in the late 1830s, railway signalling was done by men standing on the track, controlling trains in much the same way as road traffic is controlled by a policeman on point duty. (Because of their origin as policemen you may still occasionally hear signalmen referred to in railway slang as "bobbies.") As railway signalling became less rudimentary the police found plenty to keep them busy in ordinary police work on railway premises, and a smart lot they were, in the top hats and tail coats of Early Victorian police uniform, the colour of the uniform matching the liveries of the different railway companies. As the railways developed there was a growing need for police to keep an eye on goods in transit, and to deal with the wants and needs and misbehaviour of the public on railway premises. Nowadays the railway police look much like ordinary policemen and do much the same sort of job wherever there are railways to be policed, but they remain a specialised force. Keith's policeman went to a staff telephone on the platform, came back to give instructions to a guard and engine-driver about the train, and then, picking up the big portfolio, asked Keith to come with him.

"Bulky to carry, this thing," he said.

"Yes, that's why I helped her with it," Keith replied.

At intervals between bookstalls, refreshment rooms, waiting rooms and lavatories of big railway stations there are inconspicuous little doors. You seldom notice them, but they are the keys to the working life of the station, for they lead to the offices where the running of trains is controlled, freight organised, and the hundred and one things done, from arranging sleeper reservations to ensuring that trains connect with boats, that are required to move the public and its goods. The policeman took Keith through one of these doors, up a flight of stairs, to a room labelled "Police." Inside it was just like the entrance to an ordinary police station, with a counter and a bell with a card saying, "Please ring for attention." Keith's policeman ignored the bell, lifted a flap in the counter, and walked through into a big office where a sergeant was seated at a desk. The sergeant got up politely as Keith was shown in. "This is the gentleman who helped the young lady who was found dead in the Colchester train," the policeman said.

"I know nothing whatever about her," Keith added. "And I'm horribly late for work, and I really must go as soon as possible."

"Of course, sir," said the sergeant, trying to be soothing. "But you will understand that we have to find out all we can about how the unfortunate young lady came to be as she was. I understand that you travelled with her on the Colchester train?"

"Yes, I did," Keith said, becoming more and more exasperated. "But it was entirely by chance. She got into the train at Sudbury just as it was pulling out, and I helped her get that portfolio thing on board. We had to change at Mark's Tey, and I helped her because she seemed to be unwell. When we got to Liverpool Street I thought she was asleep, so I tried to wake her up. When I couldn't, I asked a porter to get help. That's absolutely all I know about it, and I wish I'd just got off the train like everybody else in the compartment."

"Come, come, sir. We've all got to help one another. You did what you could for the young lady, and I'm sure it was very good of you. Now if you'd just answer a few questions . . . May I have your name and address?"

"Keith James Tomlinson, aged twenty-eight. I'm junior partner in a firm of solicitors at Twickenham, Collard and Wellspade, and I live at 53 Canopy Court, Richmond. That's a big block of flats."

The sergeant wrote it down. "Thank you, sir. Now you say you joined the train this morning at Sudbury. May I ask what took you to Sudbury?"

"I spent the weekend with my aunt, Miss Sarah Banks, at Long Melford. That's a village about three miles from Sudbury. I got a taxi from her house to Sudbury station."

"And you met the young lady at the station?"

"I didn't meet her. I was on the train, and the train was moving. She rushed on to the platform and got on the train. I opened the door for her and helped her in. The big portfolio she was carrying made it awkward, and she nearly didn't make it."

"Dangerous thing to do—I don't mean you, sir. Still, she got on all right. What happened next?"

"Nothing happened. I mean, we just found seats in the train."

"Were there any other passengers?"

"Yes. I couldn't say how many, but several—six or eight, perhaps."

"The young lady didn't have a ticket?"

"None of us had tickets. There's no booking office

at Sudbury—it's a sort of half station. You pay on the train, like paying on a bus."

"And you had to change at Mark's Tey?"

"Yes. The Sudbury train only goes as far as Mark's Tey, I think. It's a very little train. You have to go over a footbridge to get to the main line, and you buy tickets for London, or other places, I suppose, at the booking office on the main line station. She was struggling rather as we went over the bridge, so I carried the portfolio for her. And I bought a ticket for her—I had a return ticket for myself. She gave me the money and I gave her the change."

"Did you have luggage of your own?"

"Only this," Keith indicated his canvas holdall.

"What happened when the London train came in?"

"I don't remember anybody's getting off. I opened a carriage door, let her get in, and then followed with the portfolio. It was a fairly crowded train and at first I wondered if we'd get seats. But we walked along the corridor and came to a compartment with a couple of empty seats. I was a little way in front of her. I put my holdall on one seat, and stood by the other until she came. She sat down, and I think she closed her eyes almost at once. I couldn't get the portfolio on the rack because it was too wide. I stood it in the corridor, just outside the compartment."

"Did she talk to anyone on the train?"

"On the London train I'm sure she didn't, because she seemed to be asleep. I don't know about the Sudbury train. It was a new line for me, and I was looking out of the window most of the time."

"Didn't you go on the Sudbury line when you went down to Long Melford?"

"No. My aunt met me at Mark's Tey with her car. I came back from Sudbury."

"Had you ever seen the young lady before?"

"No."

"Well, sir, that seems about all you can tell us.

Thank you very much. As a lawyer you'll know that there may have to be an inquest, and you may be called to give evidence. But you'll hear about that from the coroner's office. We needn't keep you any longer now."

Keith was thankful to be on his way to Waterloo and Twickenham.

"Funny business," said the sergeant when Keith had gone. "So the doctor's not satisfied about the cause of death?"

"No. He thinks she probably died from some kind of poisoning. That's why he wanted to look at her handbag, to see if he could find out what she'd taken. But there wasn't any handbag—at least none that we could see. He said the carriage ought to be searched thoroughly, so I asked the foreman to get it uncoupled and put in a shed when the train was shunted out. I asked the guard to see that the carriage was locked."

"Good work. The doctor had a word with me before you came in with Mr Tomlinson. I don't see that it's our case, though; she just happened to die on a train, but it's not a railway matter. I'll get in touch with the City police, and I daresay they'll want to send someone to have a look at the carriage. But I suppose we ought to try to identify her if we can. Nuisance that she didn't seem to have a handbag. Let's have a look at that portfolio."

The portfolio was a huge cardboard folder about a yard square, covered with thin black plastic sheeting, and done up with tapes. There was an address label on it, but half the label had been torn off, and all that remained was the last line of the address, saying "Suffolk." The sergeant undid the tapes. Inside were four oil paintings, with sheets of tissue paper between them. The paintings were of different sizes. The biggest, almost as big as the portfolio, was a landscape.

One of the others, rather dark in colouring, was also a landscape. Of the remaining two one showed some boats drawn up on a beach, and the other was a full-length portrait of a small boy in eighteenth-century costume. "Pretty country in the big one," observed the sergeant, "and the boats aren't bad. Don't know why they put kids in fancy dress when they want to paint them—but then painting's not my cup of tea. Not this sort of painting—I can paint a house all right."

There was nothing else in the portfolio, and nothing was written on the backs of any of the pictures.

The pathologist was puzzled. The body was that of a young woman, aged between twenty and twenty-four, and the immediate cause of death was clear enough— a substantial overdose of one of the barbiturate drugs. But there was also evidence of arsenical poisoning, not, he thought, in lethal quantity, but enough to have made her feel off-colour, and, added to the toxic effect of the barbiturate, enough to have contributed to, and probably to have hastened, death. The barbiturate suggested suicide—an overdose of barbiturates prescribed as sleeping pills is a fairly common means of suicide. But such deaths usually take place in bed, when some unhappy, emotionally disturbed individual empties his or her bottle of pills to sleep without awakening. Where had this girl taken her lethal dose of pills? The brief report that had been given to him said that she had been found dead on a train, on which she had travelled up to London from Suffolk. The railway staff doctor, who had been called to examine her on the train, had telephoned him to say that he suspected poisoning, that he had looked for a handbag which might have contained whatever she had taken, but had been unable to find one. That also was puzzling—few women travelling up to London from the country would come without a handbag. And what of the traces of arsenical poisoning? Arsenic is not a poison often used for suicide—death by arsenic is more commonly the result either of accident, such as the careless putting of some arsenical weedkiller in a lemonade bottle, or of murder, when arsenic is deliberately administered in food. The girl's death seemed to present two conflicting theories, one suggesting suicide, though the place was oddly chosen, the other a deliberate, though incomplete, attempt on her life. Arsenic is a cumulative poison, and the textbook example of murder by arsenic is the administration by a jealous wife or husband of small doses over a prolonged period. Whether the dead girl had a conceivably jealous husband he did not know. She wore no wedding ring, but that in itself meant little nowadays, and a potential murderer might as readily be a jealous lover as a jealous husband. And she had *not* been killed by arsenic—the traces of arsenical poisoning were significant of something, but of what he could not possibly say. Well, these were all matters for the police. His job was to determine the cause of death, and he was reasonably confident that he had done so.

The task of making preliminary inquiries into the girl's death fell to Detective-Sergeant Williams, of the City of London police. Having been given such facts as there were by the railway police sergeant he decided to call first on the Medical Officer at Liverpool Street station. The doctor could not tell him much. He had not yet had the pathologist's report, and all he could say was that he thought it possible that she had died from some form of poisoning. "I didn't attempt a detailed examination—the girl was dead, and it was better to get her away to the pathologist," he said. "There was no obvious sign of injury, and from the general appearance of the body I should say that she died from the effects of some narcotic drug. She hadn't been dead long, half-an-hour, perhaps. There's some evidence from another passenger that she seemed unwell on getting into the London train at Mark's Tey. The train journey is only about an hour's run, and she must have died soon after settling down in her seat. The passenger whose evidence I have just mentioned thought that she had gone to sleep—a reasonable enough conclusion. When I saw her life was definitely extinct. Her heart had stopped beating for an appreciable time—I estimate it at about half an hour—and there would be irreversible damage to the brain. I considered attempting resuscitation, of course, but it would have been futile. She was clearly dead."

"The autopsy may reveal some long-standing illness, heart disease or something, which may have killed her."

"Of course. All I can say is that superficial examination did not indicate any chronic illness, and did suggest poisoning. Naturally I looked for her handbag to see if it contained a bottle of tablets which she might have taken, but she didn't appear to have a handbag. That struck me as a curious feature of the case, and I asked the railway police to have the carriage locked and uncoupled when the train was shunted out, so that it could be thoroughly examined if you think it necessary."

"That was a good move, doctor. Thank you very much. When do you expect the pathologist will be able to report his findings?"

"I don't know. He'll act as quickly as he can. I telephoned him to give my reasons for suspecting poison, and I don't need to enlarge on the possibilities in cases where poisoning is suspected. Doubtless he'll be in touch with the Coroner's office, and I should think you'll have a report soon. It may be only a provisional report, of course."

"Of course. Well, dctor, I must thank you again

for all you've done. I think I'll go and have a look at that carriage."

Accompanied by the two railway policemen, Detective-Sergeant Williams got a lift on a shunting engine to the marshalling yard to which the carriage had been taken. He was glad to have the railwaymen with him, for they had to leave the engine and walk across the yard to the siding where the carriage had been shunted to be out of the way, and a big marshalling yard is an unnerving place to anyone unfamiliar with it. There are railway lines everywhere, and engineless trains—groups of carriages or trucks given a skilful shove by the shunter—seem to appear out of nowhere and to move almost noiselessly. Actually, the work is highly organised and beautifully timed—long experience has taught the shunters, sheepdogs among the sheep-like rolling stock, precisely where to give a push that will send carriages just where they are wanted to be made up into trains. The gangers seem to have eyes in the back of their heads, and lookout-men ensure that those working on a line are warned of approaching trains, or bits of trains. Piloted by the railway policemen, Williams made the passage to the lay-by siding safely. "Wouldn't like to do it on my own," he said. The railway sergeant laughed. "Wouldn't let you. It's part of our job to keep unauthorised public out of railway property."

Accustomed to boarding trains from the raised platforms traditional to British Railways—most other countries have ground level platforms and steps at the doors of coaches—Williams was surprised by the height of the carriage in the siding. The railwaymen swung themselves up easily, and the sergeant unlocked the door. Williams followed somewhat awkwardly, and made no bones about taking the helping hand held out to him. They entered at one end of the corridor, and went to a compartment three doors along. "This is where she was found," said the railway constable. "She was sitting back to the engine in this corner of the corridor side of the compartment."

"So she could scarcely have thrown a handbag out of the window," Williams said.

"No. And she didn't drop it on the floor, either. I had a look under both seats. Better have another look to make sure."

The railway sergeant had a torch. All three men got down and looked under the seats, but there certainly wasn't any handbag to be found. Williams was about to get up when something on the floor caught his eye. "Can I have the torch a minute?" he asked.

In the beam of the torch he saw what it was, a green stalk a couple of inches long with a cluster of small blue, or blueish-purple, flowers growing from it. It was an inconspicuous little thing, fallen from someone's button-hole, perhaps, or from a child's nosegay of wild flowers being taken back to London from the country. But it was more or less directly under where the girl had been sitting, and he picked it up. The flowers seemed quite fresh, and when he looked at the stalk closely he saw that it had been broken, not cut. "Know what it is?" he asked the railwaymen.

Neither was an expert on wild flowers. "Pretty little thing," said the sergeant, "but search me for a name to it."

"I don't know, either," Williams said. "May have nothing to do with her, of course, but she was sitting about here, and it doesn't look as if it's been picked long. Could have been brushed from her dress, or caught in her shoe, or something. Might just help to identify her, or at least suggest where she came from. So I think we'll keep it for the moment." He took a small brown envelope from his briefcase, put in the sprig of blossom, and labelled the envelope.

There seemed nothing more to be got from the compartment. "The missing handbag—if it is missing, that is, if she ever had one—is distinctly odd," Williams said. "Since we're here we'd better have a look in the corridor and the other compartments. She might have dropped it, though, and someone else picked it up."

They could have made a good haul of crumpled newspapers, sweet wrappings, and empty cigarette packets, but there was no handbag. The railway sergeant explained the messy state of the carriage. "The public's just awful about litter. Always staggers me that you can go into people's houses and find rooms kept neat and tidy, yet if you put the same people on a train they'll leave muck everywhere. The railways get blamed, of course—any newspaper will print a letter about dirty trains. But really we do our best. Normally when a train's shunted out of the terminus the cleaners go on board and it's tidied up before going into service again. The other carriages on this train will have been cleaned, but this was left as it was."

"Quite right, too," Williams said. "Well, I don't think the carriage can tell us any more—you can unlock it and let the cleaners get at it. If she did have a handbag, it's been pinched by one of the other passengers—likely enough nowadays. I'll be getting back to the office to see whether there's any news from the hospital. Many thanks for all you've done."

When Williams got back to the police station he was told that the Inspector wanted to see him. "The Coroner's Office has been on about that woman found dead at Liverpool Street," the Inspector said. "They've had a report from the pathologist—she died from barbiturate poisoning. Traces of arsenic in her, too, but apparently not enough to cause death. Seems a queer business. They want to know if she's been identified."

Williams described what he'd done. "Nothing to identify her so far," he said. "She had this big port-

folio of pictures with her—the railway police handed
it over to me. There's nothing inside but these four
paintings. Maybe an art expert can tell us something
about them, but I haven't had time to go into them
yet. The railway police also got a statement from a
passenger, a Mr. Keith Tomlinson, who's a solicitor.
He travelled up in the same train, and apparently
helped the woman because he thought she was ill.
But you can see what he says—here's a copy of his
statement."

The Inspector read it. "So she got on the train at
Sudbury—maybe she comes from there. You'd better
get on to the Sudbury police. Oh, and you'd better go
along to the mortuary first, and get a description of
her, and of the clothes she was wearing."

Williams did all this, and the Sudbury police
promised to ring back after they'd made inquiries.
They did, but it was an unsatisfactory call. No young
woman of the age and description of the girl with the
portfolio was known to any of the obvious people
who could be asked about her—shopkeepers, the public library, the schools in case she was a schoolteacher.
There were two cars left in the station yard at Sudbury, but both were accounted for as belonging to
commuters from neighbouring villages who used the
station. "Of course she may not come from here at
all," the Sudbury station sergeant said. "Since they
closed almost all the branch lines people come from
all over the place to get the train at Sudbury—she
might come from a dozen or more villages. Or she
might just be a visitor, going home after the weekend.
She doesn't seem to have come to the station in her
own car or it would be there now—she'll have been
driven there by someone else, or she may have come
in by bus. We'll do what we can, but inquiries are going to take some time. If any young woman is reported missing, of course we'll get in touch with you at
once."

No one was reported missing from Sudbury. There was that constant sad community of missing women reported by anxious husbands and parents from all over the country, but those reported missing before this girl's death seemed irrelevant, and no reports of anyone answering to her description came to the police in the following days. An inquest had to be held, but all the Coroner could do was to return an open verdict—that she had died from barbiturate poisoning with no evidence to show how the poison had come to be administered. The proceedings were brief and formal. The traces of arsenic also found in the girl's body were not mentioned, nor was anything said about the portfolio of pictures. Her portfolio, however, turned out to be of considerable interest to the police.

II

The Art Dealer and the Rugby Player

Chief Inspector Piet Deventer was on the young side
for the rank, but his promotion had genuinely
pleased his colleagues. "Really listens to anything
you've got to say; I'd sooner go to him with a problem than to anyone else in the Force," was the comment of an elderly sergeant. "High flier all right, but
he'll never take off from anyone else's back to gain
height," was the opinion of one of his seniors.

The spelling of "Piet" was a family tradition. The
first Piet Deventer of whom there is any record was a
Dutch clockmaker who had come to England in the
train of William of Orange, and although the family
had lived in England ever since they kept Dutch
forms for their Christian names. Deventer clocks are
collectors' pieces, not only because they are exceptionally beautiful but also because there are not many of
them, for the family did not stay in clockmaking. The
first Piet Deventer's son went to sea, and there followed several generations of Deventers who were master mariners in the service of the East India
Company. None of them made a fortune but they
were comfortably off, acquiring a pleasant house at
Greenwich which still belonged to Piet's mother, al-

though it was now divided into flats. The clockmaker's skill with his hands and his artistic sense
stayed in the family, and the house at Greenwich
held a fine collection of sketches and water colours
done by various Deventers on their voyages. Piet's
grandfather did not go to sea but became an engraver
of some distinction. His father had gone back to the
sea and was in command of a merchantman which
fought a gallant action with a German submarine in
1943. The merchantman, however, could not win,
and went down. Piet's father and a handful of survivors were adrift for three days on a raft, and suffering badly from exposure when they were lucky
enough to be picked up by a British destroyer.

Piet was the only child. He had a pencil or a paint-
brush in his hands from infancy, and his parents encouraged him to paint. He had just gone to an art
school when his father, who had never really recovered from his shipwreck, died. As he was only in his
fifties when he died, his widow did not get much of a
pension, and although turning the Greenwich house
into flats helped, it was on old building and a good
deal of the rent from the flats went on maintenance
and repairs. Piet's mother was ready enough to pinch
and scrape for herself in order to help Piet, but Piet
was not prepared to let her. Quite suddenly he left
the art school and joined the police. Thinking back,
he often wondered what had really prompted the decision. His mother, of course—his wish to help his
mother by getting a job for himself was certainly a
real motive. But it was not as simple as that. "If I'd
really been a great artist I'd have let my mother
starve rather than give up painting," he thought
sometimes. But that couldn't be wholly true, either.
He'd not given up painting, and he was confident
that at least some of his work was good. Good
enough? At this stage he'd stop thinking about it.
And why the police? Directly because he had seen an

advertisement for police recruiting, and fancied the life more than trying to get the kind of office job for which his school examinations fitted him. Indirectly there was much more to it—the concepts of service, of protecting others, of adventure, too—ideals which, for all the cynicism of a materialistic age, can still motivate young people.

From the start, Piet was an excellent policeman. He accepted discipline and had a natural sense of fairness, which helped both in his dealings with the public and in his relations with his mates. His artist's eye gave him an acute sense of observation, which made him outstandingly useful when he was transferred to the CID. His chance came when he was sent to investigate the theft of an important picture from an art gallery—within twenty-four hours he recovered the picture undamaged, and arrested a man who seemed a highly unlikely thief. Piet's evidence and reconstruction of the theft were so damning that the man, who had pleaded not guilty and seemed to have every chance of acquittal, changed his plea to guilty during the trial.

That led to Piet's transfer to a branch of the CID specialising in the investigation of art robberies. Now he was in charge of his own section of what was known loosely as the Fine Art Squad at New Scotland Yard, with a steadily widening range of more general responsibilities.

In the endeavours by the City Police to establish the identity of the young woman found dead in the train at Liverpool Street it was natural that her portfolio of pictures should come to Piet. It was brought by Detective-Sergeant Williams, who was a little nervous about going to Scotland Yard because he felt that he ought somehow to have made more progress with the identification. Chief Inspector Deventer was a younger man than the sergeant had expected, and this made him more nervous still, for young officers are not always tolerant of the shortcomings of others.

Piet, however, was concerned to make him feel at ease, and before opening the portfolio the sergeant found himself talking about his family and the general run of work in his Division of the City.

"Having a big main line station like Liverpool Street must make for a lot of extra work," Piet said.

"Well, it does and it doesn't, sir," Sergeant Williams replied. "There's the railway police to look after all the railway side of things, but there's always things happening at the station which are liable to bring us in—like this case, you see. The girl—young woman, I suppose I should say—happened to be found dead in a train at Liverpool Street, but apart from being a passenger in a train there was nothing in particular to connect her with the railways. So naturally we had to take it on—and I'm afraid we've got nowhere with it, sir."

"Your people sent me the papers—I don't see what more you could have done in the time you've had. It seems a very strange case, and odd that the Suffolk police haven't had any reports of a young woman's being missing. You'd have thought that she must have family or friends somewhere, and the fact that she doesn't seem to have had any luggage rather suggests that her home was in Suffolk and that she was coming to London just for the day."

"She only bought a single ticket to London, sir."

"Yes, but from what I can make out from the papers she didn't buy it—somebody else on the train bought a ticket for her."

"You're quite right, sir. That was the solicitor, a Mr Tomlinson, who carried her big portfolio because he thought she looked ill, and bought the ticket for her at Mark's Tey. But you'd have thought he'd ask if she wanted a single or return."

"I don't know. It's a point that could be put to him

if necessary. As things are I doubt if it means much. He thought she looked ill, there may have been several people waiting at the booking office window, and he may have just asked for a single without thinking. I take it you haven't gone into the question of the ticket?"

"No, sir, I'm afraid not. But I didn't interview Mr Tomlinson myself—I was given his statement by the railway police. He was called to give evidence at the inquest, but he just said he bought the woman's ticket for her, and the Coroner didn't pursue the matter."

"Well, it's another possible line of approach. Wasn't the inquest held rather quickly?"

"I don't think so. The Coroner gave us a reasonable chance to try and identify her. We might have had longer, but it's a busy district, and the authorities naturally wanted a burial certificate. And all the inquest could do was to return an open verdict, which means that inquiries have got to go on, anyway."

"You did a lot of work on the clothes."

"I did what I could, but it didn't come to anything. She was wearing a coat and skirt with a chain-store label, but the store has branches all over the country and it couldn't tell us which particular branch the clothes had come from. Same with her jumper and underclothes—all clean and in good condition, but they could have been bought almost anywhere. No laundry marks. She must have done her own washing, but then most people do nowadays."

"And the only other thing was the portfolio of pictures?"

"Yes. We took it to various shops selling artists' and architects' materials, but they all said there was nothing special about it and it could have been bought, or made up, anywhere, not necessarily even in England. The torn label suggests that it had been to or come from some address in Suffolk, which rather bears out the theory that she lived in Suffolk. But all inquiries by the Suffolk police have drawn blank."

"Did you take round the pictures with the portfolio?"

"No, sir. And you'll have seen that there was no reference to the pictures at the inquest. That was the higher-ups' decision. They reckoned that if the pictures were of any value they'd be reported missing, and since we'd no means of knowing how they'd come into the woman's possession they didn't want to put ideas into people's heads."

"Hm. It's a point of view. I'm inclined to think that they should have gone for expert examination right away, but that's just my own feeling. I'm not blaming you, sergeant, or anybody else. Let's have a look at them now."

Sergeant Williams untied the portfolio and Piet Deventer got one of the severest shocks of his life. He was looking at a Constable masterpiece. Of course it couldn't be. All Constable's pictures were recorded. John Constable was his particular love, the painter above all others with whom he felt a kind of special kinship, who spoke to him as it were in a personal, private language. He knew, or thought he knew, every picture Constable had painted. He'd made pilgrimages to most of the originals, and knew the rest from reproductions. Could there be an unknown Constable? It was possible, though highly unlikely. But this *was* Constable—no other artist could have felt and revealed, *understood* the very treeishness of a tree, such as that on the canvas before him. Yet it couldn't be.

He said nothing for several minutes, lifted the big picture carefully and studied each of the other three in turn. Then he went back to the big picture he thought of as the Constable.

"Are they likely to be worth anything, sir?" Sergeant Williams asked.

"I don't know. They may be worth a great deal, the big picture in particular. The others may be valuable, too. They'll have to be examined by specialists, and it will take a bit of time. Meanwhile it's absolutely vital that we should try to find out where they come from."

"We went through all the lists of stolen pictures, and they don't seem to match anything in the police records."

"That's not quite the point—at least, it's not the whole point. If I'm right about one of these pictures, perhaps two, they may be extraordinarily important. I don't know that I am right, of course. But if I am, they may be unknown works by very great artists. We *must* know where they've come from. They may have been stolen from someone who doesn't yet know about the theft. Or they may have been brought to London for sale, and that must be gone into because we'd like to know who was handling them. Important works of art can't be sold abroad without a licence. And other matters come into it—possible fraud on the Revenue, for instance. I'm very glad you've brought them to me."

"You think we ought to have brought them to you before?"

"Well, I'd like to have seen them, but I can promise you that I'm not going to make a fuss about it. Your Division acted quite reasonably. You're not specialists in pictures, and from your point of view the portfolio and its contents were just effects belonging to—or rather, in the possession of—the dead woman. You did your best to identify her, and in the ordinary way her belongings would have been handed over to her executors. I think there may be something very much out of the ordinary about these pictures, but it's my job now to deal with that. I hope you can feel that I'm on your side. You've done everything you could, and I think it's just as well your people decided to say nothing about the pictures at the inquest. That was good police instinct. I'll be in touch with your Division, of course, and I'll make a point of saying how impressed I am by the work you put in trying to identify her.

"And now, sergeant, we've done a lot of talking, and you'll be having a late lunch if you wait to get back to the City. What about sharing a sandwich and a beer? There's a nice little pub in a turning off Victoria Street, where the bread is fresh and the sandwiches pretty good. I'd be delighted if you'd join me."

"That's very kind of you, sir."

"Not a bit. We've both got to eat, and it will be pleasanter if we eat together. Meanwhile, I'd be grateful if you'd say nothing whatever about the possible value of the pictures. Keep your eyes open, and if you come across anything—*anything*—that you think may have any bearing on the case, give me a ring at once. I'll just get my secretary to type out a receipt for the pictures, and then we'll adjourn to the pub."

When Piet got back to his office he telephoned Wilbur Constantine, a partner in Gavell and Gainsworth, the big firm of Fine Art dealers and auctioneers. There had not been a Gainsworth in the firm since the end of the eighteenth-century, and Mr Constantine was a grandson of the last of the Gavells. He was not, however, a mere beneficiary of maternity, for he was an efficient director of the firm's picture sales, and a considerable expert, particularly on English painters of the period 1750–1850, about whom he had written *catalogues raisonnées* which were accepted as authoritative. Piet knew, liked and respected him, and he asked if he could drop whatever he was doing and come over to Scotland Yard. "It's not that I regard my time as more important than yours," he added. "I'd call on you as I've often done before, only

I've got some pictures here that I want to show you, and it will be easier if you can manage to come over." Constantine promised to extract himself in about half an hour.

The art dealer was as astonished by the big picture as Piet had been. "It's not a copy because there's no known work by Constable of this particular scene," he said. "If it's genuine—lord, we'll need to make some revision of art history. Can you place the landscape?"

"No," Piet said. "I've explored the Constable countryside pretty thoroughly, but I can't say this rings any particular bell. I'd put it somewhere in the Colne Valley—between Fordstreet and Wakes Colne, perhaps, but it could be almost anywhere on the Essex-Suffolk border. Maybe it can be placed, maybe it can't—it doesn't much matter. John Constable wasn't a photographer—he was quite capable of moving a tree if he wanted it somewhere else. All one can say is that this seems to me a perfect composition—the cottage in relation to the tree in the foreground, the rough track leading to a ford. You can't see the ford, or the river, but you just *know* it's there. At least I do. Sorry."

"There's no need to be sorry. You have a remarkable sensitivity to Constable, or perhaps to his influence on the way we look at landscape, and that's something to be cherished. I know just what you mean," Constantine said. "Whether this really is by Constable is another matter. Whoever painted it, it's a lovely piece of work." He took from his pocket a magnifying glass, a beautiful little thing that folded into a tortoiseshell case, and studied the detail in the foreground of the picture. "As far as I can see the brushwork is quite typical—there's a distinct touch of the same work in the well-known *Valley Farm*. The mood also seems to be fairly typical, though of the later work, after his wife's death. There's a hint, not of depression, exactly, but of a kind of brave melancholy—brave, because Constable was forcing himself to paint when he *was* depressed. He was often depressed and ill in his last years. The sheer courage of the man comes out in his work."

"You're talking as if you accepted the picture as genuine."

"Forgive me. I'm as shaken as you obviously are. We can't trust to instinct, we need hard, scientific work. First, what is its provenance?"

"It has no provenance so far. It came into the possession of the police because it was in a portolio carried by a young woman who was found dead in a train at Liverpool Street a short time ago."

"And no one has reported the loss?"

"No."

"Who was the young woman?"

"We don't know. We have not yet been able to identify her. But there's more to it. I want to show you these."

Piet took from the portfolio the painting of boats drawn up on a beach.

"My God! Turner!"

"And these two?"

"The portrait has a look of a Gainsborough, about the right period, and it's certainly a Gainsborough-like composition. But offhand I can't possibly say. The second landscape doesn't strike me as having the quality of the others. It suggests a Constable influence, but it's certainly not by Constable himself. Conceivably it's an experiment by Delacroix, which would make it interesting, but if Delacroix had anything to do with it, it's not a good example of his work. Again, I can't say offhand."

"What do you make of the collection as a whole? An unknown Constable, an unknown Turner, an un-

known Gainsborough and possibly an unknown Delacroix?"

"My dear Chief Inspector, I can make nothing of
it! You call me up out of the blue and show me a collection of pictures which, if genuine, are worth many
hundreds of thousands of pounds, and one of which,
whether by Constable or not, is undoubtedly a masterpiece. And you tell me they were found at Liverpool Street station, just like that. What do you expect
me to make of it?"

"I'm hoping that you will be able to help me—you
have as direct an interest as I have in protecting the
art world from forgery and fraud. There seem to me
three main possibilities. First, that all these works are
forgeries. Secondly, that they have been stolen from
some uncatalogued collection. Thirdly, that they have
not been stolen, but that the owner of them is trying
to dispose of them without raising questions of estate
duty, or the need to obtain export licences for sale
abroad. There are other possibilities, of course, but
those seem to me the main ones. Do you think they
are forgeries?"

"I can't possibly say. If the potential Constable is a
forgery, it's an extraordinarily good one, and if there
is anyone around capable of such a forgery he is
clearly a most dangerous man. Much the same applies
to the Turner and the Gainsborough—I leave out the
the word 'possible' just to save my breath. There *are*
some exceptionally good forgeries of works by famous
artists—he would be a bold man, or a fool, who swore
that all the works in great collections attributed to
particular artists are in fact by them. And 'forgery' is
not always the right word. Many great painters had
pupils, and the work of the pupil may naturally be in
the style of the master, and in the course of time the
works of pupil and master may come to be confused.
Then there are artists who, without the least fraudu-
lent intention, deliberately set out to follow the style

of someone they admire, and such works may come to be attributed wrongly, but in good faith. As you know, the attribution of paintings by men long dead is a matter of lifetime study, and what we call 'provenance', the history of how a particular painting came to be where it is, and through whose hands it passed to get there, is of the highest importance.

"If these works are forgeries, they are dangerously good ones, and it is of the most urgent importance, Chief Inspector, that you should find the forger.

"Your other possibility—uncatalogued collections—is slightly remote, but it is certainly possible. Artists of the fame of those we are discussing have been studied for so long, and their works are so valuable, that with every year that passes it becomes less likely that completely unknown paintings by them remain to be found. But it is not impossible. Turner's output, for instance, was enormous, and no one can say that unknown Turners may not still turn up in attics or on the walls of houses whose occupiers have no idea of the value of some picture they have inherited. Constable, too—his paintings were much admired in his lifetime by fellow artists, but the picture-buying public did not take them with alacrity, and many of his landscapes were unsold. He had private means and was comfortably off, so sales did not matter to him greatly. He has become so famous since his death that we may think all his works *must* have come to light, but we can never be sure of such things. I take it you have not yet sent any of these pictures for laboratory examination?"

"No. They came into my hands only today, and I wanted your impressions—I may say that I value your impressions, certainly where Constable is concerned, at least as much as a laboratory report." The art dealer gave a little bow. "Laboratory examination is the next step, but you know the difficulties here. The pictures are not ours, presumably they have some lawful owner, and in submitting pigment or canvas to the kind of tests that are likely to be conclusive it is all too easy to damage a work of art."

"Yes, but modern techniques can accomplish a great deal. It is possible to determine the age of canvas within quite narrow limits, and to discover the main constituents of pigment—which may or may not have been in use in the period when a picture is supposed to have been painted."

"Of course. And, as I said, laboratory examination is the next step. The trouble is that while it can disprove, it can't prove. It can show that a painting cannot date from the lifetime of a particular painter—it cannot prove that any painting *must* have come from a particular hand. That remains a matter for experts like yourself."

"Well, we shall have to see. If laboratory tests show that canvas or pigment is modern, then your theory of forgery becomes probable. Let us carry on from there when you have a few more facts. I hope most of all that you will soon discover the identity of the dead woman, and obtain a provenance for the pictures. I am grateful to you for letting me share your problem—it's as important to me as it is to you."

"I'm equally grateful to you for coming as you did—and I shall certainly need your help again. Meanwhile, may I ask you to keep the existence of these pictures strictly under your hat? Please don't mention them even to your own colleagues."

The art dealer smiled. "My firm has been in business for over two centuries," he said. "During that time we've enjoyed—and kept—the confidence of most of the great families of Europe. We wouldn't have stayed in business if we hadn't. I shan't be less scrupulous where you are concerned, Chief Inspector."

Piet took the pictures himself to the forensic laboratory. The scientists were not specialists in art work but they were used to being asked to turn their hands to anything. Moreover, the chief chemist was a man of international reputation in devising techniques for small-particle analysis and Piet was confident that he could deal with the pictures without damaging them. And Piet wanted to keep investigation of the pictures in his own hands for the moment—to send them to one of the recognised experts in the analysis of pigments and canvas might invite the sort of questions he did not want raised.

He got back to his office a few minutes after five o'clock, just not too late, he thought, to see if he could get hold of the young solicitor who appeared to have befriended the dead woman on her last journey. An interview might turn out to be largely a waste of time, but there were questions that he did not think had been asked, and where there was so little to go on *nothing* could be safely neglected.

So he rang the offices of Messrs. Collard and Wellspade at Twickenham. The girl at the switchboard thought that Mr Tomlinson might still be in his office, but he was very busy. Was the caller a client? Piet had to admit that he was not, but when he explained that he was a police officer speaking from Scotland Yard the girl agreed to put him through.

Keith Tomlinson was not pleased that his small Good Samaritan act on the train should intrude on his affairs yet again. "I thought all that was finished with," he said when Piet explained why he was calling. "I really do know nothing at all about the woman. I gave evidence at the inquest, and honestly, there's absolutely nothing more that I can say."

Piet was gentle and tactful. "I do realise what a pest it is to be involved fortuitously in an affair like this—particularly when you acted out of simple kindliness," he said. "But I wouldn't be bothering you if I didn't think it necessary, and as an officer of the law yourself you will understand that a witness may not always appreciate the importance of some little thing he may have noticed. There are a number of questions that I should like to ask you, and I should like to see you as soon as possible. I'm not asking you to come to Scotland Yard—I'll gladly call on you wherever you suggest."

Tomlinson was somewhat mollified. "Well, all right," he said. "I've got a good bit to do still before I can leave the office, but I should be home soon after seven. If you'd like to come to 53 Canopy Court, Richmond, at seven-thirty, I'll see you then. But please try to make this the last time that I have to be interviewed about that unhappy woman."

Piet re-read Tomlinson's statement to the railway police, and the depositions at the inquest. His story seemed quite consistent. He had helped the woman on to the train at Sudbury, he had bought her ticket for her at Mark's Tey, and he had helped to find her a seat on the London train. She had appeared to go to sleep, and was still asleep when the train reached Liverpool Street. He had tried to wake her, realised that something was wrong, and called to a porter on the platform for help. He had never seen her before she got on the train at Sudbury, and had no idea who she was.

It was not a promising statement for cross-examination, but, Piet reflected, you can't always choose the straw when you have to make bricks.

Piet was rather taken by the young solicitor—intelligent, he thought, but not in the least slick, and would develop into the traditional sort of sound family lawyer. A good type, kept himself fit, and probably played rugger. Put into words, this guess turned out to be right. Tomlinson was a trifle surprised to be asked if he played rugger, but admitted that he did. "I managed to play for Cambridge," he said. "Still turn out when I can for the local club, though I find I've got less and less time nowadays. But you didn't come to talk about rugger." He took Piet's card and studied it. "Top brass, I see."

"Not very top—somewhere about an army major, perhaps," Piet said. "But police work is so different from the Services that you can't really equate our ranks with anything else. It's good of you to see me."

"I don't think I had much choice. I thought it was rather nice of you to come here, instead of summoning me to Scotland Yard. I've tried to explain, though, that there's absolutely nothing I can tell you. What do you want to ask me?"

Piet was in no hurry to begin questioning Tomlinson on his statement. "Nice flat you've got here," he said. "Do you live alone?"

"I do now. I used to live with my mother, until she died about eighteen months ago. The flat's really too big for me, but it's so difficult to find anywhere that I kept it on. It's convenient for my office, and I was brought up in this part of London."

"My home was in Greenwich, so we've got the river in common. Do you often go to Suffolk?"

"Three or four times a year. My mother's sister—my aunt—lives at Long Melford. She's my only fairly close relation, and I try to keep in touch with her. I saw her more often when I was at Cambridge. It's not all that far from Long Melford, and she used to drive over to see me. She was younger then, of course."

"Do you normally go by train?"

"As a rule, yes. I'm not all that fond of driving across London, and the trains from Liverpool Street are pretty good. My aunt has a car, and she meets me at Mark's Tey."

"But she didn't drive you back to Mark's Tey."

"No. She's getting on, and she suffers quite a bit from migraine. She had a baddish turn on the Sunday evening, and I didn't want her to have to turn out early on Monday morning. So I got a taxi to Sudbury station."

"The girl wasn't there when you got to the station?"

"No. I've explained about that. She only just caught the train—it had started moving when she flung herself at it. I was standing at the carriage door, the window was down and I was looking out. It's a sort of ghost station. I hadn't been there before, and I was interested, I suppose. I wish now I hadn't gone there at all. But it was a good thing for her that I was at the train door, for if I hadn't grabbed her I think she'd have fallen off, and perhaps been killed."

"She was dying, anyway."

"I suppose she was. She didn't look dying then. But when we got to Mark's Tey she looked really ill. That's why I helped her."

"She died of an overdose of a barbiturate drug. So far we don't know when or how she took it. It was a fairly massive overdose and it couldn't have been very long before she went off to sleep. Could she have taken it on the Sudbury train?"

"I suppose she could, but I don't know because I wasn't looking at her. It was a new bit of line to me, and I was looking out of the window. The run to Mark's Tey doesn't take long, just over twenty minutes. She wouldn't have had much time—I mean, to get as ill as she was when we got to Mark's Tey. But I don't know how quickly these things act. If it was a sleeping pill doesn't it take a bit of time to get drowsy and go off?"

"That depends on all sorts of things. Even if you weren't looking at her, you might have noticed some movement if she took pills on the train. No container was found on her. It doesn't follow, of course, that she didn't have the pills with her, for she might have been carrying them loose. But it seems more probable that she took them just before running for the train.

The effort of running might have had two effects—if it was important to her to catch the train it might have kept her going for a little by sheer willpower, and afterwards it would probably have accelerated the action of the drug."

"It *was* important to her to catch the train. When she thanked me for helping her on she said something like, 'I don't know what would have happened if I'd missed it.'"

"You didn't say anything about that in your statement."

"I wasn't asked."

"So you see, Mr Tomlinson, it *is* worth going over people's statements, even if they don't think they have anything to add. Now I want to ask you about her ticket. Why did you get a single for her and not a return?"

"I haven't really thought about it. Let me see—I'd carried her portfolio over the bridge. When we got to the main line platform she sat on a bench, gasping, rather. Then she got up to go to the booking office window. There were several people ahead of her, and as she stood in the queue she swayed, and I thought she was going to fall. I had a return ticket for myself because I'd come to Mark's Tey, but I asked if she'd like me to get a ticket for her. She was obviously grateful, muttered something about my being kind, and went to sit down again. I think I must have asked, 'Are you going to London?' and she nodded. Anyway, she gave me a five-pound note and I got her a single to Liverpool Street. I remember thinking that we were too early for a cheap day return—it was a commuter train, you see. I suppose I got a single because I didn't know anything about her, how she planned to come back, or whether she would be staying in London. I just got the ticket and gave it to her."

"So the single was really your idea, not hers?"

"I suppose so. Yes."

"It's important because we're still trying to find out who she was. The fact that she had no luggage with her rather suggests that she lived in Suffolk, but the single ticket rather implies that she didn't. Now you've cleared that up, and we can discount whatever evidence there seemed to be in the single ticket."

Tomlinson was getting very interested. "I'm sorry I was fed up when you telephoned," he said. "I thought your visit was just another waste of time, but the way you put things it isn't."

"I'm afraid I haven't finished yet. One of the puzzling things about the case is that she apparently had no handbag. Could she possibly have dropped a handbag when you were helping her on board the train?"

"She could, I suppose. But I don't remember seeing any handbag. She had one arm round that great portfolio, and her other hand was grabbing at the door. She might have had a bag slung from her shoulder, but I think I'd have remembered seeing it. And if she had dropped her bag, wouldn't you expect her to say something like, 'Oh, my bag!' when she was on the train? Most women would be upset at losing a handbag. All I can say is that she wasn't, or didn't appear to be."

"That's a good point."

"I think there's another indication that she didn't have a bag. When she gave me the money for her ticket she didn't have to search for it. I didn't notice at the time where she got the five-pound note from, but she must have taken it from a pocket. If she'd lost her bag she'd probably have lost her money. Of course, she might have had some spare money in a pocket, but I think women generally carry money in their bags."

"Yes. How on earth did you get that portfolio on the train?"

"Goodness knows. I got the door open for her, and I think one hand was grabbing at the sill of the open window. It was a bloody dangerous situation. I got my left arm round her and just heaved. The portfolio half-jammed in the doorway, but as I got her up with my left arm I managed to get my right arm round the portfolio and hauled her in, with the portfolio. It was brute force more than anything else."

"And the experience of the rugger field. It was good work, Mr Tomlinson."

III

"A Thread of John Constable's Life"

Late as it was when he got away from Richmond,
Piet went back to the Yard. There, he found that a
telephone message had come for him from Detective-
Sergeant Williams. The message form was not ex-
plicit—it said simply that Sergeant Williams had
telephoned the Chief Inspector and would ring again
in the morning. Piet short-circuited this by getting
Sergeant Williams's home number from the internal
director and ringing him. "Sorry to bother you so
late," he said when the sergeant answered the phone,
"but I've only just got your message."

"Well, sir, I don't know that you'll think it worth
ringing up at all," Williams replied apologetically.
"But you said I was to telephone if I thought of anything, and there is one thing that I'm afraid I forgot
to tell you about. But it may have nothing whatever
to do with the case."

"What is it?"

"When I searched the carriage looking for the
young woman's handbag I found a tiny scrap of some
sort of wild flower underneath the seat. I put it in an
envelope and I've still got it. Would you like me to
bring it to you?"

"I'd like to see it, certainly. But there's no need for you to come to the Yard. I've decided to go down to Suffolk tomorrow, and I can easily call at your station on the way. What time do you get in?"

"I'm due on at nine o'clock in the morning, sir."

"Good. Well, I'll see you as soon after nine as I can make it through the early morning traffic."

That settled, Piet turned to the matter that had brought him back to the Yard—the condition of the outside of the portfolio. After hearing Tomlinson's account of the struggle he had had to get it through the train door he wanted to examine it closely.

The portfolio was constructed of two big sheets of cardboard covered in black plastic sheeting. The sheeting was of good quality, for although it was scratched in several places it was not torn. A stick-on label attached to the plastic was, however, torn in two, the tear jagged and untidy—consistent with being dragged roughly through a doorway. Piet had no reason to doubt the young solicitor's story, but it was useful to have physical confirmation of it, and the torn label and scratches on the portfolio did tend to confirm it.

There was, of course, no proof that the label had been torn during the struggle, but it seemed a reasonable assumption. If so, was there any chance that the remains of the label might still be there to be found? It was an exceptionally dry summer, and there had been no rain since the woman's last journey. If the torn part of the label had fallen on the platform it would doubtless have been trodden into illegibility, but it was just possible that it had fallen between the train and the platform, and that a search might recover it. The remaining word "Suffolk" indicated that the label had once borne an address, and if it could be found the problem of the woman's identity might be solved forthwith.

Piet considered asking the Suffolk police to under-take a search, but decided that he might just as well go himself. He had a firsthand description of the girl's struggle to board the train, and while this did not make him any better qualified as a searcher after scraps of paper it did help his imagination. Moreover, he'd already decided to visit Sudbury when he spoke to Sergeant Williams. He did not know what he could hope to learn from a visit to a country railway station which had figured briefly and incidentally in the life-story of one of its passengers, but the girl's departure from Sudbury on that Monday morning was one of the few facts known about her. The station was at least a starting point, and Piet wanted to see it for himself. He tended to think visually, and his mind needed a picture of the station. The hunt for a scrap of torn label was an additional reason for going there.

Piet had a one-bedroom flat off Ebury Street. It was enough for him, because he still thought of his mother's house at Greenwich as home, kept most of his possessions there, and went home as often as he could. But Greenwich was too far from New Scotland Yard to fit the odd hours of his work. The flat was within walking distance, and he could be on hand whenever he was needed.

He walked there now, enjoying the summer night, and wondering as he always did what private loves and hates, hopes and fears brought so many people to Victoria Station, and to the airways' terminal across the road. When he got in he remembered that he'd had nothing to eat since breakfast save the sandwich in the pub with Sergeant Williams. He cooked him-self an omelette, and felt better for it.

The CID office at Sergeant Williams's police station was a barrack-like room in a comfortless Victorian building. Piet reflected, not for the first time, on the contrast between the lavish offices of the makers of money and the conditions in which the guardians of society too often had to work. Without the police the whole fabric would come tumbling down but most people—until they needed a policeman—seemed content to regard the police as belonging in some way to the servants' quarters. Well, the police were not alone in that—until there was a war the army was commonly regarded as a waste of money, and until you needed an operation you were quite likely to think of surgeons as overpaid. Society had strange values. It was a good thing that the idea of service never quite faded out—each generation produced some men and women ready to work without thinking of material reward as the prime purpose in life, ready to spend themselves in an effort to keep the world clean.

If the physical surroundings of the CID office were cheerless, the human spirit there could be felt as brisk and alert. Sergeant Williams seemed genuinely glad to see him. "You made good time, sir," he said. "Would you like a cup of tea?" Piet didn't wany any tea, but he accepted the offer. "What's the current case load?" he asked.

"Fourteen—no, fifteen—breaking and entering, three robbery with violence, couple of suspected arson, nasty piece of work by someone who atempted to interfere with a child on the way home from school. Fortunately the child screamed and he ran off, but we've got to catch him before he does something worse. And an ugly affair outside a pub with a man stabbed—he's badly ill in hospital, but expected to recover. We've got the chap who did it, though. He's coming up in court this morning."

"And the mysterious affair of a young woman found dead in a train."

"That too, of course, sir. I'll just get the tea, and then I'll show you what I telephoned about."

Piet declined sugar, and would have preferred to

decline milk, but it was already in the teacup. While
he pretended to welcome the tea—and did welcome
the hospitality it symbolised—Sergeant Williams went
to a safe and came back with a small brown envelope.
"I'm afraid this is all it is, sir," he said.

Piet slit the envelope with his pocket knife—from
childhood he had disliked opening envelopes untidily
with a thumb—and shook out the scrap of dried wild
flower it contained. The tiny blueish-purple petals
were still firm. "I'm not an expert on these things,"
he said, "but I'd say it was sea lavender. I used to sail
quite a bit with my father when I was a kid, in the
Thames Estuary and up the East Coast as far as Yarmouth, sometimes. I've often seen it growing in the
marshes. Have you got a book on wild flowers
handy?"

"No, sir, I'm afraid we don't run to that in the office. But there's a public library only three doors
down the street. I'll slip out and see if I can borrow
one for you."

"There's no need for that, I can look in myself
when I leave. Tell me exactly where you found it."

"I was looking under the seat for the young
woman's handbag. She wasn't there, of course—the
body had been taken away, so I could only know
roughly whereabouts she'd been sitting. But one of
the railway policemen had seen her before she was
taken away, and he remembered how she'd been,
leaning back in the corner next the door to the corridor. I was using a torch to look for the handbag.
There wasn't any bag, but I saw this little thing in
the light of the torch, just about where I reckon her
feet would have been. There's no way of knowing
whether it was anything to do with her or not, but I
thought it just might have fallen off her shoe or
something, so I picked it up and put it in an envelope."

"You did very well. It may mean nothing, or it may

help to give us a line on where she'd been that morning on her way to the station. I'll give you a receipt
for it, and take it with me. There's something else I'd
like you to do for me. I know how pressed you are,
and it's probably a pretty hopeless inquiry after all
this time, but I'm surprised that no one seems to have
turned up at Liverpool Street to ask about the portfolio. I'm not satisfied that there really was nobody
there to meet her."

"The railway constable did ask on the platform at
the time, sir."

"Yes, but I rather think that whoever was there
wouldn't want to make himself or herself known to a
policeman. You're in touch with the railway men.
Could you get them to ask the ticket collectors, por-
ters, bookstall staff and anyone else who was around
when that Colchester train came in if they noticed
some man or woman hanging about and looking anxious? And try to find out if *anyone* has been to the
station since to ask where the woman's portfolio has
been taken. Nothing was said about it at the inquest.
I think someone must be getting very anxious indeed
to find out what's happened to it."

"I can try all right, but I can't promise any
results."

"Our job is ninety-nine per cent routine and one
per cent luck. But the luck doesn't come unless you
carry out the routine. Would you like me to have a
word with your inspector?"

"It would be the right thing, sir. I'll do anything I
can to help—on my own time if need be—but we've
put in a lot of work on this case already without getting anywhere, and other jobs keep piling up."

Piet knew what he was doing. He wanted Sergeant
Williams to feel personally concerned in the case, but
he had no intention of barging in on a divisional officer's territory. He devoted half an hour to the station inspector and left another ally.

Before going to his car Piet called at the library. It had a good reference section, and provided a standard work on wild flowers. This told him that there were three varieties of sea lavender, *Statice limonium*, which grew on muddy stretches of sea-marsh, *Statice spathulata*, which seemed to prefer rocks, and *Statice reticulata*, which was found only on some Norfolk salt-marshes. His specimen, he decided, was *limonium*, which would fit in with the Suffolk coast, though it was puzzling to see what connection it could have with the dead woman, for it would not occur as far inland as Sudbury. Pity it wasn't *reticulata*—that really would narrow down the locality it came from, though a Norfolk salt-marsh had even less connection with the railway station at Sudbury than had the Suffolk coast. He put the specimen in its envelope carefully in his pocket book, and at the back of his mind.

He was driving east, so his call in the City had not taken him out of his way. He went out towards Brentwood, but was able to bypass Brentwood itself, and was in Chelmsford in little over an hour. From Chelmsford it was a straight run of about twenty-five miles through Braintree and Halstead to Sudbury. He got there soon after midday, and drove to the station car park. It seemed a big car park for a very small station, but there were malthouses and mills in the vicinity, and doubtless the railway had seen better days. What was now a car park would originally have been the station yard, where drays, pulled by great Suffolk punches, would have carted produce to the trains before there were any motor lorries.

The station itself brought the same little shock of surprise that Keith Tomlinson had felt—that it should be there at all. For some reason he found himself thinking of Turner's famous painting *Rain*,

Steam and Speed. That had been painted in 1844
when railways and the power of steam seemed to offer
England a future of limitless prosperity—there was a
confidence about the picture that late twentieth-century man could not but envy. The disused track running on the Clare and Cambridge would also make a
picture, but it would be a picture of a very different
mood. Failure? Not exactly. Sadness, yes—after two
world wars and savage economic slumps confidence
had certainly been lost, and the Victorian social stability had fractured into what seemed endless social
bickering. But was Victorian stability really so very
stable? The police were needed then, as now. There
was brutality and senseless suffering—only those more
comfortably placed in life knew less about it. For
many people, the Suffolk labourers among them,
twentieth-century politics provided more than life
had ever given their families before. Did life now
provide too much? Perhaps—but what could be said
to be too much? It was a question of what you did
with what you had. People always seemed to waste
things. This little branch line had seen men, taken
men, going off to war, and brought some of them
back, hurt, often, in body or mind. Now the line itself
looked like some wizened sea-creature, stranded on a
beach, taken out of its own world and put into a
world where people thought it a curiosity. Yet the
remnants of this railway line from Sudbury to Mark's
Tey were not quite out of the world: the line was still
useful, quicker than car or bus, not hurting the countryside. And God, how beautiful it was in its forlorn
way! The picture from the train window must have
been about the last conscious vision of earth that the
unhappy woman had had—she could not have noticed
much after reaching the main line. It wasn't a bad
picture of the world to take away with you.

Piet made a conscious mental effort to halt his med-
itations. He was not concerned with reveries, he had

a job to do. He walked along the edge of the platform contemplating how best to do it.

His mind put visual images to Tomlinson's story. He was on the train, and it had started moving when the girl flung herself at the door. The entrance from the station yard was towards one end of the platform—the end from which the train went out. Presumably, therefore, the train went past the entrance when it came in, stopping about the middle of the platform. That would give a little time for someone running from the entrance to reach a moving train before it had gone too far. The struggle at the carriage door must have taken place somewhere roughly level with the station entrance, or in a sector not more than a few yards each side of the direct line from the entrance to the edge of the platform. If the torn label had fallen on the platform there was not much hope; it would have been more or less in the fairway of coming and going feet, and would almost certainly have been trodden to pieces. It might have been whisked away by the wind from the moving train, but the train had not got up speed or the girl could never have been hauled in. Piet glanced round the platform, and the blocked-up stairs leading to a footbridge across the line, not needed now that only one platform was in use. There were some scraps of paper blown against the stairs, but all save one bit was distressingly familiar litter—old sweet wrappings, an empty crisp bag, a torn sheet of newspaper. He picked up the one piece that might have been part of a label, but it turned out to be the top of a handwritten circular advertising a village fete.

A timetable by the station entrance told him that the next train was not due for an hour, so he could hunt undisturbed along the line. Again he tried to make a visual image of what might have happened. A carriage door open, with the girl, clinging to the big portfolio, being dragged in by the hefty young rugby footballer. Tomlinson had said that he got his left arm round the girl. That implied that she was clutching at the train with her right hand—for they would be opposite each other—and had her left arm round the portfolio. The piece of label still stuck to the portfolio was off-centre on the lower half; it would have scraped against the edge of the door, probably fairly low down. It could not have fallen straight to the ground—it was moving with the train when it was torn off, would have been carried forward a little by its own momentum, and have fluttered rather than dropped down. It would be on the platform side of the line, possibly beyond the end of the platform.

Piet got down on to the line from the platform, well beyond the point where he judged the struggle to board the train to have taken place. Then he walked slowly along the line in the direction of the outgoing train, scrutinising every inch. He passed what he called to himself the most hopeful sector without finding anything, and was now beyond the station. He stopped to consider for how long it was worth going on. The bit of paper might have stuck to the train and have been swept up when the carriage was cleaned, or it might have fallen off anywhere between Sudbury and Mark's Tey. Could he justify a search of the whole line? That would be ridiculous, an appalling amount of time spent on a chance probably a good deal more slender than winning a football pool. He went back to his visual image. The label was an ordinary stick-on luggage label, such as you buy in packets. It was stuck to the portfolio, so that the side which scraped against the door was not the sticky side, and even if there had been some gum left it would have been on the wrong side to stick to the train. In the struggle it might, of course, have been twisted, but still it seemed highly unlikely that it had stuck to the train, and much more likely that it had dropped off. And it was not likely to have been carried far—either it would be somewhere near where he now was, or it had been blown away and was now unfindable. It was worth looking for a little longer, but not much.

He was about to give up when he noticed something whitish caught between a shoe of the rail and the sleeper. Yes, it was a crumpled bit of paper. Telling himself to expect disappointment he bent down to it—and knew a wonderful sense of triumph. His visual reconstruction must have been more or less exact; this was the torn half of the label on the portfolio. It must have been carried along much as he had imagined, and been blown into the corner between the rail, the sleeper and the shoe. What an all-but-incredible piece of luck! Ninety-nine per cent routine, one per cent luck! Well, he'd slogged away at the routine. And the label was still legible—written with a ballpoint pen in the same hand as the "Suffolk" on the portfolio. He had a vivid mental image of that "Suffolk", and of the jagged edge above it. This piece of paper would have to be matched with that when he got back to his office, but although that was necessary to provide physical evidence to convince other people, his own visual memory was enough for him. The label was addressed to

> Mrs Shirley Vincent
> Moat Cottage Studio
> Lavenham

—the "Suffolk" that completed the address he already had.

He put the precious piece of torn luggage label in the envelope that contained the sprig of sea lavender and went back to his car.

Lavenham was not more than six or seven miles from Sudbury, and he decided to go there straight away. What a curious thread of John Constable's life seemed to stretch back from the girl found dead in a train at Liverpool Street! Lavenham was where the young Constable had been to school.

Lavenham has come well into the twentieth century, preserving a fairy-story quality from the past without looking consciously pretty. Its overhanging timbered buildings seem to have grown there, the twisting lanes between them seeming to remain just as they were trodden by the first footsteps making from cottage door to well or cabbage patch. The wealth from wool that went into the great church and merchants' houses seems somehow to have lasted from the middle ages, paying each new generation a dividend of gracious surroundings. Piet had no idea where Moat Cottage was, and as it was getting on for half-past one he thought that the best thing to do would be to call at a pub for a drink and a sandwich, and ask at the bar.

He chose the wrong pub, for the place he entered was bigger than it looked from outside and was in fact a hotel, with a flourishing restaurant trade. When he asked for a sandwich the barman said, "Sorry, sir, don't do sandwiches. You can get a meal in the restaurant."

From another point of view, though, his choice turned out to be a good one, for the customers all seemed to be at lunch and the bar was empty. "Haven't got time for the restaurant so I'll have to make do with a pint," Piet said. "Perhaps you'd join me."

"Thank you sir, I'll have a half," the barman said. "If you want a sandwich you can get one in that little pub across the road. Do them quite well there."

He pulled Piet's pint and his own glass. "Local beer?" Piet asked.

"Brewery's at Ipswich. Time was when they brewed

here on the premises—there's an old malthouse at the back. Before my time though."

"Well, it's good beer," Piet said. "I'm looking for a place called Moat Cottage Studio. Do you happen to know it?"

"Mrs Vincent's place—yes. It's a bit out of the town, but you'll find it easily enough. Go out on the Bury road, and about half a mile on you'll come to a turning on the right, little narrow track, doesn't look like a road, but it is. The studio's along it. There's a painted sign at the corner, so you can't miss it."

"Thanks a lot. Do you know Mrs Vincent?"

"Comes in here quite often with people from the studio. It's a sort of shop as well, pictures and art stuff and antiques. And they do teas—home-made scones and things. It's quite a big place, with a good car park. Mrs Vincent was in with a bunch of people last night. Cheerful lot they were, too."

This was a slight shock to Piet, for he had been hoping that he had identified the woman in the train. But you couldn't expect one strand of luck to run for ever, and at least he had a name and address to start from. "Is there a Mr Vincent?" he asked.

"Not that I know of, not to come in here. But then I wouldn't know, you see, because I only know them from coming into the bar. Mrs Vincent's not been here all that long. Came down from London two-three years back, did up the cottage and turned it into the studio place. At least, I've always thought she came from London, but I don't really know. You in the antique trade?"

"In a way . . . Well, I must be getting along. Thanks for a nice beer, and for giving me instructions to get to the studio."

Lunch time, Piet thought, would not be the best time to visit Moat Cottage. If they did teas, he'd do better to get there a bit after three o'clock. He could do with a sandwich, and there was no reason why he shouldn't take the barman's advice. He did, and found it excellent. A pleasant elderly woman served him with a plate of freshly-made ham sandwiches, and there was really fresh mustard on the bar counter. He did not pursue inquiries about Mrs Vincent.

Piet reckoned that it was still too early to make for Moat Cottage when he left the pub, but he could find out where it was, and have a look at the country round it. He had also to make up his mind what to do. The simplest thing would be to interview Mrs Vincent officially, disclosing his police authority, and asking formally for information on the portfolio that had been addressed to her and found in the possession of the dead girl at Liverpool Street. All his instincts were against this. The girl had not died a natural death, and the presence of arsenic in her body in addition to the barbiturate drug which killed her strongly suggested murder. Then there were the contents of the portfolio, a strange collection of possibly very valuable pictures, or impressive forgeries. To start questioning Mrs Vincent officially would indicate a police interest which ought not yet to be disclosed. Mrs Vincent might be entirely innocent of anything connected with the girl's death, in which case no harm would be done by keeping quiet about it. Or she might be implicated in all sorts of ways: if so a great deal of harm might be done by alerting her, and possible associates, before the police were in any position to take action. The barman had given him an idea by asking if he was in the antique trade. He would call on Mrs Vincent, he decided, as a customer with an interest in antiques, and navigate from there, as the saying goes, by guess and by God.

The barman's directions were accurate. Piet drove out of Lavenham on the Bury St Edmunds road, and soon came to the sign for Moat Cottage Studio. It was an elaborate, well-painted board, announcing

Moat Cottage Studio
Proprietor: *Mrs S. Vincent*
Antiques and Objects of Art For Sale
Art Lessons Arranged

Cream Teas With Home-Made Cakes

Good Car Park

It was still too early for the kind of visit Piet wanted to make, so he drove past the turning. The road climbed slightly, and about a quarter of a mile farther on he met another side road, also leading off to the right. He took this, and after a few hundred yards pulled in under the hedge on his near side and stopped. The other side of the road was hedgeless, with a wire fence along the verge. Beyond the fence the land fell gently to a wide valley, with a thatched cottage and various outbuildings visible through the trees that lined the track leading to them. He got out of his car to have a look. That would be Moat Cottage, he thought. With the surrounding buildings it seemed a substantial establishment. He could make out a car park, and in a field opposite the cottage there were three or four caravans.

It was a scene of quiet loveliness, typical of the soft-hued, unemphatic beauty of the Suffolk countryside. The car park and the caravans were an intrusion, but from this distance not very much; they were intelligently sited to be screened by trees. Piet wished he had his sketching block—the thatched cottage, a little off-centre in the near distance, was exactly right, and would make a perfect composition. How much nicer just to make pictures of this supremely beautiful world than to pursue the evil

people in it! But evil was ugliness, corrupting everything and everyone it touched; unless it could be
rooted out there could be no peace to enjoy beauty.
The policeman had a job to do, as creative in its way
as the artist's. No, not *as* creative—that was high-falu-
tin' nonsense. But creative, certainly, creating the security in which the artist could be free to work.
Anyway, there was police work to be done, and he'd
better get on with it.

Piet was glad to see that there were only two other
cars in the car park, and both had a look of belonging to the place. It was just on three o'clock, safely after lunch but early for tea. With luck there wouldn't
be many other customers.

What he had not seen from the hilltop because it
was screened by the cottage was a low single-storey
building linking the cottage to a barn. This had obviously been built on recently, but it was pleasantly
designed and the end nearest the barn was already
half covered with quick-growing Russian vine. The
new building was the shop. Most of the front was
glass, and through it he could see a rosewood table
bearing a pair of Georgian silver candlesticks, and
surrounded by what looked like a set of Chippendale
chairs. A bell rang as he went in, and a woman came
through an arched opening that led from the new
building to the barn. She was of that rather indeter-
minate age that might be anywhere from the mid-
thirties to the mid-forties, slightly sharp-featured, but
with a good figure and quite attractive. She had very
dark, almost black hair, severely held in a band, and
she was wearing an embroidered smock.

"Good afternoon. May I have a look round?" Piet
asked.

"Of course. The antiques, as you can see, are here.
There are pictures and some other things in the
barn."

"Your sign said that you also do teas. Is it too early for some tea?"

"No. You can have tea in the barn. What would you like—just tea and some scones? There are some cucumber sandwiches, too. They'll probably go later in the afternoon."

"I didn't have much lunch, and if it doesn't sound greedy I'd like cucumber sandwiches *and* scones," Piet said.

For the first time he got a little smile out of her. "I daresay we can manage. Will you come through?" She stood back to let him walk into the barn, and followed him through the archway.

The barn seemed huge. It was remarkably well lighted through a row of big windows skilfully let into the north wall. The other walls were hung with pictures, one wall displaying a number of high-quality reproductions of Old Masters, the others showing a mixed bunch of oils and watercolours, all discreetly priced. At the far end of the barn there were about a dozen small tables set for tea. Near the archway leading from the antique shop was a long table with a cash register. In the middle of the room were two other long tables, displaying various pieces of sculpture, hand-painted pots, and arrangements of dried flowers. The woman showed Piet to one of the tea tables, and went off through an opening in the end wall. "The kitchen's at this end. I'll be back with your tea in a moment," she said. As Piet sat down he noticed a small pile of portfolios, precisely like the one in his office, in a corner of the barn.

The woman was as good as her word, returning with Piet's tea, scones and cucumber sandwiches in no more than two or three minutes. "You have a beautiful place here. Are you Mrs Vincent?" Piet said.

"Yes. Why do you ask?"

"I saw the name on your sign. It must be a lot of work running a place like this singlehanded."

"Oh, but I don't. I'm on my own this afternoon because it's early, and my assistant has had to go to Colchester to deliver some furniture that we sold yesterday. If we get busy some of the girls or men from the studio will come in to give a hand."

"What is your studio?"

"Didn't you see on the sign? There's another barn like this where we have art classes. We have holiday courses—people can stay in the trailers."

"What a splendid idea! Why is it called Moat Cottage? I've always imagined moats round castles rather than cottages."

"Well, I think there was a castle once, or a fortified farm. It was at the back. You can still see a few ruins, but the buildings disappeared long ago. The cottage and the barns presumably belonged to them. We actually have a moat, though it doesn't go right round now. You crossed it on a bridge when you turned off from the main road, but you probably didn't notice because it's been so dry that there isn't any water in it at the moment."

Piet finished his tea, and asked, "May I look at your pictures?"

"They're mostly the work of the people who come to the art classes, but some of them aren't bad."

Piet wandered round. Most of the original pictures he thought fairly mediocre, but there was one watercolour of a cornfied that he liked, and he bought it for fifteen pounds. The reproductions were superb, and he was much attracted by a Vermeer interior. "I don't think I've ever seen such fine reproductions," he said. "Can I have the Vermeer?"

"They are good, aren't they? They're fairly new—they come from quite a small firm called Equinox Engravers. I'm afraid they're rather expensive. That one is twenty-five pounds."

"It's worth every bit of it. May I have it with my

watercolour? Oh, and could I have one of those port-folios to carry them in? How much is the portfolio?"

"They're not really for sale—the Equinox reproduc-tions come in them, and we're supposed to send them back. But I daresay I could spare you one."

She was doing up the pictures in the portfolio when a girl, her hair flying, came rushing into the barn. "Oh, Shirley, I've just brought you these," she said breathlessly. "But I haven't got a moment—I *must* get the bus from Lavenham to get the train to Sudbury."

She put two framed dried-flower arrangements on the table by the till. They were exquisite work. Both of them contained several sprays of sea lavender.

"I'm on my way to Sudbury now. I can give you a lift if you like," Piet said.

"Oh, can you? That would be a tremendous help."

"And can I buy one of your flower pictures?"

"Well, I sell them to Shirley."

"Of course you can buy one—they're for sale in the shop," said Mrs Vincent. "Which would you like? They're both the same price at twenty pounds."

Piet chose the one that had more sea lavender in it. He paid in cash—it was a good thing, he thought, that he'd just drawn a hundred pounds from the bank. His cheques had his name on them, and al-though there was no reason to suppose that it might mean anything to Mrs Vincent, it was not wholly un-known in the art world.

IV

A Bad Night for Sally

Piet put his portfolio and a rucksack belonging to the girl in the back of the car. The girl herself got into the front seat beside him. "This is really awfully good of you," she said. "I'm Sally."

"I'm going through Sudbury anyway, and it's no trouble at all to take you there. Besides, I'm in your debt for your really lovely flower arrangement," Piet said.

"Shirley charges rather a lot. She only pays me twelve pounds. Don't you think her profit of eight pounds is a bit steep?"

"I don't know—she must have pretty heavy overheads. And it might easily cost you more to advertise and sell direct."

"I suppose so—but she made eight pounds very quickly when you bought my piece. I've often thought that I'd like a little shop of my own, but I haven't any capital."

"What brought you to the Moat Cottage place?"

"It's partly run as a centre for holiday art classes. I give lessons twice a week in flower-arranging. During the summer, that is. I don't know what happens in winter, because I've only been there this summer."

"How did you come to hear of it?"

"A girl I know lives in a sort of artists' colony at a place called Poplar's Fen near the coast between Dunwich and Walberwick. It's a fascinating place, almost as much water as land. Some people live there on old boats, and there's an ancient windmill that people live in, too. It's not exactly a collective, more a kind of co-op. People pay into a fund which buys food and things, and they take it in turn to cook—there's a communal dining room in the old mill. It suits the people who live there because it's cheap, and they help each other out. When someone's sold a picture, for instance, he'll be in funds for a bit, and he'll pay perhaps the whole cost of a week's food. Then if he's broke next week, someone else will pay. I've got a job in adult education in London—I run evening courses in flower-arranging. But that's only in winter, and in summer I'm rather at a loose end. I can just about keep myself going with my flower pictures, but when Sandra suggested that I could spend the summer cheaply at Poplar's Fen, and find a lot of interesting wild flowers in the marshes, I thought that at least I could try it. She lives on a boat, and there was room for a few others. Then a man who lives on Sandra's boat—well, I think he and Sandra more or less live together—knew Shirley Vincent, and he told me that she wanted to add flower-arranging to her other art classes. He took me to see her, and she agreed to give me a trial. She doesn't pay much, but the flower-arranging classes are new, and if I do them again next year there may be more students for them. And Shirley buys my flower pictures for her shop."

They were through Long Melford and approaching Sudbury. "Where do you want to go from Sudbury?" Piet asked. "I'm going to London, and if it's any use to you I can take you on."

"Well, it would certainly be nice to save the fare," she said frankly. "Could I pay half your petrol?"

"No," Piet said, "you couldn't. It doesn't cost any more whether you are in the car or not. Whereabouts in London are you making for?"

"To tell the truth I'm not exactly sure. It's really because of Sandra. She went to London nearly a fortnight ago, she hasn't written, and she hasn't come back. It's a bit awkward for me, because of this man she's been living with. I don't like him all that much—I mean, he's quite nice to me, but I just don't like him. There's another girl on board, and when Sandra was there it was all right. The other girl and I shared a cabin, and we got on quite well. Now I think the other girl has rather fallen for the man. . . . I've been living for the last few days in one of the caravans at Shirley's place. There wasn't a fuss or anything—one of the students who'd booked had to cancel, so there was a spare berth in the caravan, and as it's a tiresome journey in three buses from Poplar's Fen to Lavenham I asked Shirley if I could have it for the week. Next week I can't, because all the caravans are booked. So I feel I've just got to find Sandra and find out what's happening. I think I know where she'll probably be in London. She's got a studio-room in a house belonging to some friends at Finsbury Park, and I expect she'll have gone there. If she's there, she'll put me up for the night."

"And if not?"

"I've got a sort of half room in a flat at Shepherd's Bush. It's a flat I've been sharing with two other girls, and when I thought I'd take up Sandra's offer for the summer I couldn't really afford to keep it on. One of the other adult education lecturers had just been deserted by her husband and was desperate to find somewhere cheap to live. So I told her that she could have my room in the flat for half what I pay on condition that I can come there when I want to. I mean, it's still my room and I shall want it again after the summer, but she has the use of it now."

"I live near Victoria, so I've got to go through the middle of London. If I drop you off at Leicester Square you can get the Picadilly Line to Finsbury Park."

"That will be wonderful."

"I hope you find your Sandra, or you'll be wandering about London half the night. Tell me about her—how did you come to meet her?"

"Sandra? Well, I was at school with her, but I went to teachers' training college and she went to a proper art school. She's a painter, and she's jolly good. I try to paint, too, but I'm not all that good. Then I started to read about flower-arranging, and got very interested in it. I went to various classes, and although I say it, I am quite good."

"Your dried flower pictures are superb."

"That's very nice of you—or perhaps you don't want to think that you've wasted your twenty pounds! Anyway, I've got an art teaching certificate, and I've got a diploma in flower-arranging, so it works out quite well."

"And Sandra?"

"She's *really* good. She had an exhibition last year, and it attracted quite a lot of notice. She ought to be having another exhibition this autumn—several galleries would put her on—but she's changed her style or something. She works away jolly hard in a room at the top of the old mill, but I don't really know what she's doing. I don't think she's very happy, and I'm a good deal worried about her."

"What is her other name—Sandra who?"

"Sandra Telford."

"I went to her exhibition last year. She certainly is good."

"Are you an artist?"

Piet took a sudden decision. "No," he said, "I'm a policeman."

"Gosh! I've never been given a lift by a policeman before! Why were you buying all those pictures?"

Piet laughed. "Policemen don't have to be Philistines! Actually, I went to an art school, too, but my father died, there wasn't much money, and I had to get a job. You're quite frank about your flower pictures being good . . . I sometimes think I'm rather a good policeman. Never mind. I've not stopped being interested in pictures, and one day I want to try to write a book on Constable. Even policemen have days off sometimes, and I love the Suffolk countryside. I wanted to paint the view from the hill above Moat Cottage this afternoon, but I didn't have time."

"Well, it was a good thing for me, or I wouldn't have got a lift to London. You're a funny sort of policeman, but I think perhaps you're rather nice."

When Piet dropped her at Leicester Square he gave her his card. "Gosh!" she said again. "A real Chief Inspector, *and* at Scotland Yard!"

"It's quite a real place. Look, if you don't find your friend, and for any reason still feel worried about her, will you ring me up? The police are very good at making discreet inquiries, and it's possible that we could help. You've told me that you're called Sally, but you haven't told me the rest of your name."

"Sally Graham. And the Shepherd's Bush address is 41C—the C means it's the top flat—Cordoba Road. I'm quite a good cook, and if you like I'll give you a meal there in the autumn to say thank you for the lift."

"I'd like that very much. And don't forget to give me a ring if you are at all worried about Sandra Telford."

Piet had a lot to think about. He was restless, and having gone to his flat intending to cook a meal he

hung up the frying pan that he had just taken off its
hook and decided to go out instead. He went to a
small Greek restaurant that would be crowded later,
but at this time was likely to be quiet. It was. He had
a table in a corner, ordered a preliminary *ouzo*, and
tried to sort out the day.

First, the girl to whom he had just given a lift. She
was a nice kid, he thought, not exactly pretty, but
vivid, with a mass of rather windswept copper-
coloured hair framing an alert intelligent face. She
had been extraordinarily frank and open about her
life—perhaps that was typical of the young nowadays.
The young! He winced slightly—he wasn't all that old
himself. But this girl must be at least ten years younger than he was, and he was conscious of the half generation between them. It was an essential part of his
job to understand people, but really he knew very
little of the way of life of the young twenties. She
seemed to have a distinctly casual life, but at any rate
she kept herself. And it was not necessarily so
casual—her group might have easy-going relationships, but it didn't follow that they were irresponsible. Painting, a close bond with his father, school,
and then the disciplined hard work of learning to be
a policeman—he'd not had much in the way of social
relationships outside his immediate surroundings in
his own youth. He hadn't really wanted them, there
was too much else to be interested in. One mustn't
disapprove of people because they happen to live differently. There was a lot to approve of in this girl,
for instance. The skill that went into her flower-arranging was not something that happened by accident—she had natural talent, obviously, but she'd
thought and studied and worked to make herself a
craftsman. However easygoing her artists' colony
might be she was sensitive to the situation on her
friend's departure, and she didn't like it. And showed
a wholly responsible concern for her friend.

He remembered Sandra Telford's exhibition very well, mostly street scenes, with sharply-understood portraits of newspaper-sellers, women weighed down with shopping bags, people waiting in a bus queue. There were a few rather precise landscapes, too, but with a haunting quality about them. Potentially they were very good indeed—odd that she seemed to have wasted a year. Perhaps there was an emotional entanglement with the man at Poplar's Fen.

Had it all ended in a drab death at Liverpool Street station? He mustn't put two and two together and make five—probably Sandra Telford had walked off in a rage because she thought the man was paying too much attention to the other girl on the boat, and was restoring herself with work in her own studio. It might be the best thing that could have happened, helping her to get back to work again. But she would have to be found—there was an uncomfortable little chain of circumstances suggesting the dead girl in the train: the portfolio from Mrs Vincent's shop, which was clearly known to people at the Poplar's Fen colony, the tiny sprig of sea lavender, which might easily have come from Poplar's Fen on a shoe.

And how did Mrs Vincent's establishment fit into things? It seemed a straightforward enough business, imaginatively planned and well run. A good deal of capital must have gone into it, and it seemed prosperous. No reason why it shouldn't be—there was undoubtedly money to be made from antiques, and the teas and the holiday art classes and the pictures and things on sale in the barn would provide a steady trade to cover overheads. But there was nothing on display there remotely resembling the pictures in the dead girl's portfolio. Apart from the portfolio itself, which might have been acquired in the same way that he had obtained his portfolio that afternoon, there was nothing so far to link the dead girl with Mrs Vincent's shop. But the portfolio needed explaining; there was a lot more work to be done on Mrs Vincent.

Piet must have ordered and eaten a meal, but he couldn't have said afterwards what it was.

He slept badly, his mind occupied with working out all the inquiries that now had to be made, and with planning how best to tackle them discreetly, so that as far as possible no one who might have reason to fear police interest should have his or her suspicions aroused.

He left early for the Yard, but although it was barely eight o'clock when he got there, the duty officer met him with the news that a visitor was waiting for him.

"Who is he?" Piet asked.

"It's a young lady, sir, says her name's Sally Graham, and that you will know what she's come about. Wouldn't see anybody else, and asked if she could wait for you. So I put her in one of the waiting rooms."

"Good. I think I do know what's brought her here. Give me a few minutes to get to my room, and then, perhaps, you'd ask someone to bring her up."

Piet had been half-expecting a telephone call from Sally, but he hadn't expected that she'd come to the Yard herself, or so soon. She looked worried and unhappy. "Have you had any breakfast?" he asked.

"Well, I've had a cup of tea, but I didn't feel like breakfast. I've had a horrible night, and I don't know what to do."

"Tell me about it, then."

"It's Sandra. When you left me I got the tube to Finsbury Park and went straight to the house where Sandra has her studio. I've been there several times, and I know the people slightly—a nice couple called Ben and Stella Morrison. I found them worried about Sandra. She'd telephoned on Sunday nearly a fortnight ago to say that she was coming on the Monday, but she never turned up. They didn't think anything about it for a few days, but when they heard nothing more from her they got a bit bothered—it's unlike Sandra to mess people up. You can't telephone Poplar's Fen because there isn't a phone there—you have to go into Walberswick to get to a phone box. After hearing nothing for three days, they sent a telegram. That brought a phone call from the man Sandra's been living with—they'd met him when he visited her at the studio. He said they weren't to worry, because Sandra had gone to France—she'd suddenly made up her mind that she wanted to paint a Normandy landscape. Then he went on to ask about pictures—were there any pictures unlike Sandra's normal work in the studio?

"They said they didn't know. They don't go into the studio when Sandra isn't there. It's a kind of annexe to the house, and though they have a key they don't use it, unless Sandra asks them to send something.

"The man—his name's Roger Leplan, by the way—rang off. The next night the studio was burgled, and somebody got into their part of the house, too. It happened while they were out late. The place was in a mess as if somebody had been looking for something. As far as they can tell nothing was actually taken, though they can't say definitely about Sandra's things, because they don't know what she had there. They telephoned the local police as soon as they got home and found that the place had been burgled. The police sent a man round almost at once, but as they couldn't say what, if anything, had been stolen, and as they couldn't get hold of Sandra, there wasn't much that the police could do.

"They're not happy about the story of Sandra's going off to France, and I'm not, either. She didn't say anything to me about it, and I'm sure she would have talked about it to me. I knew that she was going to London, but I expected her to come back, either the same day, or the day after.

"Ben and Stella gave me something to eat, and we talked about Sandra. Then I thought of another place she might be, out at Dulwich where she has an aunt she goes to sometimes. She's not on the phone. Ben got out his car and we drove to Dulwich. The aunt, who's old, had just gone to bed. She answered the door after some time in rather a state, didn't know anything about Sandra, hadn't heard from her for months. So we went back to Finsbury Park, where I slept, or as a matter of fact didn't sleep, on a sofa. I got up early, knocked up Stella and Ben, and told them that I was thinking of going to see you. They thought it a good idea, so here I am."

She sat looking at Piet, twisting her handkerchief into a tight little ball, and untwisting it again.

"Sally," he said gently, "I didn't tell you any lies yesterday, but I didn't tell you everything. It wasn't chance that took me to Suffolk—I'm concerned in a case that may relate to your friend. I hope it doesn't, because if it does, she's dead. On the Monday that your Sandra came up to London a girl of about her age was found dead in a train at Liverpool Street. She's not been identified yet, so she may not be Sandra. Could you look at some photographs and say if you recognise her?"

Sally said nothing, but she nodded slightly. Piet took a folder from a drawer in his desk. "These are not pretty photographs because they were taken after death," he said. "But they're the only ones we have."

He went over to her with the folder, opened it, and stood beside her. She needed only one quick look. "Yes," she said, and broke down sobbing.

Piet put his arm round her. "Poor Sally," he said. "You've done everything you could for your friend. Now you must help to find out how she died."

"What do you mean?"

"I mean that her death isn't at all straightforward. She died of an overdose of drugs, and we've no idea how or when she took it."

"Sandra didn't take drugs. She wasn't that sort of person."

"I'm not saying she was. All we know is that she was poisoned. If she didn't take the poison deliberately, then someone killed her. You must understand how serious that possibility is."

"Let me think, let me think."

She got up and walked over to the window. Piet's office was on the third floor, looking onto a courtyard. There wasn't much to see, but Sally wasn't looking at anything. She was seeing Sandra, in pigtails at school, sitting at her easel, walking over the marsh grass at Poplar's Fen. . . . She dabbed her eyes with her handkerchief, turned and faced Piet. "Could you die from taking travel-sickness pills?" she asked.

"I'm not a toxicologist, so I don't know. They're widely used and in ordinary circumstances they must be safe enough. Sandra didn't die from travel-sickness pills, but of a quite different drug. Why do you ask?"

"Because that was the only thing I've ever known her to take. She was liable to be car-sick or train-sick and before going on a journey she would generally take a pill. She had them in a little bottle in her handbag."

"She had no handbag with her on the train."

"She must have had a bag."

Piet didn't pursue this. He said, "Look, Sally, I'm afraid there are a tremendous lot of questions I shall have to ask you, but I'm not going to do it now. You've had a dreadful shock, you've had no breakfast, and you need someone to look after you. Where are your parents?"

"My father's dead, my mother married again and is

living in America. I've got my half-room at Shepherd's Bush."

"I don't think much of that. Have you no relations or friends you can go to?"

"Not really. But there's no need to worry about me."

"I can't help being worried about you. When do you have to be back at Lavenham for your flower-arranging class?"

"I've done my two classes for this week. I don't have another class until next Tuesday."

"There's a lot I haven't explained to you—there's a lot I don't understand myself. I don't like the idea of your going back to Poplar's Fen at the moment."

"I don't either."

Piet thought quickly. "Today's only Friday, so we've got a few days in hand before you need to go back to Suffolk. Would you be willing to stay with my mother at Greenwich? She lives by herself, she's a nice, gentle person, she'll look after you, and I shall feel that you're safe."

"It's very kind of you, but I don't know you."

"At least you know who I am, and where I work. You probably know me better than most of the people you meet at the artists' colony."

"All right. Can I be a female Dr Watson?"

Piet laughed. "I think you're much too clever for old Watson—and I lay no claim to being Sherlock Holmes. He didn't have much use for the regular police, anyway. . . . If you're ready, I'll take you out to Greenwich now. Where are your things?"

"I left my rucksack in your waiting room. I brought it with me because I thought I'd probably be going on to Shepherd's Bush."

"We'll collect it on the way out. I'll just write a note for my secretary when she comes in—we're both so early that she hasn't got here yet."

"Can I ring Ben and Stella Morrison and tell them about Sandra?"

"I think it would be better not. I'll see that they are told—I may go out to see them myself."

In the car, Piet gently questioned Sally about Sandra Telford, for although he was convinced in his own mind that the dead girl was Sandra, more formal identification would be necessary. "Tell me about Sandra," he said. "Do you know anything about her parents?"

"Not much. She didn't have any—I mean, of course she had parents, but they split up when she was a kid and I don't think she'd seen either of them for years. She was brought up by the old aunt at Dulwich—a great-aunt, really, I think."

"Sandra wasn't married?"

"Married? Good Lord, no! She was much too interested in her work. She had one or two affairs, but I don't think they meant anything until she got mixed up with this man Roger. And that didn't bring her any happiness. In fact, it upset her work."

"What a lovely house!" Sally exclaimed when they got to Greenwich.

"It's been in the family for over a century, but it's turned into flats now," Piet said. "We have the ground floor, with the garden."

He had reported with complete accuracy when he described his mother as a gentle person. Mrs Deventer was also intelligent, and fundamentally extremely kind. She asked no questions when Piet introduced Sally, but said simply that she was delighted to have someone to stay with her. Then she asked practically when Sally had last eaten. Piet left them together, saying that he would do his best to come home that evening, and that he would ring up to give a time. He was desperately anxious to get back to the Yard.

Odd how things happen, he reflected as he drove off. This was the first time he had ever taken a girl to his home.

He got back to find that a preliminary report about the pictures had come in from the forensic laboratory. He didn't study it at once, for he wanted urgently to arrange a conference about the case with the real top brass. After some telephoning he fixed up a meeting at two o'clock that afternoon with the Assistant Commissioner, the Chief Superintendent (Crime), and the Superintendent of his own Fine Art Division. Piet was in charge of a section specialising in pictures. The Fine Art Squad as a whole covered a much wider field, dealing with fraud and other criminal activities related to gold and silver articles, important pieces of jewellery, antiques and rare books. Having arranged his conference, Piet turned to the report.

"It is certainly an extraordinary case," said the Assistant Commissioner, after Piet had outlined events since the finding of the dead girl in the train. "On the evidence so far the girl's death looks like murder, and in the ordinary way the investigation ought to be carried out by the Divisional CID, calling in your people, Chief Superintendent, if they need help. But this is not in the least ordinary, and I'm inclined to think that, for the moment, at any rate, it might well be left to Deventer and his section. What do you think, Chief?"

"What exactly do you suspect?" The Chief Superintendent asked.

"Murder of the girl, forgery of at least two pictures, and theft or possibly forgery of a third," Piet said. "The forensic people have done an excellent job on the pictures found in the portfolio. The canvases all seem to be OK—that is, there is nothing to suggest that they don't date from the periods of the artists concerned, but the pigments are another matter. Spectroscopic analysis, which doesn't hurt the paintings, shows conclusively that the possible Turner and the possible Gainsborough have been painted with pigments containing a metallic oxide that was not used in paint until about ten years ago. The genuineness or otherwise of the Constable is still uncertain. It is so good that both Wilbur Constantine, who is an acknowledged expert on Constable, and I myself, for what my views are worth, find it hard to consider it a forgery. The pigments used would seem to fit the period, although one can't say that this is conclusive, for more detailed analysis can't be done without risking damage to the picture. If it is a genuine Constable it sets a number of acute problems, for it is not a work that anybody has seen before. Where did it come from? It may, of course, be stolen; but if so, from where? And why has no one, apparently, so far noticed the theft?

"The fourth picture, a rather poor attempt to emulate, or perhaps simply to suggest, Delacroix, is not important. Here again the tests are inconclusive, but it doesn't seem to matter much. It's more like somebody's experiment, and it might be just that, some art student's experiment."

"If the other three pictures were genuine, or could be sold as genuine, about how much would they be worth?" the Assistant Commissioner asked.

"Impossible to say. An unknown major work by Constable, perhaps a quarter of a million pounds, possibly twice as much. The Turner and the Gainsborough are scarcely major works, but they're good of their kind, and if accepted as genuine they might fetch anything from twenty to fifty thousand pounds apiece."

"So very large sums are at stake?"

"Yes, but it's more than that. It isn't all that difficult to steal a picture. Many important works in country houses, in cathedrals or churches, even in some galleries, are rottenly guarded. The trouble comes when the thief tries to dispose of them. All known works by major artists are recorded, and unless put on the market openly by a rightful owner they almost have no market. That's not quite true. There are unscrupulous dealers, and odd customers who'll buy something with no questions asked, but only for a fraction of its real value. With unknown works, and forgeries, the problem is rather different. If they can be given a reasonable history, they can be sold at auction, but the history has got to be one that stands up to searching criticism by experts. It's got to be high-grade fraud, and not so much a single fraud as a whole chain of frauds.

"The most serious damage is to the integrity of the art market. The British art market is enormously important, and authentication of a picture by one of our major dealers is almost like a signature of a Lloyd's underwriter on an insurance policy, a guarantee of good faith. If it turns out that such a guarantee is worthless the whole market suffers, and large sums of money that would otherwise pass through the hands of our dealers, with resulting benefits to the whole economy, go somewhere else. That's why we've just got to clear up this particular fraud."

"Deventer is absolutely right," said Piet's own Superintendent. "Work done by one artist in the style of another is not uncommon, and sometimes the imitation is as good, or nearly as good, as the original. The fraud comes with any attempt to pass it off as the more famous man's work. It's like debasing the coinage—you can have a counterfeit as good as a genuine coin from the Mint, but that doesn't lessen the damage when it goes into circulation."

"How are you thinking of tackling the suspected murder?" asked the Chief Superintendent.

"The first job is to get the girl properly identified. I think there's no doubt that we now know who she was, but some of the evidence is circumstantial—the portfolio and the bit of sea lavender—and recognition by a friend from a photograph after death isn't quite enough. She appears to have no close relatives, at least, none that we know about, except the old great-aunt at Dulwich, and she is around eighty. I'm afraid we shall have to ask her to look at the photographs, but the result may not be decisive. There is better evidence in a plaster-cast of the girl's teeth that the Divisional people had made as soon as it was clear that she wasn't going to be identified easily. She'd had dental work done at various times, and if we can find the dentist we can probably get a positive identification.

"All that's mainly routine. The more tricky work will be to go very carefully into the break-in at Finsbury Park, and to investigate that artists' colony at Poplar's Fen. The break-in looks as if somebody is after the pictures. Poplar's Fen—I've not been there yet, and I don't know what to make of it. I thought I'd try to go there as an artist. I can paint well enough to get by, and if I can get in I can keep my eyes open without raising suspicions. My own feeling is that it would be best not to have any publicity at the moment about identifying the girl. The Poplar's Fen people seem to think she's gone off to France. The only people who already know about it, or will have to know, are Miss Graham, the old aunt, and Miss Telford's friends at Finsbury Park. I can ask them all to be discreet. Obviously the news will have to come out soon—Sandra Telford was quite well known as an artist—but if it can be kept quiet for a few days while we investigate Poplar's Fen and the Moat Cottage place at Lavenham, that's really all that matters."

"Right," said the Chief Superintendent. "You've

got your plate full, young man, but I'm happy about it. If the Assistant Commissioner agrees, I'll fix it with the Divisional people through the proper channels, and if you want any help that I can give, it's there for the asking. I think you deserve a pat on the back for a fine piece of detection in identifying the girl, and I can only wish you good luck with the rest of the case."

The Assistant Commissioner agreed. Piet's own Superintendent was delighted at the way things had gone.

V

Lost Property

"You'll have to get another car," Sally said.

Piet got back to Greenwich around eight o'clock, in time to have supper with his mother and Sally. It seemed strange to find something to enjoy when he was so much involved with the dark of life, but he did enjoy the evening, and he thought that Sally did, too.

Piet's mother went to bed early, and when he and Sally were alone together after supper he asked whether she could get him into the Poplar's Fen colony for a few days. "I'd like to go there as a painter," he said. "I can take a paint box and a sketching pad, and I think I'm just about good enough not to raise any awkward questions."

"Your mother has been showing me some of your work, and I think it's a pity you decided to be a policeman; you're better than anybody else there at the moment," she replied. "There wouldn't be any problem about getting you in—the arrangements are pretty casual. If I say that you're an artist and a friend of mine, I don't think anybody will bother. And with Sandra . . . well, with Sandra gone

. . ." her voice faltered ". . . there'd be room on the boat I'm living on. I was thinking of not going back, but if you come I shan't mind so much."

"I could be quite useful. You wouldn't have to get three buses to go to Lavenham, because I could take you there."

"Yes, but not in that car—it's much too good for the kind of artist who goes to Poplar's Fen. It wouldn't look right."

It was a good point. Piet had just got a new Saab, which was admirable for his job, but he agreed with Sally—it didn't fit the part of an artist coming to join a slightly hippie art colony. "I must have a car," he said, "but I see what you mean. I'll get hold of something else. And I've got a fair collection of old clothes—you must tell me what looks most suitable."

She managed a little laugh, which Piet found oddly comforting. "Famous detective selects his disguise," she said.

"Not a bit. I sail a boat when I can, I go for camping holidays, dammit, I still am half an artist," he argued indignantly. "All I meant was that you must tell me what the art colony is wearing so that I don't look out of place."

"Why do you want to go to Poplar's Fen at all?" she asked.

Piet realised suddenly that although Sally knew of Sandra's death, she knew nothing of the pictures she had with her when she died. How much was it safe to tell her? Had he any right to tell her anything about the case? He knew remarkably little of her background—it was conceivable that she was on the other side, and that anything he told her would be relayed to the very people he was out to catch, making it unlikely that he would ever catch them. On the other hand she knew vastly more about Sandra Telford and her associates than he did, and if she was on *his* side her help would be invaluable. His instinct was to trust her, but backing instincts could be a dangerous gamble.

"You're taking a long time to answer," she said.

"I'm taking a long time, Sally, because I don't know what to say to you," he replied frankly. "If Sandra Telford was murdered, do you want whoever murdered her caught?"

"I thought that was why I was here."

The remark surprised him. If he'd analysed his motives in bringing Sally home he would have said it was because he was sorry for her, and also somewhat uneasy about her safety at the curious community at Poplar's Fen. That she thought of herself as playing a direct part in trying to solve the puzzle of Sandra's death had not occurred to him. It was a good mark to her, and he felt rather ashamed of himself.

"I'll be as honest as I can," he said, "but it isn't easy. There are a lot of other things that may be connected with Sandra's death that I haven't told you about, and I'm not sure whether I ought to tell you."

"Because you don't know anything about me, and you don't know how far I can be trusted. I understand. Poor Piet," she said. "Well, I'm showing a certain amount of trust in you by being here. You don't have to tell me anything. I'll arrange for you to stay at Poplar's Fen and you can get on with your job on your own—I shan't let you down. Sandra was my friend, I think she was probably my best friend, and if anybody poisoned her it was a horrible, horrible business. Quite apart from killing her it's robbed the world of someone who would have been—already was, I think—a great artist. I'm not a nice person about Sandra—I'm all for vengeance. You may or may not solve your case. You can do what you like. But if you don't solve it perhaps I shall. I'm not going to give up."

Piet made up his mind to do what he really wanted to do, anyway. "I told you that you were too clever to be Dr Watson," he said. "You'd make a much better Holmes. Yes, I was wondering whether I could trust you. I'm not bothered about that any more. It's a longish story—here it is." Impulsively he put out his hand to her. She took it, and held it for a moment. "Detective and detective's mate," she said. "Or should I be your sergeant?"

"There are several things that occur to me," Sally said when he'd finished telling her about the pictures. "First, if Sandra was mixed up in anything like that it wasn't because she wanted to be. There's a side of her life that I don't know about. After her exhibition last year she was on top of the world. I didn't see her for a bit because she went away for a holiday—the exhibition made some money for her—and when I did see her again she'd changed, somehow. She wasn't happy any more. I think that's really why I went down to Poplar's Fen, to hold her hand for a bit. It wasn't any good—she was fearfully withdrawn. She was certainly doing some work, but I don't know what it was, because it was at the top of the old mill, and she never asked me up there. If someone with a hold on her had made her fake pictures, do you think she was killed because she wanted to get out? I mean, could she have been taking the pictures to London to tell someone about them?"

"She could. But if the pathologist is right about the arsenic found in her body—and I don't see how he can be wrong—someone had been trying to kill her for some time. Arsenic is a cumulative poison. If you go on giving it you'll kill whoever you're giving it to in time. It's a cold-blooded, dreadful form of poisoning. Something happened which made whoever was slowly poisoning her decide that she must be killed at once. Or do you think she could have taken an overdose of sleeping pills to kill herself?"

"I don't—I don't think she ever took sleeping pills.

And I don't think Sandra would ever have killed herself. She had too much courage, and she wanted to paint. She used to say that there'd never be time to paint all the things she wanted. Someone knew she was taking the pictures to London, and decided to stop her."

"There are a lot of difficulties there, Sally. Did Sandra have a car?"

"No."

"Then how did she get to the station at Sudbury?"

"Someone must have given her a lift. Most of the people at Moat Cottage have cars."

"What was she doing at Moat Cottage? She caught an early train, remember."

"Bit of a problem, that. She told me on the Sunday morning that she was going to London on Monday, but I didn't see her go off because I wasn't there. I went to see some friends at Colchester, and the Sunday buses were so awkward that they put me up for the night. But Sandra quite often went to Moat Cottage because Shirley—that's Mrs. Vincent—used to buy her pictures."

"Right. Someone drove her from Moat Cottage into Sudbury. And she had that big portfolio with her. You were expecting her back. Wouldn't she have made some arrangement to be met? And wouldn't whoever went to meet her have been puzzled when she didn't turn up, and said something to somebody? That is, if the person who gave her a lift was innocent of anything to do with the pictures. The other possibility is that whoever gave her a lift was mixed up in the picture business. If so, why let her go off with the portfolio?"

"Because he didn't know what pictures were inside it. She may have said they were just some of her own paintings which she was taking to London."

"That's one thing which does seem to fit. The break-in at the studio in Finsbury Park rather suggests that someone is looking for the pictures, which means he didn't know at the time that Sandra took them with her on the train, but found out afterwards. Whoever it is will be very anxious to find them and get them back."

"I'm afraid I quite forgot. Did you tell Ben and Stella Morrison about Sandra?"

"Yes, I just had time to get to Finsbury Park before coming home. They're very upset about her. I asked them to say nothing to anybody else, and I think they understood how important it is not to. They were able to help me, too—they gave me the name of a dentist Sandra had been to a couple of times, the dentist they go to themselves. I don't want to distress you, but teeth are important when it comes to identification. There's no doubt in my mind about your recognition of the photographs, but legal identification requires rather more. The Divisional police arranged for a plaster cast to be made of Sandra's teeth, and now that we know her dentist it should be possible to settle things finally. I phoned the Yard to have the cast sent round, and we should know definitely some time in the morning.

"Your Ben and Stella don't know anything about the pictures, of course. The mess from the burglary in their own house has been tidied up, but Sandra's studio has been left as it was. There are signs of a considerable search, but not knowing what was there to start with, there's no means of telling what may have been taken."

"There's just a hint, I think, that they didn't find what they were looking for in the studio. If they did, why break into Ben and Stella's part of the house?"

"That's a good bit of detective work, Sally. You're probably right. It seems unlikely that they broke into the house before the studio."

"It's like a horrible sort of crossword puzzle. You've got to work out the pattern of the words before you find any clues. . . . Good lord, have you noticed the time?"

It was nearly two a.m.

Piet had an odd sense of playing truant when he left Greenwich on Monday morning to drive down with Sally to Poplar's Fen. Sally had occupied herself by making flower-arrangements for Piet's mother, but Piet had spent most of the time at Scotland Yard. The dentist had examined the plaster-cast of Sandra's teeth and reported that he positively recognised his own work, and that his records showed that the teeth were those of his patient Miss Sandra Telford, who had visited him twice during the past twelve months. In view of this Piet decided to postpone visiting the old woman at Dulwich. She would have to be told of her great-niece's death at some time, but at least she could be spared the ordeal of looking at photographs of the dead girl.

Then he had to arrange about another car. He went to see the sergeant in charge of the police garage, and explained what he wanted. The sergeant, who managed to retain a passionate enthusiasm for cars in spite of a working lifetime spent in dealing with the appalling behaviour of those who use them, had a soft spot for Piet. Like everybody else who wanted a car he always wanted it at once, but he was polite about it, understood that transport departments have their difficulties, and did his best to help. The Saab was Piet's own car. "I'd like to leave my car here," he said, "and take something older and a bit battered. That is," he added hastily, "if you ever have such a thing as a battered car."

"Well, not exactly battered, perhaps," the sergeant smiled. "But I think I can do something for you. What about my old Riley? It's a *Riley* Riley, made in the days when people actually *built* cars instead of throwing them together on conveyor belts. She could do with a respray, but everything that matters in her is tip-top. You'll enjoy driving her. I wouldn't lend her to everybody, mind." Piet decided that the old Riley would do very well.

The next thing that happened was a telephone call from Sergeant Williams. "May not have anything to do with the case," he said, "but I thought I'd better report it. We haven't had any luck with coming across anyone asking for that portfolio, but there's been an attempt to break into the Lost Property office at Liverpool Street. Chap didn't get in because he was spotted and ran off. The railway police are dealing with it."

"Could the portfolio have been in the Lost Property office?" Piet asked.

"Well it might, sir, and it might not. In the ordinary way things that people leave behind on trains and at stations—and it's astonishing what they *do* leave—go to the Lost Property office at the station where they've been found for a bit. That's to give time for the owner to come back and ask about them. But lost property isn't held locally for very long. After a bit, if things aren't claimed they go to the main Lost Property depot. If they're never claimed they can be sold. Whoever tried to break in at Liverpool Street might just have been out for what he could get—that's the most likely thing, I'd think. Or he might have been looking for something definite, not knowing whether it would still be at Liverpool Street, but reckoning that it was worth taking a chance."

"You're quite right to report it—thank you very much. It's long odds whether it has anything to do with the girl, but I think I'll go down to Liverpool Street and have a word with the railway men."

Piet saw the railway sergeant. "It seems a small matter to bring you along from Scotland Yard," the sergeant said, "but I understand you think it may be connected with the queer case of that dead girl in the train."

"I'd scarcely go so far as to say that," Piet said, "but we can't ignore even the remote possibility. That portfolio contained some exceedingly valuable pictures, and we've some reason for thinking that they were stolen. Nothing was said about them at the inquest, and whoever is concerned with them must be getting pretty desperate to find out where they are. The Lost Property office is one place where they could be, I suppose."

"It probably wouldn't be after all this time, but you're right sir, they mightn't know that. It was a funny sort of attempt at breaking in. It was last night, around eleven o'clock. A ticket collector going off duty passed the Lost Property office and saw a woman standing by the door, and a man a few yards away. He doesn't know why he looked back, but he did, and he saw the woman fiddling with the lock. He went over to her but she must have heard him coming for she ran off. He shouted and chased after her, and then the man who'd been standing nearby, perhaps keeping a lookout, came at him and tripped him up. There weren't a lot of people around just then, and by the time the ticket collector got to his feet they'd both run off. We examined the lock, and there are clear traces of some sort of wax on it, as if someone had been trying to get an impression for a key. Of course that may have been done earlier—the ticket collector thinks he heard a scraping sound as if a key was being put in the lock. He thinks it may have been that which made him look back.

"He thinks he'd probably recognise the woman, but he didn't get much of a chance to see the man, and apart from saying that he seemed rather tall and thin and might have been wearing an anorak he can't give a description of him. Here's his description of the woman—'Medium height, age around thirty, wearing dark-coloured slacks, a dark jumper, and with a scarf or something round her head.' We've changed the locks, of course, but with such poor descriptions to go on there's not much that we can do. You can't blame the ticket collector. He was pretty shaken by his fall, and in the circumstances I think he did quite well."

"I'm sure he did. I don't suppose that I can get any more out of him than you have already, but since I've come here it would tidy my own report if I could have a word with him. Is there any chance of his being on duty?"

"As a matter of fact he is. Most people nowadays would have taken a few days off after a fall like that, but he's one of the old school—joined the London and North Eastern company as a boy before it was nationalised, and puts what he still calls 'the company' first. I saw him when I came on and asked how he was feeling. He said he'd had a night's rest, and reckoned he was all right to come on duty. If you care to hang on here for a few minutes, sir, I'll go and get him."

Ticket Collector George Wright was grey-haired but walked without a trace of stoop, and wore his uniform like a guardsman. Getting near retirement, Piet thought, and then he noticed something else. Like many of the older railwaymen, Ticket Collector Wright sported a buttonhole. It was a sprig of sea lavender.

Piet said a few nice things about the ticket collector's presence of mind in going after the woman last night, and questioned him briefly about the incident. He got the same story that he had heard from the police. Then he said, "That's a nice buttonhole you're wearing. Didn't come from your garden though."

The man, pleased at Piet's interest, glanced down at it. "You know something about wild flowers, then," he said. "No, it didn't come from the garden—it came from Liverpool Street station! I picked it up after my tumble. I lived near Aldeburgh as a kid, and recognised it as a nice bit of sea lavender. Grows all over the marshes there, and it's wonderful stuff—the old people used to say that the flowers stay fresh for a twelvemonth. So when I saw this lying there I picked it up and put it in my buttonhole."

"Saw a bit of stuff like that old George Wright was wearing not long ago. Wouldn't have known it was called sea lavender, though," the railway policeman said. "Detective-Sergeant Williams picked it up when we were searching the carriage after the girl's death. There's a sort of link with your case, anyway, sir. If you can make anything of it, that is."

Piet had to arrange for his own department's work to be carried on while he was away in Suffolk, and one of the things that bothered him was the problem of communications. Isolated at Poplar's Fen two or three miles from a telephone he felt that he might be dangerously cut off. He had a long talk with his own Superintendent about this. In any real emergency a police motor-cyclist could deliver a message to him, but the last thing Piet wanted was the appearance of policemen at Poplar's Fen. His Superintendent agreed. "I think I'd better let the East Region police know that you are down there in plain clothes, in case you need assistance from them," he said. "I'll get that arranged, and I'll ask the local force to take no notice of you unless you ask. For the rest, the only thing will be for you to telephone us." Piet said he'd try to ring up twice a day, but until he knew more about the set-up at Poplar's Fen he couldn't guarantee any particular times. He would have a police walkie-talkie radio with him, but he wouldn't use it unless it seemed imperative.

Now he was on his way with Sally to Poplar's Fen.

There wasn't as much room in the Riley as the Saab,
but Sally only had her rucksack, and he didn't need
much kit. He could get all he wanted in his own
rucksack, and he took an easel and his painting bag, a
canvas holdall in which he carried paints, palette-
knife and brushes, sketching pads and a few sheets of
canvas. He put the walkie-talkie radio in the painting
bag. For clothes he settled on old sailing trousers in
the colour called Breton red, a thick navy blue pull-
over in fisherman's knit, and a canvas sailing smock, a
useful garment providing good deep pockets, and protection against light rain. Sally approved. "Our well-
dressed detectives really are quite handsome," she
said.

He changed his name slightly. He had initials—
P.D.—on both his rucksack and his painting bag.
There seemed no point in altering these, but he
asked Sally to make sure to call him Peter Devonshire
instead of Pieter Deventer. The "Piet" didn't matter—it sounded just the same spelt in his own Dutch
fashion as the common English Pete.

As far as Chelmsford his route was the same as that
he had taken from London to Sudbury, but instead of
going north to Braintree and Halstead he branched
north-east to Colchester and Ipswich. The old Riley
was beautifully tuned and had the performance of a
sports car. The sergeant was right—she was fun to
drive. But, Piet soon discovered, she could be quite
hazardous to stop: brakes of her vintage were not as
good as modern brakes, however she might excel the
mass-produced car in other ways.

He had told Sally about the attempt to enter the
Lost Property office at Liverpool Street, and as the
housing estates and suburbs of Outer London fell
away they discussed it again. "There's nothing to link
it with Sandra's death except the scrap of sea lavender," he said. "There must be thousands of people
coming to Liverpool Street from the Essex and Suf-

folk coasts who could have brought a bunch of sea lavender with them, or caught some in a shoe or something. But coincidence becomes less likely every time it occurs. A sprig of sea lavender was found near Sandra's body, and now we have it cropping up again. I mustn't let myself get obsessed by it, though."

"There's masses of it growing round Poplar's Fen," Sally said. "To get to the road for Walberswick you pass great clumps of it, and I think there's some actually growing in the path. There's quite a lot at Moat Cottage, too—not growing, but around the studio. I use it for my flower-arranging classes. I must have brought nearly a rucksack full of it."

"I didn't know that, and it could be important. I've been thinking that it must have come to Liverpool Street from the coast. It could have come from Moat Cottage."

"Yes. Some of the students put it in buttonholes, or pin little bunches of it to their dresses. It could fall off anywhere and be picked up by someone else."

"So there are dozens of potential bringers of sea lavender. Let's rule out the students and casual visitors to Moat Cottage—we don't know enough to exclude them altogether, but let's exclude them for the moment. Who does that leave?"

"Do you mean everybody at Poplar's Fen and on the staff at Moat Cottage?"

"I think so, yes."

Sally shivered slightly. "It's dreadful to think that someone I know may have murdered Sandra. But I mustn't think like that. Well, then, here goes. At Moat Cottage there's Shirley Vincent, and her assistant in the business who's a man called Jeff. I think his other name may be Wilson, but I'm not sure—it's all Christian names, you see. Shirley will say, 'Ask Jeff,' or 'Tell Jeff about it.' But I think I've heard one of the students call him Mr Wilson. Then there are two girls who come in part-time from Lavenham

to help with the teas—they're Anita and Vi. In the
studio there's Bill Wild who teaches painting, Vera
Smith who does pots, and me. Bill and Vera live locally, Vera in Lavenham itself, I think, and Bill in
Sudbury. There's an old man called Arthur who cuts
the lawns and looks after the flowerbeds—I've never
heard him called anything else. And a woman called
Mrs Marshall, who's also local, and who comes in to
help with the cleaning. That's about the lot."

"And at Poplar's Fen?"

"That's more difficult, because people come and go.
Of the people who have been there more or less as
long as I have, there's Roger and Trudi, the girl on
his boat. Trudi came after Sandra but before me. I
think it was because Trudi turned up that Sandra got
me to go down, Sandra being bothered about Trudi
and Roger. Then there's a smaller boat with a couple
called Trish—I suppose that means Patricia, but she's
always called Trish—and Malcolm. There's a sort of
dormitory at the mill with about half a dozen people,
Jim, Eddie, Brian and Simon, and a couple of girls,
Poppy and Clare. There's another girl, Jackie, but
she's not there all the time—I think she's a schoolteacher somewhere, and she seems to come mostly at
weekends. There have been other people coming for
a week or so and then going off—I don't know them
all."

"If we assume that whoever was mixed up in Sandra's death was also involved in the break-in at
Finsbury Park and the attempted break-in at Liverpool Street, then he or she or they will have been
away on those nights. Can we find out if anybody was
away then?"

"We can try. Oh, Piet, I'm not sure that I like
being a detective. It seems so mean, somehow."

"Not as mean as poisoning Sandra."

"No. . . . Don't worry. I'm not going back on
what I said."

"I didn't think you would. And Sally, I do understand. There's rather a special problem at Moat Cottage—they've seen me."

"Not dressed as you are now, and not in this car."

"That's some protection, perhaps. All the same, when I take you from Poplar's Fen to Lavenham tomorrow, I think it would be better if I took you to the bus-stop in Lavenham and you walked from there. And I can meet you again at the bus-stop. I'm afraid you'll have to do most of the detective work at Moat Cottage, finding out who, if anyone, has been away. You needn't bother with the gardener, or the cleaning woman, or the local girls for the moment."

"All right. It's not going to be all that easy, but I'll do my best."

"How many of the people at Poplar's Fen have cars?"

Sally considered. "There are some cars, but I'm not sure who they all belong to," she said. "Roger has a car, and Trish and Malcolm have a car. The mill lot seem to have two cars, but I think one of them must belong to the schoolteacher, because it's not there all the time. One of the girls, Poppy, I think, has a motorbike, and so does one of the men, but they all borrow it. It's the same with the cars, when they're there. But I don't understand the system, because although I quite often had meals at the mill, I didn't live there. I lived on Roger's boat."

"If there's a sort of transport co-operative, why did you have to get all those buses on the days you had to go to Lavenham?"

"Well, I can't ride a motor-bike. Roger took me to Lavenham a couple of times—I told you that he introduced me to Shirley, and I think he has some business dealings with her. I wanted the job with the flower-arranging class, mainly to try to build up something for next summer, and because Shirley would buy my flower pictures. So although the bus journey takes ages I thought it was well worth it, and I don't much like asking other people for things. Sometimes I'd get a lift to the bus-stop in Walberswick, but it didn't worry me if I didn't. I don't mind walking—in fact, I enjoy walking over the marshes."

They stopped at Woodbridge for lunch, and to do some shopping, for Sally said that it would help Piet to get accepted if they brought some food with them, and some bottles of plonk. So they bought bacon, eggs, butter and bread, and a half a dozen litre-bottles of Spanish red wine. Piet quoted Hilaire Belloc

> Do you remember an inn, Miranda,
> Do you remember an inn. . . .
> And the fleas that tease
> In the high Pyrenees
> And the wine that tasted of tar?

"I hope this isn't too tarry," Sally said practically.

Just beyond Saxmundham they turned right for Middleton, where they crossed the Minsmere River, Westleton, and Dunwich on the coast. Here they met true sea-marsh country, a strange world that is neither land nor water. Dunwich is a little village now, but it is easy to imagine the legendary city, once the capital of East Anglia, swallowed by the sea, the bells of whose churches, they say, can still be heard sometimes from below the waves.

The road, following a ridge of firm ground, piled, perhaps, on faggots of brushwood by some long-forgotten people, ran a little inland. To the right the flats of Dingle Marshes through which the River Dunwich wanders to the sea reached to the coast. The whole landscape, broken by innumerable streams and drainage ditches, seemed to be turning into seascape, but the land, fortified by tough marram grass, would not quite let go. The land had other allies, too, Piet stopped the car suddenly. "Look!" he said.

The grey-green of the marram grass had changed to grey-blue, where a covering of sea lavender came right up to the road. The plant was actually growing in clumps or tufts, but from a little distance it looked like a carpet of tiny flowers. Across the marshes they could see the sea, but there was no clear division where land ended and sea began. There were no sharp colours anywhere. The sky was overcast with a slight haze and the grey-green of the coarse grass merged with the grey-blue of the sea lavender—a purplish blue if you looked at individual florets closely— to give a sort of wash over everything, colour and absence of colour at the same time, that spread unbroken over the formless grey sea. There was no horizon—land, sea and sky were a single entity. It was indescribably lovely, Piet thought, but it was a loveliness you felt rather than saw.

"God, it would be hard to paint," he said.

"Why not try?" Sally asked.

"One day, perhaps."

He studied the map. "We can't have much more than a mile to go," he said. "Poplar's Fen seems to be before we get to Westwood Marshes."

"They're all mixed up," Sally said. "This road becomes a track, though you can still drive along it for a bit. We go to the end, and that *is* Poplar's Fen. About a quarter of a mile before the end of our track a rather better road goes off to the left, to join the road to Walkerswick. That's the one we use to go shopping, and that I use to get my bus."

"Well, I suppose we'd better be getting on. I can't say that I really want to."

"I don't, either."

The road ended dramatically, with a five-foot drop

into a channel known as Poplar's Sluice. Piet was unprepared for this, and so were the Riley's brakes. Quick thinking, however, swung the car round in the nick of time, and it came to rest with the nearside front wheel on the very edge of the ditch. Gingerly Piet manoeuvred into a safer position, hoping that nobody but he knew what a narrow shave it had been. Sally said nothing, but she patted his knee—she was tactful but not unobservant.

The sluice or drain was about ten feet wide, and crossed by a plank footbridge, built on old railway sleepers. Beyond the sluice was a stretch of marsh, enclosed by the sluice on one flank and by a wider watercourse on the other. The marsh here was an island of more or less firm ground, supporting an old windmill, its broken sails forlorn and stark against the sky. It was not a mill for grinding corn, but the remains of an early nineteenth-century attempt to drain the marsh, when it had worked a wind-powered pumping engine. On the watercourse—actually the River Walber—two boats were moored. One was a Dutch botter, old and squat, but freshly painted and still looking seaworthy. About fifty yards astern of her was a motor-cruiser, a good deal smaller than the rather stately botter.

"Roger's boat is the big one, the old sailing boat," Sally said. "I think it would be best if you wait here, while I go across and explain things." She went over the footbridge, and Piet walked along the bank of the sluice, taking in the surroundings.

The road by which they had come was an unmetaled track, and for most of the last mile it was wide enough for only one vehicle at a time. Fifty yards or so before it met the sluice it broadened into a fairly substantial area of dried mud, and here were parked the vehicles belonging to the colony. There were the three cars of which Sally had spoken, two presumably belonging to the people on the boats, one to the mill contingent. That assumed that the schoolteacher's car was not there, and since she came at weekends and to-day was Monday, the assumption seemed reasonable. There was one motor-bicycle. The other was presumably being used somewhere.

Not far beyond the track the sluice met the River Walber and the marsh changed to shingle. The river, augmented by water from the sluice, widened and broke the shingle beach to reach the sea. Two decaying posts marked its mouth. Broken water to seaward suggested a considerable bar, but at high tide, Piet thought, the entrance would be navigable. It looked peaceful enough that summer afternoon, but in an onshore wind it would be a horrible place.

He would have enjoyed pottering round the river, but he did not know yet whether he would be able to stay at Poplar's Fen and he felt restless and on edge. He did not want to keep Sally waiting, so after a few minutes he walked back to the road. He saw her crossing the marsh towards the footbridge as he came up. She waved to him, and ran the last few yards to the bridge. "It's all right," she said. "Roger says you're welcome to stay on the boat. Only . . . Trudi seems to have moved in with Roger, and we shall have to share a cabin. I hope you don't mind."

VI

At Poplar's Fen

The botter is a Dutch fishing boat whose design has changed little since the eighteenth century. Smaller than the old Thames sailing barge, and designed for fishing rather than carrying cargo, she shares with the Thames barge the ability to be equally at home in the North Sea and in the creeks and estuaries of the Low Countries of the continent and of the east coast of England. Her rounded shoulders, immensely strong, can take the punishing blows of the vicious short seas characteristic of the waters she was built to live in, and with lee-boards instead of a deep keel she can go wherever there is a pocket-handkerchief of water to float her. Piet's ancestral Dutch blood stirred as he walked up to the botter moored in the River Walber. He had seen her many times in Dutch marine paintings.

As a fishing boat designed for hauling nets the botter is built low aft, and the stern of the boat he was invited to board was roughly level with the river bank. In her working youth this boat would have had a fish-well amidships, but it had been taken out, and the space once occupied by the well incorporated in the saloon extended from the foredeck.

Roger met Piet and Sally on the bank. He was rather older than Piet had expected, at least in his middle forties, and with greying hair. But he seemed vigorous and fit, with no sign of going to seed. "Roger Leplan," he said. "Glad to meet any friend of Sally's."

"Peter Devonshire. It's very good of you to let me join your boat," Piet replied.

"Sally says you paint."

"Yes. Not in the Old Master class, but I get by."

Roger laughed. "Well, that's something these days. I'm just going over to the mill. Trudi's working there. You'll meet her later. Sally will show you where to put your stuff."

He went off. Piet got the rucksacks and the shopping bags on board, and followed Sally into the saloon. It was furnished as a sitting room, with a coal-burning stove in one corner; a chimney-pipe led through the deck beams of the foredeck overhead. A door at the forward end of the saloon led to a narrow companionway with cabins opening to each side. "That's Roger's room on the right," Sally said. "Ours is here."

"Quite proper. The skipper always berths to starboard," Piet said.

He was relieved to find that there were two bunks in the cabin he was to share with Sally. "Any preference?" she asked.

"Not a bit."

"Well, you're taller than me, so you can have the top one."

Piet wanted to go into Walberswick to make his telephone call. "Can I come with you?" Sally asked.

"Of course."

"I'm not frightened exactly, but I don't like being here."

"I don't blame you. I think it's very brave of you to come."

"I wouldn't have come if it hadn't been for you. I don't have to be here. I don't want to give up my classes, but I thought I'd try to get a room in Lavenham."

"We've got a job to do. As soon as it's finished I shall take you away and you need never come back—except to pick sea lavender. But you can get plenty of that on the Dunwich marshes."

"We've just about got time," Sally said as they walked to the car. "We ought to go to the mill for tea—they might think it a bit stand-offish if we didn't."

"What time is that?"

"Well, they call it tea, but it's really a sort of supper. Between six and seven. People generally work till around then, and they're ready for a meal. After tea they may go into Walberswick to a pub if anyone's got any money. Or sit around and talk."

"Right, we'll be back on time. It won't take me long to make my phone call." They left their rucksacks and Piet's painting bag in the cabin.

It took rather longer than he expected. He just caught his Superintendent before he left the office, and found that the Superintendent was most anxious to get in touch with him. Not having a limitless supply of coins for the call-box, Piet rang off and the Superintendent called him back. "That's better," the Superintendent said. "Now we can talk without being cut off. Your pal Wilbur Constantine has been round asking for you. He says it's very important—another Constable has turned up."

"The devil it has!" Piet said.

"It's been brought to his firm to sell. He says he won't do anything about it until he's seen you."

"I should hope not. Of course I must see him. I'll

come up in the morning. Can you make an appointment for me for noon? And can he bring the picture with him?"

"Yes, it's been left with him for the moment. The customer is coming back on Wednesday, so if you can see him tomorrow it will be all right."

"Good. I shall have to come back here, I think, but I'll work that out after seeing Constantine. Anything else?"

"No, that's about all. It seems enough, though."

"Well, it may help. See you tomorrow."

Piet told Sally that he'd have to go on to London after taking her to Lavenham. "Will it look odd if I'm out all day?" he asked.

"I don't think so. You can say you're working on a landscape around Lavenham."

"That gives a reasonable excuse for taking you there. I can be suitably vague about precisely where I'm painting. What time do you generally leave Moat Cottage?"

"If I'm going by bus, I have to leave at four. If you're giving me a lift it doesn't matter."

"I don't want to come to Moat Cottage, and the trouble is I can't give you an exact time. I'll try to be at the bus-stop by five, but I may not be able to make it. If I'm not there by five-thirty can you wander for a bit and meet me at that little pub opposite the rather posh hotel?"

"I know the place. They do rather good sandwiches."

"That's it. I'll try to be there by opening time, but if not you could wait quite comfortably in the bar."

They were back at the mill soon after six. "Hullo everybody!" Sally called out. "We've brought some food, and some bottles of plonk."

"Hullo, Sally!" said a rather tall, fair girl. "Brian's

cook tonight, so let him have the food. Where's the plonk?"

Piet put down the cardboard box containing the bottles.

"Oh, goody, nice big bottles," the girl said.

Sally introduced her. "This is Clare," she said. "And this is Peter Devonshire who's come to join us."

"If we could have some glasses we could have a drink," Piet said.

"Can't do glasses, but we've got some cups. Come on everybody, there's some wine."

They were in what had been the engine-room of the mill. The big pump it had once driven was still there, though so rusty that the piston would no longer move in the barrel-sized cylinder. The driving machinery had gone, leaving a large expanse of bare brick tiles, with holes here and there where some supporting piece of machinery had stood. In the middle of the room was a long trestle table, and eight or nine wooden chairs. In one corner was an ancient kitchen range, with a coal fire burning in it. A young man was working at the fire with a pair of bellows. Most of the smoke was carried away by a rusty chimney-pipe, but every now and then the bellows would send a puff of smoke to drift into the room. A flight of wooden steps without a handrail led to what was apparently a hole in the ceiling. It was the hatch leading to the next floor of the mill, which served as a dormitory for the colony. In answer to Clare's call people began assembling, a man and a girl coming down the steps from the dormitory, the others coming in from outside. Piet met Jim, Eddie and Simon, Poppy, and another girl whom Sally did not know because she was a newcomer. She was called Jennifer.

Sally took the bags of food shopping across to Brian at the range. "Where's Trudi?" she asked.

"She went back with Roger to their boat," someone said. "They'll be here for tea."

Piet had a corkscrew in his knife, and began opening the wine. Someone brought a collection of cups,
several of them cracked, to the table, and the man
called Eddie took one of Piet's bottles and filled the
cups. "Welcome to the happy home," he said, raising
a cup to Piet. "Are you staying here in the mill?"

"No," said Sally. "He's with me on Roger's boat."

Nobody seemed to think this a matter for comment.

The wine, Piet thought, could have been worse. Most
of the others were on their second or third cups, but
he drank slowly, studying his companions through the
slight smoke haze. They all seemed fairly young—the
girl called Jennifer looked no more than eighteen or
nineteen, and he doubted if any of them was over
twenty-five. It was an odd set-up, but perhaps would
not have seemed so odd to him if he had been ten
years younger. It was not uncommon nowadays for
groups of students to come together in communes for
more or less collective living, though they seldom
lasted long, and young people with any purpose in
life tended soon to outgrow them. Perhaps it did no
great harm, perhaps it was part of the process of
growing up in a society rejecting, or pretending to re-
ject, so many of the older values. It was a way of life
that instinctively repelled him because it was sloppy
and untidy, and fundamentally irresponsible in its approach to human relationships. It would tend, he
thought, to make the inadequate even more inadequate. But these youngsters were not quite hippies.
They seemed to do some work, and if they liked living in a kind of human ant-heap, that was a matter
for them.

The tall girl, Clare, who seemed to exercise some
sort of leadership in the community, called him over
to her. "Have you got a jar, or a small tin?" she
asked. "A tobacco tin would do."

"Sorry, I'm afraid I haven't," Piet said.

"Well, we must see if we can find something." She took him to the corner by the range, where there was one shelf holding packets of cereals, tins of baked beans and other foodstuffs, and another stacked with odds and ends of crockery. On the crockery shelf was a small collection of cocoa-tins and similar receptacles, each labelled with a piece of sticking plaster with a name on it. "Sugar," she said. "We share everything else, but some people are so bloody greedy for sugar that we make it a rule that everyone looks after his own. Let's see if we can find you a sugar tin." She searched the shelf, but there didn't seem to be an empty tin. "These all belong to people. Here's Sally's—I suppose you could share with her till you get one of your own," she said. "No, wait a moment." She reached to the back of the shelf and brought out a small rectangular tin—originally a mustard tin— with Sandra's name on it. "This is really Sandra's but she's away, and I don't know when she's coming back," she said. "You take it, and we can get her another one when she needs it. Now for the First Aid box."

The First Aid box was a biscuit tin containing sticking plaster, a few bandages, and a tube of antiseptic ointment. She took out a small square of plaster and stuck it on the tin. "Got anything to write with?" she asked. He produced a ball-point pen, and she wrote "Pete" on the plaster.

"Thank you very much," he said.

"You'll probably think it rather silly to have rules and regulations," Clare said. "We don't have many, but I got so fed up with running out of sugar that I got people to agree to look after their own. We share the cooking, but someone's got to look after the catering, and I do that—to see that there's generally something to cook, I mean." She laughed.

"It must be a job," Piet said.

"Not really. It's all right when we have any money,

but naturally it gets a bit difficult when we're all broke at the same time."

Piet gave her three five-pound notes. "I haven't put anything in the kitty yet," he said. "Can this be my contribution for the moment?"

"You seem to be in funds."

"Well, you know how it is. I sold a couple of pictures last week, and when I met Sally in London I thought we might have a bit of a holiday together. It's a working holiday for me, though. I'm doing a series of county pictures. I did Kent last year, and I'm doing Suffolk this. Tomorrow I want to do one near Lavenham. It's not great art, but I can sell them for calendars, and they go quite well at local exhibitions. People actually buy pictures of places they know, though they won't spend much on them."

"Seems a good idea. I do portraits, mostly, and I find it damned hard to make anything out of them. I'd like to have a talk with you about the calendar side of things. But tea's ready. Get a plate and a knife and fork, and help yourself from whatever Brian's cooked."

Brian had cooked Piet and Sally's bacon and eggs. People collected plates, filled them, and took them to the table. While everyone was busy getting food Piet slipped the sugar tin in the deep pocket of his sailing smock.

Roger and Trudi had turned up while Piet was negotiating with Clare, and were already sitting at the table when he got there with his own plate. Roger beckoned Piet to a chair beside him. Trudi was sitting opposite. Sally was involved in conversation with the girl called Poppy.

"Do you know this part of the world?" Roger asked.

"Not well. I used to sail a boat with my father when he was alive—we kept her on the Orwell—and I know the coast a little up to Lowestoft and Yarmouth."

Roger was at once interested. "What do you think of the old botter?" he said.

"I think she's lovely. I've never sailed a boat with lee-boards."

"I bought her in Holland, and brought her over. Of course you don't get the performance of a keelboat when you're on the wind, but it's remarkable how well the lee-board holds her. And you get all the advantage of not having a keel in shallow water. It would be nice if I could take you for a trip, but I don't know whether I shall be able to get away. How long are you likely to be down here?"

"How long are you likely to want me on board? It's jolly good of you to put me up at no notice at all."

"It's no trouble, and with Sandra away there's plenty of room. I expect Sally told you about Sandra."

"Yes."

"She's very gifted as an artist, but inclined to be moody. She made up her mind suddenly that she wanted to paint in Normandy, and went off."

"I saw some of her work in an exhibition in London last year. You're right—it was outstandingly good, I thought."

Roger was silent for a bit, then he said reflectively, "We nearly got married once. But it wouldn't have worked out. She didn't like boats—I mean, she quite liked living on the botter at a mooring, but she didn't like going to sea. Poor kid, she was dreadfully seasick. She'd get travel-sick on a car or train journey, too."

"Do you live on your boat all the year round?"

"As much as I can. I've had her for nearly three years, and the last two winters I've gone south to Cornwall. I think I shall again this year. That's the joy of a boat—you go where you want, and take your home with you."

"As long as you're not tied to a job, or a studio."

"Well, I couldn't make a living out of painting—not good enough, I'm afraid. On the other hand I'm not bad at selling pictures, and sailing around as I do I pick up paintings, or sometimes antiques, here and there. A friend of mine has a place at Lavenham where she does quite a good trade in art and antiques, but there's always the difficulty of getting stocks. It's easy enough to get stuff of a kind, but not easy to get good stuff. That's where I come in. We're not exactly partners, but we work together."

Trudi called across the table. "Tea up, Roger. And tea for you, Pete?" She handed them two mugs. Piet didn't take sugar in tea. Roger shook some into his cup from a tin. As he put down the tin the sticking-plaster label was turned towards Piet. It had "Sandra" written on it.

The meal was about finished and people were getting up and leaving the table. Trudi came over and sat down next to Piet. "We haven't really met yet, but Sally pointed you out to me," she said. "I'm so glad that you are going to be with us for a bit."

"It's a wonderful holiday for me."

"What sort of pictures do you paint?"

"Landscape, mostly. Run of the mill stuff, I'm afraid, but with calendars and things it keeps me going. I'm doing a Suffolk series at the moment, and I want to do one near Lavenham. Sally's got to go there tomorrow, so I thought I'd drive her there and stay and do my picture."

"Sally's very talented. I wish I could do her flower pictures, but I think I haven't the patience. I like quick, broad brush strokes. I'm trying to do some seascapes."

"I'd like to see them."

"Well that's easy enough, but not now. I've packed up for today."

Piet couldn't put a background to her. She was older than Sally, late twenties, he thought, and good-looking in a slightly hard way. She had a mass of dark brown hair, and wore a pair of big, somewhat barbaric, earrings, made out of carved wood. She had a set of bracelets of the same wood on one arm. They suited her. The other girls were all in jeans, but she wore a long skirt. Piet was about to ask if she and Roger would like to come out for a drink when Clare settled things for him. She clapped her hands and called out, "Pete and Sally are in funds. Let's have a kitty for the pub." Sally came up and explained, "Clare looks after the money. People give her what they can, and anyone who wants to go to the pub comes along."

Piet handed over another five-pound note, and most of the others gave Clare something, though one or two did not. Roger contributed a pound, but said, "If you don't mind, I think Trudi and I won't come tonight. We've got rather a lot of things to do on the boat." To Piet he said, "Don't worry about what time you get back. The boat won't be locked."

The pub party went off in Piet's car and another car. The pub was a friendly old country inn, and they spent a pleasant evening there. The man called Eddie got rather tight and tried to fondle the girls, but they seemed used to him and there was no real unpleasantness. The others kept their drinking within bounds, and there was a flow of bright talk, sometimes with an edge of cattiness, mostly about people Piet had never heard of. There was not much serious discussion about anything. Poppy did try to start a conversation about whether the French impressionists had actually created anything, or merely applied correctives to other people's vision, but it got lost in the general atmosphere of relaxed enjoyment of the pub. With the possible exceptions of Clare and Poppy, who seemed to have more to them than the men, Piet couldn't see any of the mill company as likely to have the qualities necessary for serious artistic fraud, let alone the poisoning of Sandra.

Back at the Fen, the others went off to the mill, leaving Piet and Sally to make for the botter. It was a lovely summer night, and Piet said, "If you're not too tired, let's walk down to the sea before turning in." Sally slipped her arm in his and they followed the line of the sluice to the beach. It seemed the most natural thing in the world that they should be together.

The tide was in, and there was no sound but the slight fret of wavelets stirring the pebbles. The beach here was fairly wide, a good fifty yards between high-water mark and the marram grass of the Fen. There was a half-moon, and Piet was confident that anyone near enough to be within hearing on the open beach would be visible. There was no one. They walked on slowly, and Piet said, "I should be surprised if anyone at the mill knows anything about Sandra's death. I'm less sure of Roger. What do you really know about him? He doesn't seem to fit in with this slightly hippie lot."

Sally didn't answer at once. Then she said, "He doesn't fit in. For one thing he seems to have a good deal more money than the others. I don't know much about him. I met him once at Sandra's studio—I don't *know*, but I think she met him at her exhibition, and that he offered to act as a kind of agent for her, selling pictures on commission. They got close quite quickly, and there's no doubt that Sandra was fairly seriously in love with him. Whether she still was at the end I don't know. She was certainly upset about Trudi, though when I was on the boat with them Sandra was still Roger's girl, and Trudi just a hanger-on. At least, that's how it was officially, but Trudi used to act sometimes as if she owned Roger. That's what upset Sandra."

"Where did Trudi come from?"

"I haven't any idea. She'd been studying in Paris, or so she said, but whether she'd just come from Paris, or it was some time ago, I don't know. Roger takes his boat across the Channel, and he may have picked her up in France. I told you I didn't like the set-up. I don't much care for either Roger or Trudi, though they've always been quite nice to me."

"What about the people on the other boat, Trish and Malcom, I think you said? We haven't met them yet."

"No, they weren't at the mill tonight. They don't come all that often. Their cruiser is a modern boat, beautifully fitted out, with a bottled-gas stove in the galley, all that sort of thing. They're friendly enough, but they seem to like being on their own. We'll see them tomorrow, I expect."

"Are they married? What is their other name?"

Sally laughed. "Are we married? People accept couples, but they don't go around asking to inspect marriage lines. Trish and Malcolm seem to have a more or less permanent relationship, but whether they're married or not, goodness knows. As for their name, well, you've seen how difficult it is tonight. I think it's something like Malcolm Winterer, but I'm only going by something Roger once asked me. I'd come back from Lavenham, and he said, 'Did you meet Malcolm Winterer at Lavenham today?' I didn't, and I said no."

"Do you think Roger was ever in love with Sandra? He told me this evening that they nearly got married once—that was how he put it. He went on to say that it wouldn't have worked out because Sandra was moody, and she didn't like going to sea because she was always seasick. It seemed a funny thing to say to a chance acquaintance."

"That's because you're not used to this world, Piet. People are always pouring out their souls to chance acquaintances. It doesn't surprise me a bit—he may have felt that he had to say something to explain why he seems to have teamed up with Trudi. Yes, I daresay he was a little in love with Sandra once. She was very attractive. But he couldn't have been much in love. If you're really in love it seems a rotten reason for not marrying someone, just because they get seasick."

"Was Sandra moody?"

"She could be. Who isn't sometimes? She may have seemed moody to him because she was upset over Trudi, but you can scarcely blame her for that. Whether Roger ever thought seriously about marrying Sandra, I don't know. Sandra probably thought about marriage, but I doubt if he did."

They turned back, and Piet said, "You know, Sally, I don't think you really belong to this set-up either."

"I do wish Sandra had never asked me to come here. It seemed a good idea at the time, but oh, Piet, it's turned out to be just horrible."

They walked back to the Fen, and crossed the foot-bridge over the sluice. Even in thin moonlight, Piet's sharp visual memory told him that something had changed. The motor-cruiser belonging to Malcolm and Trish was not there.

VII

Sally at Lavenham

Sally didn't have to be at Moat Cottage until her first class at eleven-thirty, but since Piet had to be in London by noon they got up early and were away soon after seven o'clock. Roger and Trudi had not stirred. It was too early for breakfast at the mill, but there was an oil stove in the botter's galley, and Sally made a pot of tea. It wouldn't matter, she said, if she got to Lavenham early—she had an unfinished flower picture there, and could get on with that. And she had her own detective work to do in finding out who had been away from the studio recently.

They were careful not to discuss anything but tea on board the botter, but when they were safely in the car Piet asked if the Trish and Malcolm cruiser often left her mooring on the Fen. "I don't know what you mean by 'often'," Sally said. "And I can't say that I've ever recorded her movements—I've not been that much interested. In the two months or so that I've been here she may have been away a couple of times—at least, I *know* she's been away twice, because Trudi went with her to get impressions for seascapes. She may have been out more, of course. I haven't been here all the time."

"How long does she go away for?"

"Oh Piet, it's awfully difficult! She was away for two nights on one of Trudi's trips—I know that because Sandra was so happy to have Trudi out of the way. The other trip that Trudi went on was simply a day outing. All I can say is that Trish and Malcolm have generally been around."

"You don't know where they go when they leave the Fen?"

"No."

Not wanting to be seen again at Moat Cottage for the moment, Piet dropped Sally at the bus-stop in Lavenham, promising to get back as soon as he could for their rendezvous at the pub. "It's going to be a very lonely day without you," Sally said.

"I'm going to miss you, too, Sally, and much more than I can say. When this wretched business is over I want to talk to you about all sorts of things."

"What sort of things?"

"You're not much of a detective!" He kissed her hand lightly, and drove off.

He had to call on all his powers of self-discipline to stop thinking about Sally and concentrate on the case. As a matter of fact, he couldn't stop thinking of Sally, who stayed as a warm glow in his mind. But he could make other parts of his mind go over the various problems that had emerged at Poplar's Fen. Why did Sandra apparently have two sugar tins? And why was Roger using one of them? The tin in his pocket had been right at the back of the shelf, and the shelf was in a dark corner of the mill. Could she have lost one tin, and got another? And if someone wanted to remove Sandra's sugar tin, could he have found and taken one tin, not realising there were two?

What a curious dichotomy there was in the Poplar's Fen colony! There seemed two sharply distinct

groups of people—the boatowners and the mill crowd.
He hadn't met the owners of the cruiser, but from
what Sally said of them they seemed to relate more to
Roger than to the slightly hippie element in the mill.
The man Roger seemed much more like a prosperous
businessman keen on yachting than a happy-go-lucky
artist. The botter was in good conditon, and her
maintenance would not be cheap. True, she might
save the cost of a home on land, particularly if she
could find free mooring, but she would still need
money spent on her. Roger gave the impression of
being well-to-do—what on earth could he find to attract him in the rather childish group of people in
the mill? Did he own the mill? There was a faintly
proprietorial air about him, although he seemed to
accept Clare's leadership of the mill group docilely
enough. The mill colony could simply be squatters,
but there wasn't the feel of an illegal squat about the
place. Someone had installed the kitchen range, and
equipped the mill with furniture of a sort. If Roger
owned the mill—whoever owned it, for that matter—
occupation by a colony of young artists could scarcely
be regarded as a reasonable investment.

He was no nearer answering any of his own questions when he got to London, but concentrated
thought made for a quick journey and he was at Scotland Yard by eleven. The first thing he did was to
send the sugar tin to the laboratory with a request for
immediate analysis of its contents. He had a word
with the chief chemist on the phone, explained the
urgency of the matter, and was promised a preliminary report early in the afternoon. Then he reported
to his Superintendent, and got ready to receive Mr
Wilbur Constantine.

The art dealer was a very worried man. "I'm thankful
to see you, Chief Inspector," he said. "I wouldn't
have believed it possible that I could be in doubt

about a Constable, but I am. This is the picture that was brought to me yesterday." He opened the portfolio he was carrying and carefully laid a painting on Piet's desk. It was slightly smaller than the painting recovered from the train at Liverpool Street, but in a similar style. It was another landscape, the foreground showing a rutted road with a man leading two horses, great patient Suffolk punches, clearly tired after a day's work. Just as the other picture had suggested a ford without actually showing it, so this suggested the approach to a farm, man and horses nearly home, thankful for the rest ahead of them.

Piet looked at it for a long time. Then he said, "I see what you mean. I have the same feeling about the other picture. It *is* Constable, and yet there's something . . . not lacking, almost something added."

The art dealer nodded. "It would seem to belong to the same period as the other, a late period near the end of his life. He died in 1837 at sixty-one. *If* he painted this it would have been, I think, when he was approaching sixty, absolute master of technique and materials, his vision still unclouded, but his mood saddened by the death of his wife and by his frequent bouts of illness. You can *see* fatigue in those plodding figures; they're heavy with weariness, but it's weariness bravely borne. They know they've got to go on.

"I agree with you, Chief Inspector, though perhaps for somewhat different reasons. You are judging instinctively, and you *feel* that there's something you have never met before in Constable's work, not exactly non-Constable, but an unknown Constable. I am judging technically. I know—at least, until last week I should have thought I knew—every nuance in John Constable's *oeuvre*, but there's something here that defeats me. If this picture, and the one you showed me the other day, are genuine, then we've got to revise a whole chapter of art history. I'm not saying that revision isn't called for. I am doubtful of the facts."

"You have not yet submitted the painting to any tests?"

"It is not my property. I took it home last night, and I have been living with it ever since. I am not prepared to say that it is by Constable, but I am not prepared to say that it isn't."

"Tell me how it came to you."

"It is an extraordinary story. Yesterday morning a woman came to our galleries and asked to see me, asked for me by name. That is not uncommon—most people concerned with English painting have read my books. My secretary went down to see what she wanted, and came back with her card. I have it here—Mrs Shirley Vincent, Moat Cottage Studio, Lavenham. Antiques and Fine Art. She told my secretary that she had a picture which she wished my firm to auction for her, and that she was sure I would be interested in it. I agreed to see her, and she brought in this painting. Naturally, I was intensely interested. She said that she believed the picture to be by Constable. I was non-committal, and asked how it had come to be in her possession.

"She was prepared for this. She told me that she runs an art centre and antique business at Lavenham in premises that were once part of the Moat Grange estate. The house, supposedly an Elizabethan building, had long been in ruins, and she bought the ruins with the cottage and about five acres of land some three years ago. She wanted to build on to the cottage. Getting the necessary planning consents, and then getting the building work done, took about two years, and she opened her place for business in the spring of this year. Now comes the almost unbelievable part. In building on to her cottage she used some old stone from the ruins of the Grange. There was nothing habitable above ground, but in demolishing a wall for stones they came across the entrance to a cellar. It was quite dry, and contained a mass of old junk, including some big wooden boxes. The builders made a bonfire of most of the stuff, but she had the boxes taken into her cottage. She says that she was too busy to look at them, and forgot about them until a few weeks back. Then she opened them, and found a number of pictures, of which this is one. She wants my opinion on it, and to know if we will handle it for sale."

"Even if the story is true, her title to the pictures would seem highly dubious," Piet said.

"Yes, but she says she has gone into that. The Moat Grange estate was broken up before the First World War—the house has not been inhabited during this century. The family which then owned it appears to have died out. The land was sold off to various local farmers. The ruins hung on the market, and were finally sold just before the Second World war to a building company. Nothing could be done during the war, and after the war, when they wanted to build houses there, they ran into planning difficulties. The original building company sold the place to another property company, which had an idea of building a country club. Again there were planning difficulties, the company ran short of money, and finally went into liquidation. She bought the place from the receiver. She had a canny lawyer who drew up a very wide conveyance setting out that the sale included the ruins and any articles found on the land above or below ground. She says that this was because the site was archaeologically interesting, and she might want to excavate it one day. It seems a remarkably wise provision, as things have turned out."

"It seems too clever by half. And if anyone else could produce a serious claim to the pictures his lawyer would argue that the receiver had no title to the pictures when he sold the property. However, that is purely speculative. No doubt the lawyers could argue about it for years. If no other claimant turns up her title might stand, I suppose. What have you done to check her story so far?"

"She is coming back tomorrow with the conveyance. She has given me the name of her builder, and says that he will confirm the finding of the wooden boxes in the cellar. There has been no time to go into this yet."

"He can't confirm what was in the boxes, because they weren't opened in his presence. As far as the provenance of the pictures is concerned, his evidence is worthless."

"You think the whole story is a fake?"

"Don't you?"

The art dealer paused before replying. "In the records of my firm there are a number of extraordinary stories, at least some of which are true," he said. "I agree that her story is improbable, but the improbable is not necessarily untrue. At present I have no evidence on which to believe or disbelieve what she told me."

"What do you know of Mrs Vincent?"

"Nothing, apart from her trade card and what she said of herself. She is not a member of our association, but that in itself means little—many reputable small dealers are not in the association. We have, as you know, a trade protection branch, and I have inquired about her there. They have nothing against her. She has bought and sold goods from time to time—always antiques, I think, not pictures—with member firms, and the transactions have been perfectly satisfactory. But she has not dealt much—on her own story, she has not been in business long."

"What is your next step?"

"I shall see her tomorrow afternoon at five o'clock—I made the appointment as late as I could because I wanted to see you first, and I was not sure then when I should be able to. She will presumably bring the conveyance she talked about, and that will confirm her title to the Moat Grange ruins. It will not go far towards establishing a history for the picture. Genealogy is often important to us, and we are in touch with a number of genealogists. I have asked a man who is considered the leading expert on the families of East Anglia to find out what he can about the former owners of Moat Grange. It was occupied for some two centuries by a family called Carless, and he believes that that particular Carless family is, indeed, extinct. He is conducting some research into the matter, but it will take a little time. We shall try to discover whether any member of the family was known to collect pictures, or had any known association with John Constable. If it is impossible to authenicate the picture, and it seems unlikely to have been painted by Constable, we shall, of course, decline to put it in a sale with any attribution suggesting that it may be by Constable. But I have sufficient doubt not to want to let it go too easily. If by any chance it can reasonably be attributed to Constable it is a most important find, and we would naturally want to handle it. I shall explain to Mrs Vincent that much research is needed, and hope that she will leave the picture with me."

"I think you will find that there *is* a Carless-Constable connection, of a sort that can be neither proved nor disproved easily. I can almost tell you what it will be. John Constable was at school in Lavenham, and some Carless then living at Moat Grange is believed to have befriended him—it will be something like that. And I shall not be surprised if the Moat Grange hoard does not soon produce a Gainsborough. His home was not far away, at Sudbury, and doubtless the Carlesses invited him to dinner. Later there may be a Turner connection, though it is geographically less clear."

Mr Constantine was both pained and excited. "You talk, Chief Inspector, as if you have unearthed a conspiracy."

"I am not sure. I have reason to be deeply suspicious of the pictures you saw the other day, and of the new Constable that has been brought to you. It is conceivable that the Constables at least are genuine, though I have a theory that may account for the puzzling features about them. It would be improper for me to say more at present—I have said too much already, but we are allies in the same cause and I know I can trust your discretion. I would advise you to be very much on your guard in any dealings you may have with Mrs Vincent. And I have a request to make: would it be possible for me to be present at your interview tomorrow, in such a way that I can see and hear without being seen?"

The art dealer considered this. "It would be possible, I think," he said. "My secretary's room opens from mine, and you could be in there with the door slightly ajar. Mrs Vincent is due at five—could you be at my office at four-thirty? We may need to make one or two small adjustments to the furniture."

Piet undertook to be there.

He had lunch with his Superintendent, and got back to his own office to find the telephone ringing. The call was from the chemist at the forensic lab. His tin contained sugar, probably beet sugar, but it would require further analysis to determine its precise origin. With the sugar was an admixture of arsenic tioxide, which certainly could not occur naturally in sugar, either beet or cane.

"Don't worry about the sugar," Piet said. "Tell me about the arsenic. What sort of quantity is there? Would it be a lethal dose?"

"Well, we haven't had time to do a full quantitative analysis, but as far as I can estimate the total it would undoubtedly be lethal. Arsenic tioxide is highly toxic."

"What would happen if it wasn't taken all at one time—say a spoonful or two of the arsenic-sugar mixture once or twice a day?"

"The mixture is fairly well dispersed—there wouldn't be a great deal of arsenic in one spoonful, and if taken in tea or with a breakfast cereal probably not enough to taste. But it would remain toxic, of course, and over a period of some days the cumulative effect would be lethal."

"That's what I needed to know. Thank you for being so quick with your preliminary report. We'll want a full analysis, but get that done when you can. You've given me the really important information, and it's an immense help to have it so promptly."

"I hope you find out who's mixing arsenic and sugar like this. It's not a nice mixture."

Piet hoped so, too. It was something to have discovered how arsenic had been administered to Sandra Telford, but, he reflected gloomily, he was no nearer knowing who had given it to her.

With daytime London traffic to be got through he was anxious to start his journey back to Suffolk, but he had another job to do first. He called at the Yard's criminal records department and spent half an hour looking at photographs.

He was too late to meet Sally at the bus-stop, but he got to the pub in Lavenham a few minutes after opening time. He felt an immense flood of relief to see Sally in the otherwise empty bar. He had no particular reason to fear that whoever had murdered Sandra might wish to hurt Sally, but there was so much he did not know that he was exceedingly worried about her. On the way to the pub he had noticed a small corner shop still open. Telling Sally that he would be back in a minute he slipped out to the shop and bought a packet of sugar and two small tins of cocoa. The cocoa he didn't want, but he did want the tins: He was determined that whatever sugar Sally had should not come from the mill.

It would have been a rush to get back to Poplar's Fen in time for the evening meal, and he didn't want to stay in Lavenham in case any of the Moat Cottage people should come in for a drink. So he suggested to Sally that they should go back through Stowmarket, not quite on the direct route to Poplar's Fen, but not far out of the way, and get a meal there. She was so happy to be reunited with Piet that she didn't mind where they went, though she didn't want him to feel that he had to spend money on her. "I don't know how rich you are, but I do know that I have to be very careful about money," she said. "You and your mother have spent an awful lot on me already, so if we're going to have dinner in Stowmarket you must let me pay my share."

"I'm not at all rich," Piet said, "but I earn enough to get by, and I think it will run to taking you out to dinner. Besides, I want to talk to you."

"I've been doing some work, too," Sally said.

He had not told her yet about the sugar. In the car he said, "I'm afraid I've come across something horrible. I know how Sandra was given arsenic." He explained about the tin. Sally went white. "And that was the tin that Clare gave to you!" she said.

"It doesn't seem likely that she knew anything about it. You don't give arsenic to chance strangers."

"No, but you might so easily have taken it! Oh Piet, oh Piet. . . ."

"I was suspicious of anything that Sandra might have eaten. What really puzzles me is why there were two tins."

"It could happen easily enough. Clare's got a thing

about those sugar tins, a mean streak, or something. People are always taking them away and losing them. Sandra liked sugar—she may have taken her tin to the boat for coffee, or sometimes she'd have breakfast on board and she'd want sugar for cornflakes."

"That might explain why Roger had her tin. Or there might be other reasons. . . ."

As a dinner in the sense of a pleasant occasion spent with an attractive girlfriend the Stowmarket meal was not a success. Presumably the food was well enough cooked and adequately served, it might even have been delicious, but Piet ordered and ate mechically. Although he did not realise it at the time, the meal was, however, an important small landmark in the case. Sally explained what she had done to try to find out about the movements of people at Moat Cottage.

"As an instructor," she said, "I get a free lunch. The students who are staying at the place pay for lunch with the fee for accommodation, and the instructors can have lunch with them. Shirley doesn't charge us—she thinks it a good thing that we should mix with the students. So I was able to talk to people quite naturally. I asked if anyone had been to that big Roman Exhibition that's just opened at the British Museum. A couple of the students had, but I don't think they're likely to come into it. Bill and Vera both said that they hoped it would still be on in the autumn, because they found it hard to get to London in the summer—they gave the impression of not having been up for ages. Jeff Wilson was still away— he was away most of last week, so he could have been in London, but I don't know about this. Shirley couldn't have been in London, I think. She's arranging an exhibition of work done at Moat Cottage since it opened, and with Jeff away that has kept her very busy."

"Yet she was in London yesterday," Piet said.

"Yesterday? She couldn't have been. She was framing and hanging pictures all day—she showed me what she had done. Why do you think she was in London?"

"She called on Wilbur Constantine, the art dealer, and gave him her card. At least, he showed me her card, but of course—I didn't see the woman who gave it to him."

"Well, I suppose it's possible, but it doesn't seem likely. Nobody spoke of her being away, and I think they would have. I suppose she could have done a lot of work on Sunday and pretended that she'd done it yesterday. But there were people around all the time, and when she was telling me about it nobody said, 'But Shirley, you weren't here yesterday.'"

Piet didn't pursue the matter. "What about the others?" he asked.

"Today was a busy day for teas. Anita and Vi were both on, and Vi said, 'I think it's even busier than we were on Friday.' Anita said, 'At least we didn't have that awful couple who complained of everything.' Then they laughed. Obviously they were both there on Friday, and as far as I know they were there all the week."

"That seems sound detective work. Well done, Sally. It leaves the cleaning woman and the gardener."

"Old Arthur may have been to London in his lifetime, but I doubt if he's been much away from Lavenham in the past fifty years. Mrs Marshall comes in every day, even on Sundays. There's nothing to suggest that she's been away recently. When Shirley was showing me how she was getting on with hanging things for the exhibition Mrs Marshall came in about something, and when she'd gone Shirley said, 'I don't know what I'd do without her. She's getting on, and I have nightmares about her being ill, or something. But these Suffolk people are tough. She came originally from somewhere near the coast, and she says it was the sea air as a girl that keeps her well now. She's wonderfully reliable.' That doesn't look as if she's been away at all."

"So apart from Jeff Wilson, who may or may not have been in London, the rest of the Moat Cottage lot seem to have been at work at Lavenham."

"It certainly looks like that, yes."

It was after eleven when they got back to Poplar's Fen, and the mill and the botter were in darkness. After he'd turned out the lights of the car and his eyes had got accustomed to the night Piet could see that the motor-crusier had not yet returned. They went on board the botter as quietly as they could, and got to their cabin without disturbing anybody.

Piet had to be in London for his appointment with Wilbur Constantine at four-thirty, but that didn't need an early start, so there was time for a leisurely breakfast. They were up before Roger and Trudi and went across to the mill. On the way Piet said, "Let's have a look at the sea before breakfast. I want to talk to you, and I don't want to talk on Roger's boat, or in the mill." He was worried about Sally. She had no class at Lavenham that day, and normally she would have stayed at Poplar's Fen, getting on with one of her flower pictures. But he didn't want her to be alone at the Fen, and with his late appointment in London he didn't want to have to come back that night. He didn't know what might have to be done after the meeting in Constantine's office, and he'd have to keep himself free. He explained this to Sally on the way down to the beach.

"I don't see any real reason why I shouldn't be here on my own," she said. "It's a bit cowardly, but I agree with you. I don't much like the idea of staying on alone."

"I don't think it's at all cowardly. Your friend was

murdered here, or if not here the actions that led to her murder seem to have taken place here. We don't yet know how or why, but we know enough to suggest that there's something very nasty going on. I've *got* to be in London this evening, and . . . and . . . well, I don't think I can concentrate on my job if I'm worrying about you all the time."

Sally laughed. "Poor Piet, what a nuisance I am!"

"You could say that you are an important witness, and it's perfectly proper for the police to be concerned with the protection of witnesses. Could you come to London with me, and spend tonight with my mother?"

"I could do that, yes. But what about tomorrow? I've got a class at Lavenham tomorrow."

"Can we leave tomorrow to look after itself? If I'm free I can leave early and get you to Lavenham for whatever time you want. If not—you could telephone and say that you're ill. Please, Sally, I really do want you to be away from here."

"All right—I did volunteer for the job of detective's mate, after all. I suppose I've just got to obey orders, though to be honest they're orders that I rather want to obey."

"Thank you, Sally. Let's have breakfast and chat to whoever happens to be around, and leave about mid-morning. We can have lunch on the way to London. What shall we say about having to be away?"

"We don't need to say anything, it's a pretty casual community. But it would do no harm to have a reason—I know, I can say that I'm hoping to have an exhibition of flower pictures, and that I've got to go to London to see people about it. You can say that you've got to see your calendar printers, and it's reasonable enough to combine the two jobs."

The mill group differed a good deal in their getting-up habits, and only Clare and one of the men were having breakfast when Piet and Sally got there.

Breakfast was not a cooked meal. There were packets of various brands of cereal on the table, some bottles of milk, a sliced loaf, some butter, and a big pot of tea. "You can make some toast if you like—I think the range fire is still in," Clare said. "But I don't recommend it—you'll get smoked bread rather than proper toast. There's some jam on the shelf. People do their own washing up after breakfast."

Piet had the tins of sugar he'd prepared for himself and Sally in the pocket of his smock. He went to the shelf to get the sugar, but was careful to come back with his own tins. He noticed that both Clare and the man with her had heaped sugar on their cereals. "This is where the sugar goes," Clare said. "You can understand why we have the rule about separate tins. Sandra is awful about it—I think she sometimes has more sugar than cereal."

While Piet had been doing his careful subterfuge with the sugar tins Sally had poured out two mugs of tea. "Where did you two get yesterday?" Clare asked.

"Sally had a class at Lavenham, and I'm doing a Lavenham picture for my Suffolk calendar," Piet answered. "I made two starts, but they just didn't come right. Then I did get it right, and I went on as long as the light lasted. Sally came and found me, and I'm afraid she got rather bored. So we went to a pub, and then it was really too late to get back here for supper. We got some food in another pub. Everyone was asleep when we got back—at least, the mill and Roger's boat were all in darkness."

"We're going to be away again today," Sally said. "You know I told you there was a chance of an exhibition of my flower pictures in the autumn—well, it seems that there really *is* a chance. I telephoned the man who thinks he may be able to arrange it from Moat Cottage yesterday, and he wants to see me about it. Piet's got to see his calendar printers, so we're both going up to London today. We'll stay the night in London, I think."

"Nice to have someone wanting you," Clare said. "I've got a couple of pictures in the exhibition Shirley Vincent's putting on at Lavenham. I hope to goodness someone buys them."

Roger and Trudi came in. "Morning, everybody," Trudi said. "I heard you come back last night, Sally, but I must say you were very quiet."

"I'm sorry we disturbed you at all," Piet said.

"You didn't, because I wasn't asleep."

"Well, we won't be bothering you tonight," Sally said. She explained about their trip to London. Piet watched Roger shaking sugar over his plate of cereal. He was using his left hand, and Piet noticed something that he hadn't seen before. The top joint of the little finger of his left hand was missing.

"You said you'd show me some of your work," Piet said to Trudi. "We don't need to start all that early. If you've got time after breakfast I'd love to see your pictures."

"Sure. I'm pretty well through now. I'll take you up to the studio."

Roger stayed at the table, eating and chatting to Sally. "Don't swig all the tea," Trudi said. "I'd like another cup when we come down."

Piet followed her up the unrailed stairs. "Not good for anyone who's had a bit too much," he said.

"Oh, you soon get used to them. There's never been an accident, as far as I know. Stick by the wall if you feel worried. I remember I did at first."

The stairs led through an open hatch into a huge room. What it had been used for Piet found hard to interpret. Since the mill had been a pumping station and not for grinding anything, it would scarcely have needed a granary. Maybe, though, the place had once served for storage as well as housing the pumping engine on the ground floor. It might conceivably have been a sail loft in the days when fishing boats worked under sail. A length of decayed belting that had once carried the drive from the windmill down to the pumping engine still hung from a hole in the wooden ceiling. Now the great room was a dormitory. There were two or three camp beds, and several mattresses, with sleeping bags on them. Two were still occupied. "Some people just can't get up in the morning," Trudi observed. No one took any notice. She prodded one of the unoccupied mattresses with her foot. "Bet you can't guess what that's stuffed with," she said. "It's dried grass from the marsh. Makes a wonderful bed. I'd sooner have that than a camp bed any day."

She walked through the dormitory to another set of stairs at the far end. Like the stairs from the ground floor these had no handrail, and they led up to another hatch. Piet thought they must be getting near the working top of the mill. He was right, for most of the open space above the hatch was taken up by a hand-worked windlass, a train of rusty gear-wheels disappearing into the rafters. "Above here the whole top of the mill can be turned," Trudi explained. "They used to turn it for the sails of the windmill to catch the wind. I don't suppose it would work now—I doubt if anyone's even tried to turn it for a century."

The windlass-room, however, was not the only space on this second floor of the old mill. The curious construction providing for the huge room underneath was continued here, and instead of tapering to the turning-head of the windmill tower the floor-space here was also large. Unlike the dormitory it was not a single room. There were doors at each end of the windlass compartment, fitted, Piet noticed, with modern locks. Trudi unlocked one door, and Piet followed her inside. This room was a well-equipped studio, with a fine north window, not noticeable on coming to the mill either from the road or from the botter, for the road was south, and the botter's mooring about southeast. There were three easels, two empty and one with an unfinished painting on it, and a number of finished pictures stacked against the walls.

"This is mine," Trudi said, going to the unfinished painting. "And here are some finished ones." She took a framed picture from a group and stood it on one of the unoccupied easels. It was a seascape, the waves, Piet thought, improbably blue, and a sailing boat dead centre in the picture an irritation rather than of any value to the scene. The composition he considered appalling, but the drawing and the brush-work were competent enough. Tactfully, he did not disclose his private thoughts. "What a splendid mass of colour," he said dishonestly.

"Yes, that's what I try for," Trudi said. "You've got a good eye to go for the colour first." She was obviously pleased. "Let me show you some more."

Piet looked first at the unfinished work on the easel, another seascape, but with an angrier sea, and with a flight of dreadfully white birds wind-driven over the waves. She produced two more finished paintings, both much the same in style. Piet thought nothing of any of them, but politely said all the right things. "Do you have this studio to yourself?" he asked.

"Not exactly," she said. "Sandra used to work up here and I suppose she'll use it again when she comes back, but I never found it easy to work with her around. I let Clare come up, and one or two of the men sometimes, if they've got something that particularly needs a studio, but they have to ask me first. I'll let you come whenever you like, I'm sure I could work with you here," she added generously.

"That's very nice of you," Piet said. "But it won't be today because as you know I've got to take Sally to London, and try to get some money out of my calendar printers. It's something I'll look forward to."

She gave him a friendly smile. "That's settled then. Let's get down before those greedy people have finished all the tea."

The door locked automatically behind them. She did not open the other door before they went downstairs.

VIII

Mrs Vincent's Call

Mr Constantine's office was a finely-proportioned room in one of those lovely eighteenth-century town houses still to be found in Mayfair, although most of them are now dress shops of the most expensive sort, or belong to embassies. From the outside, apart from a discreet brass plate with the name of the firm, the headquarters of Gavell and Gainsworth still looked like a private house, and Mr Constantine's room on the first floor might still have been the drawing-room. A panelled door in one corner opened into an annexe now occupied by his secretary. Piet arrived a little before four-thirty, and found Mr Constantine standing in the middle of a superb Persian carpet studying a glass-fronted cabinet holding a collection of figurines in Meissen china. "I think this will do," he said. "The back is in these panels, and they are easily removable. If we take out one, and stand the cabinet just to one side of my secretary's door, you should be able to see through the glass front. The cabinet will disguise the fact that the door is slightly ajar, and we can arrange the figurines so that nobody looking from the front will notice an observer at the back. You will have to crouch, and it may be rather uncomfortable, but it's the best we can arrange. Let us move it now. The cabinet itself is not heavy, but first we must remove the Meissen figures."

He opened the cabinet, and Piet, feeling that he would be in debt for the rest of his life if he dropped one of the precious pieces of china, helped him to take out the figures and stand them on the carpet. Then they carried the cabinet across the room, and Mr Constantine slid out one of the back panels. When the figurines were put back Piet found that he could see between them perfectly, and Mr Constantine arranged a chair in front of his desk so that it was in the direct line of sight from Piet's observation post.

"That seems all right," he said. "I can't see you at all from here. Do you know, I'm not sure that I don't like the cabinet better there than where it was before—it looks right, somehow. But it would get in the way of the door, I fear, so it will have to go back.

"I've written a letter for my secretary to deliver by hand to an address in Hampstead," he went on, "and since she lives in Hampstead I've told her not to bother to come back. It seemed to me wise that no one should know of any possible interest in Mrs Vincent other than as a customer. When she comes, the receptionist downstairs will bring her up. She'll ring through to me before she does, though, so there will be time for you to disappear. We've got about ten minutes in hand before she's due. Come and have another look at the picture—I want to show you something."

The possible Constable was on Mr Constantine's big desk. "Consider the foreleg of the leading horse," he said. "Above the fetlock it is a chestnut-brown in colour, the body-colour of the whole horse. But look at the knee. Here and there on the rest of the paint-work there are tiny hairline cracks, such as you are liable to get on old oil paintings that have not been carefully preserved. They are not very noticeable, but they are there. The knee, and about half an inch above and below it, are entirely free of them. Also, there seems to me to be something not quite right about the knee. It seems very slightly out of proportion. I didn't notice it before because I was thinking of the picture as a whole, but since our meeting yesterday I have practically lived with it, and I find the knee puzzling. Have a look at it under the glass."

Piet began to look through Mr Constantine's magnifying glass when the telephone rang. "That will be Mrs Vincent, I expect," Mr Constantine said. He answered the phone. "Can you please bring her up in about five minutes?" he told the receptionist. And to Piet, "We'll have to discuss that knee later. Now I think you'd better make yourself scarce."

Piet retired to the secretary's room and knelt down behind the cabinet. "Fine," Mr Constantine said. "You wouldn't notice that the door was ajar unless you were looking specially at it."

A couple of minutes later there was a knock on the main door of Mr Constantine's room and the receptionist brought in a woman. Piet got a severe shock—he had never seen her before.

The art dealer was at his blandest. "I'm delighted to see you again, Mrs Vincent," he said. "You are very punctual, and I am sorry to have kept you waiting."

"But you didn't, at least not more than a minute or so, and I think I was a scrap early," said the woman called Mrs Vincent. Mr Constantine politely held the chair for her, and she sat down. His politeness also served to ensure that the chair remained in the right place.

She was certainly not the woman from Moat Cottage whom Piet knew as Mrs Vincent. This was a considerably younger woman, fair haired where Mrs Vincent was dark, and with a rounder face than Mrs

Vincent's rather fine-drawn countenance. Dark hair can be bleached and clever make-up can do much to alter the look of a face, but Piet was quite sure that this was not his Mrs Vincent in disguise. "So Sally was right about Mrs Vincent's not having been in London," he thought.

"I have brought the conveyance I told you about," the woman said, handing over a document with green tape and a red seal attached to it. "You will see that it confirms my title to anything found in the ruins of Moat Grange. Have you decided yet whether you can handle the sale of my picture for me?"

Mr Constantine hedged. "I have thought of little else since you brought it to me," he said. "I am disposed to regard it as a genuine work by John Constable, but if so it is totally unknown, and before we can offer it for sale as such the most detailed research will be required to find out as much as we can about its history. You will appreciate that an unknown work by Constable would be a major art discovery, and would arouse enormous interest internationally. If we are to catalogue it and offer it under our name as a guarantee of authenticity it is imperative that we should try to date it, and ascertain how it came to be where it was when it came into your possession. It is very much in your own interests that this should be done. It could be offered, perhaps, as an unattributed work of the English school of the early nineteenth century, and it might fetch a few hundred pounds. As a work by John Constable—even a probable work by Constable—it would attract a very large sum of money. There would be keen international bidding for it. But you must see that this cannot be done forthwith. Naturally, we should like to act for you, but you brought the picture to me only the day before yesterday, and I cannot yet give you a definite decision. You already have our receipt for the picture. If you are willing, I should like you to leave it with me for at least three months. It will be perfectly safe in our strongroom, probably safer than it would be in your keeping. Will you agree to act as I suggest?"

"I don't quite understand. You are considered to be our leading expert on Constable." Mr Constantine bowed. "You have had the picture for two days—surely that is long enough for you to make up your mind?"

"Regrettably, madam, it is not so. It may take years to determine the attribution of a painting, and sometimes it can never be conclusively determined. I am grateful for your remarks about my own small expertise, but in a matter of this importance I must consult the directors of our leading galleries, as well as a number of art historians. There is also—" Mr Constantine coughed slightly "—the somewhat delicate matter of precise legal ownership."

"This is absolute nonsense—indeed, it is almost an insult. There is no possible doubt about my ownership of the picture. The conveyance you have on your desk sets out everything that was conveyed to me when I bought the property, and you have my permission to consult the firm of solicitors who drew up the conveyance if you are in any doubt about it."

"Forgive me, madam, but it is not the conveyance that occasions me any concern. My doubt—no, that is the wrong word, it is simply a matter of legal caution—is whether the previous owner of the property was necessarily the owner of the pictures that you say were found in a cellar beneath the ruins. If this picture, as I think may well be the case, turns out to be a genuine Constable its discovery, and ultimate sale, will attract a great deal of publicity. It would be a serious matter, for yourself as well as for my firm, if some other claimant came forward. Your claim to ownership might be established, but there might be costly litigation first. We have long experience in these matters. I am simply offering you the advice that I should give to any important client."

"Well, I don't like it. I'm offering you a chance to make a lot of money out of your comisssion on the sale, to say nothing of adding to your reputation by identifying what I'm quite sure is a genuine work. All you do is to lecture me about pettifogging legal ifs and buts. There are other dealers, and if you don't want to handle what may be the most important art find for years, I'll go to someone who does—who understands things better. You've just wasted my time. Can I have my picture back, please?"

"Certainly, madam, I'll ring for a packer. And perhaps you would return my receipt."

Mr Constantine telephoned for a man to pack the picture, and the woman hunted in her handbag. As she handed Mr Constantine his receipt she said, "I'll have the picture packed in my presence. I don't trust you an inch."

When the packer came Mr Constantine asked him to bring packing materials and do up the picture where it was. He returned with a big cardboard portfolio, tissue paper, brown paper and string, and made a neat, expert job of packing the picture safely. "Shall I label it, sir?" he asked.

"No," said the woman, "I'm taking it with me." She didn't even thank the man for his work. As soon as he had gone she grabbed the picture and walked out of the room, slamming the door behind her.

Piet rushed from his observation post. "Must try to find out where she goes," he said. "Sorry—we'll talk about things later."

Mr Constantine's room was reached by an elegant flight of stairs from the hall on the ground floor. As Piet got to the top of the stairs the woman was at the bottom. She walked straight out of the building and he followed her. Outside, she was standing on the edge of the pavement, obviously looking for a taxi.

Piet took no notice of her, but turned and walked away towards Grosvenor Square.

It was not a good time for taxis—people were leaving offices, going home after shopping, or going off to early cocktail parties. Three taxis came by—all occupied. Then Piet had a stroke of luck. He spotted an empty cab with its "For Hire" light showing, and beckoned to the driver. The man drew up beside him. As he did so the woman with the picture came running down the pavement. "I want to go to Liverpool Street," she said.

"Sorry, miss," said the taxi-driver. "This gentleman has already booked me."

"Nonsense. I saw you coming, and I waved to you. Besides, I'm in a hurry."

The taxi-driver was firm. "I didn't see you at all, miss. I did see this gentleman, he signalled to me and I came to pick him up. 'Fraid you'll have to wait for another cab."

Piet offered a compromise. "I'm going to Bishopsgate," he said. "If the driver doesn't mind I'll be delighted to offer you a lift. Liverpool Street will do fine for me—I can easily walk from there to where I want to get."

"O.K. But make up your mind. Can't wait here in this traffic all the bloody evening," the taxi-driver said.

"It's extremely good of you. Of course I'll pay my share," the woman said. Piet opened the door for her, helped her with the big picture, and followed her into the cab. After it had moved off he tried to make polite conversation. "Are you an artist?" he asked.

"Oh, no. I've just been buying a picture as a wedding present for a friend," she said. "It's a bulky thing to carry. That's why I needed a taxi."

She showed no readiness for further talk. Piet, who thought that she had behaved rather stupidly with Mr Constantine, was interested in another stupidity in her lie. A picture as a wedding present—reasonable enough. But if you go to Gavell and Gainsworth to buy a picture you are probably going to spend a lot of money. She had implied that it was the picture which made her want to travel by taxi, that she would not normally do so. The sort of person who would go to Gavell and Gainsworth as a private customer would be more likely to take taxis as a matter of course.

At Liverpool Street Piet again helped her with the picture, and got out of the cab, too. "You can drop me here," he said to the driver. "I've only a short way to go, and it will save you making an awkward turn in Bishopsgate traffic." Not wanting any argument about extra payment for letting the woman share the cab he paid the man twice the fare shown on the clock.

The woman waited while the cab drove off. "How much do I owe you?" she asked.

"Well, I had to come here anyway. Let's forget it."

"That's very kind of you. The lift has been a tremendous help. Thank you very much." For the first time she gave him a genuine little smile. It made her rather hard face much more attractive. "Goodbye, then," Piet said, and walked off towards Bishopsgate.

He did not go far. Fortunately it was a crowded time for people hurrying to the station, and after two women and a man had passed him he turned round. The woman who called herself Mrs Vincent was easily identifiable by the big package she was carrying, and she was still in sight. Piet followed her discreetly, making sure that there were always several other people between them. He hoped that she would go to the booking office, but she did not. It was after six o'clock now, and the station bars were open. She went into one of them. It had a big plate-glass window, through which Piet could follow her movements clearly. She went to the bar, ordered what looked like a gin and tonic, carried her glass to a small table and sat down, propping the picture against the table.

Piet wanted badly to telephone for assistance, but he couldn't risk taking his eyes off the woman while he went to a phone-box. He considered what to do. On the wall near the entrance to the bar were pasted a set of timetables, which he could read while still keeping an eye on the door. He went over to them. There was a train leaving for Colchester in five minutes, one for Cambridge in twelve minutes, and one for Norwich and Yarmouth in thirty-five minutes. The woman would scarcely have sat down for a drink with five minutes to catch a train, so he thought that Colchester could be ruled out. Cambridge was possible, but she would still be cutting it rather fine. The Yarmouth line seemed the best bet, leaving her comfortable time for a drink but not long enough to do much else. She had not seemed hurried in the taxi—she had glanced at her watch once, but that was all. True, she had told the taxi-driver that she was in a hurry, but that could have been simply an argument to persuade him to abandon Piet and take her. Having to get through London traffic from the West End to the City she might well have been worried about catching either the Colchester or the Cambridge train, and kept on looking at her watch. But she hadn't, which was another indication that she was making for neither of them.

Piet had another look through the bar window. She was still sitting comfortably over her drink. Of course she might not be going anywhere by train, but have arranged to meet someone in the bar. Or she might be going to Southend, or to any of half a hundred suburban places served from Liverpool Street. He would just have to go on watching her. He tried to assess the probabilities of a suburban journey. The Liverpool Street lines are much used by commuters, for convenience and to avoid the problems of car parking, but she didn't look as if she had just come from an office, and she would have had to leave early to keep an appointment with Mr Constantine at five o'clock. That wasn't impossible, and if she had a season ticket to Liverpool Street she would naturally use it to get home. But there were dozens of suburban trains, and if she wanted to get home it seemed improbable that she would waste time by sitting in a bar. He couldn't rule out a suburban destination, but decided that the probabilities were either a main line journey, or the use of the bar for a meeting place. If a main line journey, the Yarmouth train seemed quite likely.

If she went by train, he would have to go too. And he couldn't afford to be ticketless. Production of his warrant card and a word of explanation would doubtless get him on the train, but it would mean delay at the barrier, and might draw attention to him. There was time to go to the booking office. Where to book a ticket for was a gamble, but it might as well be Yarmouth. It was the end of that particular line, it would get him on the train without fuss, and if she got out at Norwich or some other intermediate stopping place it wouldn't matter much—he could just tell the ticket collector that he'd decided to break his journey.

The few minutes at the booking office were a panic of anxiety, with infinite relief when he got back to the bar to see that the woman was still there. There were now twenty-five minutes to go before the train. If he had guessed rightly, she ought to be moving soon, for the train would probably be in, and she'd want to be sure of getting a seat.

With twenty minutes to go she did get up, collected her picture, and left the bar. While she was walking from her table to the door Piet slipped back to the timetables, and stood studying them with his back to the door. He allowed a moment of extra time for get-

ting the bulky picture through the swing door, and
then turned. She was making for the main line platforms, and he felt the thrill of the successful hunter
when he saw that she was going towards an entrance
over which an indicator-board announced a train for
Norwich and Yarmouth. She must have had a return
ticket, for the ticket inspector let her through, and
she walked along the train. Piet watched until he saw
her get into a carriage, and then followed her to the
train.

She had chosen a carriage about the middle of the
train. Piet decided to get into the rear carriage: he
need then look only one way when the train stopped
to see if she got out. He couldn't relax until the train
started, in case the whole business of going by train
was an elaborate blind, and she intended to go back
before the train pulled out. He let down the window
in the door of his compartment, opened the door,
and stood on the platform behind it looking through
the open window. The door effectively masked him,
and he doubted if the woman, getting out from
several carriages along, could notice that she was
being observed.

Unless a train is very crowded, people seldom
choose the rear compartment. This may reflect a kind
of folk-wisdom in avoiding a point of danger should
one train run into another, or it may be simply that
people want to be nearer the station exit when they
get to where they are going. This was not a particularly crowded train, and no one else made for Piet's
compartment. He stayed where he was until there was
half a minute to go, when he returned to the compartment, shut the door, and stood looking out of the
window. There was no sign of the woman, and no
one got out of the train before it left.

With his destination still unknown, at least the
journey had started. Piet now had time to feel hungry. Having to take Sally to Greenwich before going

on to keep his appointment with Mr Constantine, they'd made do with a sandwich in a pub for lunch, and that seemed almost a lifetime ago. There was a restaurant car on the train and the fact that he *could* have a meal made Piet hungrier still, but he decided that he could not risk it. It seemed more than likely that the woman would go to the restaurant car, and if Piet were there she would almost certainly recognise him. A policeman's lot, Piet reflected, traditionally is not a happy one, and it wasn't the first time that he'd had to go hungry on duty, and probably it wouldn't be the last. Worse than being hungry was his anxiety about Sally. He had told her that he would telephone during the evening to let her know what was happening; he had warned her that he might get so involved that he couldn't manage to phone, but that wasn't much comfort, because no one without actual experience of police work can really understand that there are occasions when it is just impossible to find the few minutes needed for a phone call. Sally would be worried, and uncertain about her class at Lavenham tomorrow. But there was nothing he could do about it until he left the train, and since he had to try to follow the woman to her destination it might still be hours before he could safely take time off to find a telephone. Mentally he kicked himself for not having his police radio with him—alas, that was in his car. Thinking that he was going to overhear a conversation between the art dealer and the woman he knew as Mrs Vincent of Moat Cottage, he had not envisaged any need to follow her when she left the building, he had not thought of a situation in which he might be left completely cut off. That was a bad mark against him—he ought to have thought about it, and although he was in plain clothes he ought to have had his radio. In his defence, he told himself, there would not have been much opportunity of using it. There wasn't time before he left Mr Constantine's office because he had to go after the woman at once, he couldn't have used it in the taxi without telling the woman that she was a suspect, and he could scarcely have used it at Liverpool Street without drawing attention to himself. He had a defence of sorts, but he didn't think much of it, and convicted himself of a bad piece of carelessness, of taking too much for granted.

What else was he taking for granted? He ought to have paid more attention to Sally's evidence that Mrs Vincent might not have been in London the day before yesterday, but having seen what was apparently her card in the art dealer's possession he had discounted the possibility that Sally could be right. He went back over his conversation with Sally. Mrs Vincent's assistant, the man called Wilson, was an absentee from Moat Cottage, but unless he was a brilliant performer at female disguise he could not have been the woman who had called twice on Mr Constantine. Sex is not always easy to determine, but Piet had no practical doubt that the woman he was now following, the woman he had listened to in the art dealer's office, the woman with whom he had shared a taxi, was indeed a woman. Had Sally told him anything else about the Moat Cottage crew the significance of which he might have missed? He didn't think so. They had ignored the students, which was perhaps unwise, but there had not been time to go into the movements of everybody, and whatever was being done with the pseudo-Constable paintings was not a casual matter, likely to relate to the students and holiday makers who came and went. Then he thought of a chance remark of Sally's which had no obvious bearing on anything else. Reporting Mrs Vincent's reference to the cleaning woman, Mrs Marshall, she had described her as coming from somewhere on the coast—it was the sea air in her girlhood which kept her well. Why not? It was just the kind of remark that one woman chatting to another might make. Mrs Vincent had been speaking of her fears lest the invaluable cleaning woman should fall ill, and comforted herself with the reflection that Suffolk folk are tough, adding a particular reason for toughness in Mrs Marshall's case. Again, why not? But it was another curious link between the Moat Cottage group at Lavenham and the coast, like the sprig of sea lavender that already seemed to link them. Could Mrs Marshall ever have had anything to do with Poplar's Fen? It was possible, but even if she had spent her youth around Walberswick or Dunwich, what could it matter? Apparently she had been living at Lavenham for years, and it was hard to see that her place of birth could have any significance whatever. Nevertheless, Piet was so shaken by his earlier neglect of Sally's observation that he decided it would be just as well to go into Mrs Marshall's background. That could be done easily enough by the local police. It certainly couldn't be done now.

The train's first stop was at Norwich, a run of some two hours and twenty minutes. When the ticket inspector came around he said that they were running a bit late—there had been a hold-up caused by the derailment of some goods waggons earlier in the day, and he was afraid that it would be nearer three hours before they made Norwich, and they might be nearly an hour late at Yarmouth. This did not particularly matter to Piet as far as following the woman was concerned, but it worried him because it would make it later than ever before he had a chance to telephone. However, there was nothing to be done about it, and at least his mental criticism of himself gave him something to think about, and made the time pass relatively quickly. When they did draw into Norwich he did as he had done at Liverpool Street—opened the carriage door and stood behind it to watch the people getting out from farther up the train. It was getting late in the evening and the light, even on the lighted platform, was not all that good, but Piet was reasonably confident of seeing the big parcel of the picture, and he was satisfied that the woman had not left the train at Norwich.

After Norwich the train ceased to be an express, and stopped at a number of country stations—Brundall, Lingwood and Acle. Not many people got out at any of them, and although it was dark the platforms were lighted, and Piet was sure that the woman was not among the passengers leaving the train.

By the time they reached Yarmouth it was close on eleven p.m. Piet adopted different tactics here: he was out of the train before it had quite stopped moving, and through the barrier at the exit before any other passengers got there. Beyond the barrier, and a few yards to one side of it, was an automatic vending machine, dispensing chocolate. Piet stood against the wall on the far side of the machine, confident that he could see everybody coming through without himself being noticeable. The woman with her picture-parcel was among the last group of people to emerge—presumably the awkward parcel had prevented her from walking quickly. Piet watched her go out of the station, and then followed. In the stationyard was a queue of about half a dozen people waiting for taxis. The woman took her place at the end of the queue.

The taxi trade seemed fairly brisk, and the queue cleared in about ten minutes. It was a nuisance that the woman was at the end of the queue, because it meant that Piet could not join the queue with a safeguarding knot of people between him and the woman, but in another way it helped, because when her turn came two taxis drew up at almost the same moment. Piet slipped behind the second taxi and was near enough to hear the woman tell the driver of the first, "Can you take me to the Yare Haven, please?" She got in and the cab drove off. Piet got into the sec-

ond cab, asking for the Yare Haven, too. There was
not much traffic at that time of night, and for most of
the way he could see the lights of the leading cab
ahead of them. For a few minutes another car came
between them, but it didn't matter because Piet knew
where the woman's cab was going. Indeed, he thought
that probably it was rather a good thing, in case the
woman should be looking back, though he had no
reason to suppose that she had any idea that she was
being followed.

The town of Yarmouth is really on an island, or
rather, on what was once an island, a long thin finger
of higher ground in the complex of shoals and sand-
banks off the mouth of the River Yare. The river
curls southwards to get round this strip of land, and
the town is, as it were, between the river and the sea,
providing splendid shelter for the lower reaches of
the river. The Haven, sought thankfully by seamen
since Saxon times, and probably by our prehistoric
forebears fishing from coracles, is really in the river.
It is a busy port now, its traditional trade in fish and
timber augmented by supply ships serving the oil-rigs
in the North Sea. There are fine quays along the
river, with bollards for the mooring of ships.

The woman's taxi stopped at a gate leading to one
of the quays. Reckoning that a woman, having to get
money from her handbag, takes longer to pay a cab-
driver than a man, who has simply to take money
from his pocket, and that this woman, having to
struggle with her big parcel, would take longer still,
Piet asked his taxi-driver to go past. "I really want the
next gate," he said.

That was at the end of a row of sheds, about a
hundred yards ahead. Piet paid his man quickly, with
a generous tip, and doubled back in the darkness of
the wall of sheds. He was right in his calculations, for
he had almost reached the other gate by the time the
woman had finished paying off her taxi. Not wanting

to be caught in the headlights of the cab, he pressed himself against the wall, turning away his head so that the whiteness of his face should not show up. As soon as the cab had gone he ran to the gate.

The main gates, for vehicles, were closed for the night, but a little wicket-gate, for people on foot, was unlocked. He had not lost much by having to wait for the departure of the cab, for the woman had to put down her parcel to open the wicket-gate, and he got there a few seconds after she had gone through it. He could see her walking a few yards ahead, and then turn right along the quay in front of the sheds. As soon as she was clear of his direct line of sight he followed her through the gate, turned right also, and picked her up again about twenty yards in front of him. She went about halfway along the quay, and then made for the waterfront.

There were vessels moored all along the quay, but it was near low water, and there was no sign of a boat where the woman went. Astern was a bigger vessel. her superstructure still above the line of the quay. Piet slipped into the shadow of this and looked ahead. Moored below where the woman was standing was a motor cruiser—the cruiser, he was sure, from Poplar's Fen. The cabin portholes were curtained, but light was showing through them.

At low water the deck of the cruiser was several feet below the quayside. Rungs of vertical iron steps, set into the wall of the quay, made it easy enough to go on board, but the woman did not make for them. Instead, she hunted about on the ground, found a pebble or small stone, and threw it on to the cruiser's cabin-top. A moment later the door leading aft to the cockpit opened, and a man came out. Piet was near enough to hear everything. "You're dreadfully late, Trish. I was getting very worried about you," the man said.

"The damned train was late. And I've had to

bring back the picture. Can you help me get it down?"

"What went wrong? But you can tell me about it later. Hold on, and I'll come up and you can hand the thing to me."

The man climbed a few rungs of the iron ladder, took the picture from the woman, and laid it carefully in the cockpit. "You'd better take my bag, too, and then I'll come down. I need both hands for the ladder," she said. A few moments later she was on board. "God, I need a drink. I've had a hellish day." She almost spat out the words. Without even bothering to collect her handbag she went into the cabin. The man, still holding the bag, picked up the picture and followed her, shutting the door after him.

There seemed no sign of the cruiser's imminent departure, and in any case Piet doubted if they would leave at night. But they would have to be watched. He couldn't stay on the quay all night by himself, and there were many things that he wanted to do. He had noticed a phone-box near the entrance to the quay, and as the occupants of the cruiser were presumably having a drink and discussing the day's events, he reckoned that it would be safe to leave them for a few minutes. He telephoned Yarmouth police station, and explained who he was. The precautions taken by the Yard paid off. "Yes, we had a message about you from the Metropolitan Police a couple of days back, asking us to give you any assistance you might need," the duty officer said. "What can we do for you, sir?"

"I'm speaking from a box on the quay at Yare Haven, just inside Gate No. 3. It's imperative to maintain a watch on a boat moored here. Can you send an officer to take over from me, and a car to take me to your station?"

"Do you want the watch all night?"

"I'm afraid so, yes."

"And do you want a uniformed man, or a man in plain clothes?"

"Plain clothes would be better."

"Right, sir. I won't call a patrol car, but send one of the duty men from here, with a driver to bring you back. He should be with you in about a quarter of an hour. Where can he meet you?"

"At Gate No. 3. It's locked at night so the car won't be able to come on to the quay, but that's just as well, for we don't want to show ourselves. You can get on to the quay on foot through a side gate. I'll be waiting just through the gate."

"I know those gates. Very good, sir. We'll get a man to you as soon as possible."

Piet was tempted to telephone Sally at Greenwich, but he'd been away from the cruiser for several minutes, and although he didn't think that anything much could be happening on board, he wanted to get back. He returned to his old post in the shadow of the ship astern. There were still lights in the cabin of the cruiser, but he could hear nothing. He waited for ten minutes, and then walked to the gate. Yarmouth police were as good as their word. In slightly under the promised quarter of an hour a car drew up at the gate, and a CID man in plain clothes met Piet on the quay.

"Chief Inspector Deventer?" he asked.

"Yes, and very glad to see you," Piet said.

"I'm Detective-Constable Hart. The duty officer said I'd get instructions from you."

"About halfway along the quay there's a motor-cruiser moored—I'll take you to her in a minute. There's quite a good observation post in the shadow of a bigger vessel lying astern. On board the cruiser are a man and a woman—as far as I know they're the only people on board, but I can't be absolutely sure. The woman's Christian name is Trish—for Patricia, I suppose—and the man is called Malcolm. The surname is Winterer, or something like that. We suspect them of being concerned in an elaborate art fraud, and possibly implicated in murder. I want you to keep an eye on the cruiser. If she shows any signs of leaving, telephone your HQ and the harbour authorities at once. If either the man or the woman comes ashore without carrying anything, it will probably be to telephone. Do what you can to make out the number dialled, and to overhear anything of the conversation. You probably won't be able to do much about either, but if you can pick up anything it will be useful. If either of them comes ashore carrying a picture in a big parcel, about a yard square, follow whoever it is and try to discover where he or she goes.

"But I don't expect either of them to come ashore, and I doubt if the boat will leave before daylight. I'll be back, I hope with some help and another boat, well before then. I'm afraid you'll probably have a dull few hours of just watching. But you know how it is—and this is a job that's just got to be done."

"I understand, sir, and of course I'll do my best."

"I'm sure you will, and I'm very grateful to you. I'll show you the boat, and then I'll use your car to get to your police station. The sooner I get there, the sooner I'll be back to relieve you."

Somewhat to his embarrassment Piet was taken to the Superintendent's office where he found a small reception committee awaiting him. The duty officer explained. "This is Superintendent Barnes and the other gentleman is Detective-Inspector Lennard," he said. "In all the circumstances I thought I'd better inform the Superintendent of your call, and he decided to come down."

"And I picked up Lennard on the way," the Superintendent added.

"Lord, I'm sorry to have got you out of bed," Piet said.

"Not the first time, my boy." Superintendent Barnes was a kindly, much-liked officer, within a year or so of retirement. "Tell us about it, and we'll see if we can help. Wait a minute, though—you look a bit done in. When did you last have anything to eat?"

"Oh, some time this morning."

"You mean yesterday morning—it's well after midnight. We don't have the canteen staff on at night, but at least we can manage a cup of tea and a couple of cheese rolls, though it will have to be yesterday's bread. Slip up to the canteen, Bill, and see what you can get," he said to the duty officer. "Make a big pot of tea—we could all do with a cup."

When the man had gone he said to Piet, "We had a message from the Metropolitan Police saying that a Chief Inspector Deventer would be pursuing inquiries in our area in connection with a case in London, and asking us to assist if he called upon us. Are you Chief Inspector Deventer?"

"Yes. I'm not really poaching on your manor."

"Come off it, young man! Sorry, I ought to have said Chief Inspector, but you must make allowances for age and length of service. What's it all about?"

The tea came, and with it a plate with a cheese roll and a small pork pie. "I'm not listening to a word more until you've eaten something," the Superintendent said.

Piet was thankful for the food, and ate it quickly. Over a cup of tea he gave a brief outline of the finding of the dead girl in a train at Liverpool Street, of the inquiries that led to her identification, of the curious colony at Poplar's Fen, and of the pursuit that had brought him to Yarmouth. "It's a horribly complex case," he went on. "The girl was undoubtedly murdered. The fact that no container of any sort for pills was found points to murder rather than suicide, though that alone is not enough to rule out suicide. The arsenic revealed by the autopsy seems to make it certain that someone intended to kill her. The pictures she had with her, and the other picture taken to London by the woman I followed this evening, suggests a carefully worked out scheme for dealing in either stolen or forged paintings. One would think that the girl's death was related to the art frauds, but I'm afraid I have no evidence yet to explain how. On the other hand, I think I am in a position to make an arrest, though it will have to be on a holding charge."

"Do you want to arrest the man and woman on the boat here?"

"No. There is strong suspicion that they are involved in the art frauds, and that's why I need to have them watched. I expect the motor-cruiser to leave Yarmouth in the morning, and I was going to ask if you can get hold of a sea-going boat to follow her."

"We can get a boat all right. There's a small fleet of tenders serving the oil-rigs. They're powerful, sturdy craft, and I'm sure we can borrow one. Where do you expect the cruiser to make for?"

"I don't know. She's capable of the crossing to Holland, but she may go no farther than Poplar's Fen—that's about twenty miles down the coast. The vital thing is that we should discover where she does go."

"Well, the oil-rig tenders work in the North Sea in all weathers, they have fine crews, and they could certainly get over to Holland if necessary. Get on to the Harbourmaster, Bill. Tell him the sort of boat we want, though you'd better not say anything about why. Say we need her now, ready to sail at short notice, perhaps at first light. The Harbourmaster's a good sort, and I'm sure he can fix it for us. Ask him to ring back as soon as possible with the name of the boat and where she's lying." To Piet he said, "How many men do you want to go with you?"

"Two would be enough, I think. And I rather feel that they should be armed."

"Where do you expect to make your arrest?"

"Probably at Poplar's Fen. I doubt if a seagoing oil-rig tender could get over the bar, and in any case it would be better not to follow the cruiser into the Fen. If the cruiser goes there we could be put ashore at Walberswick, and go on by road. If she doesn't make for the Fen then I'd like myself and one of your men put ashore, leaving one officer on the tender to see what happens to the cruiser."

The superintendent studied a big map hanging on the wall. "Poplar's Fen is well south of Lowestoft, and not in my division," he said. "I can certainly help with the boat, and provide a couple of men to follow the cruiser from Yarmouth, but I think I'd better ask my opposite number at Lowestoft to have some men waiting for you at Walberswick—you will be going ashore there, anyway. And if the cruiser's got to be followed beyond Poplar's Fen I think both my men ought to stay on board. They will have to follow your customers when they land, and they can easily split up. Do you want the Lowestoft men armed?"

"I think it would be safer, yes."

"Well, it's not for me to teach you your business, but if there's a possibility of real trouble, two men are not going to be enough. I'm going to ask Lowestoft to have four men waiting for you at Walberswick, shall we say from eight o'clock onwards?"

"That's immensely good of you. Eight o'clock should be all right. Even if the cruiser leaves at first light, I don't see how she could be there before eight. She'd have to average over rather than under ten knots—possible, but I doubt it."

"The oil-rig tender will be capable of a good deal more than that, so you'll have power in hand to get ahead of her and keep her in sight. By the way, I'd better tell Lowestoft that you'll need a car with their men, or rather, two cars. There'll be five of you, and you'll need another car if you succeed in making your arrest."

"Would you like me to go with the Chief Inspector on the tender?" Detective-Inspector Lennard asked.

"You took the thought out of my head! Can you get one of your lads to go with you?"

"Yes, I'll see to it now."

"And I'll get on to Lowestoft. I'd better do that myself, because we're asking quite a lot of them."

"I told your man watching the cruiser that I'd get back to relieve him as soon as I could," Piet said.

"I don't know how you work in the Metropolitan Police, but in my division Chief Inspectors are supposed to get a bit of rest sometimes. You'll be busy enough as soon as we've fixed up the tender. You stay here and have another cup of tea. We'll see to the relief."

"I can only say thank you again. I also want to make a call to London. Can I use one of your phones?"

"Of course. Use the phone in here, and I'll get on to Lowestoft from the duty room."

Piet rang his mother's home at Greenwich. It was dreadfully late, but he half-hoped that Sally might be waiting up for the telephone to ring. In any case, his mother had an extension phone beside her bed. It was his mother who answered.

"I'm awfully sorry to wake you up, but can you get hold of Sally for me? It's quite important," Piet said.

"But she's not here! She left around ten o'clock. She was expecting a call from you all evening, and when it didn't come she said she thought you might need her, and that she knew where you'd probably be. She asked where she could hire a car at that time of night, and I said she could have my Mini—you know I hardly ever use it nowadays."

IX

At Sea

Piet's instinct was to get hold of a car at once and drive to Poplar's Fen, but he couldn't undo all the arrangements he'd just made, and there was no certainty that Sally would even be at the Fen. Where else could she possibly have gone? To look for him at New Scotland Yard? That was absurd—she wouldn't need a car, for at ten o'clock there were still trains and buses into London, and she would know that if he could get to his office he'd have telephoned, or got someone to telephone for him. To Lavenham for her art class? She couldn't possibly have wanted to leave at ten o'clock at night for Lavenham. For some sinister purpose that he couldn't even guess? He admitted to himself that he was more than a little in love with Sally—had he been a fool to trust her? He knew next to nothing of her background—was she really working against him, reporting everything he said and did to someone else? Quite possible, but he couldn't bring himself to believe it. It was at least equally possible that she had felt that something had taken him out of London, and that he had some urgent reason for returning to the Fen. Well, if she was as close to him as he felt himself to be to her she was right about his having to leave London, but wrong in calculating that he must have returned to the Fen. If his other suspicions were anything like right she could well be in considerable danger in turning up at the Fen in the middle of the night. Should he get a police party sent there forthwith, to search the place and try to find Sally? That might invite the very danger he feared—it doesn't take long to shoot someone. And he still didn't really *know* enough: he knew what he wanted to do when he got back to the Fen, but he couldn't possibly explain the instincts, feelings and suspicions that had been building up in his mind to an unknown police officer at the other end of a telephone. To invoke a dramatic police invasion in the middle of the night might wreck everything, and scatter all the evidence he hoped to find. The harsh truth was that there was *nothing* he could do immediately to help Sally. If she had gone back to the Fen she'd have to take her chance, poor kid, and he could only pray that he'd get there in the morning in time to prevent the worst of his fears from being realised. He'd been banking on the fact that no one else at Poplar's Fen could yet know precisely what he was beginning to understand. Reason told him that he was probably right, and if so Sally might be in no immediate danger. But reason is one thing, imagination another, and imagination here was not greatly comforted by reason. Yet reason had to win. He must stay where he was, wait for his plans to be carried out, and do nothing to alert those it was his job to pursue even if it meant doing nothing at the moment for Sally.

The teapot was quite cold now, but worry made him thirsty, and pouring out a cup of cold tea at least gave him something to do. He was drinking cold tea when the superintendent came back. "All fixed up, my boy," he said. "The tender *Daffodil* is waiting for you at the Lower Quay—that's only a few hundred yards from where your cruiser's moored. She's fully crewed and was going out anyway in the morning, but they've managed to switch her job to another boat. So she's all yours. It'll cost the ratepayers a bit for the charter, but I'll see if I can send the bill to the Metropolitan Police. No need to worry about that now—and if the public wants to be protected against crime they've damned well got to pay for it. Lowestoft's been jolly good, but they don't like your idea of coming ashore at Walberswick."

"I was thinking of doing that in a dinghy from the tender," Piet said.

"Yes, but they don't think much of it. They say you'd do better to let the tender take you into Southwold. She can get in there, it's only a wee bit north of Walberswick across the River Blyth, and as far as getting by road to Poplar's Fen is concerned they reckon it makes next to no odds. So if you approve, Detective-Sergeant Skinner with three men and two cars will be waiting for you on the quay at Southwold from eight o'clock on. All we've got to do is to phone back and say if you agree."

"Of course I agree—they know the coast far better than I do."

"Good. That's all laid on, then. At this end Jim Lennard and a constable are ready to go off with you to the *Daffodil*. I know her skipper slightly—go fishing with him sometimes. He's a man called Mick Mallory—but everybody calls him Mick. Give him my regards, and he'll do anything for you. He's a Yarmouth man, and reckoned among the finest seamen on the coast."

Piet glanced at his watch. It was just after four a.m. "It's getting on towards dawn, and I think we'll go off now," he said.

"Right. I'll phone Lowestoft about the change to Southwold. Good luck."

"I can't begin to thank you properly."

"Get away with you! We're all policemen, doing

the same job. Come back and spend a holiday in Yarmouth. And we'll go fishing with Mick."

Daffodil was a small diesel-engined tug, workmanlike in looks, and specially built for the job of serving oilrigs in the North Sea. She could tow heavy floating equipment, carry engineering stores, or food and water. It was work that called for seamanship of the highest order, for loading or unloading anything from a rig meant going as nearly as possible alongside, with the constant risk of being carried on to the vulnerable legs of the rig by the vicious North Sea swell.

The tide had risen considerably since Piet had left his observation post on the other quay, and it was only a step from the quayside on to *Daffodil's* after deck. Skipper Mallory met them as they came on board. "Don't often get a police job. How's my old pal the super?" he asked.

"Particularly asked me to bring you his regards," Piet said. "I'm Chief Inspector Deventer of the Metropolitan Police. You probably know Inspector Lennard of the Yarmouth force, and this is Constable Macleod."

"Glad to meet you. Mick's the name here. Come into our grand saloon for a bit of breakfast and tell me just what you want us to do."

The "grand saloon" was an all-purpose cuddy under the bridge deck forrard, with a table bolted to the deck, a settee-berth along one side and a passageway on the other. There were three doors, one leading to the fo'c'sle, one to a tiny cabin, and one to the galley. The table was laid for a meal, and almost as soon as they got there the deckhand/cook appeared with a huge pot of tea, went away and came back with a tray of plates of bacon and eggs. "Not knowing when you want us to sail, thought we might as well start with

breakfast. Never go anywhere without breakfast—
that's my motto," Skipper Mick said.

The bacon and eggs, and a thick slice of bread and
butter, made Piet feel better. He explained that he
wanted *Daffodil* to follow a motor cruiser moored on
the Upper Quay, which he expected to sail soon after
daylight. "We'll be able to see her from the bridge,
with glasses, anyway, when it's light enough," the
skipper said. "We'll go up after breakfast, for it's getting light now. Where's she making for?"

"That's the point—I don't know," Piet said. "My
guess is that she'll make for Poplar's Fen, just south
of Walberswick, but I don't know."

"Not going into Poplar's Fen in *Daffodil*! I know
that entrance because I've done it in a small fishing
boat. There's a dangerous bar, though there's quite a
good anchorage in the river when you get inside."

"I'm not suggesting that you should go in. I want
to see if the cruiser goes there. If she does, I'd like
you to drop us all off at Southwold, and then your
job's done. If she doesn't, I want you to drop me at
Southwold, and follow the cruiser with Inspector
Lennard and Constable Macleod."

"Won't take long to nip into Southwold. I'd suggest
we get ahead of her and hang about off Southwold.
Then we can see what she does, and act according. I
know that coast pretty well, but come up on the
bridge and we'll have a look at the chart."

It was light enough to see across the river. There
were no yachts lying to the Lower Quay—all craft
there were working boats, like *Daffodil*. On the Upper Quay there were several yachts, with some working vessels, among them the small freighter in the
shadow of whose superstructure Piet had stood to
watch the cruiser. He identified the freighter first,
and having found her it was easy to spot the cruiser.
She was lying as he had left her, though with the ris-

ing tide she was more nearly level with the quayside. There was no sign of any movement on board.

Piet pointed her out to the skipper. "I'll get my mate to keep an eye on her," he said. "He can see if anyone comes on deck to unmoor. As soon as there's any sign of that we'll get out into the stream. We can hang around for a few minutes, and then follow at a safe distance. Now for that chart."

The mate took post on the bridge to watch the cruiser, while Piet and the skipper studied the chart. "What do you reckon she can do?" the skipper asked.

"Well, I've never been on her, so I don't know. But she seems to be built for comfort rather than speed. I'd give her around ten knots, perhaps twelve going all out."

"Without a tow we can do well over twenty," the skipper said. "Even if we have to lose time putting into Southwold she won't be able to get away. See, it's just like I thought. We can be off Southwold a couple of miles ahead of her, and wait to see if she's making for the entrance to the Fen. She's low in the water, but there's no mist this morning and visibility looks like being good. From a position off Southwold, with the glasses, we should be able to see pretty well to the Poplar's Fen entrance. If he's really going in there, sooner him than me."

"He's done it several times before—he has a mooring on the river."

"Well, good luck to him. Or perhaps you don't want him to have good luck."

"I don't want him to be wrecked on the Fen bar. I suspect him of being a bad lot, but we should have to try to rescue him, and that would be a lot of trouble for everybody, besides standing *Daffodil* into danger."

"We should have to do it all the same. So I'll say good luck to him, in a navigational sense, anyway."

At eight o'clock there was still no sign of movement

on the cruiser, but a few minutes after eight the mate called out from the bridge, "Looks like she's getting under way."

The skipper had a look through his own binoculars, and then handed them to Piet. The man had already cast off forrard, and the woman was holding the stern line. There was no wheelhouse proper on the cruiser: she was steered from a wheel set to port on the cabin bulkhead, at the fore end of the cockpit, over which a canvas canopy could be extended to provide some shelter from the weather. The canopy was not extended now. Piet saw the man give the bow a push from the quay with a boathook, and then go to the wheel, handing the boathook to the woman in the stern. She hauled in the mooring line, gave another shove with the boathook, and the cruiser moved out slowly into the stream.

Having taken his own look, the skipper did not wait for any further news from either Piet or the mate. He ordered *Daffodil* to cast off and get under way, and took the wheel himself. "Tide's still making," he said, "and we've got to be careful passing the south pier, because of the eddy there. Can be troublesome to a biggish vessel, because your bow can be pushed one way while your stern is still trying to go another. Doubt if it will worry him much, he's not long enough. And it won't bother us, because I know all about it. I think we'll wait to see him through before we follow."

With skilful use of wheel and engine he held *Daffodil* in midstream while the cruiser gathered way and made towards the entrance to the Haven. Watching through the glasses Piet saw her tossed about a bit as she caught the eddy mentioned by the skipper, but she got through safely and made towards the open sea. *Daffodil* put on power and followed her out.

"He's going south all right," the skipper said, "he's making for the Hewitt Channel. That's the main channel for anyone going south'ards—runs between the Scroby Bank and the Corton Sands. Runs east-south-east near enough, for two or three miles, until you pick up the North Corton buoy. With his draught he could probably get over most of Corton now, but if he's any sense he'll stick to the channel until he picks up the buoy. He's got to get a good offing to get round Lowestoft, and ESE is as good a course as any for him at the moment. We'll stay well behind him in the channel, and see what he does when he gets to the buoy."

Daffodil slowed down, keeping roughly half a mile astern of the cruiser. The sands blanketed the swell to some extent, and with the glasses Piet could make out two figures in the cockpit. The man was at the wheel, the woman sitting aft. They seemed to be in no particular hurry, going at about eight knots. At this rate it would be three hours or so before they could make the Fen. The sergeant and his man at Southwold would have a long wait. That couldn't be helped. The cruiser might have left a couple of hours earlier, she might be faster than she seemed, and if he was right he couldn't afford to take risks.

If he was right. . . . He tried not to show it, but he was in an agony of anxiety. If he was right the cruiser must be making for the Fen, but there was still so much he didn't know. He hated to keep men hanging about, particularly men from another force who were simply obeying instructions without knowing how they fitted into the scheme of things. "These bloody chaps from the Yard—think they own us mere yokels in the country," he could hear them saying. He was comforted to feel that they probably knew now that the cruiser and her pursuer had sailed. The Yarmouth superintendent would have kept a man watching the cruiser until she left, and he'd certainly let Lowestoft know. Suddenly he was worried by another thought—handcuffs. They might need handcuffs, and he'd forgotten to ask for any. Inspector Lennard was on the bridge beside him. "I've been a fool," Piet said. "It's quite possible that we're going to need handcuffs before we're through, and I forgot to ask you to bring any."

"Not to worry," Inspector Lennard said. "You said you might be going to make an arrest so we brought a couple of pairs as a matter of course. You can reckon that the Lowestoft men will surely have some, too." That was one fear relieved.

There were many which could not be relieved. What was happening, or had happened, to Sally? She might not be at Poplar's Fen at all, but he feared that probably she was. If he was wrong in his guesswork she might be in no danger at all. But if he was right, or even partly right, then danger to her would be real. The period of greatest danger, though, would probably not come until after Malcolm and Trish in the cruiser had got back to the Fen—they might not decide what to do with Sally until then. And by the grace of God he and the Lowestoft men could get there in time to rescue her.

There was nothing to be gained by pursuing such thoughts now. He tried to concentrate his mind on the cruiser, still well ahead of them. And he had a momentary distraction when the deckhand came round with mugs of steaming tea—a North Sea tender is apparently fuelled by tea almost as much as by diesel oil.

"There's the North Corton buoy, fine to star-board," the skipper said. Mick Mallory was over rather than under sixty, but his eyesight was superb. He'd picked up the buoy without glasses. Pointed out to him, Piet could see it, too, but he'd never have spotted it for himself. The cruiser passed the buoy, and made no immediate attempt to alter course. "If she holds this course, she'll be making for Holland," the skipper said.

That was a new worry. Piet had considered it theoretically possible that Trish and Malcolm might be heading for the Continent but he hadn't really believed it. Well, if they were, his contingency plans could still work. He'd pick up the Lowestoft men at Southwold and go with them to the Fen, leaving Lennard and the constable to follow the cruiser. "I'll get through to the Yard as soon as I can and get a message sent to the Dutch police," he thought. "If they're really going to Holland there should be time enough for that."

The cruiser held her course ESE for about another twenty minutes, then she did change course to the south. "Looks as if you're right," the skipper said. "He'll probably go more or less due south until he's clear of Lowestoft and then, if he's making for the Fen, he'll go about south-south-west. If he does turn SSW we can be pretty sure that he's going where you think he is. I reckon we'll get ahead of him now, and keep an eye on him astern."

Daffodil put on speed, and a few minutes later passed the cruiser, keeping well clear of her. Piet slipped into the little chartroom just behind the bridge as they came up. He had no reason to suppose that the people on the cruiser had the slightest interest in a tugboat going about her business in the North Sea, and at the distance they passed it would probably have been impossible for anyone in the low cockpit to recognise any figure on *Daffodil*'s bridge, but he acted instinctively. *Daffodil* had more than twice the speed of the cruiser, and the skipper kept up speed on a course of ESE until the cruiser was no more than a speck astern, and slightly to starboard of them. Then *Daffodil*, too, turned south, reduced speed, and followed a course parallel to that of the cruiser, well to the east of her. "He's low in the water and I doubt if he can even see us," the skipper said. "But we've still got a good view of him through the glasses. I reckon we want to get well ahead of him, to make time for putting into Southwold. Doubt if it matters much if we lost sight of him for a bit. On this course he's clearly not making for Lowestoft, and he's not going to Holland either, though I suppose he could still be making for Belgium or France. But we know where he is, and if we do lose sight of him we can go slow and soon pick him up again."

It was a strange pursuit, to be ahead of the quarry. Piet went over his reasoning anxiously. He could understand Yarmouth—with its access to the Broads, and its character as a holiday town as well as a port, it was a reasonable place for a motor-yacht to go, and if one wanted to get a train to London, who would know, or care, about it? It was not all that far from Poplar's Fen, but far enough for it to be unlikely that anyone from the colony there would be visiting the Haven. Lowestoft was nearer, but a yacht might attract more attention there, and he remembered from a sailing trip as a boy with his father the complexities of the tides sometimes at the entrance to Lowestoft. They could go south to Harwich, but it was a lot farther away. If you had a seagoing boat and wanted to go to London from Poplar's Fen without anyone's knowing about it, Yarmouth was about the best rail-head to make for.

It couldn't always be like that, though, for the cruiser was lying in the river on the afternoon that he and Sally got to the Fen, and that was the day when Trish, calling herself Mrs Vincent, had first visited Mr Constantine. The cruiser had been there, but Trish and Malcolm had not—at any rate, they hadn't met them that first evening at the mill. That was consistent with the woman having been in London, though on that occasion she had not travelled from Yarmouth. Sally said they had a car—perhaps they varied the procedure. Then he remembered Sally's remarks when he had asked if she knew their surname—Roger had asked if she'd met Malcolm *Winterer* at Lavenham. So they had some connection with Moat Cottage: what more reasonable to go to London via Lavenham and Sudbury as Sandra seemed to have done on her last journey?

Reasoning held together so far. Were Trish and Malcolm the couple in that curious attempt to break into the Lost Property office at Liverpool Street station, and in the burglary (if anything was taken) of Sandra's studio at Finsbury Park? Possible, but he had no means of knowing whether they were or were not at Poplar's Fen over those dates, because it was before he got there, and Sally had no real recollection of the cruiser's absences. Both performances struck him as somehow out of character with the rest of the case, though if he was right in his other assumptions he could see a possible reason for them.

Daffodil was now off Southwold, a couple of miles ahead of the cruiser, and about a mile to seaward of her. The skipper reduced speed to give *Daffodil* no more than steerage way. "I reckon we'd best hang about here until he passes inshore of us," he said. "We should be able to make out what he's going to do, and with the swell and his lowness in the water I doubt if he'll even notice us."

"I don't think it matters if he does," Piet said. "He's no means of knowing that we're interested in him."

It was a long twenty minutes before the cruiser was roughly level with the tender, well inshore of her. "He's going in all right," the skipper said. "Do you want me to put into Southwold now?"

"I'd like to make absolutely certain that he enters the Fen. Could we close the coast a bit?"

They did, until they could clearly see the breakers on the bar at the entrance to the Fen. "Wind against tide now," the skipper said. "Not a nice place. But with his draught, if he knows the entrance, he ought to get in all right."

They were well astern of the cruiser now, but still considerably offshore of her. She was making for the breakers, disappeared for a moment in a flurry of spray, and was then through. "That's that," Piet said. "Now for Southwold."

As *Daffodil* turned to make for Southwold Piet automatically glanced round the horizon. A speck in the distance made him suddenly feel sick. "Give me the glasses, please," he asked urgently.

He focussed the skipper's glasses, and saw that what he feared was real. The botter, under full sail, was standing out to sea.

"I've got to change my plans," he said. "Do you see that small sailing boat? I've got to get on board her before we do anything else." *Daffodil* put on speed, the botter became clearly visible, and the distance between them lessened rapidly. Piet had a hurried talk with Inspector Lennard. "I know that boat, I know the man on board her, and I've got to get hold of him," he said. "We must close her, and I'd like to go on board with Constable Macleod. The two of us will be enough to handle her, and I'll put back to the Fen. You must take charge of the Southwold party. After Macleod and I are on board the sailing boat—she's a Dutch boat, called a botter, and I suspect she's making for Holland—I want you to make full speed for Southwold. Collect the Lowestoft party, and get to Poplar's Fen as quickly as you possibly can. The cruiser will be moored in the river by then. Arrest the man and woman on board her—they're called Malcolm and Patricia Winterer, or at least that's the name they go by—on a charge of being concerned in attempting to defraud a firm of art dealers in London called Gavell and Gainsworth. Be very careful, for they may be dangerous and violent. If they give any trouble, arrest them for resisting the police, if you like. It doesn't matter what charge you arrest them on, for there'll be other much more serious charges to come. But get them in custody, handcuff them, and hold them till I can come. There'll be five of you. Three should be enough to hold the Winterers, and send the other two to guard the old watermill near where the cruiser's moored. There's a sort of artists' colony there, not quite hippies, but hippie-types. No one is to be allowed to leave the mill, and if anyone comes he or she is to be detained. I don't think you'll have much trouble with them, and I don't think— though I can't be sure—that any of them is mixed up in the other matters. You've got your revolver, and the Lowestoft men will be armed. I'm afraid you've got a horrible job ahead of you, and don't hesitate to shoot if you've got to. I take full responsibility for giving you these orders."

The skipper had again taken *Daffodil*'s wheel. He closed the botter, carefully coming up to leeward of her so as not to interfere with her handling. Piet and Constable Macleod went down to the tender's low after-deck, kept clear for the manipulation of towlines. "Take the loud-hailer," the skipper said to Piet as he left the bridge.

They were about thirty yards to leeward of the botter, and the skipper reduced speed to keep level with her. The man called Roger Leplan was standing at the high, curved tiller of the botter. Trudi was sitting in the cockpit beside him. Using the loud hailer Piet called out, "Please come alongside. I want to come on board you."

Roger had no loud-hailer, but his angry shout was audible enough. "Go to hell. I don't want you on board. I've got right of way under sail, so clear out."

"I am coming on board," Piet called.

"Then you'll get this." Roger produced an automatic pistol and fired a warning shot slightly astern of *Daffodil*.

"Don't be a fool," Piet shouted. "I've got an armed police party on board, and you can't possibly get away." Piet heard Trudi scream at Roger, "Shoot him! Or give me the gun and I'll shoot!"

The man at the tiller neither gave her the pistol, nor fired another shot. He held up one arm to signify that he was going to obey, freed the mainsheet and turned the botter into the wind so that she lay wallowing in the swell. The skipper ordered his crew to throw out fenders, and with consummate skill he brought *Daffodil* up to the sailing boat. "I want a line," Piet said. Roger threw a line, *Daffodil's* deckhand caught it, and put a turn round a belaying pin on the tender's counter. There was not much difference in height between the tender's low stern and the botter's narrow side-deck. Piet waited for the right moment of swell, and jumped. Trudi clawed at him, and he hit her roughly, knocking her to the floorboards of the cockpit. A moment later Constable Macleod was on board the botter, too. "Handcuff the woman and keep her quiet," Piet said. "I'll deal with the man."

Roger made no effort to resist. "I'll have that gun," Piet said. It was handed over, and he put it in his pocket. "Thank you," he said, "I'm afraid I want you handcuffed, too." Roger held out his hands meekly. "Thank God it's all over," he said.

"I'm sorry, but I'd prefer your hands behind your back." Roger obeyed this order with the same docility. "I'm not having you jump overboard with manacled hands. I want both you and Trudi in the cabin, and Constable Macleod can keep an eye on you. I must warn you that he is armed," Piet said.

Trudi was still lying on the floorboards, her hands also held by cuffs behind her back. "You weak-kneed swine! Why didn't you shoot when I told you to?" she said to Roger. He took no notice. The jib had not been backed when Roger turned into the wind, so the botter, although stopped, was not hove-to. Now the headsail was bringing her round, and the boom of the mainsail, although free so that there was no drive in the sail, swung viciously across the cockpit. Piet saw it coming. "Duck!" he shouted. Roger slumped on one of the cockpit lockers, and the constable, who, as a Yarmouth man, knew something about boats, got down beside Trudi. The botter was beginning to gather way from the headsail, and the line holding her to *Daffodil* had to be cast off.

"Are you all right?" the skipper called from *Daffodil.*

"O.K.," Piet called back. "Situation under control."

"Do you want a tow?"

"No thank you. I can handle things, and it's not far back to the Fen. I want you to go full speed ahead to Southwold—you'll be faster without a tow."

The skipper blew a blast on his siren. "Good luck," he and Inspector Lennard called together.

Piet hardened the mainsheet and tidied the jib sheets for the new tack. Then he took the tiller. "Go forrard into the cabin," he ordered Roger.

"You're doing quite well," Roger said mildly, "but I think you haven't much experience of sailing botters. You've forgotten the lee-board. You want to winch up the one that's down and let down the other."

"Thanks, I'll do it when you're safely in the cabin. Get forrard now." He couldn't understand the man's extraordinary docility, and didn't trust him an inch.

"You can't get into the cabin. It's locked, and I threw the key overboard," Trudi said from the floor.

Constable Macleod tried the door. It was certainly locked. Then he and Piet both heard a sort of scuffling noise coming from the other side. "I think there's someone else on board," Macleod said.

"Give the key to the constable," Piet ordered Trudi.

"How can I, with my hands like this? Besides, I haven't got it. I threw it into the sea."

With his left hand on the tiller, Piet drew Roger's pistol from his pocket. "Get down on the floor," he ordered Roger. "Break down the door, constable."

Constable Macleod weighed fourteen stone, and played for the local Rugby football club. The botter belonged to a period when boats were built of seasoned wood but three heaves from Macleod's powerful shoulders were enough. The wood split away from the lock and the door burst open. Inside, roped to the cabin table, with a handkerchief stuffed in her mouth, was Sally. The scuffling was her efforts to work herself free. Piet let go the tiller and ran to her. "Take the tiller," he said to Macleod. He snatched the handkerchief from Sally's mouth, got out his knife and cut the rope that bound her. She threw her arms round his neck and kissed him. "Oh Piet, Piet," she sobbed.

Piet said nothing. He felt nothing but a surge of infinite relief at finding Sally alive, mixed with a wave of anger at the people who had bound her, locked her in, and were taking her . . . where? He picked her up and carried her into the cockpit, putting her down on the after locker, next to the tiller and as far as possible away from Trudi and Roger. At least now she was in fresh air. There was work to be done that could not wait.

"I'll take over," he said to Macleod. "Get those two below. If they won't get up, heave them in."

With the movement of the boat and his hands cuffed behind his back, Roger found it hard to get to his feet, but at least he tried. Macleod hauled him up, and he went below on his own. Trudi mulishly refused to move.

"Let me help you to get up, madam," Macleod said politely.

"If you so much as touch me I'll sue you for assault

through every court in England," she screamed back at him.

"The Chief Inspector wishes you to go into the cabin," Macleod replied quite gently.

"That other pig can go to hell, and so can you."

Macleod put his arms under her and lifted her. With her hands tied she couldn't claw at him, but she bit his cheek as he bent over her, and drew blood. Macleod had to shake her to break free, but although her bite hurt and blood was streaming down his face he continued to handle her without roughness. Piet, watching enraged from the tiller, thought he behaved magnificently. He put the woman in the cabin, on a settee on the opposite side of the table from Roger, and came back into the cockpit.

Piet took out his own handkerchief. "Seawater, Sally," he said. She dipped the handkerchief over the side and cleaned up Macleod's wound. "I should hold the wet handkerchief over the bite," Piet said. "It may sting a bit, but seawater is a good disinfectant. If you feel up to it I'd like you to stay in the cabin to keep an eye on those two specimens we've got there."

"I'm all right, sir. If you'll pardon the expression, miss, that woman's a fair bitch."

"What happened, Sally?" Piet asked when Macleod had gone back into the cabin.

"When you didn't ring up I got very worried about you."

"I couldn't ring up. Do you remember how puzzled I was when you told me that you didn't think Mrs Vincent could have been in London on Monday? Well, that was because a woman calling herself Mrs Vincent, and using one of Mrs Vincent's trade cards, called on Gavell and Gainsworth, the art dealers, on Monday, to try to persuade them to sell a picture for her. The picture is ostensibly an unknown Constable, but there's something very funny about it. Wilbur

Constantine, the expert at Gavell and Gainsworth, naturally got in touch with us, and I saw him on Tuesday. He stalled off Mrs Vincent for a couple of days, arranging for her to come back yesterday. I was in his office—well, actually in his secretary's room opening off it—when she came. *And it wasn't Mrs Vincent—she was somebody I'd never seen before.* I had to follow her at once and keep her in sight—I never had a chance to go to a phone-box. She went to Liverpool Street and got a train to Yarmouth. I had to go too. And now I think I know who she is. She went to the yacht harbour at Yarmouth, and went on board the motor-cruiser that I first saw moored at Poplar's Fen. The man on board called her Trish, so I suppose she's the Trish of your Malcolm and Trish."

"Oh Piet! I think I'm beginning to understand," Sally shuddered.

"I don't think you *can* understand everything yet. But you can understand enough to know that you were among some very nasty people. What happened to you?"

"Well, I told you I was worried about you. I thought that you'd probably decided to go back to Poplar's Fen, and didn't want me with you because . . . well, perhaps because you didn't altogether trust me. I wanted to show you that you *could* trust me, and if anything dangerous was going to happen to you I wanted to be there, too."

Piet needed only one hand for the tiller. He ran the other over Sally's hair. She went on, "I hoped you'd be on board Roger's boat when I got there, but you weren't. Roger and Trudi were. They were quite nice to me, made some cocoa for me, and asked where you were. I said the wrong thing. I said that we'd separated in London, and arranged to come independently. I said that you'd probably got held up in London, and would be back first thing in the morn-

ing. They asked how I'd got back, and I said I'd borrowed a friend's car. Then Roger asked, 'Have you
come back to warn us?'

"I said, 'I don't understand. What on earth do you
mean?'

"Trudi said, 'Well, your boyfriend's a copper, isn't
he?'

"I said again that I didn't understand, that I'd
known you for ages as an artist, and that I was quite
sure you weren't a policeman.

"Roger said something like, 'I don't know if I believe you, but even if that's what you think, you're
wrong. If he'—he meant you—'is coming back in the
morning we've got to get out first. And I'm afraid you
will have to come with us.'

"I began to get cross, and I said, 'I'm damned well
not going anywhere with you. I'm clearing out now.'
I got up to go, but Roger caught hold of me. While
he held me Trudi put a handkerchief in my mouth
and tied a gag round it so that I couldn't scream, and
she and Roger tied me up. They had a discussion
about whether to leave straight away, but Roger
didn't like the idea of crossing the bar at night so
they decided to wait till morning. They thought
you'd be coming by road, anyway, and that they'd be
out of sight at sea before you got here. I still don't
understand how you came to be on board that boat."

"I'll explain that later. What happened to you?"

"They just left me tied up. I don't know exactly
what they did, because I was in the cabin and
couldn't see, but I could hear them on deck, and either one or both of them seemed to make several
trips ashore—I could hear coming and going from the
river bank. I don't know where they went—to the
mill, perhaps, but I don't know. Soon after it got
light they began to move the boat. There wasn't
much wind—less than there is now. We were tossed
about a lot in getting over the bar, but Roger is good

with the boat and we got out all right. Because there wasn't much wind we didn't get very far until you caught up with us. They didn't seem to bother about me. Until you started hailing from the other boat they left the cabin door open. When you came up they shut the door and locked it. I haven't any idea what they were going to do with me."

"I'm afraid I have," Piet said. "Thank God we got to you in time."

With the wind increasing, they made good progress back to the shore, and Piet could see the line of breakers on the bar some way ahead. Constable Macleod came out of the cabin. "The man says he wants to talk to you," he said to Piet.

"All right. You take the tiller. Hold her as she goes, we're doing well enough as we are."

Piet went below, and Roger said, "You don't know the bar, and I do. If you'll untie my hands and let me take her in, I'll guarantee to get you over safely."

"Why do you suppose I should trust you?" Piet asked.

"I haven't resisted so far, have I? Trudi's hand-cuffed in here, and there are two of you, with guns, to look after me—three of you, if you count Sally. The most important reason, though, is that since Sandra's death I don't really care a damn what happens to me."

"You swine," Trudi said. "What you could ever see in her is beyond me."

Roger made no comment. "How did you know I was a policeman?" Piet asked.

"You made a mistake, a rather silly mistake. When you went ashore that first evening, and went off to the pub, you left your things on board. Not knowing anything about you, naturally I went through them. And among a lot of painting things in one of your bags there was a police walkie-talkie radio. How did you know about me?"

"You made mistakes, too. You've obviously had some cosmetic surgery, and you've altered the shape of your nose quite well. But I really am an artist as well as being a policeman—at least, I've been to an art school, and learned how to look at people before doing portraits. You couldn't alter the shape of your skull, particularly at the back of your head. I thought I'd seen that shape before, and I saw it again in photographs in our records. I couldn't be absolutely sure, of course, but you made a worse mistake."

"You mean my finger?"

"Yes."

"I got careless, I suppose. I did have an artificial joint made and wore it for some time, but it was never comfortable, and I could use my hand better without it. After three years there seemed no likelihood of any danger at the Fen, so I just gave up using it. . . . But we must be closing the coast. Are you going to let me take her in?"

Piet knew enough about sailing on the East Coast to accept the value of local knowledge. He had never entered Poplar's Fen from seawards and although he had studied the chart on board *Daffodil* the channels through such bars change frequently. Roger was undoubtedly a competent sailor, he had brought the botter out of the Fen only that morning, and if anyone knew the passage, he did. With himself on one side and Constable Macleod on the other, there didn't seem much that Roger could do to escape.

"All right," Piet said. "Come aft and we'll unlock your handcuffs. But remember, we're both armed. Any funny business, and I'll shoot." With the sway of the boat Roger found more difficulty in keeping on his feet. Piet had no intention of removing his handcuffs in the cabin. He put a hand on Roger's arm and helped him to the cockpit.

X

The Secret of the Fen

"My hands are a bit stiff from being tied," Roger said. "Do you think you could harden the jib sheet a little?"

Piet took half a turn around the winch. The jib certainly set better, and although they were not going very fast they closed the land steadily. They were about half a mile offshore, the breakers of the bar dead ahead, and, beyond them, details of the land stood out sharply. "In case you ever want to do this again," Roger said, "keep the tower of the mill on a bearing of 320 degrees." He glanced at the compass. "We're about right as we are."

Piet wondered if Inspector Lennard and the Lowestoft men had got to the Fen, and what had happened when they got there. It might be awkward if they had not arrived, but the botter's speed compared with what *Daffodil* could do going all out was so slow that there should have been ample time. Well, they would soon know.

The breakers were only about fifty yards ahead . . . thirty yards . . . ten yards. At the last moment Roger put the tiller hard over. The botter swung almost broadside on to the breakers and there was a dreadful crunching sound as she struck the shingle bank. It was hard shingle, not sand. The breakers kept on coming at her, with that kind of deliberate viciousness that the sea sometimes seems to show towards a vessel in distress. She heeled to her beam ends, the mast went, and water began pouring into the wreck of splintered wood and tangle of ropes and sails. Roger made no move, just standing where he was, waist-deep in water.

"Get the woman out of the cabin and unlock her hands—you have the key. We must give her a chance," Piet shouted to Macleod. But the constable didn't need telling, for he was already fighting his way to the cabin through the wreckage. He found Trudi with water up to her shoulders, and managed to drag her to the cabin door, through which the sea was now swirling. Piet went forward to help him, and together they contrived to lift her on to the cabin top, still a couple of feet above the sea. "I think I've broken my arm," Macleod said. "Can you get the key out of my pocket?" Piet found the key and freed Trudi's hands, so that at least she was able to help herself by clinging to the cabin top. Piet got hold of a broken shroud that had fallen across the cabin, tugged at it, and found that it was still holding to the chainplate. "Hang on to this with your good arm," he said to Macleod. Then he went back for Sally.

She had kept her head, and was holding herself above water by clutching what was left of the main boom, still half in the boat. She couldn't have held on long, though, for the breakers were clawing at her, and driving the remains of the boom over the side. Piet got a line from the mess of cordage—it was one of the jib halliards—and took it with him. Gripping the line with his left hand he got his right arm round her shoulders. He had a fairly firm foothold on the windward coaming, the higher side of the steeply-heeled wreck. "O.K. now," he said. "When the next wave comes let it lift you up to the boom. I've got you safely." As an extra precaution he looped his end of the line under her arms, and with the lift of a wave drew her to him. Then they clambered up to the cabin top, and Piet got Sally to cling to the same bit of broken shroud that was supporting Macleod. "Look after him as well as you can," he said. "His right arm's badly hurt."

Trudi was lying across the cabin top, with a good grip on the base of a ventilator. She seemed all right for the moment. Piet looked for Roger. He had not moved, and was standing trance-like in the stern, holding the high, curved tiller, still miraculously intact. Water was lapping his neck. "Come up here," Piet shouted at him. "I'll throw you a line." Roger took no notice.

No wooden boat, however lovingly built, could long withstand the battering of heavy breakers on that cruel shingle bank. One particularly steep swell lifted her, and sent her crashing down again on the stones. On the lee side her timbers were already broached. Now the planking on her weather side began to give, and the sea tore a huge hole in her just below the cabin, splitting the cabin top. She was breaking up.

Trudi was the first to go. The woodwork round the ventilator top to which she was clinging was wrenched away. She clutched at the broken wood but the next wave swept her and about one-third of the cabin top into the sea. Piet, Sally and Macleod were huddled nearer to the stump of the mast. Piet reached out and tried to grab Trudi as she went overboard, but the gap in the planking was too wide and he could not reach her. He threw her the end of the halliard. She made a grab at it, missed, and disappeared in the swirl of breakers. Roger must have seen it all happening. He did nothing whatever.

It could be minutes only before the rest of the little

group on the remnants of the cabin top were carried away. The planking round the chainplate holding the shroud was gone, and although the plate itself was through-bolted to a rib, the wrenching away of the planking and the battering on the stones of the shingle bank had broken the rib. The shroud that had been supporting them was useless now. Piet got one arm round the stump of the mast, but that, too, was giving, as the bottom of the boat was ground to pieces. With his other arm Piet held Macleod. Sally worked herself into a position with her feet against the mast, and did what she could to help Piet support the injured constable.

There was no respite from the vicious breakers. "It's no good, sir," Macleod said gamely. "You'll have to let go of me, and maybe I shall be carried ashore somehow."

"Thanks, but I'm not having it," Piet said. "When we go, we'll go together—with one arm you wouldn't stand much chance in those breakers. I'll do my best to keep you up, and Sally will try to make it on her own."

Man proposes. . . . The words were hardly out of Piet's mouth when the sea settled the matter by sweeping Macleod out of Piet's grasp, and he was gone. Piet was about to go after him when, to his bewilderment, he saw Roger come alive and plunge into the sea. The man was a powerful swimmer, and clearly he knew something about life-saving. He was up with Macleod before he went under, supported him, and struggled with him to the beach.

Piet and Sally followed—there was nothing more to hope for on the broken boat, and no sign of rescue from the shore. Piet could swim well, but it was all he could do to keep himself up in the maelstrom of breakers, and he could feel a savage undertow trying to drag him down. He was determined not to let go of Sally, and he didn't, but their chances of getting ashore seemed slim. The old boat herself, or rather, a plank from her, was their salvation. Piet saw the plank, grabbed it, and dragged it to them. It was not enough to support both of them, but with Sally lying across the plank and Piet holding on to it they could keep their heads above water, and swim with their legs. Inside the breakers the sea became much calmer, and once clear of the troubled water on the bar it wasn't long before Piet felt one of his feet touch bottom. Two more strokes and he could walk within his depth, pushing the plank with Sally lying across it to the beach.

As soon as Sally was safely within her depth Piet left her, to go to the aid of Roger, who was having a far harder struggle with the injured—and much heavier—Constable Macleod. With Piet's strength added to Roger's they got Macleod to the edge of the shore. Sally ran to help, and the three of them carried the injured man safely above the tide line, and made him as comfortable as they could with his back against a tussock of marram grass. The four of them, soaked, and momentarily exhausted, lay there panting.

"That was a magnificent act," Piet said to Roger.

"I had nothing against him. Why should he drown?"

Piet went on. "In the circumstances it is appalling to say this, but it is my duty to arrest you. I have reason to believe that you are Rupert Lexington, sentenced to fifteen years' imprisonment for your part in a bullion robbery at Southampton, who escaped from prison shortly afterwards. I need scarcely add that your act today in saving the life of Constable Macleod will be brought to the notice of the authorities."

"That doesn't matter. Has Trudi gone?"

"She doesn't seem to have got ashore."

"Good. She poisoned Sandra. That's why I got Sandra a new sugar-tin."

"She found out about that. There was arsenic in the new tin. I had it analysed."

"Then I hope she's safely in hell by now."

"But she didn't succeed in killing Sandra."

"What do you mean? Of course she killed her. She was jealous of her, partly because of me, mainly because Sandra really could paint. She knew who I was, and I could do nothing because she could simply go to the police. And that would mean that other people, quite innocent people, morally at any rate, if not legally, would suffer, too. So I didn't do enough to stop her killing Sandra."

"But Sandra didn't die from arsenic poisoning."

The man called Roger or Rupert had no time to ask Piet what that meant, for a panting Inspector Lennard came running up. "We saw your boat go on the rocks," he said, "but we could do nothing, for we had a full-scale battle on our hands. I had four men—I could have done with forty. Are you all right?"

"There's a woman missing from the boat. She was washed overboard and doesn't seem to have got ashore. I don't think there can be any hope for her, but the coastguard must be informed and a helicopter sent up to search as soon as possible. Constable Macleod has a broken arm—he owes his life to this man here, who risked his own to save him. I'm afraid that the man himself has to be under arrest. He is Rupert Lexington, the escaped prisoner, whom police all over the world have been looking for."

The Inspector gasped. "The Southampton bullion robbery!"

"Yes."

Piet got up. "We must get Constable Macleod to hospital," he said, "but he will be all right here for the moment. Stay with him, Sally, and we'll send some dry blankets as soon as we can." To Roger he said gently, "I'm sorry, but you must come with us. We must get an ambulance for the constable, and we must organise a search for Trudi. There is a great deal to be done."

Roger nodded. "I shall give you no trouble," he said. "While you're about it you might like to get some salvage men to work on the wreck. There's the best part of a million pounds worth of gold bars lying on the bottom. You ought to be able to recover most of it if you get to work quickly."

"What happened to you?" Piet asked the Inspector. They were walking side by side, Roger, still exhausted after his swim with Macleod, plodding a few yards ahead.

"We got to the motor-cruiser as instructed, and I went on board," Inspector Lennard said. "The cabin door was open, but there was no one there. As I got off the boat on to the river bank a man and a woman came up. They were carrying parcels, which turned out later to be gold bars. They didn't wait to be challenged. They both had pistols, and they opened fire. One of the Lowestoft men was hit and gravely wounded. There were four of us left. I told two of my men to run like blazes and get behind them from different sides. The other man and I took cover on the boat and fired back. One of us had a lucky shot and knocked the pistol from the man's hand. I'm afraid his hand was rather hurt, but I can't say that I've any sympathy for him. Then it was all over. My chaps were marvelous—simply rushed them and took them. The woman fired again and hit one of my men on the arm, but it was only a graze. We got handcuffs on them and two of my men are guarding them. The third man went to the mill, again as instructed. We radioed for an ambulance and for reinforcements, and they should be here any moment now. I don't know what happened at the mill because I didn't wait to see. I had to get down here to see if I could help you."

"Cast your mind back to the bullion robbery trial," Piet said. "Four men were arrested and tried, one of whom was Rupert Lexington. There were several references to a 'Mr Big', a criminal organiser behind the whole thing. The accused all denied knowledge of him—under cross-examination none of them squeaked. But it was fairly obvious that there was such a Fifth Man, only he was never caught. I believe that your prisoner, the man we know as Malcolm Winterer, is that man. The gold bars they were carrying when you arrested them are damning evidence, and I hope we shall get a lot more when we can search the mill. All we have to do at the moment is to get them all locked up. The Winterers can appear in court tomorrow on charges of attempted murder and assaulting the police. We can bring further charges later. This man doesn't need to be charged. He has not denied being Rupert Lexington, and fingerprints will make it certain. He has already been sentenced, and we've simply got to keep him in custody to await an escort to take him back to prison. He'll have to appear before the prison authorities, of course, in connection with his escape, and there may have to be new charges relating to offences committed while he was on the run. But we must do what we can for him. He undoubtedly saved Constable Macleod's life, and at least he's told us how to try to recover some of the stolen bullion. Can your people organise a salvage party to try to recover the gold from the wreck?"

"It had better be Lowestoft, I think. I can radio about that. And when the reinforcements come we'd better have some men on the beach to watch the wreck in case anybody else knows about it."

"I doubt if anybody does, except the woman who's missing, presumed drowned. But you can't be too careful. The ambulance for your wounded man can look after Macleod, too. I think I can see it on the road now."

The Fen seemed to be swarming with policemen. When the bedraggled little party from the beach got to the wooden bridge over the sluice they found the wounded man being lifted into the ambulance. Piet asked if the ambulance men could collect Constable Macleod, but a doctor with them said, "I'm afraid not. This man is so badly hurt that his only hope is to be rushed to hospital, and I think I *must* go with him. I'll send another ambulance as soon as possible."

"The injured man on the beach is soaking wet," Piet said.

"One of the ambulance men can stay—he knows how to lift an injured patient, and can probably get some of the wet clothes off him and make him more comfortable with dry blankets. There are plenty of spare blankets in the ambulance. He ought to be all right—I'll send help as quickly as I can."

The ambulance drove off.

The Superintendent from Lowestoft had come to the Fen with the reinforcements. Inspector Lennard introduced Piet to him. The Superintendent knew nothing yet beyond the shooting charges against the Winterer couple. Piet told him about the recapture of Rupert Lexington, and of the further charges likely to be brought against Winterer.

"I don't understand it all at present, but you seem to have pulled off a remarkable job, Chief Inspector," the Superintendent said.

"Your men did the pulling. Can you get the prisoner Lexington into custody straight away? He's soaked to the skin and he is suffering from exposure. He saved Constable Macleod's life at real risk to his own. He needs some dry clothes and a hot drink. At least he deserves that."

"Of course. I'll send him off now, with a driver and two men."

"And can you ensure that he has no chance of contact with the Winterer couple while he awaits his prison escort? I'd like them held in different places, if possible."

"I can arrange that."

The man Piet had known as Roger got into a police car with the same surrender to fate that he had shown all along. He did not look back at Piet.

From another radio car Inspector Lennard sent off messages about a search for Trudi and the dispatch of a salvage party to the wreck.

The Superintendent came back to Piet. "If I may say so, Chief Inspector, you're looking pretty well done in yourself. I recommend that the next job is to get you some dry clothes."

"There's a girl looking after Constable Macleod who has done a lot to help me. She was in the wreck, too, and also needs dry clothes."

"We've plenty of men here to look after Macleod. I'll send you both into Southwold, where we can certainly fit you out with something, and a policewoman can look after your girl. Do you want to question the Winterers before we send them away?"

"I don't think so. I shall have to interview them later, but I'd like to search the mill first, and there are important inquiries to be made at Lavenham."

"Right. We'll send off the Winterers to be locked up. The man will need some treatment for his hand, but I don't think he needs to go to hospital. A doctor can see to him in his cell at the police station. Now I want you and your girl to get away to Southwold. It won't take long for you to be fixed up. I'll stay here, and we'll hold all the people who appear to be living at the mill until you get back. I expect you'd like to make the search yourself?"

"I think so, yes."

"We'll wait for you, then. Can we do anything for you at Lavenham?"

"I want to know the maiden name of a woman called Mrs Marshall, who works as a cleaner at a place called Moat Cottage Studio at Lavenham, but I don't want anyone to question her directly. She's lived at Lavenham for years, the local police are bound to know her address, and can get her Christian names from the electoral register. As I don't know where she was married, it will be a matter of getting on to the Registrar General's department for a copy of the marriage certificate. The Records Division at the Yard can handle that. If you can get hold of the woman's full names, I'd be awfully grateful if you could ring Records and ask them to find out about the marriage for me. Tell them it will probably have been about fifty years ago."

"I'll ring Lavenham as soon as we've got you off. Anything else?"

"I want to try to find out the real name of the woman who runs Moat Cottage Studio—it's a sort of combined tea-place, art gallery, and antique shop. She calls herself Mrs Vincent, but I doubt if that really is her name. Again, I don't want anyone to question her, so it had better wait until I can get to Lavenham. It's not so urgent as discovering Mrs Marshall's maiden name."

Sally was shivering as they sat in the back of a police car. Piet put his arm round her. "Comforting, but not much drier!" She tried to laugh and didn't succeed. "Oh, Piet, how long have you known about Roger?"

"I was slightly suspicious on that first evening when we met him. In profile, the back of his skull has a slightly unusual curve. He's been a very much wanted man since his escape from prison, and photographs of him were circulated to all police divisions. I've always had a good visual memory, perhaps because of painting. I checked on the photographs the first time I went back to London, and I thought I was right. I knew for certain when I saw his little finger at breakfast in the mill yesterday."

"Was it really only yesterday?"

"You've been through a lot, Sally. Do you feel that you know me any better?"

"Yes. But I think I could be rather afraid of you. Unless . . ."

"Unless what?"

"Unless we were always on the same side."

News travels fast in the police force, and Piet was a hero to the men at Southwold. They hadn't known about Sally, but when he told them how she had been in the wreck, and nursed Constable Macleod until other help came, she at once became a heroine. Piet thought that they'd better try to buy some clothes, rather than borrow them, but Sally's handbag had gone down with the boat, and when he looked at his wallet the notes it had held were a mass of soggy pulp. So was his cheque book.

"Look, sir," said the station sergeant, "don't worry about that. I know the bank manager, and I'm sure he'll fix you up." It turned out that the bank was a branch of Piet's own bank, and when the sergeant had explained things, the manager, thrilled to be among the first to know of the recapture of Rupert Lexington, and sworn to secrecy (though every newspaper would soon be carrying the news), was delighted to help. A policewoman took Sally to a local draper, where she was re-equipped with underclothes, a skirt and rather pretty blouse. She had lost her shoes, and was wearing a pair of police boots, many sizes too big for her. A shoe shop almost next door to the draper soon put that right. Piet found a men's outfitter, and emerged looking, he thought, reasonably respectable for the work he still had to do. The shoe shop re-equipped him, too, for his own sodden shoes had been more or less cut to pieces on the sharp shingle in the effort to get Macleod ashore and carried up to the beach. He wanted to get back to Poplar's Fen, but hot coffee was waiting for him and Sally at the police station, and it would have been churlish to decline it. They were also glad of it, and for some excellent ham sandwiches that the policewoman got for them.

"Do you want to go back to the Fen?" Piet asked Sally. "I can get a police car to take you back to London from here, if you like. It might be better so."

"I want to stay with you."

Had she not stayed, the mystery of Sandra's death might never have been cleared up.

The art colony at the mill were a subdued, pathetic group. As Piet had thought, they gave no trouble at all, and were shocked by the events that had been taking place around them. They were also rather shocked to discover that someone they had accepted as one of themselves turned out to be a Chief Inspector of the Metropolitan Police. "Never thought I'd go drinking with a copper," one of the men muttered. "I thought him quite a decent bloke."

Clare, more practically, asked, "Shall we be allowed to go on living here?"

"I don't think any of you were mixed up in the matters that brought me to Poplar's Fen—I think you, and your way of life, were used as a cloak for the criminal activities of other people," Piet said. "But you will all have to be interviewed, and give an account of yourselves. That will be done as soon as possible by other officers. You will be interviewed individually. After that you will be free to leave, unless, of course, anything comes to light to give reasons for detaining any of you. I hope it doesn't. You can help yourselves best by being absolutely frank in answering questions. Please don't be afraid of the police. It is our job to enforce the law—the law that makes civilised life possible—but no one wants to trap you into anything, or to make difficulties for you. As for going on living here—for tonight, certainly, but there is a great deal of investigation to be carried out, the mill will have to be under police guard for some time, and you might find all this very inconvenient. You would be wise to move out. If any of you really has nowhere else to go, the police will put you in touch with organisations that may be able to help. Do you know who the mill belongs to?"

"I don't. I always thought it belonged to Roger, but I don't know. We never had to pay rent to anybody."

"Well, I don't think you can count on it as offering a permanent home. Try not to worry. This is an appalling experience for you, but it is experience of life, and it may turn out to be gain in the end." Privately he hoped that it would persuade at least some of them that contracting out of the more normal responsibilities of life seldom offers much of a future.

When Malcolm Winterer was searched a bunch of keys was taken from him. Among them were keys to his car, to his boat, and several that were not immediately identifiable. When these were tried, one of them was found to unlock the door on the top floor of the mill tower that Trudi had not opened when she was showing the place to Piet. The room here was also a studio, but it contained many other things as well. There were stacks of gold bars remaining from the great bullion robbery. Rupert Lexington had presumably taken what he regarded as being his share. The Winterer couple had been removing the rest when Inspector Lennard and the Lowestoft men arrived. They had not had time to complete their business—gold is heavy stuff to carry. Important as the recovery of the gold was, more interesting to Piet was a pile of unfinished canvases, that looked like genuine sketches and pieces of work in progress by John Constable. There were other paintings, all unframed, in the manner of Gainsborough and other famous artists.

The room had to be photographed as it was, and then everything had to be carefully checked for fingerprints. All this was left to the Regional CID. Having had a look at the room in the tower, Piet and the Lowestoft Superintendent walked over to the motor-cruiser. Sally went with them. While the men looked in the lockers and under the floorboards in the cockpit, finding several more gold ingots, Sally stayed in the cruiser's well-furnished little saloon. On one of the settees, in a corner, apparently left as it had been thrown down, was a woman's handbag. Sally called out urgently. "Piet, please come! I've found Sandra's handbag."

XI

The Skein of Tragedy

Sally's identification of Sandra's handbag loosened the key thread in the unravelling of a dreadful skein of human passion, greed and jealousy. Had the bag been found by Piet or one of the other CID officers engaged on the case its contents would, of course, have been examined, but it held nothing to link it positively with Sandra, and it would reasonably have been assumed that it belonged to the woman on the boat, who would undoubtedly have claimed it. Why Trish hadn't thrown it away remained a mystery. Sally thought that it was probably because it was rather a nice bag, and that may indeed have been the reason—yet another example of the pettiness so often mingled with much larger human affairs.

There was nothing particularly out of the ordinary in the bag—about thirty pounds in notes and coin, an unmarked handkerchief, a comb, a small mirror, the usual lipstick, face powder and things, and a bottle of anti-travel-sickness pills. Such pills are, perhaps, a little uncommon in the contents of everyday handbags, but not on a boat. As soon as Sally saw them, she said, "Remember how I told you that Sandra was always liable to be travel-sick, in cars or on trains as well as at sea? She always carried travel-sickness pills, and those are the ones she always used."

Piet wondered why there was no latchkey in the bag. Then he thought of the robbery or attempted robbery at Sandra's studio in Finsbury Park. Before setting off for Lavenham he collected the unidentified keys from Winterer's key ring, and took them with him.

Since Piet had come to Yarmouth by train the old Riley was in London. The Mini which Sally had borrowed from his mother was still safely on the Fen road, and although the key had gone down with Sally's handbag the local police soon fixed him up with a spare. So he took the Mini to go on with Sally to Lavenham.

On the way he stopped at a phone-box in a village and telephoned the Yard. Put through to Records, he spoke to one of the men he knew and asked, "Have you had any luck in tracing the marriage certificate of that Mrs Marshall?"

"Oh, yes. It turned out to be quite easy, because you were almost right about the date—it wasn't quite fifty, but it was forty-nine years ago. She was Emily Beatrice Winterer, of the Mill House, Poplar's Fen, near Walberswick."

"Thanks a lot. You've helped enormously."

Some late teas were still being served at Moat Cottage. Mrs Vincent wasn't in the tea-room. "Do you know where she might be?" Piet asked Sally.

"Probably in the cottage. Shall I go and see?"

"No. Stay here and talk to people as if nothing had happened. I shall have to see Mrs Vincent alone."

Piet knocked on the door of the cottage two or three times. Nobody answered. He tried the door. It was unlocked, and he walked in. As with many country cottages, the door opened directly to a living room. Mrs Vincent was sitting with her head in her hands. A radio was turned on, but she wasn't listening to it. It was some talk about orchid-hunting in the Amazon forests. Piet had heard the radio news earlier, in his car—it had been full of the recapture of Rupert Lexington, and of the shooting at Poplar's Fen. He learned to his sorrow that the wounded constable had died. The Winterers were not named. It was stated simply that a man and a woman were helping police with their inquiries.

He turned off the radio, and Mrs Vincent looked up. "What do you want?" she said. "I've seen you before."

"Yes, I had tea here and bought some pictures from you last week. I should explain that I'm a police officer. I'd like to ask you some questions."

"It doesn't matter. It's all happening again. Have you come to take me away?"

"That depends on your answers to my questions. What is your relationship to Malcolm Winterer?"

"He is my husband."

"And Mrs Marshall is his aunt?"

"Yes. If you know everything about us, why do you want to ask questions?"

"Because there is very much that I don't know. I'm inclined to think that you may have been more sinned against than sinning," Piet said gently, "but I can't be sure unless you tell me the truth."

"What has happened to Malcolm?"

"He and a woman with him called Trish—or Patricia—have been arrested on very grave charges, which must now include the murder of a policeman. Did you know about the Southampton bullion robbery just over three years ago?"

"Know? God knows. You asked me to tell you the truth—it is very hard to know what is the truth. I knew Rupert Lexington, of course. He was a friend from the old days. Yes, I suppose I did know. I knew

Malcolm was a bad lot. There were other things. He was . . . he was not very nice to me. There were always other women. I left him—or he left me—about two years before the affair at Southampton. I could have divorced him, and perhaps I should, but I'm a Catholic, and I cannot bring myself to divorce. Although we have long been separated, he still turns up sometimes. He has been here. I try not to think about him, but I can't help wondering . . . wondering if, when he comes to see me, he wants an alibi for being somewhere else. That may be unfair. Before you came, the police have never been to me about him. He's very clever."

"How did you get the money to buy Moat Cottage?"

"My great-uncle died and left me some money. I've always wanted to do something like this, and I thought I'd put my money into it before Malcolm could get at it. I didn't have quite enough, but Aunt Emily—that's Mrs Marshall—I've always liked her, and we've got on together—was able to lend me the rest."

"Whose idea was that extraordinary clause in your contract about buying with the property anything found below ground?"

"It was Malcolm. Aunt Emily helped to bring him up, and she's about the only person he's always been fairly nice to. She has a soft spot for him, in spite of knowing what he's like. She told him that she was helping me to buy Moat Cottage. To my surprise he said it was a good idea, told me that with these old properties you never know what may turn up, and suggested that we insisted on a clause to safeguard my rights. But how on earth do you know about the contract?"

"You must accept that I do. I suppose Poplar's Fen belongs to Mrs Marshall?"

"Yes, but she hasn't been there for years, and I've

never been there. Her mother died when she was a child, and she lived in the old mill with her father. He seems to have been rather an eccentric. She never had much schooling, but her father was an educated man, and he used to teach her. The Winterers were a good family once, but they had this vein of eccentricity and they fell on hard times. Aunt Emily's father died when she was about seventeen. There was nothing but the old mill and a bit of surrounding fen, and nobody wanted to buy it in those days. She went into service with some people who then lived at Southwold, but soon afterwards they moved to Lavenham, and she came with them. She married here. Her husband was a lot older than she was. He was wounded in the First World War and had some sort of pension. I think he had a little money of his own, but it wasn't much. He did have the cottage where Aunt Emily still lives, but when he died she didn't have enough to live on so she went back to work. Domestic work was all she knew about, but she's a hard worker and very good at it, and she always found people who wanted her as a daily. She's a careful, saving person, which was how she had the money to lend me when I needed it."

"And when Malcolm asked if he could use the mill, she just said yes?"

"It wasn't quite like that. Malcolm said he thought the mill could be used as a sort of holiday camp, to provide a bit of income for her when she was too old to work. She told him to go ahead. Of course he never gave her anything—I don't think she ever really expected anything."

"Did you know where Rupert Lexington was living after his escape from prison?"

She didn't answer at once. Then she replied with a question. "Did you follow the trial closely?" Answering herself, she went on, "Of course you must have done. So you'll remember that the others got twenty-five years, but Rupert only fifteen. The gold, some in bars, some in South African gold coins, came by ship, and was being sent to London in two big security vans. Just outside Southampton the road was partly blocked by a faked road accident, with smashed cars, an ambulance, and men in police uniform to direct traffic. The security vans were stopped, and the guards tricked into getting out to help the police release a man they said was under one of the smashed cars. Then the 'police' got into the vans, and drove off. One of the security men tried to stop them, and was shot. He was wounded, but wasn't killed. Rupert didn't go off in the vans with the others, but stayed behind to drag the wounded man off the road and do what he could to stop the flow of blood. Then he got away in the fake ambulance. The wounded security man had recovered by the time of the trial. He identified Rupert, and told how Rupert had tried to help him. A doctor gave evidence to say that without Rupert's help the man would almost certainly have died. That was why the judge reduced Rupert's sentence."

"You haven't said if you knew where Rupert Lexington was living while he was on the run."

"Haven't I told you enough? I have said that Rupert was an old friend. He did wrong things, but wasn't bad, like Malcolm. He was weak, I suppose. His father had a flourishing business, and Rupert had too much money at Cambridge. Then something went wrong, his father died, the business was bankrupt, and there wasn't any money. His mother had gone off years before, divorced and married someone else. Rupert left Cambridge without taking a degree. He was used to having money, and I think he didn't care much how he got it. Do you know how he lost the top joint of his little finger?"

"No."

"Trying to mend my bicycle chain when I was about eleven."

Piet changed his line of questioning.

"All the security guards said that there were five men in the group that tricked them. Only four were ever caught. Do you know who the fifth man was?"

"I've told you that I don't *know*."

Again Piet changed his questions.

"Have you met the woman called Trish who is apparently living with your husband?"

"I've met *a* girl called Trish, but only briefly, and I didn't know she was living with Malcolm. It was some little time ago. She came here early one morning with another girl called Sandra Telford, whom I do know quite well. She's a painter, and a good one. I've sold several of her pictures, and I had some more for sale, but she took them away because she said she wanted them for an exhibition in London. I lent her one of those big portfolios to carry them in—like the one I gave you last week. The next morning she came back, with the girl called Trish, who was driving her to the station to catch a train for London. Sandra just introduced her, something like, 'This is Trish. She's one of us at Poplar's Fen. She's taking me to Sudbury for the train.' Sandra was in rather a state. She said she'd lost her handbag, and wondered if she'd left it here, forgetting it because she was carrying the portfolio. Sandra, Trish and I all looked for it, but we couldn't find it. Sandra was upset because it had her money in it. I said I'd lend her some. She said she could get some more in London, but could she have enough for the train and a bus or tube at the other end? I gave her a five-pound note, and enough in change for the little train from Sudbury to Mark's Tey. Then Trish said, 'We'll have to drive like hell if you're going to catch that train,' and they went."

"Have you had the money back?"

"No, but Sally—that's another girl from Poplar's Fen who gives some art classes here—tells me that Sandra seems suddenly to have made up her mind to go and paint in Normandy. I'm sure I shall get it back, though, because I think a lot of Sandra."

Piet got up. "To have knowledge of criminals on the run without disclosing it can be a very serious matter. I can make no promises, but my own feeling is that you have told the truth, and that in the circumstances it is unlikely that proceedings will be taken against you. I shall have to check your great-uncle's will—and you will understand that I must be certain that you have not profited in any way from the proceeds of theft."

"I haven't had a penny from Malcolm for years—not since we were first married. And even then he had money from me, more often than not. I was working for an antique dealer in London, and I kept on my job after we were married. That's how I know about the antique trade. My great-uncle was Sir Arnold Travers, a retired member of the old Indian Civil Service. His solicitors were Messrs Harmsworth and Headington, of Lincoln's Inn. You can check his will easily enough."

"Thank you. I don't say these things to hurt you, but because it's my duty. I think you've been hurt enough. May I give you some advice? Try to carry on here as normally as possible. There will be pain for you and Mrs Marshall when Malcolm Winterer is brought to trial, but try to find comfort in the faith that prevented you from seeking a divorce, and look to the future, not the past. Rupert Lexington will have to return to prison, but there were special circumstances about his arrest which may help him later. My personal views don't matter much, but I may say that I'm inclined to agree with your assessment of his character. Good luck."

"They gave me some tea, and they brought some for

you, but it's stone cold. Shall I get some more?" Sally asked.

"No, thank you. Please, Sally, I want to go away from here."

"What do you want me to do? I can stay here—there's room in one of the caravans again."

The thought that his adventure with Sally was over had not occurred to Piet. She remained an important witness, of course—her identification of Sandra's handbag would be vital when the case came to trial. But that was months away. There was no need for her to string along with him any longer. "You've been nearly drowned, you're dead tired, and if you want to stay here I shall wholly understand," he said. "But if you ask what I *want*, then I'd like you to let me take you back to London."

Sally said nothing, but got up from the tea-table and went with Piet to the Mini.

They drove through Lavenham and Sudbury in silence—to both of them the route seemed one that they'd been living on for half their lives. On the way from Sudbury to Halstead Sally asked, "Where are you taking me?"

"Home," Piet said simply.

"That's my half-room at Shepherd's Bush."

Piet stopped the car. "I'm not taking you to Shepherd's Bush," he said. "If we're going to be married your home is my home, or my home your home, whichever way you like to put it."

"Are we going to be married?"

Piet put his arms round her. "My dear, beloved Sally, if you want me to get out of your life you have only to say so, and I'll take you—yes, I *will* take you—to Shepherd's Bush. But at least you suggested earlier today that you could contemplate our being always on the same side. I love and admire you more than anybody else in the world. And I want to be on your side as long as this life lasts, and in any other life there may be."

"That's what I want too. Only . . . only . . . I could feel that you're under a dreadful sort of strain, and I didn't want to take advantage of it."

Piet went on kissing her until she gasped, "My darling, we're not on a lay-by. It wouldn't do for a Chief Inspector to be run in for obstructing traffic."

Old Mrs Deventer was delighted. She had long been worried about Piet's apparent lack of interest in finding a wife, and she felt instinctively that Sally was the right one for him. She went off for a few minutes and returned with a magnificent single-stone ruby ring, that Piet's great-grandfather had brought back from one of his voyages to the east. She gave it to Piet, and he put it on Sally's ring-finger. It fitted as if it had been made for her. "You see, it's just been waiting for you," Mrs Deventer said.

Piet had a long interview with Rupert Lexington at Wormwood Scrubs. Piet now understood what he had meant by saying that people who were "morally if not legally innocent" would suffer if the secret of the Fen came out, but with Malcolm Winterer arrested he was ready—indeed, he seemed almost glad—to talk. "I'm a bad hat—selfish, gilded youth—bad company—standard morality play," he said. "Only thing I was ever really any good at is sailing—perhaps if I'd spent more time at sea I wouldn't have got into such trouble on land. Yes, I'm a bad hat all right, but Malcolm—he's got the devil in him. Attractive devil, though. Tragedy that young Shirley fell for him. I knew her as a kid, you know—or probably you don't know. She's convent-educated, not far off being a saint. Malcolm treated her like dirt. Used to beat her up. Shirley's father left her quite a bit of money. Malcolm got through the lot, and before he thought up schemes for getting into the big money himself he tried to make Shirley into a call-girl. That's when she left him. Old Aunt Em—she's a scout. Malcolm got the mill from her—not a bad place for the loot, though. I'm afraid I thought up the idea of the artists' colony—rotten artists, most of them, but who'd have thought of a hippie lot like that sitting on a few million pounds in gold? Can't think how you got on to the place."

"Why did he go on calling himself Winterer?"

"Why not? Winterers have had the Fen for donkey's years—natural for a Winterer to be there. Used to have a lot of land in Suffolk, round the Essex border, too, Constable country. Malcolm's great-great-grandfather was a friend of Constable, watercolourist himself—not much good—but interested in painting, and in Constable's last years, when he was miserable after the death of his wife, old Winterer used to go and see him. Got a lot of unfinished pictures off him, things that Constable didn't think were going right, or had put aside to go on with later."

"How did Sandra come into it?"

Rupert Lexington said nothing for a bit. When he went on it was in a tone quite different from his earlier, slightly bantering manner. "Sandra was a bit like Shirley, less of a saint, but you could see her becoming a saint. I fell for her—and she wanted to rescue me. I didn't really want any more of Malcolm's bloody gold, I know a little about pictures, and I thought up a scheme for using some of old Winterer's stuff that was still in the mill. Sandra could paint anything—in any style. Because she wanted to rescue me she was prepared to finish off some of the Constables, and have a go at Gainsborough and a few others. I planned to sail them over to France, and unload them on the Continent—not strictly honest, maybe, but I could have made enough to live with Sandra somewhere safely abroad, without touching any more of the gold. Unhappily, Malcolm found out about it, because he knew about the pictures in the mill, though he didn't realise what they might be worth. He didn't try to stop me, though—said he understood my feelings, and wished me luck. Then Trudi came along—she's a friend of Malcolm's bloody Trish, thinks she can paint herself, fell for me and hated Sandra, and everything went wrong."

"Did you know that Malcolm Winterer was trying to sell a faked Constable, presumably touched up by Trudi—fortunately rather badly—for himself? And covering up by involving Shirley Vincent? Trish called herself Mrs Vincent, had trade cards in Mrs Vincent's name, and took the picture to a London art dealer for sale?"

"If I had known that I think I would have killed the lot of them and given myself up. I'd reckon life imprisonment a small price for keeping Shirley out of it."

Trudi's body was washed up on the beach near Orford Ness. With Trudi beyond interrogation the question of who first decided to kill Sandra could never be wholly answered, but that didn't matter much, for the pattern of events was clear. The details of the final act were put beyond doubt by the discovery on Malcolm Winterer's boat of a small bottle of sleeping pills. They appeared to be a normal barbiturate prescription, but, on analysis, each pill was found to contain a lethal dose of the drug. Malcolm Winterer admitted nothing, but access to a bent doctor or chemist was entirely likely in his world, and as the specially-formulated pills were in his possession it was reasonable to assume that he had obtained them. Piet wondered whether they were intended in certain circumstances for Aunt Emily.

The story of the lost handbag, and Shirley Vincent's recollection that it was Trish who had driven Sandra to the station on the last morning of her life, was damning evidence of what had happened. Sandra, already ill from arsenic poisoning, and fearful that the train journey would make her sick, would have been near panic. "Look, I've got some travel-sickness pills—I use them on the boat. Have one of mine," Piet could almost hear Trish saying.

Interviewed in prison on remand, she was nearly as tough as Malcolm Winterer, but not quite. At first she denied all knowledge of Sandra's trip to Sudbury, but when told that her call with Sandra to look for the handbag at Lavenham was known, she decided to remember having driven her to the train. The rest she put on Trudi. "If Sandra was poisoned, then Trudi did it," she declared. "Trudi hated Sandra." As for the handbag, well, Trudi must have put it on the cruiser, to divert suspicion from herself.

Sandra had been living with Trudi on Rupert Lexington's boat, and it seemed probable that it was Trudi who had actually taken her handbag. She could have given it to Trish to make sure that Sandra couldn't find it. But Trudi was slowly killing Sandra with arsenic—why suddenly join up with Trish to finish her off? And do so in a way in which poisoning was almost certain to be detected? It seemed to Piet, as he had felt all along, that there were really two distinct and separate cases, which, for some reason, had coalesced. He thought back to what Shirley Vincent had told him—that she had lent Sandra a portfolio to remove her own pictures from Moat Cottage. But the pictures in the portfolio at Liverpool Street were not Sandra's paintings—they were the touched-up Constable and other fakes. Sandra had clearly taken away her pictures from Moat Cottage, but she had not taken them to London next day. Why?

The detailed search of the mill at Poplar's Fen brought to light several canvases that were undoubtedly Sandra's own work, in the style of her paintings at the London exhibition. Shirley Vincent identified them as those she had had for sale at Moat Cottage, and which Sandra took away. Therefore she must have substituted them for the pictures found in her portfolio before she left Poplar's Fen. Why had she done this? Why had she decided to go to London at all?

"I don't know what I should have done if I had missed this train." That was what she had said to the young solicitor who had helped her to board the train at Sudbury. Why the urgency? Sally's view was that all at once everything had become too much for her. She was deeply in love with Rupert Lexington and prepared to misuse her art to help him, but she hated doing so, and she was not prepared to compete with Trudi as a rival. This was borne out to some extent by Lexington himself. Sandra had told him she was going back to London, he said, and he thought this was the best way of getting her out of Trudi's reach. Trudi's blackmailing power was that she could inform on him at any moment—and his recapture would almost certainly have meant a search of the mill, and probably the arrest of Malcolm Winterer, with more suffering for Shirley and Aunt Emily. Short of killing Trudi, there seemed nothing he could do but encourage Sandra to go.

To Sandra, this must have seemed like victory for Trudi, and added to her despair. Had she herself decided to go to the police, taking the pictures with her as evidence? Probably not, Piet thought, but she did not intend to allow those particular pictures to be sold as genuine. To Malcolm Winterer a distraught Sandra, knowing what she did about the mill, was too dangerous to live. He intended her to die on the train, but neither he nor Trish nor Trudi knew that the pictures she was taking to London were the fakes and not her own.

*   *   *

One of the keys found on Winterer fitted the lock on
the door of Sandra's studio at Finsbury Park. It must
have come from Sandra's handbag, and, added to the
lethal pills found on his boat, it was firm evidence
against him. Piet thought he could now understand
the apparent robbery at Finsbury Park, and the
clumsy attempt to break into the Lost Property office
at Liverpool Street. Neither was a serious attempt to
recover Sandra's pictures—*both were desperately serious efforts to concentrate police attention on London.*
The art frauds were secondary to the prime purpose
of the mill in providing an apparently safe place to
keep the hoard of stolen bullion, and perhaps the
proceeds of further robberies.

Winterer, Piet concluded, knew more about the potential value of the pictures in the mill than Rupert
Lexington had realised. Here, again, there appeared
to be two cases—Lexington's plan, with Sandra's help,
to use the pictures to break away from Winterer, and
a cold-blooded plan of Winterer's own to have the
pictures found on Moat Cottage property. That
served two purposes—it diverted attention from the
mill by giving the pictures a provenance that was
nothing to do with Poplar's Fen, and it overcame the
slight legal difficulty that in fact the pictures belonged
to Mrs Marshall. The lethal pills were a further insurance against any complications from her, and perhaps intended also for Shirley if she rebelled against
the scheme. On her death the Moat Cottage property
would go to Winterer as her husband—the pills,
indeed, may have been an integral part of the scheme
from the start.

Winterer and Trish were charged jointly with the
murder of the Lowestoft policeman, Winterer for his
part in the original bullion robbery, and Trish with
being an accessory after it. They were also charged
separately with being concerned in Sandra's murder,

but in the end, to Piet's infinite relief, for it meant that neither Sally nor Shirley Vincent had to give evidence, that charge was not proceeded with. After the Crown's case concerning the shooting of the policeman was concluded, counsel for Winterer and Trish called no evidence for the defence—there was really none to call. Counsel for Trish, making a plea in mitigation, said that Trish admitted having given a possibly harmful substance to Sandra, and asked that this admission should be taken into consideration in her sentence. Winterer, knowing that he would be sentenced to life imprisonment for the policeman's murder, said arrogantly that he did not care—the court could take into consideration anything it liked. Both were sentenced to life imprisonment, the judge recommending that Winterer should serve a minimum of thirty years and Trish a minimum of twenty. Justice? There seemed little to choose between Trudi, Trish and Winterer. Trudi was dead. Trish's admission, which did serve to reduce her sentence, probably owed more to the skill of her counsel than to any feeling of remorse on her part. It did, however, save a certain amount of pain for other people, and removed the slur of possible suicide from Sandra's memory. But nothing could bring back to life the young policeman, nor Sandra. All that could be felt was that some very evil people had been put away.

Something like eight hundred thousand pounds-worth of gold was recovered from the wreck. Piet had another long interview with Rupert Lexington in prison. "If you suspected me of being a policeman from that first night, why did you wait?" he said.

"Well, a police radio is one thing, a policeman is another. We couldn't be absolutely sure. I told Winterer, of course. I didn't know that he was already engaged in trying to dispose of faked pictures in the scheme involving Shirley. You see, I didn't know that

Sandra was dead—I thought that once away from Trudi she'd pick up, and be all right. Trish told me that she'd decided to go off to Normandy. I believed it—at least I wanted to believe it. Knowing what I do now I can see that everything Winterer did was to protect the mill. If there were to be police inquiries, he wanted them at Lavenham and in London. And there was the gold—he didn't want to leave any of that. Otherwise he could have sailed away from Yarmouth. He gambled either on your not being a policeman at all, or not having time to act before he could get away with the gold. I didn't know what he was doing by then. I decided to get out the night Sally came back alone, but Trudi wouldn't go without as much gold as we could take. It took a devil of a time to load even what we did take. I'd have got away earlier, but for that."

Piet shivered slightly. Then he said, "I think you've summed up your own character faily well. You've done a lot of harm, some of it not altogether your fault. But you've also done some good. You'll have to serve a few years, but the authorities take a favourable view of your action in saving Constable Macleod, and also of your telling us about the gold left in the wreck. If you behave yourself, it's quite on the cards that you'll get parole. Try to keep in touch with Shirley Vincent. If anyone can keep you straight, she can."

Mr Constantine was delighted to handle the sketches and unfinished paintings found in the mill—they had a credible provenance, and a reputable legal owner in Mrs Marshall. The fakes, with her agreement, were burned. The painting touched up by Trudi had lost a good deal of its value by her insensitive treatment, but some of it was certainly genuine, and Mr Constantine thought that it might be possible for her additions to be identified and removed. With one exception, all the other works were sold. They realised a considerable sum for Mrs Marshall, most of which she insisted on giving to Shirley.

The exception was the part-Constable painting in Sandra's portfolio. It could not be regarded as genuine because it was known that she must have added to it, but her work was so sympathetic, so beautifully done and so perfectly in keeping with the mood of reflective sadness in the later Constable that the completed painting was a lovely thing in its own right. Mrs Marshall and Mrs Vincent between them decided to give it to Sally in memory of her friend.

Piet and Sally were married before the trial, but Piet's work was so imperative in tidying up all the complex ramifications of the case that there was no time for a honeymoon. As soon as he could after the trial Piet demanded leave. Sally had never been to Holland, so for their first holiday together Piet took her for a visit to his beloved ancestral countryside. He wanted her to arrive by sea, so they made the traditional passage from Harwich to the Hook. The train for Harwich left from Liverpool Street. For this important private journey Piet decided to travel first class, and they had a compartment to themselves. In the last few minutes before the train pulled out Sally put her arms round her husband and burst into tears. "Oh Piet, Piet," she sobbed, "it seems so dreadful that I should be so happy when ... when ..."

"Is it wrong to be happy?" Piet asked.

"Not exactly, but ..."

"The 'buts' make life, my darling. There is much sadness in the world, and much evil, but even on battlefields flowers grow."

Comes the Blind Fury

John Saul
Bestselling author of
Cry for the Strangers
and *Suffer the Children*

More than a century ago, a gentle, blind child walked the paths of Paradise Point. Then other children came, teasing and taunting her until she lost her footing on the cliff and plunged into the drowning sea.

Now, 12-year-old Michelle and her family have come to live in that same house—to escape the city pressures, to have a better life.

But the sins of the past do not die. They reach out to embrace the living. Dreams will become nightmares.

Serenity will become terror. There will be no escape.

A Dell Book $2.75 (11428-4)

Dell BESTSELLERS